"Sure, I know Kate Goodfellow is a fictional character—a most intriguing one at that—but she's based on one of my real-life heroines: Margaret Bourke-White, whose gutsy assault on the all-male bastion of photojournalism in the early twentieth century helped open the field to the rest of us. This stirring account of a singular woman breathes new life into that turbulent era and reminds us of what it took to get here."

—Lynn Sherr, ABC News *20/20*

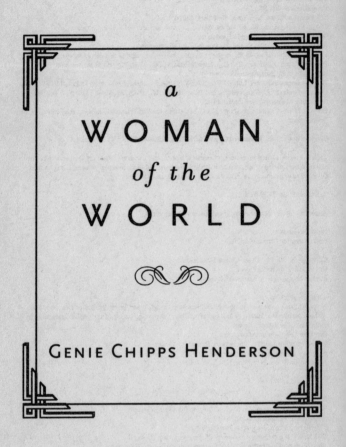

a WOMAN *of the* WORLD

GENIE CHIPPS HENDERSON

BERKLEY BOOKS, NEW YORK

THE BERKLEY PUBLISHING GROUP
Published by the Penguin Group
Penguin Group (USA) Inc.
375 Hudson Street, New York, New York 10014, USA
Penguin Group (Canada), 10 Alcorn Avenue, Toronto, Ontario M4V 3B2, Canada
(a division of Pearson Penguin Canada Inc.)
Penguin Books Ltd., 80 Strand, London WC2R 0RL, England
Penguin Group Ireland, 25 St. Stephen's Green, Dublin 2, Ireland (a division of Penguin Books Ltd.)
Penguin Group (Australia), 250 Camberwell Road, Camberwell, Victoria 3124, Australia
(a division of Pearson Australia Group Pty. Ltd.)
Penguin Books India Pvt. Ltd., 11 Community Centre, Panchsheel Park, New Delhi—110 017, India
Penguin Group (NZ), Cnr. Airborne and Rosedale Roads, Albany, Auckland 1310, New Zealand
(a division of Pearson New Zealand Ltd.)
Penguin Books (South Africa) (Pty.) Ltd., 24 Sturdee Avenue, Rosebank, Johannesburg 2196,
South Africa

Penguin Books Ltd., Registered Offices: 80 Strand, London WC2R 0RL, England

A WOMAN OF THE WORLD

A Berkley Book / published by arrangement with the author

PRINTING HISTORY
Berkley edition / November 2004

ISBN: 0-425-19913-4

BERKLEY®
Berkley Books are published by The Berkley Publishing Group,
a division of Penguin Group (USA) Inc.,
375 Hudson Street, New York, New York 10014.
BERKLEY is a registered trademark of Penguin Group (USA) Inc.
The "B" design is a trademark belonging to Penguin Group (USA) Inc.

PRINTED IN THE UNITED STATES OF AMERICA

10 9 8 7 6 5 4 3 2 1

For Lily,
On the threshold of her world

Remembering Pam,
Whose world ended too soon

AUTHOR'S NOTE

This is entirely a work of fiction. Nothing in the narrative is necessarily true, yet much in the novel is derived from the romantic, turbulent, extraordinary life of photojournalist Margaret Bourke-White.

She began her career as an industrial photographer in the 1920s and secured her fame at *Life* magazine in the '30s and '40s. Her adventures and daring were breathtaking, and her career took her to the forefront of every important world event in the mid-twentieth century.

Essentially, this novel attempts to find the driving spirit behind a real-life heroine—a fictional tale loosely based on one of the twentieth century's most remarkable and admired women.

GCH

PROLOGUE

THE SMOKE HUNG faintly blue in the room down in Chelsea. On this night all of New York's café society was jammed into Gaby Leigh-Bell's like chickens in a market crate—and just as loud. The party swayed in a constant motion of elbows and craning necks and faces leaning toward one another and arms passing bottles of champagne overhand as in a fire brigade. No one seemed to want to behave. They were gay with a special febrile gaiety, laughing a great deal, content for these few hours to "put their worries on the doorstep" while they could. All things considered, 1935 had been a lousy year for just about everyone.

Leaning against a wall between two elaborately draped windows, a young woman surveyed the scene with restless eyes. She was splendid-looking and she knew it. Red hair, tight black gown ornamented simply by a diamond bar pin and her own faultless figure—she compelled the eye, seeming at once to dare you not to stare at her and to triumph when you did. Beside her a small owlish man was trying to hold her attention, and from time to time she inclined her head in his direction, but she was more interested in the crowd and her eyes boldly traveled about the room.

Weaving through the crowd, smiling, greeting, exchanging hoots and hoorays, was a short, fat woman in a bright orange dress. She looked like someone's cook with a ruddy, pug-nosed, immensely jovial face. This was Gaby Leigh-Bell, and this face, which once may have been charmingly girlish in youth, was now elongated with chins and as supple as soft rubber, so that there was nothing Gaby could not do with it. Essentially a funny face, it was more glib than speech and much more effective. She could always make you laugh. She had the best taste in people and she loved giving parties.

She seemed unafraid—of being ugly, of being fat. She was even unafraid of poverty. The sickening thud of 1929 had sent prosperity down the drain, but money meant less to Gaby than it did to most people. She was fueled by a will to make the most of what she had. She had arrived in New York just as the Jazz Age took off in the early twenties, a wealthy widow from Louisville, Kentucky. She knew no one of particular importance in New York, but she was well-off and eager to spend. She invested in the theater, and because she loved music and was a good judge of it, her investments paid off in the form of hit musicals. She coddled her casts and threw big, happy, elaborate galas in celebration of their talents. Gaby wore funny clothes and said outrageous things. Theater people loved her. People like Noël Coward and Irving Berlin and Gertrude Lawrence. Soon all of New York loved her.

As the thrill-crazy twenties roared to a devastating close, Gaby was the reigning queen of all that was giddy and smart and fabulous. On paper she felt the crash badly, but unlike the really rich who were desperate to divest themselves of their unmarketable commodities—yachts, polo ponies, town cars, and country estates—Gaby was able to hang on to the one thing that mattered to her the most—her townhouse. The paintings were sold one by one, servants were let go, and, at her lowest ebb, the grand piano had to be hocked, but the house remained and it continued to remain a Mecca for fun-loving people. There the party went on even as the Depression deepened. Everyone said Gaby Leigh-Bell was remarkable. And she was! She gave you something to feel good about in these dark days.

Just before midnight a man appeared at the door. Every

woman in the room instantly noted his arrival. The red-haired woman dressed in black suddenly straightened as if someone had run a cold finger down her back. She couldn't help staring, and then quite unexpectedly their eyes met and she felt a heat rush to her face. She quickly looked away and did not allow herself to look again. She did not want to give him the satisfaction.

"That's Hopper Delaney," said the owlish little man, though it was entirely unnecessary to identify him.

"Who?"

"Don't tell me you're the only girl in New York who doesn't know who Hopper Delaney is."

"Of course I know who he is, but I had no idea"—she was about to say she had no idea he was so attractive, but she didn't—"he was so young," she added rather lamely. This too was true. Hopper Delaney's name had been around for as long as she had been in New York, and it was so well-known that surely if she had thought of him at all she would have imagined a much older man. But there was nothing aging about this man at all.

She waited a moment and then allowed her eyes to once again return to the figure still standing in the entranceway and was quite unreasonably annoyed to see that he was being kissed by an elegant and remarkably beautiful woman who, by the looks of her gown, was a woman whose husband could still afford fashionable clothes. Ah, but now he looked back again in her direction, and this time she let her eyes linger for just an instant longer, long enough for him to perceive how cool she was; and then, abruptly, she turned away, her long white back shown to perfection against the plunging line of the black satin gown. She let her turned back speak for her. "I've seen good-looking men before," it said, "and I've met famous writers before, too. I'm not impressed."

But she was terribly impressed. She had read his books and seen his long-running play and read the columns in which he appeared on a regular basis, and now here he was in the flesh and almost too dazzling. She liked dark men and he was very dark, with a face marked out in black—black eyes and eyebrows and black curly hair. She liked height and he had that. She liked the aura he projected when he entered a room. There seemed to be no flaw in his perfection on sight, and she could find none now still studying him in her mind. It wasn't as if he was perfect, like a matinee idol; there was an irregularity about him, a wary cast to his eye. He had the look of a man who had been there . . . and back again.

He'll be insufferable! she thought, and hoped she would have a chance to find out.

Hopper would have agreed with her. He was in an insufferable mood, but the effect of stepping into Gaby's large living room was like a tonic. No matter what the state of her bankbook, the room was the warmest and most welcoming he knew. Brightly lit, comfortably plump chairs and sofas splashed in color, low-slung coffee tables, flowers, masses of flowers, and the buzz of conversation; it was a room to be happy in, to have fun in, to fall in love in. He should know. He had done all of these things and more in this room over the years. In the corner, dominating the scene, he saw the grand piano out of hock once again. Gaby was in full tilt at the keys and the sight of her rowdy gray head bobbing back and forth as she sang out some popular rollicking tune made him feel fabulously young. Gaby loved music. She could sing and play the piano with unusual verve, her podgy fingers striking mighty chords that seemed to hit the ceiling and explode. She sang everything— Tin Pan Alley, blues, even light opera like a pro. Once during the time when the piano was in hock, she invited a slew of people to hear the score of a musical she was trying to find backers for and performed the entire show slapping it out on her plump thighs.

He signaled an enthusiastic wave to her and she answered with a mighty trill of chords, but in truth Hopper's momentary ebullience was fading fast. He was in no mood for Gaby's party tonight. Already he was mentally calculating, even as he acknowledged half-a-dozen faces, how soon he could reasonably leave. Out of habit, his eyes traveled the room but without real interest. And then, suddenly, his vision filled with the sight of a young woman in black with hair so astonishingly red it seemed to him like the Greek goddess Athena herself had blazed forth, and he felt his heart lurch and instantly set his mind against it. But he couldn't stop looking at her. His eyes locked with hers. Who was she? he wondered. Not an actress, though she looked theatrical. He knew every actress in New York one way or another. Someone's wife? He hoped so. He wanted no more of women for a while.

"Hopper, it's about time you showed up." Gaby's voice was loud in front of him as she demanded to be kissed. "Why are you just standing here? I want you to meet someone. Now, where is she . . . ?"

"Don't you dare. I'm a single man again and I want to keep it that way." He leaned down and pressed his lips to her cheek. Gaby fluttered her plump hands, her face a fever of excitement and delight in the hubbub. "Well, you're going to meet her anyway, because I promised." As she scanned the crowd, he glanced back and saw that the woman was staring at him still, and he started to acknowledge that stare, but then she turned her back and Hopper felt his throat tighten. The effect of that bare white skin! Gaby was still flapping about, and in the din of the room Hopper couldn't hear a word she was saying but knew it didn't matter. He gave her a devilish wink and signaled he was going to the bar, but halfway through the crush of people he changed directions and started for the big bay window. He had to know who she was.

She willed herself not to turn around but began talking intensely to the man beside her whose name she couldn't remember. Something told her he was coming over to her, and she must signal to his vanity that this advent was not of the slightest interest. Then, because she couldn't bear it another minute, she turned around and there he was, towering just behind her. She also saw that he quite understood why she had turned. He smiled.

The man at her side now turned useful. A haze of introductions and distantly sounded responses . . . "Hopper, good to see you. . . . Do you know Kate Goodfellow? Kate, Hopper Delaney."

And there it was. Kate Goodfellow lifted her steady gaze into the dark eyes of Hopper Delaney. Up close he seemed a little awkward, which was completely disarming. His tailor had emphasized the broadness of his shoulders, but there was no hiding the loosely held arms, big bear-hug arms that now seemed not quite to know what to do with themselves.

"Kate Goodfellow." His voice was surprisingly soft for a

man so big and the Southern drawl just enough to make her smile. He took her hand in both of his and held it for a moment looking down at it curiously. "I should know your name," he said with real concern, "I should know you."

The degree of his self-assurance was exactly right, as if he did not quite expect but only hoped that she would like him. She could not help herself. She was flattered, as he had meant for her to be. He turned smoothly to her partner. "You don't mind if I steal her away, do you?" And then, without consulting her, he took Kate's elbow and propelled her to a small alcove, where his large frame blocked her view of the party.

In her most distant and mannered voice she started to protest. "Do you always behave this way?" she demanded to know. "As if I were waiting and ripe for the plucking?"

He smiled again. "Always when the spirit moves me."

"That would be rather often, I should think. You seem very practiced."

"You seemed deeply interested. Don't forget that."

"I don't know what you're talking about."

"Yes, you do. Cigarette?"

She shook her head and then watched as he cupped his hand around the match and inhaled the blue smoke. For a second the cigarette hung at the edge of his mouth, and his eyes squinted as the smoke trailed upward. He stared at her hard and she could feel her mouth start to go dry. Then she lowered her eyes, not wanting him to see the exultant light that surely was in them.

"You had the most alarmed and searching look just now when you turned around to see if I had come to you. Did you think I might not?"

"I simply don't know what you're talking about."

"You lie, Miss Goodfellow."

Kate heard herself saying coolly, "I knew you'd be insufferable."

Hopper laughed. "I've been called insufferable before but never with such conviction." He stopped a tray of drinks going by and commandeered two Sazeracs in thick, frosty glasses. Kate felt her heart pounding so hard she knew if she looked down she would be able to see it pumping under the tight black dress. Out of the ceaseless march of men through all of her days, this one, she knew, had been appointed and predestined for her.

They would talk about this meeting afterward, asking each other the immemorial lovers question—"When did you first know you cared?"—and they both agreed, "When I first saw you." It was a recollection they would smile and marvel at, remembering often this fascinating moment when Fate had brought them together. They who did not believe in Fate, they who were not sentimentalists and never fools. But then, of course, they were wrong.

PART ONE

1942

"... and all the ships at sea."

CHAPTER ONE

THE SEA RAGED. Breaking green water swept across the deck of a ship, cascading over the side in a carpet of suds so that the ship wallowed clumsily like a pig rooting in mud. Waves piled up in rising cliffs with spume sixty feet high. Even the troopship captain, who had spent all his life at sea, had never met such a continuously savage storm. Down in the trough the ship rolled drunkenly from one direction to another only to shoot up again to the curl peak of the next roller-coaster wave.

It was a ship built for peacetime pleasure cruises. Her graceful hull once white topped with three tall azure smoke-stacks was now painted a wartime putty gray. On her decks there had been beautiful brass fittings and deck chairs of polished teak, but now, stripped of all such luxury, she was performing a wartime miracle by stuffing an unheard of number of British and American troops, nurses, and a handful of news correspondents below decks and in the hold.

Five days earlier, a flotilla of ships had set forth from Southampton on an uneventful sea en route to Gibraltar and the Mediterranean resembling not so much a modern-day war convoy but a giant feudal family moving with all the pomp of a royal parade. Queen of the flotilla was the pleasure cruiser; airplane carriers, troopships, and destroyers flanked her on all sides. Flags snapped smartly in the breeze, and somewhere a brass military band played all the marching songs of battle in sprightly resonance.

The sheer size of the convoy had made it an obvious target for enemy torpedo attack, and every sort of defensive maneuver had been evaluated and debated among the commanders. Twice the ships had made ready to sail and twice they had delayed. The navigational course was designed to confuse and confound the enemy but no one had reckoned on the storm. It came sweeping in from the middle Atlantic almost without warning—a shift in the wind, a rise in temperature, a falling barometer, scudding clouds on the horizon; then a wall of rain-laden squalls of unusual ferocity. In the distance, coming in and out of the gloom, you could just make out the other ships bobbling about like rubber toys in a child's bath. Outside, crew were lashed to the decks. Inside, and below deck, some 4,000 men and women clung to anything that was battened down—and prayed.

Ensign Cal Holden was scared. They had taught him none of this at Annapolis. Not about fear. Not about being trapped. Not about wanting to run when there was no place to run to. He was sure he was going to die and he couldn't bear it. He was just twenty-one and he wanted to go home. Holding on to the railing and trying to keep his legs steady as the ship rolled and bucked, he walked the length of the corridor as he was meant to do on watch. He could hear people moaning from their bunks and smell their vomit. When at last he reached the end of the corridor, he turned. At the far end he saw a man trying to push open the door onto the deck.

The blood rushed to Cal's face in relief at having something to do. "Hold it, Mac. Hold it right there," he bellowed, and though he knew he must look like the comic character of a drunken sailor as he lurched uncontrollably in the dim light, he didn't care. His orders were to let no one on deck for any reason.

"Where do you think you're going?" He bore down on the figure.

"The deck" came the short reply.

"The shit you are! No one goes out and I don't care who, what, or why. Those are direct orders. No one on deck unless there's a drill." The man in question turned around and Cal did a wide-eyed double take. He saw an explosion of red hair spilling from a brown leather flier's cap, its flaps pulled down to cover her ears. Cal instinctively amended his tone. "'Scuse me, I mean, ma'am?"

She looked at him and smiled. A sunny, optimistic smile. In one beat she had taken his measure. She saw a young man with a nice face—the kind they liked to put on military recruiting posters making war look like a wholesome activity for young men. She saw an Adam's apple bobbing uncertainly under his collar. His inexperience was written all over his hapless face. Her smile widened. Here was a boy unprepared to handle this situation. This was her kind of boy.

"You wouldn't make those rules apply to me, now would you?' It was not a question but a gentle cajoling voice. She stepped toward him, tapping the insignia she wore on her lapel. "I'm a war correspondent . . . *World* magazine." She stuck out her hand. "Kate Goodfellow. What's your name?"

Cal puzzled a moment entirely thrown off. *World* magazine? That was big-time stuff. "Un . . . Holden. I mean Cal. Cal Holden. Ma'am."

She laughed. "I like the ma'am. Sounds like you're from the South."

"That's right. I'm from Kentucky, ma'am, but I have to tell you, you can't—"

"They never say 'can't' in Kentucky. Oh, I know Kentucky. I was down there in . . ." The roll of the ship suddenly threw her against the young man, and she clung to him helplessly. Then, after steadying herself against him, she tilted her head up and locked his eyes in hers. "Tell you what we're going to do, Cal. You're going to tie this rope around my waist and hold on to it while I go out on deck. I can tell you're strong enough to hold me. I won't be long. But I have to get a picture for my magazine. It's very important. You understand." She put her hand on his shoulder and stared deep into his eyes. They were partners now with a mission to complete. In the split second Ensign Cal hesitated, she had already started wrapping the rope around her, and he found himself securing a slip knot around the slim waist of the woman with the red hair.

"Hold me tight now, Cal. If I tug twice, give me some slack. If I tug once, haul me in. I'm depending on you." She turned and gave him a quick wave and a flirtatious wink, and before he could quite think about it, she was out the door and into the howling tempest. Cal couldn't figure out how that had happened, but one thing for sure, he hung on for dear life.

Outside, the wind ripped at Kate's jumpsuit in an instant, tearing the aviator cap from her head. In less than a few seconds she was drenched in seawater. With her free hand she wiped her eyes of the salt spray. Her heart was pounding in fear and excitement. Her camera was in her musette bag. She would need both hands to hold on to it. A little farther along she saw stairs leading up to the bridge. She gave the rope two sharp tugs and inched her way toward them. Then, wedging her legs between the railing and the steps, she allowed her eyes to take in the scene. The sky and the sea churned together the color of thick, gray oatmeal set in a bedlam of sounds as if a hundred banshees were on deck, moaning and screaming and whistling in hideous discord. She raised her camera to her eye just as the ship's bow plunged down into the trough. Perfect. Kate pressed the shutter and the peanut bulb flashed—an infinitesimal beacon in the murky twilight.

At that very moment some three thousand miles away in New York, the counterman at Schrafft's on Madison at Fiftieth finished placing the luncheon special in the pronged holders at each table in the restaurant. Today, November 6, 1942, they were featuring: Shrimp Cocktail, Tomato Soup, Steak with Mushroom Caps, Potatoes and Peas, Endive and Orange Salad, Gingerbread, Strawberry Shortcake, and Coffee at the inflated wartime price of $2.50. Over at Radio City Music Hall, Irving Berlin's *White Christmas* had just opened, and between Madison Avenue, the mall of Rockefeller Center, and the immense, ornate movie palace, New York was alive with people. It was a clear day with the smell of roasting chestnuts drifting in air just cold enough to put a smart snap of color in your cheek.

Some twenty stories above Schrafft's and its busy lunchtime crowd, a man sat alone in his office. He was a pale timber wolf of a man and he sat very still except for a single finger tapping a slow beat on his desk. Shaggy eyebrows hung over eyes the color of slate. He did not look like a man who smiled much. A quick glance around his office and one would note it was devoid of clutter or personal effects. The desk took up most of the space, and it was clear save for a telephone and a complicated-looking intercom system. Behind him fat, speckled pigeons pecked and cooed mindlessly on the sill of a window tightly shut on the chill November day.

It was impossible to know what he was thinking, but it could have been about any number of surprising things. A new dance called the jitterbug had young people jumping, the boys in zoot suits, the girls in swirling skirts and bobby socks. Gas rationing had just gone into effect, and car owners would have to make do on four gallons a week. The cathedral city of Canterbury had been blasted in the biggest daylight raid against England since the Battle of Britain two years before. Names like the Sudan, El Alamein, Guadalcanal—until now unheard of places to some 150 million Americans—were headlines in the news. A vast workforce of women, over two million, had mobilized to take up the jobs the men had left behind. "Rosie the Riveter" was a national symbol, and women were getting equal pay for equal work. One wondered if that would outlast the war.

Americans were wondering about a lot of things they had never thought about before, and it was his job to know what they were wondering. It was his genius to create their wonder. But on this day, none of these thoughts and concerns penetrated the intense concentration of the man behind the desk high above Madison Avenue.

There was no name on the glass plate of his door. There was no need for one. Everyone concerned was well aware that this was the office of the publisher of *World* magazine . . . and *World* magazine was the most widely read weekly news magazine in existence. The large glossy red-and-black format of *World* was as well known to most Americans as was the face on the dollar bill. Each week *World*'s mammoth presses stretching for the better part of two underground city blocks churned out twenty million copies of photographs depicting the world's news as Otis Bennett chose to tell it.

In his magazine, stories unfolded through the medium of pictures, not words. Good pictures, sharp and clear and visually exciting. No expense or care was spared in the getting and making of *World*'s eye-stopping photography. The magazine's handpicked group of photographers went places and saw things most people would never go nor even imagine seeing. Week in and week out *World* magazine held a mirror up to the times in a singularly clear, brilliant, and revealing tone. Seven days of certain events, certain people, certain emotions true to that particular week.

Launching the magazine in the relative calm of 1936, Otis had concentrated his first issues on American know-how and exuberance and all that was sentimental and charming and endearing about American life. Readers looked forward to stories about country doctors and radio performers and aspiring actresses in New York and Chinese schoolchildren in San Francisco and baseball heroes and presidential garden parties and family reunions—stories to warm the heart and maybe even shed a tear over. When *World* reporters covered political events and major disasters, they never did so in the blood-and-guts style of the daily newspapers. *World* gave *meaning* to disaster. In its large, glossy pages no building burned without a heroic fireman; no tornado hit without a last haunting image of a child's tattered doll in the rubble; sudden and tragic death was always coupled with the miracle of birth, and always, the indomitable human spirit glowed from beginning to end of each issue. As Otis Bennett often said to his staff, "There is nothing wrong with normal, decent, pleasant behavior."

As the decade ground to an end, however, behavior in the world at large had become distinctly unpleasant. By 1939, *World* correspondents were fanned out all over the globe, and the images they brought home were bloody and ugly and heartbreaking. From China and Spain came arterial bombardment of civilians, from Berlin a Nazi rampage of fire and murder against the Jews, from Prague the conquering Third Reich and the end of Czechoslovakia. The fall of Poland, the blitz over London, a state of siege in Moscow—and then, Pearl Harbor.

The world was at war and photography had become the principal means by which the public could see what was going on. There were the newsreels, to be sure, but these were fleeting images left behind in the darkened theater. A magazine came right into the home, and its pictures could be studied and pondered over by every member of the family. *World* magazine told the story of the war in magnificent images—churches in ruin, soldiers in the trench, sacked villages, fleeing refugees, medics on the front lines, crying orphans, tense generals, bombing missions, invasions, bravery, and in every issue, a hero.

Getting a weekly magazine out was a killing business. Each issue of *World* contained two major news stories, one photo essay, a series of short human interest pieces, and one text article. All of this had to be fitted in and around the presold advertisements. Everything—the stories, the human interest, the essay, the advertisements—had to be distilled into one cohesive whole with what, in magazine parlance, had "jump." Jump meant pace, impact, a kind of ignition that not only fell into the overall philosophy of the magazine but propelled each issue so that it stood alone.

Add to this the colossal logistics of covering news of the war. It tested and taxed correspondents and editors to their limits. Other magazines relied on the newly formed wire services for their pictures; Otis Bennett wanted exclusives. No longer mere eyewitnesses to the scene, news photographers were now interpreters, social commentators, cultural arbiters. They had to be tough, aggressive, and smart. Most of all, they had to be willing to risk their lives.

Twenty million copies a week marched out of this office and into the homes and hearts of America. At least triple that number read the magazine. No other form of media reached that many people. Everyone was aware of the power it wielded and everyone, including the government and the military, stood still for a *World* photographer—who could argue with that much influence? *World* photographers were celebrities in their own right; the bright stars of the show constantly out front, highly visible, raising a cloud of dust wherever they were working. They were the ones who met royalty and presidents, who hobnobbed with newsmakers, who got to go anywhere and do anything. But there was a price to pay for being out front. A person could get killed. It was no wonder that egos ran large and demanding.

With space limited in each issue, competition among war correspondents was fierce, and they demanded only one thing of their editors back home—sacred assurance that no other *World* photographer scoop their stories. Otis Bennett's solution was to assign each of them a territory. The territories were inviolable.

Otis suddenly reached forward and punched a button on his intercom. It squawked for a second and then he heard his managing editor's voice. "Any word yet?" said Otis. It was all he needed to say. They both knew he was talking about Kate.

"Nothing yet" came the short reply.

CHAPTER TWO

KATE NO LONGER went up top. There was no sense in it.
She had lost one of her cameras in a lifeboat drill. The captain
ordered two and three drills a day, indifferent to the sickness
and turbulence down below. At first she had been given permission to roam the boat at will taking pictures of whatever
she wanted, but now this was forbidden because of the storm.
She had tried working from her drill station, but the camera,
one of her best, had been swept out of her hand by the lashing
wind and rain as she clung to the ropes. She couldn't risk losing more of her equipment. It was better to stay in the bunk
and try to keep safe from the seething turmoil around her. She
tried to rest, to sleep even, but it was impossible. It wasn't the
fear, the noise of people being violently ill, or the moans of
others sure they were about to die that made sleep impossible;
it was another voice, an inner echo that kept her tossing and
turning. *"Don't go, Kate."* His agonized words rang in her
ears. *"You can't leave. You can't leave us."* She lay in her bunk
and heard his voice as close as if he were standing next to her,
his face lost in the shadows of the night, his voice reaching out
for her and holding her heart.

Two months ago—a lifetime. Another lurch of the ship and

the dim lights from the passageway flickered and went out. She mustn't think of Hopper. If she did, she would go mad.

She was in a first-class cabin meant for two but billeted with nine Scottish nurses. However crowded, they all considered themselves lucky to have a cabin at all. Elsewhere, soldiers were in bunks tacked up in passageways, kitchens, laundry rooms, broom closets, and worse. By those standards Kate and the nurses lived in relative luxury, though the stateroom's prewar elegance had been stripped almost bare. Bunks fastened to the walls replaced the once large luxurious beds. Interior doors, mirrors, and drawers had all been removed, though no one knew quite why. Still, mahogany panels, the marble sink with its golden leonine fixtures, and the toilet were still intact. The latter, though only curtained off, still provided some degree of privacy, and this in and of itself made the women feel downright pampered.

In the first two days of the storm Kate had not suffered from the paralyzing seasickness that gripped almost everyone and had gone up to the grand saloon for the twice-daily meals taken by those who had the confidence they could keep their food down. But dining aloft exposed one to the hazards of unpredictable flying objects. Plates flew from one table to the next, scattering soup and food generously as they went. Tables and chairs slid about like marbles in a pinball machine, and the grand piano, one of the few reminders of past elegance, turned into a fierce charging beast eluding a group of infantrymen who tried to ambush it, until finally, with a deafening chord, it crashed against the wall with its legs broken.

The violent motion of the ship was compounded by dim light or, often, pitch darkness. Those who could still walk and talk tried to buoy each other up. "We're lucky," they said. "We don't have to worry about getting torpedoed in a storm like this. No sub could hold its aim long enough to hit us." It was true about the torpedoing, but it was not true about the luck. The storm couldn't have hit at a worse time. The Allies were planning a surprise invasion of North Africa, and though the operation was one of the best-kept secrets of the war, so secret that most everybody on board thought they were bound for Sardinia or Sicily, Kate Goodfellow knew otherwise.

Hitler had conquered Europe. Now he could be attacked

only from Britain, from Russia, or from North Africa, yet the Germans held all three fronts with a seeming impenetrable strength. It was a dark time for the Allies. Then, in 1942, the break came. In one of the greatest Allied victories of the war, the British 8th Army under the command of General Montgomery defeated the Germans at El Alamein in Egypt. German General Rommel, aka the Desert Fox, was pushed westward. If the Allied troops, commanded by Dwight Eisenhower, could take North Africa, they could close in on Rommel from the west, trapping him in a pincers movement. They had to move quickly and with deadly accuracy in order to surprise Berlin. Hitler would know the cost of losing Africa, and he would pour thousands of airborne troops into a counterattack.

On the American side of the Atlantic, few civilians, including Kate's editors at *World* magazine, had any inkling of the invasion, just the break Kate needed to jump from one territory to the next without their permission. After all, she reasoned, she couldn't risk security by cabling trans-Atlantic, could she? She was a war correspondent . . . she should follow the troops. And follow them she would, right down to the front line.

All her life she had been a first, and now she was going to be the first American woman allowed into battle. Of course, there was that other matter . . . the problem of infringing on some other photographer's territory, but all that seemed so trivial now. After all, rules were made to be broken.

Her assignment was to cover the landing of the first American troops in Britain. Otis gave her two months and then he wanted her back in New York. So for weeks she had been singing the patriotic theme of *World* with photographic human interest stories about American GIs in beleaguered England, but all the while she had been looking for an opportunity to get a combat assignment. She was desperate to see battle, real battle. She wanted to be in it, see it as it happened, feel it, feel the fear of it, smell it. She was electrified by the sheer drama and spectacle of war. "If I'm good enough to be a war correspondent," she argued to anyone who would listen, "I'm good enough to get shot at." The military shook their heads. She cabled Otis in New York begging him to use his influence. He cabled back he would do no such thing. "*World* is not just a battle magazine," she could hear his editorial growl coming through the cable, "it's a celebration of the human race. Forget macabre interest in disaster. Your job is to provide just the opposite. Keep up the good work."

"Bullshit!" She wadded the paper in her fist and threw the cable across the room. The young English operator who worked the trans-Atlantic Teletype grinned. "B-u-l-l-s-h-i-" He pecked at the black keys as if typing a reply. Kate was not amused. She flew at him in a fury, grabbing his shirt by the neck. "You bloody men make me sick. Arrogant, self-serving, the whole lot of you. I've done more in my life in a day than you will ever do in a lifetime. I've risked my life hundreds of times and for what? So that I can sit on the sidelines of the biggest story of the century? He won't say out and out it's because I'm a woman, but the message is clear. And I say bullshit!" Tears of rage and frustration spilled down her cheeks. The young operator reached in his pocket and pulled out a large handkerchief and handed it to her. Kate took it and blew her nose loudly. "Christ, Charlie, I'm sorry. It's not your fault."

"It's alright, luv. The messenger always gets shot. For a pack of Camels, I could be persuaded to overlook the whole messy affair."

American troops had poured into England rolling in cigarettes, canned goods, chocolates, Kleenex, and goodies the harassed English hadn't seen in years. Kate bartered these goods for stories.

"Okay, Vicar, stand tall and look straight into the camera lens. You boys with the lights, we want to pick up the rubble and the bombed altar. I want all the rest in shadow, and for God's sake keep those people out of my sight lines. I only want the vicar, the GI, and the kids. Now listen, Dave, on three hold the Hershey bars up so the kids can see them. Got it?"

The resulting picture, which made the cover of *World* two weeks later, appeared to be the spontaneous effort of a roving camera, and it tugged at the heart of every reader. A bombed-out church, moppet-haired children in drab wartime woolens gathered close to the kindly vicar, all eyes looking eagerly at the proud American soldier. The blatant sentiment bothered no one. The message telegraphed to the American people was assuring. Americans liked seeing themselves as saviors.

Kate had her two months to capture the flavor of wartime England. Death was verboten. Heroism and humor her mandate. Soldiers grappling with English money, English tea, English girls. She sat in bomb shelters, rode trains north with evacuated children, stood with women in rationing lines, and every photograph was a tireless tribute to the indomitable English and the lovable Americans. In short, she was allowed access only to subjects that did not encroach on the last frontier of the male domain—the battlefield. The threat of being left out of the action almost drove her mad.

Toward the end of her two-month assignment, the big break finally came. It was a cold, damp, and discouraging day. The press had been called into duty to photograph King George VI while he inspected the newly arrived heavy bombers from America. These big, lumbering, elephantine airplanes were capable of flying great distances carrying massive bombs. It was no wonder they were called the Flying Fortresses. Every reporter in England wanted to get a closer look at them. They were something new, they were important. The army was convinced their Fortresses were going to win the war.

"Who is that woman with the remarkable red hair?" the king asked his aide as he inspected the first thirteen bombers on the tarmac. The aide, not used to such questions from the pale, humorless, stuttering monarch who had so recently been thrust onto the throne after the abdication of his brother, glanced quickly to the cordoned-off reporters and photographers kept at a respectful distance. Red, indeed, and dressed to the nines in a spanking-new officer's uniform, brass buttons polished to a glittering shine, skirt fitted without an inch to spare exposing a damn sight pair of good-looking legs.

Word was quickly sent down, and before long Kate was drawn from the ranks and brought forward to photograph the king and his entourage up close. The grousing from the press corps was audible. "That says it all, don't it, boys? She's got one piece of equipment we don't have." Kate put an extra little wiggle in her walk just to let them know she'd heard. If they were going to treat her like a woman, she was going to show them just how much a woman she was.

She was charming, ladylike, and professional as she photographed the king and his aides. After their departure, the mood relaxed and Kate was just flirtatious enough with the American brass to warrant a special invitation from one of the officers to lunch with them. She lost no time in making good use of this sudden windfall. The higher the rank, the more these commanders reminded her of the gods of old—headstrong, mighty, and childishly vain. Everyone, it seemed, wanted to be singled out by *World* magazine for a story. By the time lunch was over, she had secured an invitation from the army air commander to do a story on the Flying Fortresses from their secret base in the countryside of England.

Kate rolled and punched at the bedding in her bunk, trying to find some way to wedge her body so that it wasn't so at the mercy of pitch and role of the ship. She was cramped and the air in the cabin was suffocatingly vile. On impulse she reached into the canvas camera bag which she kept close to her at all times, deep into the side pockets until she felt the smooth silky fabric jammed to the very bottom of the bag. It was a foolish thing to carry around—foolish and comforting.

"Hop," she whispered his name in the dark of the bunk, gripping the satin fabric. Just saying his name made her eyes fill with tears. She missed him. She missed him like hell. Where was he tonight? With someone else? The thought of Hopper in bed with another woman was almost more than she could bear. She wouldn't think about it—but she did. His hands on someone else, his mouth, his soft, summer voice. His stories and his laugh. So hard to coax out of him, and yet when it came it was like a brilliant sun bursting out from behind a cloud.

She started crying, now in earnest but silently, so none of the others could hear. If only she could snuggle up to Hopper and let him hold her, making her small against his large warmth. If only he could stroke her head and tell her it was all right. That he was there, waiting for her to come home.

She remembered his ebullient arrival in her office one afternoon and under his arm the parcel from Saks Fifth Avenue.

"I had to buy it," he said, thrusting the package at her with a childish grin. "It was too beautiful to leave behind on a stiff form with a bright pink throat and no head." Inside under the masses of white tissue was a soft and silky thing, beautiful and sexy and rich.

"Try it on, Katie. Please. Right now."

"Here? In the office?" The impatience she always felt when her day was interrupted was clear. She was on deadline. For a week she had been sloshing around the streets of Louisville, Kentucky, in one of the worst floods on record. The Ohio and Mississippi rivers were on a rampage; a million people were homeless, hundreds had died. She was working on pure adrenaline, editing her pictures, making sure they told the story the way she wanted it told. Now, at the eleventh hour, here was Hopper asking her to put on a satin nightgown in the middle of the afternoon on a busy day. And she had!

Stepping behind the door to the closet, she had changed out of her slacks and jacket and minutes later emerged with her hair falling free and the gown clinging to the curves of her tall, slim body. Outside her door all the clatter of a busy editorial office: the telephones ringing, the typewriters clacking; inside, the look on Hopper's face, his sharp intake of breath, and then *World* with all its urgent deadlines and complexities had fallen away. They had made love right there against the door, and she remembered it now with a clarity that left her breathless.

Caressing the satin gown made her feel so lonesome she thought she might die. If she did die, she would never see Hopper again, never feel his hands on her, never hear that easy voice telling her all the wonderful things she loved to hear, teaching her, teasing her, whispering the magic words of love into her ear. She dug her hand deeper in the bag and pulled the gown out. It was her one link to Hopper now. If she was going to die on this miserable ship, she wanted to die as close to him as she could get. In the dark she fumbled with her regulation slacks and thick undershirt. The cool, elegant feel of the gown as she wiggled into it was a shock. Her wardrobe consisted entirely of army-issue uniforms—bulky, itchy undershirts, and hideous panties with wide elastic bands at the waist, slacks, wool skirt, a tailored jacket, and an officer's greatcoat. She had forgotten the way satin made you feel, how sensual it was clinging like the very promise of love to your body.

* * *

Flying low in a light aircraft, Kate could barely hear his words, but the pilot, an Englishman, was determined to show her the sights nevertheless. "Gloucestershire . . . Vale of Evesham . . . Cotswolds . . ." most of his dialogue lost in the whine of the motors. He kept pointing and she looked and nodded. Certainly the English countryside was beautiful. Hedgerows trimmed fields that seemed like soft pieces of green felt, small villages clustered around old stone churches, sheep grazing on hillsides. "There!" he shouted, pointing off to the left. Seeped in the morning mist was an immense house, a castle, complete with towers and turrets and a beautifully crisp formal garden. The tranquility of it all made it impossible to believe that this country was going through the ugliest of wars, but moments later when they came to the base and Kate stepped out onto the busy tarmac, the peaceful countryside was immediately forgotten. Here at last was the world she had longed for—the crews, the machinery, and all the dramatic activity of a military at war.

Kate's arrival on base afforded her an instant celebrity. If she had caused a stir simply by being a woman in other circumstances of her life, here it amounted to an eruption. For the next few days she was followed everywhere, ogled all the time, treated with elaborate courtesy and all the while every man on the base dreamed of what she would be like in bed.

Kate basked in her celebrity. She had never lost the thrill of being the center of attention, but she couldn't go on indefinitely being the pinup girl. She needed a story, a hook, something about these bombers that would read back home. The airplanes were immense, formidable, but clumsy-looking on the ground. There was certainly nothing sexy about them and she wanted sexy. Something that humanized them. The hook came in the form of a note delivered to her room one afternoon from the twelve-member crew of one of the bombers. In it, she was invited to name their airplane.

All over the airfield, crews were coming up with names like *Berlin Buzzbomb* and *Deutscher Cleanser* for the bombers that would take them into enemy territory. It was serious business, and imaginative artwork began to individualize each plane. Kate was flattered and gave a full night's thought before settling on *The Flying Flashgun*. The crew loved it and went to work immediately painting the nose of their B-17 with a glamorous pinup model, a mass of red hair flowing, her eye winking out at the world from behind her camera, having just blown up Hitler and Mussolini with a lethal, outsized flash attachment.

An official christening ceremony was scheduled, and Kate got herself all dolled up in dress grays for it. The boys had found a piano and wheeled it out onto the runway, written a speech that would be read by the commanding officer, and decided in lieu of champagne to have Kate crack a bottle of Coca-Cola over the nose. "More typically American," they all agreed, and far more accessible. It was a heavy overcast day, and the CO, due back from a week's absence in London, was late. Kate was already up on a ladder with the cola bottle in hand when the piano player struck up a boogie-woogie riff. Then the CO leaped out of a jeep and began reading the speech. "May *The Flying Flashgun* bring as much honor to . . ." Kate's head swung around and for a moment she almost teetered off her ladder. She looked down at the officer who was reading with great expression and dramatic gestures. She couldn't see his face, but there was no mistaking the voice. ". . . as its godmother has brought to the 97th." He looked up and grinned. "Your cue," he said. There were enormous tears in Kate's eyes. She swung her bottle over the right front machine gun. It broke as clean as if it had been cut by a jeweler.

"Eddie?" She reached her hand down to him.

He stood looking up at her. "It's me." In that brief moment it was as if an eternity of years fell away. For once in her life, Kate was utterly speechless.

He held up his hand. "I feel the same way. I don't know what to say except that you look like nothing else on earth. My God, you're more beautiful than ever."

"Eddie. Is that really you? I . . . I don't believe my eyes." But she did. He was different and the same all at once. In a flash she was in his arms, oblivious to the wolf whistles that rose up from the crew surrounding them. Colonel Chester Edding allowed himself the indignity of the embrace in front of his men before gently disentangling himself from her arms.

* * *

Lying in her bunk, Kate's eyes misted up again just thinking about Eddie. Funny how things worked out. She had done everything humanly possible to get an assignment close to battle and nothing had worked. Then, as if by magic, Eddie had shown up in her life again and here she was on her way at last. But not even Eddie could get her assigned to a bombing mission. "We'll get you as close as we can, Kate. Then it's a toss-up whether they'll let you go out on one." They were nearing Gibraltar. Maybe tomorrow they would be in the relative calm of the Mediterranean. Another lurch of the ship and the lights from the passageway flickered back on.

She could hear Maggie in the bunk below her, and so she tried to lie very still, willing the girl asleep. Maggie had the most disconcerting way of popping her head up, "just for a chat," as if they were college roommates. She too belonged to the small proud minority of those on board who could keep their meals down. "I come from the Isle of Skye," she said, as if this said it all. "My folk are deep-water men. So, now, tell me, Kate, tell me more about the movie stars. Did you really meet Clark Gable? You never finished the story." Her voice was sweet and the accent was blurred in the Scottish way. Maggie loved Kate's stories.

At first Kate did not mind the small, slight girl who looked far too young to be a nurse, let alone one heading off to war. Maggie McKye was delighted her bunk mate was a famous photographer. For two days, before they set sail, Maggie had followed her everywhere and Kate had not minded at all. Indeed, Maggie served a purpose. Her constant chatter and avid devotion kept Kate's mind off the fact that she was breaking one of the most rigid codes of her profession. She was going to scoop a story in another reporter's territory. Willie Madden was *World*'s man in North Africa. Not a bad guy and one of the best war photographers in the business. He had been in the trenches, he'd been on missions over Germany, and now he was in the desert witnessing Montgomery's stunning victory over Rommel. He was only twenty-five and already his work dominated the battle coverage in the magazine. Anger and frustration made it easier for her to board the ship ignoring the cables from *World* urging her back to New York. It wasn't fair. Madden and others like him were going to walk away with this war, and she was damned if she was going to let it happen. Why, even nurses like Maggie had a better chance of seeing the action than Kate did.

It was hard to imagine Maggie under siege. She had a sweet face with an upturned nose and a rosy complexion set off by a cloud of soft brown curls. *Pert* was the word that came to mind, *pert* and *winsome* at the same time. Maggie and her fellow nurses were kept on close watch by their matron, a severe taskmaster of the old school. The nurses grumbled under her unyielding authority, her most damning edict being that she did not allow her "gels" to wear slacks. The nurses, or "sisters," as they called themselves, were openly envious of Kate's regulation slacks and her freedom to wear them whenever she wanted. They too had been issued slacks, but Matron had forbidden their use, insisting her nurses appear in off-duty skirts, blouses, and jackets.

Because the ship had remained in port for two full days before sailing, Maggie had attached herself to Kate like a little mascot. She followed her all over the ship as Kate prowled about with her camera; she carried her equipment for her, and she would have waited table for her if Kate hadn't put her foot down.

"Don't wait on me, Maggie. Come sit here and talk to me." They were in the main dining saloon set aside for officers and news correspondents. Here there were a few reminders of the bygone cruise days. The chairs were cushioned and gold gilt; there were linens for the tables and enough musicians routed up from the troops below to keep a pretty good combo playing from the risers where the ship's orchestra had once played. The nurses were supposed to eat in the second-class dining room with the rest of the enlisted men, but no one questioned Kate's authority as she waved her little friend in behind her. "Sit down and let the mess boys carry the trays. There's a good girl." Kate patted the seat next to hers. She at once saw that Maggie had never been in such surroundings before even though they were a mere shadow of what had once been and suspected that Maggie McKye had never been anywhere and never seen anything before the times had catapulted her and millions like her out of their secure villages and traditions onto the grand-scale stage of war. Maggie made her think of her boys in *The Flying Flashgun*.

"Tell me about yourself, Maggie." The girl was wolfing down a mound of mashed potatoes and something gray and gristly-looking that was being passed off as Salisbury steak. "How did you get here?"

"Oh, well, ma'am," Maggie said, swallowing a forkful and turning her bright blue eyes on Kate. "There's nothing much to tell. When my Jamie signed on, I did, too. I was in my last year of nursing school. Aren't you going to eat your steak, ma'am?"

Kate looked down at the mystery meat and shook her head. "You can have it if you promise not to call me ma'am. It makes me feel a hundred years old."

"So how old are you?" Maggie asked.

Kate laughed. "I'm thirty-six. Does that seem very old?"

"Oh, no." But obviously it did because Maggie turned a bright pink under Kate's direct eyes. "I turned twenty on my last birthday," she added hopefully.

"Is Jamie your husband?"

"Well, he soon will be," Maggie said with a laugh. "That is, when the war's over. I would have married him before he went, but he wouldn't hear of it. Jamie says there are enough babies on the way as it is. He wanted to wait. Jamie says . . ." And Maggie was off and running at the mouth like a little steam engine. Kate nodded and smiled, but she was hardly listening. She had little interest in what Jamie had to say even though from the sounds of it Jamie had a great deal to say about everything. Maggie and Jamie were like two characters out of a pretty little romance novel. They had met over a garden fence. "Jamie was visiting his auntie and her fence bordered up to m' dad's. So there we were hanging over the fence and fallin' in love. Jamie says he doesn't believe in love at first sight, but sure it was lovin' from the minute we saw each other." Later, when Maggie had shown her Jamie's picture, she would have laughed out loud if the raw-boned, gangly Jamie Lloyd hadn't reminded her so painfully of that boy from Kansas—one of her boys.

Her boys. The crew of *The Flying Flashgun*. Kate

photographed them all in the days before their mission. She was good with people who were not used to presenting themselves in front of a camera. Soon their stiff, self-conscious poses relaxed as Kate smiled and laughed and drew their stories out. Watching their faces through the ground lens of the camera, she saw so clearly what they could not—fuzzy-faced, freckled, fresh-eyed youth, so eager to please and swaggering with bravado, these were the men who flew bombing raids deep into German territory. These were the men the civilian world was relying on to win the war. God, they were young.

"That's right, soldier. All I want you to do is sit in that chair and talk to me. Start with where you're from. Kansas? I know Kansas. I've been all over your state. . . ." "Kansas" said he was a farmer's son, least ways until his daddy lost the farm in the Depression. He had put himself through two years of agricultural school by playing piano in a whorehouse in Topeka. Kate laughed. "Did you enjoy it?" she asked. "Yeah, kinda." He grinned and his big ears caught the light from the window in a way that was more endearing than humorous. The camera snapped. Kansas was a front gunner.

Rear gunner was an Irish kid by way of Boston by way of reform school. "Pickpocketing?" "Sure I'm good, but I'm sort of out of practice now." His round blue eyes, meant to melt hearts, gave Kate the eeriest feeling that she just might be missing something. (She was.) The small notebook and tiny gold pen she kept in her hip pocket for quick notes was returned to her pillow in the room where she slept with an awkwardly scrawled note asking her for a date. The navigator, a tall, skinny kid from Tennessee, had been editor of his college newspaper and class valedictorian. His dad was a horse trainer and he had grown up around the tracks as a hotwalker. He launched into a long and quite interesting story about breeding Tennessee walkers. He had volunteered the day after he graduated from Vanderbilt.

There was a boy from Vermont, the youngest and only boy in a run of six girls, a religious straight arrow from Mainline Philadelphia, and a tough-guy ladies' man from Brooklyn. "Brooklyn" was the bombardier. It was his job to operate the bombsight and pull the trigger that released the bomb. These were the men that flew off early one morning with Kate there to photograph their big, lumbering bomb-laden plane as it roared down the runway and up into the empty sky.

Eddie stood with her. "Your boys are on a hazardous mission. They're after an airplane factory and they'll get quite a reception."

"I wish I could go. Oh, I wish I could," she said fervently. "I wouldn't mind the danger. I wouldn't mind anything if I could just get permission to go up once."

"I've heard you want to be the first woman on a bombing mission."

Kate was suddenly all ears. "You bet I do. Is that something you can arrange for me?"

"Nope. I tried. Word came back you'd have to get clearance from the Pentagon." He saw the hurt look come over her face. "Look, I know dozens of newsmen who haven't been given clearance, if that makes any difference."

"It doesn't," Kate said shortly, "because I know dozens more who have. I don't understand it, Eddie." She looked in his eyes expectant, insistent. "What do you think I'll have to do to get into battle?"

Something caught in Eddie's throat. He saw a girl from years before, her face set in determination, her hair bunched up under a man's hat, her body bent over a large, clumsy camera and both girl and camera precariously close to the edge of a slippery slate roof some three stories high. But that had been a long time ago. Looking at her now, with the morning sun in her hair, she seemed more beautiful to him than ever. She had lost the girlish dishevelment and the awkward staccato of her younger self and acquired ease, self-possession, and assurance. No longer merely pretty, she was striking with high cheekbones, pale skin, and piercing, intense eyes. The almost hawklike intensity of her face was saved by the loveliest mouth. A mouth that had not changed in his view one bit. It was the kind of mouth that fiction writers never called big, but always called "generous." He knew if he leaned over and kissed her, which was exactly what he wanted to do, that he would be kissing a dynamo.

Eddie had work to do and left her on her own for the morning planning to meet up again at lunch. She wandered about watching the ground crews but found little to photograph. She noticed the whole rhythm of the base changed when a mission was in operation. Everyone went about their business, but every eye and ear was cocked toward the sound of a distant engine. Along about two o'clock they heard what they were waiting for. The first of the bombers was coming back to base. Everyone started pouring out of Quonset huts, their eyes, like Kate's, straining to make out who had made it back. One after another they came straggling in. The flight crews, Kate could see, were climbing out of their planes silent and sullen. Things had not gone well. She had been around long enough to know one should not talk too much if things had gone badly. After the men had disappeared into the debriefing hut, she stood on the tarmac alone and watched as the sky deepened to twilight. *The Flying Flashgun* had been hit, its crew ditching in the North Sea in heavily patrolled German waters. There was no other word.

At dawn she started her story. It was the most powerful story she had ever filed because it had touched her in a way far deeper than her other stories. Here was the immense beauty and ominous power of the bombers, the youth and vigor and camaraderie of the crews, the tension on the ground, the long wait, the homecoming for some, the empty sky for others, and finally a long shot of a tough and lonely man sitting at a desk in a Quonset hut writing letter after letter. *Dear Kansas and Boston and Cleveland and Tennessee and Brooklyn, Your son is missing in action. . . .*

Eddie leaned back from his desk. He was exhausted, she could see. "Still want to go bombing?" he asked.

"Of course. More than ever."

"Then I have an idea for you. Something big is about to happen. It's top secret and if they let you go, you'll have to go under wraps. This is bigger than anything we've done so far."

And there it was—laid in her lap like a gift. The invasion of North Africa. This was her chance. She listened to Eddie describe what he knew of the logistics of the invasion, but her mind was racing over the equipment available to her, the supplies she would need. "I'm going by air, but they won't let you fly. So you have clearance to go by boat on one of the troop ships," he continued, winking at her, "the safe way."

On the eve of her sailing, two cables reached her. One

from *World* magazine. NEXT ASSIGNMENT IN OREGON, it read cryptically. The other was from Hopper, not cryptic at all.

> HAVE REACHED MOST DIFFICULT DECISION OF LIFE-
> TIME. PARTNERSHIP MUST DISSOLVE UNLESS IMMEDI-
> ATE PROMISE OF FUTURE. YOU ARE MY ONLY LOVE
> AND ALWAYS WILL BE. PHOEBE AND I BEG YOU. RE-
> TURN CABLE YES OR NO.

Now she regretted putting on the nightgown. It was a dangerous thing to do. Allowing the undisciplined pleasure and agony of Hopper into her thoughts was dangerous. She must shut her mind to him. But here in the discomfort of the bunk and the jerks and jolts of the rolling ship, Hopper was everywhere. And then, too, there was Phoebe, the night child, the moon goddess. This was the name they had given to their child who was to be. A child of their secret devising, the child who sometimes seemed so real it was as if she were awaiting them just around the bend. They had named her Phoebe and he had even dedicated a book to her. But Phoebe was still waiting.

Kate dozed and in a fitful half sleep dreamed she was on a train and the train was speeding through a tunnel. In the windows her face was reflected back on her like a black mirror, and the face she saw was not her own face but that of a plump child. Then, with a lurch, the train careened around a corner and into the light. She knew Hopper was waiting for her at the station and she was excited and just a little giddy. She peered out to get a first glance of him. Just ahead, she could see that the tracks ended not at a station but at a large body of water. The train never slowed down but plunged off the tracks, jettisoned into a murky sea. Down it went with a shriek so that her screams of fear and panic had no effect. She clawed at the windows to get out, but they were bolted shut. The sound of a voice made her whirl around in the cramped compartment, and there sitting on a seat of red plush and bouncing a little like she was having a wonderful time was the child. "Don't go, Kate." She giggled. "Don't leave *us*."

CHAPTER THREE

HOPPER DELANEY WOKE up with a start. Had he been dreaming? If he had, he couldn't remember the details, only that a large and ugly monster was fighting to get out of his head. He lay still in the unfamiliar bed, trying to reconstruct the last twelve hours of his life. His eyes were like slits and refused to open wide. The upper and lower lids parting only enough to tell him he was in a place he had never seen before. Tiny pinpoints of pain began to shoot in and around his eyeballs, probing deep into the burning red center of his brain. This was going to be one hell of a hangover. He tried to lick his lips, but his mouth felt as if an entire roll of toilet paper had been shredded into it. He tried to swallow, but the taste of stale tobacco at the back of his throat made him want to vomit. *Can't do it anymore,* he thought. *Old man now. Forty-two years old.* Now he remembered. He had been celebrating (if you could call it that) his birthday. Bourbon. Wine. Some sort of licorice, sticky drink they called a Stinger. His stomach gave another strong warning, like rolling waves deep in his gut.

Okay. Make your peace. Lie still and be quiet. These things he told himself he could do. He forced his mind to think back to the preceding day. It was a lecture hall. Faces, hundreds of them all staring up at him, laughing, applauding, asking questions. All those questions! He'd give everything he had for a tall glass of shaved ice and a Coke. After the questions, he'd called a buddy who worked for one of the daily newspapers in Chicago and they had agreed to meet for dinner. It was someplace down in the old part of town, an Italian joint. There was some sort of party going on, maybe a wedding? Yes. He remembered dancing with the bride, and the bride's mother, maybe even the bride's father. Then he remembered the proprietress, a small, plump woman called Mama Louise. Such a nice mama, he had cried in her lap. She had roared with laughter and propped him up at a table. "Give him spaghetti. All he want," she called to the waiter. "But don't give him no more wine." So they had gone from one bar to another—hotels, dives, clubs . . . he couldn't remember the details, just a series of images and cars and bars and then a fight somewhere and a bloody nose. Then nothing. His dry tongue licked one more time at his lips, and he forced one eye open to see where he was.

"Good morning, Mr. Delaney."

It was a voice bright and cheerful and it came from somewhere in the room. Hopper squinted into the dim gloom. A girl was sitting in a chair next to the window. Now she got up and started to reach for the blinds, which were closed.

"Don't do that, honey," he groaned. Her hand dropped quickly.

"I guess I'd better not," she agreed. "How do you feel?"

This seemed to be an idiotic question, but it was too much trouble to say so. She came over to the bed and stared down at him, smiling. "Why don't you let me run a hot shower for you, and I'll order up some coffee and breakfast if you want."

"No food . . . just coffee." He inched his feet and then his legs gingerly over the side of the bed. It was like moving a giant mass of Jell-O upright. When he was finally in a sitting position, he noticed that he was naked. He pulled the sheet around him, wondering how long it was going to take him to remember who this girl was and what, if anything, had happened between them. She was pretty—and very, very young. Hopper decided not to think about it until after the shower. She disappeared into the bathroom and he heard the water running. Then she came back with a terry robe compliments of the Palmer House.

"Here." She offered it to him. "I'll just go down to the coffee shop and get you the coffee. I'll bet the room service is really slow. Don't run away, now." She wagged the room key happily at him and dashed out the door.

He waved a hand in no particular direction after she had left and considered putting his head back on the pillow. Two Alka-Seltzers later—showered, teeth brushed, his own paisley robe wrapped chastely around him—Hopper allowed the girl to pour him a second cup of coffee. "Okay, honey," he said gently, "you've got me. I don't know who you are and I hope that doesn't upset you. Most of all, I hope I didn't . . . ah . . . take advantage of you last night or . . ."

She laughed. "Mr. Delaney, I don't think you could have taken advantage of anyone last night. You were, well, very inebriated when they brought you back to the hotel. I had been waiting for the longest time. I told the manager I was your niece, and so he let me take care of you. You looked awful . . . I mean . . . I think you were in a fight or something. There was blood all over your shirt but I washed it out."

"You were waiting for me?"

"Oh, yes. I was supposed to take you to the play readings last night. Remember? You were going to critique our plays. Then you were supposed to have dinner with the head of the department. By the way, I'm June Michaels. I was in your seminar yesterday, but you probably didn't notice, there were so many of us."

"Us? How many June Michaels are there?"

She laughed politely. "Students, I mean. Mr. Delaney, don't you remember? You're here at Northwestern University lecturing on the theater. I'm a senior. I can't tell you how much we all thought of your talk. We broke into small groups afterward, and we must have talked all afternoon. It must be so exciting living as you do, knowing all those people. Anyway, I waited and waited and then after you came in, I called the school and said you were ill. I hope you don't mind. It seemed nicer—"

"Very nice. I don't mind at all. Then what?"

"Well, I got you into bed, but you didn't want to stay. You wanted to go out again, but I stopped you."

"Good lord, how did you do that?"

"Oh, I hid your trousers." She lifted her perfect arched

eyebrows, and despite himself he laughed. Then she laughed. A real laugh this time. "I told you they were downstairs with the valet and would be up soon. In the meantime, we talked."

"Was I capable of talking?" The dull throb in his head was beginning to lift, and he reached for his cigarettes. Instantly she was up finding matches for him. He found it was rather nice being looked after by a college girl.

"Oh, yes. Quite capable, only you were rather unhappy—I didn't know it was your birthday—but we talked about a lot of things. You told me all about Hollywood and the new play you were writing. I was very honored to hear about it."

"Yes," he said dryly, inhaling the smoke deep in his lungs. "Well, I'd like to hear about it, too. You see, honey, I haven't written a play in seven years. What was the play about?"

"Oh, it was lovely and very sad. Would you like some more coffee? Would you like for me to tell you about your play?"

He nodded cautiously, not entirely sure he wanted to hear whatever drunken garbage he had spewed out the night before, but she was so eager to please and so damned pretty, he didn't want her to stop talking.

"It's a fable, you said, set in one room, sort of a hunting lodge somewhere in the middle of a forest. The forest is very important, you said, very primal. The man, the main character, is on stage at rise, puttering about, fixing it up, straightening out things. It's his house and everything in it is his. He is happy in his solitude. Then there is a sudden loud knocking at the door. A woman walks in." June stood up as if she were the actress playing the part. "The woman is all decked out in mountain-climbing clothes. She has stumbled onto the cabin in the woods. At first he thinks she is lost and tries to help her, but she isn't lost at all. She knows exactly where she is and what she is after. She seduces him." June turned a little pink. "You were very explicit about the seduction scene."

"I apologize."

"Oh, don't. I mean, I didn't mind. It's all art, isn't it?"

"No, honey. It's sex. You can call it art or anything else you want to, but sex is sex. Don't ever confuse it for something else. Listen, I think I know the end of this little playlet. You don't have to tell me any more."

"I can't anyway." June smiled. "I'm afraid you passed out

before you got to the end. All I really remember was the part about love . . . real love between a man and a woman. It was beautiful," she said fervently. "You talked about loving beyond ourselves, about love beyond 'time and breath and tears . . .' then you fell asleep."

"Thank God." Suddenly he was exhausted by her youth. He wished she would go away. "Was that all, then?"

"Not exactly. You called out a name. Over and over again in your sleep. That's why I didn't leave. You seemed so upset. I didn't want to leave you like that. I didn't want to leave at all." Her eyes filled with emotion.

"Kate. I suppose that was the name."

She nodded. "I know who Kate is. I mean, everyone knows about Kate Goodfellow."

Hopper got up. "Listen, June. I think I'm going to go back to bed and get some more sleep. You've been very kind to take care of me this way, but I think you had better get back to the campus and your classes and whatever else it is you do. I apologize for crying in my beer last night and you were sweet to listen to it, but I think it's time to let me nurse this head of mine in my own way."

June Michaels stood up. She was a picture-perfect college coed circa 1942. Blond hair combed in a smooth pageboy to her shoulders, regulation bobby socks and saddle shoes, a skirt with a large pleat on the side, and a soft blue lamb's-wool sweater that matched her eyes and tucked in neatly at the waist. She was really very, very pretty. He wondered if she had a boyfriend—probably many. He wondered if she had brains or ambitions. He hoped not. He cursed ambition. Her breasts under the sweater were full, and her skin glowed with all the health and vitality of a Midwest farm girl. He could see wheat fields in her eyes and smell the warm honey in her skin. His blood rushed through his veins. Suddenly, though neither one of them had moved, everything changed.

"You'd better go now, Miss June," he said softly, not meaning it, and she knew he didn't mean it. They stood looking at each other for only the briefest moment, and then he strode across the carpeted room.

"Do you know what you're doing?" he demanded.

Her cheeks were a very high color and her mouth, slightly

open, was full and moist. She was so clear-eyed it hurt. She gave a small, breathless gasp and nodded. Then he pulled her into his arms. Her body came against his like a warm eager animal. He could forget Kate now. He would forget her for however long this girl could make him forget.

CHAPTER FOUR

THE TORPEDO CAME almost softly, penetrating the ship with a dull blunt thud, yet there was no mistaking what it was and what it meant. For maybe five seconds the women in the cabin didn't move, and then, as if a signal gun had been fired, legs, arms, bodies bolted from their bunks. A sudden list catapulted Kate into the shambles of the stateroom. One of the nurses found her flashlight, and by its wavering light the women struggled into their clothes. Kate, instead, started for her equipment. Her camera bag was large, but she knew from past drills she would not be allowed any of her big cameras. Too heavy and too large, they said in the drills, enough to displace a person. So she emptied the bag and threw in her smallest camera plus rolls of film and a handful of flashbulbs. Another list of the ship, screams of terror from the nurses, and the bulbs went rolling about the cabin. Kate steadied herself. She needed those bulbs; otherwise the camera would be useless. She reckoned it was near midnight. She had to hurry now. She went on her knees and started searching for the bulbs. The nurses marched single file as they had been instructed to do in the passage outside. Kate recovered a few of the bulbs, but it was not enough. It was almost pitch dark again. She groped her way back to the bunk and her hand went for one last thing—it was the big, long telephoto lens. A Hasselblatt—one of the best ever made. She had used it over the years fitting it to successive cameras. This lens had gotten her through more difficult situations than she could remember. The steel mills in Cleveland, the flood in Louisville, the Arctic Circle. When she had been just another hustling photographer in New York working the night beat, this was the lens that got her through. Eddie had given her this lens and she was damned if a German submarine was going to take it away from her now. They had been instructed to keep their musette bags ready at all times packed with soap, extra socks, a flashlight, a whistle, water and food rations, and a first-aid kit. But Kate threw out the socks and her food rations and jammed in her precious lens. She saw that her hands were trembling, and for the first time she registered the danger she was in.

She moved quickly now because she was alone in the cabin. A solitary MP appeared in the door with his flashlight and angrily ordered her out of the room. She saw in an instant that this was no green kid she could cajole. Kate reached for her officer's greatcoat and threw it on, at the same time hoisting both the camera bag and the musette bag over her shoulder.

Up top she and everyone else was astonished to see the moon shining so brightly it gave the illusion of dim daylight. The storm was over, the sea relatively calm, and the air was warm. They must be very close to Africa, she thought, and it was reassuring, somehow safer in the warmth. Kate went in the direction of her lifeboat but on impulse broke the line and made her way up to the bridge. Before sailing, the captain had given her permission in case of enemy attack to go up to the bridge to cover the attack from there. This was it. Despite so few peanuts bulbs, she thought the moonlight just might provide enough light for her to shoot. She could feel the ship list and she knew it was gravely wounded, but work always made her forget the danger she was in. She grinned. Taking action always did that to her. Immediacy. That was her antidote for danger.

She worked steadily for more than five minutes before she realized she was alone. Where was everybody? It was as eerie a sensation as she had ever known. Alone in the shimmering light of the full moon like a tiny speck in the universe. She held her breath, straining to hear something—voices? Footsteps? But all was silent. A sudden cold chill gripped her. She was far from her lifeboat station. Maybe it had already gone over. The bow seemed to be jutting higher and higher in the sky. Was the ship sinking?

In the distance she heard a blurred voice filtered through a megaphone—a mournful, desolate sound made all the more desolate in the brilliant moonlight. "ALL HANDS ABANDON SHIP." Kate struggled to steady herself, clinging to whatever she could in the sharp slant of the deck. She pulled her way toward the sound. The ship was tilted so that the guns resembled big, black industrial smokestacks pointing skyward. "REPEAT, ABANDON SHIP." Her camera bag fell away and she reached wildly for it, but it slid outside her reach closer and closer to the edge of the ship's rail. In the distance she saw lifeboats going over the edge. When she turned back to her case, she saw it teeter for just a moment and then it flipped over the side. She was stunned. Her camera was gone. Gone. Without it, what was she to do? All her life the camera had given her strength. There was nothing she couldn't do as long as she had that box in her hand. She started wildly back toward the stairs, intent on going back to the cabin where the rest of her equipment was, but within seconds she realized it was no use. Some primal instinct told her she was in great danger and to get to her station now! *Why is my mouth so dry?* she wondered. And then she realized that this was fear. Fear raw and naked and uncompromisingly real. Survival instinct kicked in. If she could only make it to her lifeboat station in time. She kept barking her shins on metal debris and running into piles of wreckage that had to be climbed over. She dreaded that she would find her lifeboat already launched.

When she got close enough to see her station, she let out a cry. Her lifeboat was still there and beside it all the faces that had grown so familiar to her during the drills. Gratefully, she slid into place and stood in silence with her companions. The boat, now that they needed it, looked so pitifully small for the sixty people who stood silent and tense. Kate saw that most of the other lifeboats had already been launched. Why was hers still tethered to the ship? An American nurse turned and told her tersely that the lifeboat had been flooded by the torpedo and damaged. The crew was deciding whether it could be launched at all.

Though they must have waited only a few minutes, it seemed interminable. It was the sort of moment where people start to bargain with God. Kate did not pray, but what she felt was something entirely foreign to her. The last of her infamous bravado had disappeared, and in its place a Kate she had never known herself to be came to the surface. This Kate was fragile. As fragile and unsure of herself as a lost child.

At last the officer in charge decided that although the lifeboat was half full of water they would risk it but not at full capacity. The women would go first and then the men. The nurse behind Kate protested. "We should go as we were assigned. This is not the *Titanic*. We're all part of the same army." But the officer turned and barked his orders again. One by one the women clamored into the boat to find they were sitting in water up to their waist. Only half the men followed in their preassigned order. Slowly the ropes started to let them down the long descent into the sea.

The scene would cling to Kate for the rest of her life. For all photographers their greatest pictures are the ones never taken, and now, despite the dire situation she was in, she could think of nothing but the magnificent picture unfolding before her. The powerful hull of the ship curved up in a towering perspective. From where she sat, clinging to the sides of the lifeboat, it seemed larger than any skyscraper. It dwarfed the hundreds of human forms scrambling to escape down rope nets flung over the side. Every visible surface was encrusted with human beings clinging or climbing for their lives. The water itself was alive with people swimming, people in lifeboats, people hanging on to floating debris, crying out for help. She saw the familiar uniforms of the Scottish nurses now hanging on for dear life at the bottom of the nets, their boat having capsized in the descent to the sea. One poor girl on the lowest rung of the rope ladder was dizzily twirled about and dragged underwater with each wave. In between waves she had only one moment to breathe before getting pulled under again. Kate gasped. It was Maggie McKye.

"Can't you get over there?" she screamed at the officer in charge of her boat.

He saw what she was pointing to, but he shook his head. "We're having enough trouble staying clear of the suction from the ship!" he shouted. "The rudder broke—we can't steer. It's all we can do to keep clear of the ship."

"But she's in trouble. She can't last. One of them can . . ." But he had turned away from her and was giving orders for all hands to bail out the boat. Two seamen were straining at the oars, trying to pull the boat out of harm.

Kate lost sight of Maggie and the other nurses as her boat passed around the front hull of the ship. It was bedlam. "Over here, oh, God, help me, please, can't someone help me?" "I can't hold on, please help." Kate and everyone in her boat were alternating the bailout and straining to see and to help. But the lifeboats were full. The unlucky ones in the water had to be passed by.

Every effort went toward getting clear of the ship. Suddenly a loud explosion sounded over the water. Everyone looked up. The ship was going down. She was burning out of control and all eyes turned to the blaze. The stern of the ship had already sunk below the waterline, and the bow towered up out of the water, a great and powerful giant brought to its knees. As if she knew what was happening to her, the ship began sending off her own distress signals. Parachute flares skyrocketed from her decks, great arching beams of light crying for help. Kate had not realized how human the ship had been—more than human. Throughout the storm, when it seemed as if there was no way she could keep from capsizing, she had righted herself and headed into the next onslaught. For five grueling days she had met the elements head on and she had prevailed. She had kept her family safe in her bosom. Now the great diva of the sea was dying. Kate saw that her portholes were melting, and as they melted they began to flow, great tears of molten glass.

She sank quickly. And then there was nothing but a big, golden full moon shining down on the sea.

By some miraculous stroke of luck the lifeboats that had not capsized or been dashed to bits by the side of the ship had all pulled together so that when they had cleared the ship they could see each other and call to each other. Somewhere in the flotilla someone started to sing. "You are my sunshine."

Everyone in every lifeboat and even those hanging on to rafts and floating planks picked up the refrain. "My only sunshine! You make me happy when skies are gray." It seemed that the vast sea had become some waterborne theater supporting an enormous floating cast and chorus.

"Look!" A sailor shivering next to Kate pointed to something floating nearby.

They all peered into the area he was pointing to and saw the underside of a lifeboat, its planks jagged from the break floating close to them. Hanging on to the side was a figure. The oarsmen pulled the lifeboat alongside. "She's dead," someone who was close to the figure said. "She's got herself tied on, but she looks dead."

The midshipman in charge signaled them to row on, but just as the lifeboat drifted by, Kate saw again the familiar insignia worn by the Scottish nurses.

"Wait, Officer, please. Can't you see for sure if she's dead? She might just have passed out. Please. I think I know her."

He brought the boat alongside the wreck again and reached over to the limp body. He lifted her head and Kate saw instantly that it was Maggie. In the dim light she seemed dead, but the very act of lifting her head made the inert body gurgle and then sputter as dark, oily liquid dribbled from her mouth.

"Please. Please let her on board," Kate begged. "I know her."

"There's no room," someone said. And then more joined in. "No room . . . we're crowded enough as it is . . . she won't last . . ."

Kate felt the blood rise in her face. "The hell she won't. She'll last and there is room. I can make room. Let her on board." Her voice was steely and commanding. There was a moment of silence, then the oarsman reached down and grabbed Maggie's collar and hauled her small body over the side. She was passed over to Kate and an American nurse next to Kate. They laid Maggie down between them, and the nurse began mouth-to-mouth resuscitation.

"God," she said after a few minutes as she spat out the liquid coming up, "she's swallowed a lot of oil."

"Maggie. Maggie? Can you hear me?" Kate brought her mouth close to the girl's ear. She was rubbing her wrists. Maggie sputtered and coughed and choked, fighting the noxious poisons she had swallowed. Finally she began to vomit, and together Kate and the nurse rolled her over and held her head over the side of the boat.

"Let her get as much of it up as she can. Jesus, she must have taken in the entire tank of oil. You know her, do you?"

"Yes. We were in the same cabin. She was hanging on to the ropes after her lifeboat smashed. I can't believe she survived."

The American nurse, who was named Pat Sommers, shook her head. "I'm not so sure she has. I've seen this before. Some men brought in off of Lake Michigan to the hospital where I worked in Chicago. Two freighters collided and the men took in a lot of water mixed with gas and oil. Not a pretty way to go, I can tell you."

"They died?"

"Mercifully after excruciating stomach pain. And we had morphine."

Kate didn't say anything but looked down on Maggie's face. Such a sweet little face even now, and with her hair wet and matted to her head, she looked like a puppy that had fallen in a well. Kate wiggled out of her greatcoat and wrapped the girl up in it tight. Then she cradled Maggie's head in her lap.

Pat Sommers began to laugh. Kate looked up, shocked. She saw that everyone else in the boat was staring at her. She looked down. She was still wearing the blue satin nightgown Hopper had given her. In a lifeboat in the Atlantic in the moonlight with sixty other hapless souls, she was wearing a slinky gown from Saks Fifth Avenue. She didn't know whether to laugh or cry, so, hugging Maggie close to her, she did both.

CHAPTER FIVE

"MR. DELANEY IS in Chicago, Mr. Bennett. The operator has rung his hotel room several times, but there's no answer. He hasn't checked out. I'll keep trying."

Otis Bennett uncharacteristically slammed down the phone. "What the hell was she doing on a ship heading into the Mediterranean? Can anyone answer me that?"

"We all know Kate. She was on to something, a story." Diz Damian, managing editor of *World,* paced back and forth in the large corner office, stopping only long enough to open two Alka-Seltzers into a paper cup of water. He watched the white spheres dissolve into a million fizzy bubbles as if they held some message for him, and then he tossed down the potion and resumed his pacing.

"Of course she was after a story. She wasn't on a pleasure cruise. There's a top-secret story here and Kate was on to it. But why didn't she get clearance from us? Where in the hell was that ship heading for? I want answers. Why doesn't anyone have answers?"

The door opened after a brisk knock and Virginia York came in. She handed a memo to Diz. "More than half the passengers have been accounted for either dead or alive," she announced to no one in particular. "Kate is still on the missing list."

A silence settled over the room. Virginia glanced around, her eyes lingering for just a minute on Rolly, who stood hunched at the window. No one could possibly be feeling more pain than he. She wished she could go to him and put her arms around his shoulder, but, of course, such a display would embarrass Rolly, and Virginia, too. They were, neither of them, demonstrative people.

Otis tapped the end of his pen against the desk. Diz crumpled the paper cup in his hand and threw it into the wastebasket. It missed. Rolly took his glasses off, pinched the bridge of his nose in a gesture he had done a thousand times before, then adjusted his glasses back on with the utmost care. Virginia cleared her throat.

"We have a report coming in by courier this afternoon. It's been filed by a colonel in the Air Command stationed on the base where Kate filed her last story. I understand it will shed some light on why she was on that ship."

"Well, why didn't you say so in the first place?" Otis growled.

"Because in the first place I thought you would like to know that she was not on the latest casualty list," Virginia answered mildly. "Reports from survivors say she was seen in a lifeboat, which means, we hope, she got clear of the ship before it sank. The majority of the deaths were caused by suction and fire from the ship. Ninety percent of the known survivors were in lifeboats. The lifeboats are equipped with food and water and first-aid supplies. There are flares on board and blankets. The air temperature is unseasonably warm for November in that part of the Atlantic. Unfortunately, the weather, which was clear when the ship sank, is heavily overcast, and search efforts are limited. General Gold in Washington is sending us information top priority. In the meantime, this colonel's report may give us some useful information."

Everyone felt better. Now at least there was something they could do. Analyze the report. Disseminate information. Ferret out the facts. This is what they were trained to do. In the meantime, there was a magazine to get out.

The office emptied quickly.

* * *

On any given Monday morning, Rolly Stebbins would take a
look at the week's mock-up, which told him how many pages
the coming issue of the magazine would have, where the advertising fell, and where the open spaces were. Then he would
roll up his sleeves and go to work. It was a mammoth juggling
act—a giant, intractable puzzle. Move something in the back
of the magazine, and pages in the front would also move.
Sometimes it led to real problems, like the time he decided to
go an extra page on a photo essay about the poaching of big
game in Africa. It was a powerful story and masterfully shot
by a photographer who had spent months in Kenya working
on it. The last picture in the essay was a full-page stopper. In it
natives were butchering a hippopotamus. It was a shocking
and grisly picture, but one on which the entire essay hung.
Unfortunately it fell opposite a four-color ketchup ad showing a man biting into a juicy hamburger. The ad, which had
been presold to that space, could not be moved, nor could the
essay be cut. The essay was jettisoned. Photographers naturally screamed their heads off when that happened. Layout
wasn't the only problem. News of course has its own impera-
tives. There was no shaping it. What happened, happened. Yet
in order to pick the photo essay, Rolly had to second-guess
on Monday what his big news stories were going to be Friday, the day before the magazine went to press. This meant
coordinating dozens of stories about the war and matching
them with film coming in. Even when the story was obvious,
there was no guarantee that the photographers could get the
shots they wanted, pass prints through the censors, and get
them on their way back to New York before the event turned
stale. A great war picture was useless if it arrived too long after the action.

World had circumvented some of the logistical problems
of access by arranging to have their correspondents assimi-
lated into the military as officers. This meant World photographers could get transported to where they needed to be and get
their work shipped back to the U.S. on a priority basis. This
did not, however, free the work from military censorship, which
had become a mandatory part of routine editing. Censorship

was tight, and dirty work by the Allied troops, such as the charnel of air-raid victims behind enemy lines, was never passed through for publication. Photographs of dead Americans were also strictly forbidden. Photographers screamed about that, too. Mercifully, Rolly didn't have to handle photographers. That was Diz Damian's job.

Everyone called Fitzhugh Damian "Diz" because he was fidgety, breezy, and seemingly awash in disorganization. Newspaper clippings and notes overflowed from every pocket. He had a new idea every minute, and if for one minute he did not, he borrowed one from someone else. He talked nonstop, telling stories, finishing people's sentences for them. He could, in the movie parlance, *smell* a story. He embraced incongruity, loved folly, and had a natural instinct for the mass appeal.

As the managing editor at *World,* he was the perfect antithesis to picture editor Rolly Stebbins. Diz had no clear idea of what made a good picture, he only knew one when he saw it. Rolly, however, knew exactly what made a good picture. Diz often told the story of walking through Times Square late one night with Rolly. "I asked him what photographers see that I can't see. After all, I have eyes . . . why can't I see the pictures around me? Rolly, who we all know is not a loquacious man, said characteristically he didn't know. Then"—Diz always took a pause here to make sure everyone was with him—"he casually points up to a perfect half-moon in a purple black sky. Below is all a gaudy manmade mess of neon light, but this moon far outshone every bit of street illumination. It was a perfect picture, brilliant . . . and of course, I hadn't seen it at all."

Rolly was a shy man. Being shy, he kept the world at a distance, meeting it instead vicariously in the hundreds of photographs that passed over his desk each week. While Diz chose the stories for each issue, and photographers translated them into images, Rolly had the final word. If the pictures did not live up to the story, the story was cut. His remorseless progress through stacks of pictures was something photographers and department heads learned to dread.

Now on this Monday in November of 1942, slowly, methodically, Stebbins began to sift through the pictures before him. The essay had been selected, as had the human interest stories. The two big news stories would begin to form on Wednesday. He closed his mind to photographers now—to who they were, and what they risked and how many times they had appeared in the magazine and how temperamental they were. Now he was looking for his images. He went into what amounted to a trance—nothing else penetrated his mind or his eye except the pictures at hand. And for every given story, there were hundreds of photographs.

World photographers habitually overshot. No one knew out in the field exactly how Stebbins would put their story together because building a photo essay was not merely a stringing together of pictures. It had to have a coherent story line, a strong opener setting the mood, builders, show stoppers, pacers, and a finale. No one knew what the layout would be, so best shoot long ones and wide ones and thin ones. But it was not just for variety that they overshot—no photographer wanted to have his story killed because he missed something obvious. "For God's sake, you knew the story was about leaving home. Where's the shot of the soldier eating his last home-cooked meal?" An oversight like that could not only kill a story but jeopardize a career.

Stebbins came to the end of the pile. His usual method was to stand at his desk and go through the pile steadily without editing. Then he would stretch, go to the window, and peer out at the New York skyline. Not that he ever saw it; what he saw was an instant replay in his mind of the pictures he had just seen. Already, the issue was taking form in his head; he had an uncanny memory and a maestro's sense of rhythm and form. Without actually having made firm decisions, the decisions were all but made. Then he would go back to his desk, call in the paste-up man, and go through the pile again. Often, stories were laid out in less than two minutes. Today, however, he did not go to the window. Instead he remained sitting at his desk and took off his glasses, which were thick and gave him the myopic look of the very nearsighted. Without his glasses the clear sharp definitions of sight blurred and familiar objects slipped into light and dark shadows, but in his mind, as though intensified by some inner magnifying glass as strong as the spectacles he wore, he saw a girl with vivid red hair. A breathless girl rushing through the door of a camera shop in Cleveland, Ohio, demanding of him the loan of a camera. He had fallen in love on sight with that girl, and from that moment on, his life had taken on a singular purpose.

They waited all through the day for the colonel's report to come in, hovering around Virginia's office, no one going out for lunch. Hope, even jocularity, embraced some of the staff. They were all cheerful, some even envious of Kate's coup. "I'll bet she's out there single-handedly rowing through the Straits of Gibraltar," they said. "She wouldn't miss a deadline!" . . . "Kate's going to land feet first with a scoop like this!" . . . "Wonder what she'll call the book. . . ."

Virginia went about the business of her day as she always did, but her mind was, unlike the others, on the very real possibility that Kate might not survive this ordeal. She would have never called it intuition because Virginia was not given to unexplained phenomena, but she felt a sense of dread nonetheless and could not shake it. No one had yet said they would do a story on Kate, but Virginia knew they would if she died. Mentally, she began researching such a story. She was an organized woman and thrived on order. Kate lived in the moment, propelled and motivated by an agenda known only to herself. Virginia lived according to precise checks and balances. Kate wore her emotions on her sleeve and had no trouble at all with throwing fits of anger or weeping as it suited her. Virginia's emotions were buried under layers of carefully laid out and evaluated plans. Her emotions were as in check as was her neat hairstyle and sensible Peck & Peck suits.

The public side of Kate's life would be, if not easy, at least readily accessible if it came down to putting a story together, Virginia reasoned. Kate was a master of self-promotion. Ever since coming to New York she had molded her image, constructing an attractive but often misleading myth about herself. Then there was the private Kate. What did Virginia actually know about her? She had walked into Kate's life nine years before. Walked in and hung up her hat and coat and gone to work. She had no reason to regret it. Not that it had been easy or especially gratifying to work for Kate. In the main, it had not. Kate Goodfellow was in the business of Kate Goodfellow and was not a woman given to anyone's needs but her own. She was often demanding to the point of rudeness. She once told Virginia, "If anyone gets in my way when I'm making a picture, I become irrational." How true that was! Once at the Bronx Zoo, Kate was doing a picture story on two Bengal tigers just arrived from India. The animals were restless, howling, and ferocious, made even more so by the bright lights set to illuminate them for the camera. Kate simply could not get the lights in the right place to suit her, and no matter where they were placed, it was wrong. Finally she turned to Virginia and insisted she go into the cage with the flashgun. The zoo keeper was horrified—the tigers would tear anyone who went into the cage to pieces. Kate flew off the handle, screaming at him and Virginia alike. "You people are all the same! Always thinking of yourselves, as if you mattered. You and your problems will be forgotten tomorrow, but my pictures will live forever!"

How Virginia had hated her then. Now the story only made her laugh. There were dozens of stories about Kate and dozens if not hundreds of people to tell them. But who, Virginia pondered, were the key players in Kate's life? Friends? Once *Vogue* magazine had done a story on Kate. The editors wanted her to throw a party so she could be photographed in her apartment wearing a long, slinky designer hostess gown. The "friends" Virginia had hired from a casting agency.

Lovers? In the early days of her career in New York, Kate had taken more lovers than Virginia cared to think about. Men literally lined up at the door of the studio, but they meant little. Kate treated her lovers as objects, useful, even important objects, but objects nevertheless. How often Virginia had seen her talking to them, turning on her quick radiant smile, but as soon as she turned away, the smile would disappear as with the flick of a switch. She turned her personality on and off only as it suited her. Often she overbooked and one suitor would arrive before the other had left, and then the three of them would have to sit around having a drink and a chat with elaborate civility.

"What about love, Miss Goodfellow?" asked the writer from *Redbook*.

"Love? I'm in love with life," Kate answered.

"Marriage?"

"It doesn't fit into my schedule." The reporter was delighted. Here was a headline her women readers could marvel over. Imagine! Career over marriage.

Of course, all that was before Hopper Delaney. Virginia did not wonder that Kate had married him, but she did wonder that even the great Hopper Delaney had not made a significant change in Kate's busy career. Virginia could not explain Kate Goodfellow any more than she could explain herself. They were opposites . . . maybe that was why she had remained so loyal to her for so long.

Virginia's intercom buzzed and she snapped back into the present. It was Otis's secretary. "The report from Washington is in," came the voice. "Mr. Bennett wants everyone back in his office."

"Thanks, Jenny." It took her only a few moments to walk down the hall past layout, past reception, past the small cubicles allotted to editors, but her feet felt slow and leaden. She could not shake the premonition that Kate was not safe, that Kate might, at this very moment be dying—or dead. When she got to the large corner office of the publisher, she saw that the others were gathered.

"It tells us nothing," Otis growled. He was pale with frustration. He was a man used to getting his way, and for a man of such brilliance and vision, he had remarkably little patience. The room grew very still. He thrust the paper into Virginia's hand. "Read it aloud."

" 'To Admiral Gold, State Department, Washington, D.C., from Colonel Chester Edding, 97th Bombing Division, (censored).' "

Rolly looked up. "What?" he said incredulously.

"The exact location of the 97th Bombing Division is censored out," Virginia explained.

"No, not that. What was the name of the colonel?"

"Colonel Chester Edding." Virginia looked back down at the paper and then back to Rolly, but his face was impassive. She continued.

" 'Lieutenant Goodfellow, United States Army Correspondent, was assigned to the bombing base in (censored) England on October 19, 1942. Lieutenant Goodfellow lived on the base for two weeks covering a story on the Flying Fortresses. Lieutenant Goodfellow made a professional request to fly on a bombing mission. It was denied. However, in grateful appreciation for the fine coverage she did on the work of the United States Army Air Corps, Lieutenant Goodfellow was given clearance to board Troopship (censored) as a representative of the United States Army in coverage of the (censored).' "

"That tells us nothing!" exploded Otis. "Except that the censored boys haven't run out of ink. Get me Gold on the telephone. Maybe I can get him to loosen up some of this mumbo."

But Admiral Gold was unavailable. He had left Washington for an undisclosed destination. His aide, however, had updated information on survivors of the torpedoed ship. New word reported Kate's lifeboat had been seriously overloaded, half-filled with water and apparently without any means to steer. The other lifeboats had hung together. Those passengers had been rescued, but Kate's boat had disappeared.

CHAPTER SIX

THROUGHOUT THE VOYAGE, Kate had harbored the comfortable and completely groundless theory that if they met with any attack, the other ships in the convoy would gather about like worried members of a family to aid those stricken. She was shocked to find that the exact opposite was true. Seeing her ship struck and sinking, the rest of the convoy had sped on so as not to provide the enemy with additional targets. Rescue was not their mission—they were needed for the invasion of Africa.

In the last dark hours of the long night, with a useless rudder, Kate's boat drifted away from the community of lifeboats and set on its own course. At the first dull hint of dawn over an empty sea, it was time to take stock of their situation. The day promised to be overcast and gray so that the sea and the sky met in one continuous color. There was no compass. There was no bearing. There were few flares. The lifeboat was seriously overcrowded and many on board were injured.

The officer in charge, a funny little man who had been quartermaster on the ship, was now skipper of the lifeboat. His name, Alfred Biggs, belied his short stature. He positioned himself in the front of the boat and assumed command

as if he had been doing this sort of thing all his life. He began
by taking a roll call of rations and medical supplies. Kate had
none. She remembered she had tossed most of them out of her
bag in order to make room for her camera lens. Now she felt
foolish. She had not only lost all of her camera equipment, but
from the looks of it she was the only person on board who had
not secured water and concentrated food. Even Maggie had
been hauled on board with her musette bag strapped to her
shoulder. Though someone had given Kate a sweater to wear,
she was still dressed in her silk nightgown. Her teeth chattered
in the cold gray dawn, but she would not consider the use of a
blanket. It was bad enough she had no rations, she was not
about to deprive someone wounded from what little warmth
there was in an open boat at sea.

All through the first day, spirits ran high and all eyes scanned
the horizon and all ears strained to hear the sound of a ship's
engine or an airplane. Everyone knew that if rescue came it
would most likely come in the first twenty-four hours. In the
meantime, Alfred Biggs, having assessed the state, rank, and
ability of his passengers, began issuing orders. The boat held
fifty-two human souls. Caretakers and the injured were placed
aft. Pat Sommers was in charge of the medical supplies. Kate
and six of the other women, five nurses and a driver for one of
the British commanders, were under her charge. Pat assigned
each one or more of the injured. All other able-bodied men
and women were sorted into teams for rowing by day and the
watch at night. For a while everyone felt useful, reassured by
the swift organization of Alfred Biggs.

At the first ray of light the next morning, they all looked
around expecting something, anything that might smack of
land or rescue. There was none. The mood grew somber. Then
a little Welshman called out for breakfast orders describing
the aroma of his coffee and the sizzle of his sausages until
everyone got in the spirit . . . "kippers and toast here" . . .
"eggs over easy and hash browns" . . . "bagels and lox, oh
man, what I wouldn't give . . ." "just a big ol' mess of ham and
grits, right heah." That last from a Georgia boy with enormous
feet. "Almost didn't get in the army with my feet," he drawled
and held up one leg so all could see. "Say, we could use those
for paddles," came an observation. They went around the boat

and told their names, where they were from, and what they did in civilian life. At noon a rationing of water and high-calorie sticky bars made of coconut, dried fruit, and rendered beef fat were passed around.

The day lengthened. One by one they were allowed to stand and stretch. The jocular talk waned and by nightfall the mood reached its lowest ebb. Overcast skies meant that they had not even the stars to guide them in some direction.

Kate alternately dozed and tried to care for Maggie. Pat Sommers had done everything she could to help her. She was cheerful, kind, and humane, but the look in her eyes when Maggie was asleep was not reassuring. Maggie was very sick, anyone could see that, but beyond keeping her warm and making her take tiny sips of the rationed water there was nothing anyone could do. She lay with her head in Kate's lap, and when she was sleeping she looked so like a child that Kate found herself doing all those things that mothers automatically do for their sick children. She stroked her cheek and kept dipping a cloth into the cold seawater, wringing it out and laying it against the hot forehead. When Kate's leg cramped and she felt she must stretch it out and twist and turn her body into a more comfortable position, she held still if Maggie was asleep.

When Maggie was awake her distress made Kate's heart ache for her to have to suffer as suffer she surely did. She had swallowed too much water thick with oil and gasoline spewed out from the sinking ship. The poisons had seeped into her body and the pain and nausea were constant, but Maggie hardly ever complained. She only gripped Kate's hand. She found that talking helped. Maggie was weak and couldn't say much, but she loved listening to Kate. It helped her to rise above the nausea and pain. And so Kate talked. Sometimes she was so tired and sore and cramped and thirsty and hungry she hardly knew what she was saying, but Maggie kept tabs. It was amazing how alert her mind was even as her body seemed to shrink before Kate's very eyes.

The high point of the next day was when Kate discovered six Hershey bars in the lining of her greatcoat. A supply officer had shoved a handful of them into her pockets in grateful appreciation of the picture she had taken of him to send back to his wife just before they had set off from Southampton. The discovery now of such luxurious bounty was cause for much cheer and the precious candy was carefully divided and passed around. The low point was that by nightfall of the third day they had seen nothing in the amorphous gray of sea and sky. It seemed impossible that they were without a compass to point them in some direction, and there were angry outcries laying the blame on naval inefficiency. Mr. Biggs reminded them that their boat had been badly damaged by the splash from the torpedo and filled with water. Hundreds had not made it into boats, hundreds more had died, many of them had been trapped in the hold of the ship. The anger subsided into silence. Someone had a harmonica and played "Row, Row, Row Your Boat." And that made everyone laugh. They all took up singing, going in rounds until they were exhausted with the song, and then they sang the popular tunes of the day: "That Old Black Magic," "White Cliffs of Dover," and "Praise the Lord and Pass the Ammunition." That night the sky cleared, and overhead the stars gave them the first hope of setting on a course. But by dawn all was a colorless mist again and the men were exhausted from rowing. Water rationing was severe and there were those not inclined to be so generous with the seriously sick.

"Kate?"

"Yes, dear?"

"Oh, Kate, I was having the loveliest dream. But it didn't feel like a dream. It was so real. I dreamed I was at home and I was running down the path that leads to the back of the farm. Jamie . . . Jamie was there with me and we were talking about . . . I told you about Jamie, didn't I?"

"Yes, you did. You mustn't talk, Maggie. You must rest."

"Please, Kate . . ." Her voice came in tiny gasps and her face was contorted with pain, but she tried to struggle up to a sitting position ". . . please . . ." Maggie's color was like chalk.

"I think she wants you to look in her pocket," Pat Sommers said. "She keeps trying to get her hand in there."

Maggie looked so relieved that Kate instantly felt annoyance with herself. She put her hand down into the deep pocket of the nurse's uniform and felt a small hard object. When she pulled it out she saw it was a small oval picture frame with Jamie's picture in it. He was staring out into the world with the Scottish Highlands firmly planted on his features. Though still a boy's face, one could see the man to come in his ruddy complexion and high forehead and prominent nose. Kate wondered what it was in that stolid face and bearing that made Maggie love him so. She handed the picture to Maggie, who didn't need to look at it, only to hold it in her palm and fold it to her heart. Thus comforted, she drifted off again into sleep. Kate stared at the girl's face. All they had ever asked is that they might love each other and laugh together and marry and have a family and a life. But this was going to be denied them. Kate smoothed Maggie's hair back and wetted her mouth once more. She was like a little doll.

The water was calm and the fog shrouded the boat. There was nothing to look for and no direction to go in. In that moment of disembodied peace, the gentle slaps of the water against the side of the wooden boat, the smell of the sea and the rocking motion, Kate let her mind slip free of worry over Maggie and closed her eyes against the hopelessness of the scene.

It would be late afternoon in New York. She could imagine each and every one of them in the office. Surely they knew by now that she had been on that ship, that she was lost at sea, that the invasion of Africa was about to begin. Did they understand why she had done what she did? Were they worried and distraught? Unlikely. It wasn't that she didn't need their affection, but she had never required it, preferring to compartmentalize her relationships. It was a mental trick she had learned as a young girl when one day she had wandered into the post office in her hometown and had been utterly transfixed by the repeating patterns of tiny glass doors that lined one entire wall. Its appeal was instant. The little doors, so many of them, each so perfect, each repeated a hundred times, each with brass knobs and little scrolled keyholes—this image was immediately and vividly fixed in her mind.

She had often used the image of these doors to structure her life, fitting everyone and everything into a compartment. And it had worked . . . up to a point. It hadn't worked with Eddie, it certainly didn't work with Hopper, and now, the small light weight of Maggie's head in her lap, there was no ready compartment for this. She could feel the tears coming up from her belly and then she felt something else—a hunger so strong it almost made her gag.

CHAPTER SEVEN

"MR. DELANEY, HAVE you had any more news about your wife?" "Will you go to England?" "Why was she on that troopship, Mr. Delaney?" "Over here, Mr. Delaney." They had been waiting for him on the sidewalk when he came out of the Palmer House. They swarmed around him at Union Station shouting questions and flashing bulbs in his face. Hopper brushed by them. He boarded the train ahead of the other passengers thanks to a friendly porter who knew him from previous trips.

The train between Chicago and New York was running late. Late because now, with the war on, trains ran late due to last-minute schedule changes and military priority and crowded stations and long goodbyes. Inside, the cars were packed with soldiers on the move, and Hopper was the only man in sight in civilian clothes. Clothes that read "too old for war." It seemed to him incredible and sudden and startling that he was over forty years old. He had a helpless and indignant feeling that he had been put on the shelf before his time and that all these downy-chinned youngsters were considered better than he was or stronger or more able to fight. Up to now he had dismissed the whole problem as though it were no problem, but the fact

of the matter was, it was a problem to Hopper Delaney. He had
been a fighter all his life, a fighter with words. Words did not
count for much in wartime, except for the speechmakers. It
was only after wars that the people turned to their writers
again for explanation and consolation. *Why?* they would ask,
and the great thinkers and wordsmiths would spew forth with
books and articles and lectures filled with answers and speculations explaining conquest and slaughter and misery, famine,
and death. Words were useless things now. The nation was at
war and war was not about words, it was about deeds, about
heroics and patriotism and proud fathers and weeping mothers
and the seduction of guns and the heightened urgency between lovers and a dreadful, dreadful sentiment that would
keep wars in business for a long, long time.

At last, some five hours late, the train dragged itself and
the heavy load aboard out of the station past the stockyards
and South Side tenements of Chicago toward the white smoke
and burning furnaces of Gary, Indiana. The years of the Depression and deprivation were over. Factories were working
overtime transforming scrap metal into the nuts and bolts of
battle. Jobs were plentiful. The great god Mammon had returned on the back of death.

Hopper rocked and swayed in the monotonous motion of
the train trying hard not to think of these things or, indeed,
about anything. Kate was missing. Missing now for five days.

"Can I get you anything, Mr. Delaney? A drink? Coffee?
Man, we've never been so jammed up as this. There's no pri-
vate compartments at all. Just this roomette and you're lucky
to get that, I reckon. We can only hold on to it for you until
Pittsburgh, but that'll get you most ways through the night.
Are you all right, Mr. Delaney? Let me get you a drink."

Hopper shook his head. "No . . . thank you, George . . . just
want to be alone . . . thanks . . . I'll ring. . . ." The tiny room was
hot and uncomfortable, but he supposed he should be happy he
was able to manage a room even if only to Pittsburgh. It was not
at all what he was used to. Hopper Delaney traveled first class
when he traveled. When had he grown so used to luxury? he
wondered. He who had jumped boxcars as a boy traveling from
Memphis to New Orleans, New Orleans to Atlanta on to the
coast and down into the Carolina lowlands and Florida. Then it

had been empty cattle cars and on top of coal bins on freight trains stopping at every whistle stop in the South. The thought of buying a ticket and riding in passenger seats had never even crossed his mind, and now here he was feeling sorry for himself because he had a roomette instead of his usual suite.

He had grown used to the attentive ministrations of the porters who all knew him and liked him, liked his generous tips and easy manner. Used to the large bed that folded out from the wall, the linen smelling of fresh soap, and the heavy silver coffeepots that came on trays to his double stateroom in the morning. He liked large china cups and buckets of ice and crystal tumblers for his drinks. He liked the big overstuffed armchairs, the desk with his typewriter facing the window. He liked working as the train swayed and the wheels sent their steady clickety-clack message of speed up to him. He liked looking up from his work and seeing America flashing before his eyes as he sped coast to coast and all the stops in between. These were the things that poor boys liked when they grew up and became rich and famous. "All the comforts," he had explained to Kate on their honeymoon, "might as well have them while the havin's good."

He pressed his hands to his face rubbing them hard against the rough stubble; he supposed he looked a wreck, he felt it for sure. He had been trying to get to New York ever since his friend had called him from the *Chicago Tribune* with the Teletype news on the torpedoing of a ship. A ship they now knew was bound for North Africa with troops and supplies for a massive invasion. A ship now sunk to the bottom of the sea with more than a thousand dead—or missing. It was the "or missing" that haunted him. It seemed to him he should know, should be able to feel in his very soul whether she was one of the missing or one of the dead. But he felt nothing. So little emotion it scared him. He tried to think, but all he heard were the words, his last words to her, like a litany in his brain. *You can't leave, Kate. You can't leave us!*

These were the prolonged and tedious words of his marriage. Their familiarity played in his mind like a stale old vaudeville routine. The immemorial battle of the sexes. He said, she said played over the sad and bitter punch lines of love. Was she dead? Even now while he sat crunched up in the tiny roomette, was his Kate dead? Crushed, burned, eaten up by fire, bloated by drowning. *You can't leave, Kate. You can't leave us!* Her face loomed up before him as it had been in their last minutes together. "Hop, don't make this any worse than it is. I'll only be gone a few months."

Five days adrift at sea. Lost, without food, without instruments to guide them—there was no longer pretense of goodwill among the survivors. At first there had been that extraordinary human spirit of camaraderie. The songs, the jokes, the immense and generous sharing of comfort and rationing—but now things were different. Each person seemed to grow inward—irritable and lethargic all at the same time. They had had too much time to think, too much time to lose hope. They were alive, but for how much longer? After all this time, one could still drown, or die of exposure, of weather, of sharks. The religious ones made piteous appeal to God, others unloosened a flood of invectives. No one was listening. Three people had died so far. For the first there had been sorrow and prayers as a boy, a sailor not more than eighteen, had been lowered into the sea. Now, there was no sorrow over the dead, only relief in lightening the load in the boat and the drain on precious rations and water.

Kate swallowed hard, but the fuzz in her mouth would not go away. She had been awake most of the night with the fitful pangs of hunger. Just a bite, just a chew of something to cheat hunger of its grip. Worse than the hunger was the thirst. The rationing held them to two ounces of water a day. It was not enough. A soldier had been caught in the night stealing more water for himself, and in the ensuing scuffle two precious cans of water had gone overboard. Dehydration was a swifter foe than hunger, causing the muscles to lose all strength. Kate found that she had developed a fixation on water that logic could not overcome—seawater is wet, she reasoned; how could it hurt me? She was so bored with surviving. And then she would indulge herself with a vivid fantasy of an impossible meal. Around her the faces told the same story.

That night it rained—a blessing to the parched throats, but now in the wan first light of day six, the sea stretched glassy and empty around them. There was nothing—only the limitless stretch of water and occasionally a few seabirds gliding high in the overcast sky. One by one, those who could stood unsteadily and stretched and then huddled down again, wet, silent, and growing weaker. Surely drowning was not so bad.

Kate was aware of a fogginess in her head. She found her thoughts were all askew and disproportionate. They jumped and ranged as if she had taken a hallucinating drug. At first they had all been afraid of being picked up by the enemy. If you've been torpedoed, you know there are people in those waters who want you dead—maybe they'll find you and kill you outright; maybe they'll capture you and take you to a concentration camp so they can think your death over. But now, she reasoned, if she were to be picked up by the Germans, she would get her full officer's pay. War correspondents had to be captured to collect officer's pay. With the check she was going to have her hair done, and, yes, she needed a new pair of shoes. Spectator pumps she thought would look nice. But they would be angry at the office because she had sent no pictures. She kept reaching for her camera only to remember over and over again that it had been lost with the ship, and she could feel her eyes tear up, but it was not for her equipment, she realized; she cried for her beautiful cosmetics case now at the bottom of the sea. It was fitted with exquisitely carved ivory jars, a gift from Hopper two Christmases ago and the case covered in ostrich skin. But she would not think about Hopper.

"So you married him, Kate?" Maggie's voice was weak, but she was smiling.

"Yes, dear. I married him."

"Oh, tell me about it. Did you have a wedding, then? A big wedding in New York?" She tried to lift her head.

"You lie quiet now, Maggie." Kate laid her hand on the burning forehead of the girl. But Maggie wouldn't be still. It was as if she was possessed of a restlessness struggling from within to break free. All night the girl had moaned and tossed in a fretful state, calm only for minutes at a time when she seemed to be calling on other people as if she were visiting them. Her face was a deathly white, and though Kate kept dabbing her lips with precious water, her mouth was cracked and parched. Pat Sommers shook her head. There was nothing more she could do for her. The medical supplies were gone. There was nothing anyone could do.

Pat gave Kate a weary smile. "You'd better tell her about the wedding. I think your voice is the only thing that calms her."

Kate looked down into Maggie's expectant eyes, willing her to go to sleep so she herself could sink back into the phantasm of brain. She was so tired, so tired of talking, sick with fatigue and the cold and her cramped aching muscles. Her tongue was swollen in her mouth; her throat felt like a cardboard tube. Her saliva was thick and foul-tasting, but she cleared her throat and licked her dry lips. "No, it wasn't a big wedding. Nothing like that. We had a little wedding. We got married in a ghost town in Colorado." But that wasn't that wedding she saw in her mind. It was the other one. The chapel on the edge of the campus and the borrowed blue dress and somewhere someone was crying.

It was painful to remember the wedding because everything was so scrambled up anyway. She didn't like thinking about weddings.

She had married Eddie because she had never loved anyone before in her life. She had married Hopper because the time had come when it was too troublesome to remain unmarried. His need for her was so intense, and then, too, she was half blinded for love of him. What was love anyway but maybe a colossal joke on all mankind? Whatever force that bound them together seemed the same force that had been their undoing. She had somehow known that all along and still she had said yes. Her constant longing to be with him won out over any misgivings.

"We were on our way cross-country on a whistle-stop lecture tour," she began, recalling the train and all the attendant luxury that had gone with their celebrity. Walter Winchell predicted they would marry, and the morning they left New York the station platform was crawling with reporters, some with tape measures to gauge the exact distance between their two adjoining staterooms. "Marry the guy, Kate!" one of them shouted as the train pulled out of Grand Central. By the time the train had reached Denver she had said yes.

"We got our license in Reno but decided to drive up into the mountains until we found a place that we liked. We drove for hours, then all of a sudden we rounded a curve and there, hanging on a bluff above us, looking so charming that both of us knew that this was the perfect town to get married in, was a place called Silver City. So we drove in and discovered that, except for a few durable citizens, Silver City was a ghost town. It was mostly boarded up, but there was a church.

"It was enchanting. The altar was covered in dust and cobwebs. Through the windows we could see for miles, and it was just like heaven up there on top of the mountain, just like being on top of the world. Over the next hill was another town where the proprietor of the general store doubled as the circuit court judge. Hopper told him we wanted to be married in the church at Silver City that very hour. The sun was starting to set, you see, and Hopper said, 'Cattle trading isn't legal after sundown, is it, Judge? And I want this marriage legal.' Well, the judge thought that was funny, so he called his wife and we all piled in our car back up to Silver City. The sun dipped down behind the mountain just as he pronounced us man and wife, so we just made it under the wire."

Kate stopped for a minute and dabbed her lips with the wet cloth she had been using on Maggie's forehead. For a minute she thought Maggie was asleep because her eyes were closed, but she squeezed Kate's hand and rolled her head slightly back and forth.

The boat rocked in the water, and all you could hear were small waves slapping gently against the wooden hull. It was impossible to tell where the sky ended and the sea began, and just for a moment it seemed to Kate as if they were drifting through a world of pearly radiance.

She looked down at Maggie. The girl had opened her eyes and was staring out, focusing on nothing, apparently oblivious to all that surrounded her except the warm, strong hand. Perhaps she was somewhere in Scotland, leaning on a garden fence, her pretty mouth laughing, her eyes gay with flirting with the boy on the other side. If it were so, then this moment would now stretch into eternity. Maggie McKye was dead.

* * *

They buried her at sea, as they had done the others. They could not spare a blanket to wrap her up in, so Kate removed the blue nightgown under the greatcoat now no longer needed to warm the girl and wrapped Maggie's head and torso in its satin loveliness. They tied her body with a small length of rope and Officer Biggs recited the official prayer for burial at sea. Then two men lowered the body over the side and into the cold, slate water. *Blessed are the pure in heart* . . .

Pat put her arm around Kate and she leaned into her, unable to cry, unable to feel much of anything, but it was nice being held. She awoke with a small jump some hours later. Nothing had changed except the trusting little hand that had stayed in hers for the past six days was gone. What happened to the dead? Where had Maggie gone? Surely somewhere the heavens had opened to receive her and comfort her and absorb her lovely light. Somewhere a God? Kate had never thought much about these things. Religion had never entered into a childhood filled with science and nature. The only person she had ever known who ever talked about God was Hopper. "God is not answers," he said. "God is silence."

All was silent now and Kate wandered into a dream. She was walking down a street of giant elms. She saw a house with a red tiled roof and a large porch painted a deep, cool green. Walking onto the porch, she entered the house into a room filled with large and sturdy chintz chairs, and books crammed onto shelves and piled high on tables. Over the mantel a carved wooden sign read LISTEN TO THE SONG OF LIFE. On the wall was an immense map of the world. A woman was reading from a book and a child sat on the floor in front of her listening. Kate leaned into the scene and heard her mother's voice and saw herself in the child. *There was a child went forth every day,* read her mother, and both Kate, the child, and Kate, the woman, smiled, for it was their favorite poem by Mr. Walt Whitman. A wonderful, joyful poem about the child who goes out for a day, *or a certain part of the day/Or for many years or stretching cycles of years*. And every object and every sound and every person became *part of the child who went forth every day*. The voice faded to a whisper and now Kate grew uneasy and tried to find a way out of the house. But it was dark and she could see nothing. Still, she could hear the whisper in her ear.

PART TWO

1925

"There was a child went forth. . . ."

CHAPTER EIGHT ·

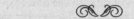

A SMALL LAMP on the bureau cast a circle of light on the quiet bedroom drama. Kate Goodfellow sat by her father's bedside and watched his impassive face. He was dying. Just five days ago he was fine. Sunday evening after dinner he went to his chair, the chair he worked in, read in, and thought in. Throughout dinner they had been talking. This was unusual, for Frank Goodfellow was an abnormally silent man. He was so absorbed in his work, so deeply immersed in his world of machines and inventions that he seldom allowed himself the indulgence of conversation, but Kate was home from college and this evening the drafting tools and sketch pads and notebooks would be put aside for his daughter.

Kate was overflowing with enthusiastic talk about her classes and her professors and the access to libraries and equipment and all that she had learned of the very latest in scientific findings. Her academic bent was toward the study of snakes, frogs, and insects. In this she had her father's blessing. Ever since she was a child he had encouraged her interests, and in many ways it was their only means of real communication. The long nature walks, the learning of birdcalls and the names of stars, the legions of butterfly eggs that populated the house, the glass containers of harmless snakes in her bedroom. He had given her books and helped her study from them. Fabre's *Lives of Insects, A Handbook of Nature Study, Amphibians and You*—these were the titles of her bedtime reading. The natural world was limitless, she discovered, and one in which she planned to become an expert. Kate, the naturalist, would go on expeditions of great scientific importance. Expeditions that would lead her into exotic lands. She didn't know it then, but it was mostly the travel aspect that intrigued her. For as long as she could remember she had pictured herself going off into jungles bringing back specimens for natural history museums. This need to see the world had been her mother's legacy. They rarely mentioned her mother now, she and her dad, but in this quiet evening of homecoming when at last Kate had wound down from the enthusiasms of college life, her father had leaned back and gazed at his daughter. She knew he was thinking about her mother, and her cheeks went very high in color because it always flustered her. She wished she looked more like her mother, but she didn't. She was plump, whereas her mother had been slim. Kate's features were too much like her father's, prominent and bold, but she shared her mother's radiant red hair and her gray-green eyes. She had only one picture of her mother. In it the youthful twenty-year-old Winnie O'Neill appeared in a starched shirtwaist and leg-of-mutton sleeves, but even the stilted setting of the photographer's studio could not hide the eager, full-lipped, and wide-eyed young woman who peered out at the world as if everything was new and fresh and worth investigating.

"You're so like her, Katie," he said suddenly. "Your mind is open and inquiring. You must never lose that." And then in a rare moment of emotion his eyes filled with tears, and, embarrassed, he got up and patted her head absentmindedly before moving away to his chair. Kate cleared the table of their dinner quietly, knowing he needed to be alone. Suddenly the quiet was interrupted by a strange noise, a sound that was something between a whimper and a yelp. When Kate thought back on that evening, it was the incongruous hiccup of distress, a sound that might come from a child or an animal but not from her father, that had frightened her the most. It took her a few seconds to understand that the little bleating noises were being made by Frank Goodfellow. Then she heard a high-pitched babbling that was even more shocking. For one second she clutched at the table's edge and then ran to her father's chair. He was slumped half in, half out of the chair, his face ashen, and for a few seconds she thought he was already dead. Kate willed herself to be calm as she searched his wrist for a barely discernible pulse and was briefly reassured when his chest heaved and he uttered a groan. The doctor came quickly.

"Looks like he's had himself a stroke," the doctor said. "Let's get him into bed. The next twenty-four hours are critical."

So Kate began a roller-coaster ride of hope and despair. Frank Goodfellow remained unconscious for the next two days. When he did regain consciousness, he was far from being himself. The stroke had paralyzed his right side and had cruelly impaired his speech. It was agony for Kate to watch and wait as he tried to piece together a simple sentence. Clearly it was an even greater agony for Frank. His intelligence was intact, but the means to communicate had been removed, as was his naturally patient and gentle personality. He was irritable, inconsolable, and rude. Laboriously he had pieced together a phrase that spoke volumes to him and was gibberish to Kate. "Unleash the umbrella!" he shouted over and over, the urgency and insistence in his voice increasing with each barked command. After many frustrating hours of trying to decipher this puzzle, Kate found the solution. She dismissed the words as irrelevant and tried to guess what would be so important to her father that he could not rest until it was attended to. In a flash she knew. It had to do with his work.

"Listen to me, Dad. I'm going to go talk to Mr. MacIntosh and see if he has any messages for you, or anything he wants you to know about." Her father nodded gratefully and relaxed. He sank back in his pillows and closed his eyes. The message she brought back from Mr. MacIntosh had reassured him even further. Frank Goodfellow was the key engineer on a big project that all concerned hoped was going to revolutionize the printing press. The message from his boss was "Don't worry. We're putting everything on hold until you get back." After that, Frank Goodfellow was a lamb. He ate and slept and even tried to smile on the half of his face that could still move. The doctor had been cautiously optimistic. "I've seen this happen before," he said. "If he's got the will, lots of rest and time will get him back to normal." If anyone had the will, Frank Goodfellow did, but he never got a chance to use it. The next day he suffered another stroke. Not only had he not recovered consciousness, but with every passing hour his pulse got weaker and it seemed to Kate that he was slowly and irrevocably receding like the tide going out to sea.

Kate and a nurse took turns sitting by his side—the nurse taking the days while Kate sat vigil by night. The nighttime hours would always be the most congenial to her.

By the age of five Kate Goodfellow had already contracted the habit of insomnia. The fact was, she didn't need much sleep and usually three or four hours at a time was enough. When she awoke it was never a slow, cautious edging into consciousness but rather an instantaneous leap as her mind engaged anything and everything. One moment she was asleep, and the next she was thinking about the caterpillar she had found and installed in a glass jar with airholes punched in the lid. Her father told her that it would eventually turn into a butterfly, and she tried to imagine how this could be true. Could she watch it or was it the kind of activity that could only take place in darkness and in private? As she continued to lie awake, she might think about her pet snake, the cool dry feel of it as it moved in her hand or up her arm. Snakes too did wonderful things in private. A snake could shed its entire skin, like a woman removing a silk dress. What happened then? Was there a ready-made skin like underwear ready to become outerwear?

Kate had kept her nighttime wakefulness a secret from her parents. She knew it would distress them. "A little girl needs her sleep to grow and be smart," they told her. Sleep was like food, a kind of fuel for the machine of the body, but as far as she could tell she was growing anyway. Her mother constantly had to buy new boots, new dresses, new coats, because her other ones, not really old at all, no longer fit her. And she didn't worry about being smart. Her daddy was the smartest person she knew and he hardly slept at all.

Sitting beside her father on this wintry night, her heart filled with sadness and foreboding, she remembered another night, a dozen years ago, when she had been no more than three or four years old. That night had been warm for so early in June, and the windows were open. She had awakened to find the light of the full moon pouring into her room, and had run to the window. The moon made the night bright with light and shadows, and the garden looked like a stage set. She could hear insects buzzing; the deep throated croaking of frogs and an occasional *whooo* from a curious owl. There were other noises as well—voices murmuring and gentle laughter. Her parents were outside, probably on the bench beneath the elm, their words and occasional laughter blending perfectly with the other night sounds. All the world was awake and outdoors, and she wanted desperately to join them. She went downstairs and opened the door, but her progress was arrested at the doorstep. The garden, familiar in daylight, now looked dark and mysterious. Every familiar landmark—the brick path, the hydrangeas, the blooming tulip trees, the huge elm in the distance, the fragrant lilacs—all looked strange and a little threatening. The world was bathed in a dark light of the moon, and Kate was afraid of the dark.

"Is that you, Katie? What are you doing up at this hour?" It was her dad's voice.

"Come on out here, darling," her mother spoke. "We're looking at the stars. I can show you the Big Dipper."

Kate remained frozen in the doorway. She wanted to go to her parents, to melt into her daddy's bear hug, to hear her mother tell about the stars, but to get there she had to cross an ocean of darkness. She wasn't even sure her parents were really there. She could hear their voices, but they were disembodied. What if it was all a ghostly trick, wicked wood nymphs trying to lure her into the darkness . . . ? Then she saw her father's figure looming out of the darkness, his arms outstretched, as he called for her to come to him. She ran and kept running. Just as he was almost within her reach, he'd move away and disappear, into the darkness, behind a tree, somewhere so she couldn't find him. Then her mother appeared. Relieved, she ran to her mother, until she, too, would suddenly hide. They were playing a game, hide-and-seek, in the middle of the night, by moonlight, when every shape and every shadow looked as if it might be something other than its ordinary self. But they were laughing and Kate laughed, too. And as she ran barefoot on the moist grass, seeking first her father, then her mother, searching in the moonlit night, she forgot to be afraid. Her eyes grew accustomed to the darkness and it was congenial to her. Then they were reunited. Her daddy scooped her up in his familiar embrace. Her mother, laughing, brushed the wispy hairs off Katie's forehead, and everything was safe and normal in the garden, by moonlight, in the early morning hours of June 1910.

"Never be afraid" was the constant lesson of Kate's childhood. "If something scares you, go right up to it and look it in the face" was the moral her parents repeated to her day in, day out. They taught courage as if it were a skill, like proper table manners, or using a handkerchief when you sneezed. Well, Kate was scared now. To lose her father was unimaginable to her. She had lost her mother and that had been awful, confusing, and sad. To make up for it, she had become her daddy's girl. To the outside world she might look like an awkward teenage girl who was too tall, too plump, and too serious looking to be popular, but to her father she was a princess. And not just an ordinary princess but a princess with a scholar's mind and a scientist's inquisitiveness.

Both her parents had been devoted to the idea of learning and self-improvement for their little girl. Every moment of every day was an opportunity to be seized to acquire knowledge. From as far back as she could remember her mother had filled the house with books, pictures, and maps. Indeed maps of the world covered every available wall surface of every room. Winnie Goodfellow was a romantic, a woman who had married for love, content in most ways save her passion for foreign lands. As a child, Kate had sat hour upon hour at her mother's feet listening to stories read aloud of adventure in exotic places. The heroes of such stories—explorers, wanderers, and soldiers of fortune—were people who lived life on a robust plane, embracing all, fulfilling all, casting in one bold throw all or nothing. Together they studied the picture books and maps that brought them the visual reality of the stories.

Egypt, a country filled with camels and pyramids and intrigue; China with its towering Buddhas and Great Wall; Greece, the land of antiquity and truth and beauty, where mortals aspired to the passions of the gods. "Follow your instincts always, Kate. Never let convention control you. The world is out there waiting for you, and it is larger than you ever imagined," Winnie counseled her little girl, fervently, longingly.

"Can we see the world together?" Kate asked. "Will you come with me, Mama?"

"I'll always be with you, Katie."

Among Kate's favorite pastimes when she lay in bed at night was to recreate in her mind's eye the features of a particular map. She liked to picture the twisting blue lines that were the great rivers, cutting across continents and spilling out to the seas. What would happen, she wondered, if she followed the brook that ran through the meadow behind her house? Would it lead her eventually to the Raritan River which ran just outside the edge of town? And if she followed the river, would it lead her to a larger river still and eventually take her all the way to the ocean? The ocean could take her all around the world. She would try it. She would follow the brook as far as she could, and someday she would follow the zigzag of the big rivers and at last sail out on ocean waters of the world.

"Adventuring," they called it. Every weekend the three of them took long walks in the woods that stretched for miles behind their house. In the distance they could watch the play of light and shadows on the rolling Watchaung Mountains. Frank Goodfellow taught his daughter that the world around her was full of mystery and wonder. Miracles and magic were not tucked away in fairy tales but happened every day right under your very nose if you had the eyes and the sense to see. An ordinary withered brown leaf on the floor of the woods might conceal an entire colony of ants—a whole universe all its own. They collected butterflies, bugs, snakes, anything that caught their fancy that they could take home to study. At home a corner of the parlor had been turned into a laboratory of sorts with an assortment of jars and stoppers, vials and tweezers, and their proudest possession, a real microscope.

When Kate had been not yet quite six, she had done some adventuring on her own. One summer day she walked down the road that passed in front of her house, determined to walk to the end of the world. She had ended up in town, and that had been so interesting that she had stayed away most of the day—exploring the railroad station, the riverbank, and the full length of Main Street. In the late afternoon a neighbor who recognized her brought her home. Her mother welcomed her back effusively and never uttered a single reproach. She wanted to know in detail everything she had seen and discovered. It sounded like a good adventure, she told the little girl. Then the family had a powwow, the result of which was to pin a piece of paper to the back of Kate's sweater with her name and address and the words "Please help me to get home safe." She always did, pleased with her adventure, her fat little cheeks glowing with the pleasures of exertion and fresh air.

As much as he loved nature, Frank Goodfellow loved machines even more. Science, progress, and technology were his religion and he worshipped them passionately and whole-heartedly. He worked for a company that manufactured printing presses, and his job was to invent ways to improve how the press worked. As far as Kate knew he had only two loves in his life: his family and his work, and they were always intertwined. His family supported his work and vice versa. Their home life revolved around her dad. Winnie and Kate both knew that when he got a certain faraway look in his eyes, they were to be quiet and never, never interrupt. Something was happening in his mind, and it was as real an event as a thunderstorm or a rainbow. If Frank Goodfellow got an idea during dinner, he would freeze with a fork full of food poised in midair and remain as immobile as if he were playing a game of statues. Silence fell at the table and Winnie watched him eagerly, quickly bolting down as much of her dinner as she could until Frank put down his fork, leaving his dinner untouched, got up, and walked away to his study. At that point Winnie dropped everything, and followed him, pencil and notebook in hand to take down in her precise shorthand whatever thoughts he might want to record.

When Kate was thirteen years old her dad took her to a foundry to watch the manufacture of printing presses—he had invented most of the huge machines that she saw huffing and puffing, shuddering and steaming—watching him among his machines he seemed to her like a god, striding confidently in the din and smoke. They climbed up on a high iron balcony and peered over into the mysterious depths below. "Wait," said her father, "and don't take your eyes off that spot." She waited, poised in anticipation. Then suddenly there was a rush in the blackness, and she saw flowing metal and a burst of flying sparks as flames from the furnace illuminated the dark and a fiery river of melted iron pouring like water into waiting forms. It was magic and the effect on her was instantaneous. Kate knew that this was not something that most other children her age ever got to see, and most girls probably never did, but to her that sight represented the beginning of a true understanding of beauty—in the ever changing flow and movement of life, there were single extraordinary moments. Later, she would credit the sight of the river of iron with the beginning of all that she had become, the memory of it so vivid and alive that it shaped the whole course of her career.

That night she rushed into her house filled to the brim with excitement over the day spent in the factory. It was almost suppertime and she was hungry for one of Winnie's robust soups and the homemade bread she baked almost every afternoon. Hungrier still to tell her mother all about the day's adventure. But the house was strangely silent. The table had not been set. There were no delicious odors coming from the kitchen. Minutes later, Kate found her mother lying across her bed upstairs, too ill to undress.

In 1918 the world, still reeling from the devastation of the Great War, was hit with an even deadlier scourge—a pandemic virus that claimed the lives of an estimated twenty million people. It hit with terrifying speed. Four ladies playing bridge of an afternoon—three of them dead by midnight. People out shopping, walking, visiting, attending church were taken ill so suddenly many had no time to get home. Winnie Goodfellow hung on to life through the night. The doctor had been summoned, but there was nothing he could do. Nothing anyone could do. There was no medicine, no inoculation, little hope. In the early dawn Winnie died. Kate and her father were by her bed, each holding a hand. She broke through the incredible illness only once, her face pale and drawn as she raised a shaky hand to Kate's cheek. "I'll see the world through your eyes," she whispered. A few hours later she slipped away from them so quickly, so silently, that for many minutes they did not know she was dead.

After her mother's death, her father's silence seemed to break only when he was experimenting with some new gadget he had invented or exploring new avenues of thought. Her only way of communicating at all with him was to become his assistant. Father and daughter became a team. He knew little and cared less for the growing social needs of a young girl, and Kate, like her mother before her, tried very hard not to bother him with her own cares. His world became her world and it was filled with ink rollers and pressure cylinders, musty patent offices and the intricate mesh of gears and camshafts.

When Kate was in high school, father and daughter discovered a love for photography, but while other families filled albums with snapshots of birthday parties and the family dog, Kate and Frank Goodfellow took their camera out into the world around them. Down came Winnie's faded maps and up went photographs of machine parts, landscapes, factories, caterpillars, and scenes from their field trips together. Frank taught his daughter to see that there was beauty in the most unlikely places. She learned about the drama of light and shadow and discovered that she had a natural talent for composing and arranging a picture. On a trip to Montreal, where her father was overseeing the installation of one of his presses, both father and daughter took exposures of skylines and smokestacks and architecture which they both loved. "What people are like," her father told her, "is shown by what they build. Architecture is the grandest of human gestures."

In Montreal they found much to photograph. They positioned the camera low to the ground aiming it high so that people and cars were outside the scope of the lens. Verticals of roofs and window frames cut sharp patterns against the sky and gave awesome power and beauty to brick and mortar.

Once, in a poor part of town, just as they were beginning to pack up their equipment, a group of tattered French Quebec children came rushing up to them waving their little hands in the air, palms up, and chanting a singsong "I wan'a, I wan'a, I wan'a . . ."

Kate was fascinated by the scene. "Wait, Dad. Let's take their picture." The camera was a large, boxy affair which required intense attention to focusing, and the children froze as soon as it dawned on them what she meant to do. Then they ran for cover in the nearby doorways.

"It's no use, Katie. You'll never get people to relax in front of the camera. It's too intimidating."

"Wait a minute," she insisted, digging down into the pocket of her coat. "Here, show them this." It was a bright penny and Frank held it up for all to see. The children came running, holding up their hands in a mad scrabble. Kate uncapped the camera lens and took the picture. When he saw the results later in the darkroom, Frank laughed out loud. The photograph was a delight. "You constantly surprise me, Kate. This is very good." It was a heady moment for Kate, for her father was not an indulgent man and never given to praise unless it was deserved. Being good at your work was the highest goal. It surpassed all other aspirations and it certainly surpassed trivialities such as parties and beaux. But it was hard not to think of these things.

Especially in a world where unprecedented prosperity was on the rise. Spurred on by the giant new advertising industry, people were spending their money as fast as they could make it on luxuries unimagined just a few years back—washing machines, refrigerators, vacuum cleaners, 12 million radios, 30 million cars, and untold millions on phonograph records and tickets to the movies. Young people, intent on having fun, were kicking up their heels in this new fast-living world of freedom and glamour that their grandparents could never have imagined. American women had won the right to vote. Hemlines were on the rise and astonishingly closer to the knee than the ankle. Dancing had become the national pastime, the crazier and more frenetic the better.

All through high school Kate longed to go to just one dance. She loved dancing, and when her father wasn't in the house, she practiced by the hour with a windup Victrola and a high-backed dining room chair for a partner. The girls at school talked about the dances they had been to and demon-strated the new steps they had learned. At night, lying in bed, Kate hugged her pillow and imagined the arms of a boy encir-cling her waist, but by her senior year this had not happened. She decided she was never going to be asked to dance and tried every possible way of assuring herself that it didn't mat-ter. The biology lab after school and her darkroom at home consumed her time and left her smelling faintly of formalde-hyde and developing chemicals. Often, she carried her snakes to school or got permission to rush home if a chrysalis was about to hatch so she could photograph the event, and this made her a favorite with her teachers. While her classmates wan-dered restlessly through adolescence, Kate seemed like some-one with a destination. Yet all the while she yearned to go dancing, to tip her head just so next to her partner's cheek, to feel his breath on her skin, to wear a swirling dress, and to float effortlessly to the dreamy strains of a waltz.

Spring came. All seniors were invited to enter an essay contest, the grand prize being fifteen dollars' worth of books to be awarded at commencement just before the senior prom. Kate labored intensely on her essay. If only she could win. It wasn't for the prize, it was so that the boys would notice her. Kate Goodfellow, the winner. Kate the star. Winning would be her key to romance; the prize her passport to popularity.

Commencement arrived. All the girls at Pierson High School wore white gowns to graduation and carried flowers. The au-ditorium was alive with students and parents when Kate and her father made their entrance. Frank detested large gather-ings, and Kate had assured him he could sit in the back of the auditorium so that he could make a quick exit after the scrolls had been given out and the prizes announced. Then she made her way to the front. In her eyes she had never looked so beau-tiful. Unlike the other girls who wore soft organdies and pale ribbons, Kate had chosen a stiff, ballooning taffeta gown more suitable for a fancy ball than a high school graduation. The other girls carried small nosegays of roses or daisies, but Kate had fashioned for herself an immense crown of white carna-tions. It sat perched on top of her flowing red hair, which hung wild and free down her back. The effect was ridiculous.

In due course the seniors received their scrolls; then a series of lesser prizes were handed out and then came the grand prize. Kate, so sure she was going to win, was already half out of her chair even before they announced her name and so flushed and triumphant that she did not notice or hear the titters of her classmates.

Then the chairs were pushed back, the lights romantically lowered, and the band struck up the first waltz of the evening. As couples paired up and dissolved into a swaying throng in the center of the auditorium, Kate took a position confidently at the edge of the dance floor, her prize—three heavy leatherbound books—clutched to her bosom. She stood serene, expectant during the first dance, and again through the second. Then, as the third dance, a foxtrot, began, a small anxiety raised its worrisome head. She swallowed hard.

Waltzes followed foxtrots. Two-steps followed waltzes. The floor churned with swaying organdy and black bow ties. The books grew heavy in her arms, but she dared not put them down. These were her credentials, her magic carpet into the new life of boyfriends and parties and moonlit kissing.

Fewer and fewer girls stood on the sidelines, and yet in an inexplicably perverse way, the stag line seemed to grow longer. Only the seasoned wallflower knows how painful the sight of a long stag line can be. Kate fought down the tears, too proud to go to the powder room, where unpopular girls went to dawdle, fixing their hair or finding snags in their hems to mend.

"May I ask the loveliest girl I know to dance?"

Kate turned and went crimson. It was her father! He had stayed after all. It was the worst moment of her life. Here, on this night of hope and expectation, the only person to ask her to dance was her father. This was the supreme badge of failure— her wonderful, dear, absentminded father. He took the books from her arms and set them on a chair and then, as if they had been dancing together all their lives, he glided her out onto the shiny floor.

And now, less than a year later, he lay dying. Kate looked at her dad. His face was peaceful and he looked content, relaxed, as if he were having a pleasant dream. She wondered what deep in his coma he was thinking—perhaps he was solving his latest problems with the workings of a color press or maybe he was in the night garden with her mother. Then,

without much ado, as if he had never been sick, Frank Goodfellow opened his eyes. He looked at his daughter and she saw
a glimmer of a smile, then with his one good eye he winked at
her, just as he used to do when she was just a little girl. It was
over in an instant. A gentle sigh escaped him and he was gone.
She waited. The room grew very still. Then she pressed his
eyelids shut as she had read was right to do. She kissed him on
the cheek and whispered, "I hope you'll have some great adventuring, Daddy."

CHAPTER NINE

THEY MET IN a revolving door. No one called him Chester.
Everybody called him Eddie. He was tall and fair haired and
moved with the leisurely loose-jointed grace of the self-
assured. You could imagine he danced well. In fact, you could
imagine that he did most things well; there was just that degree of jauntiness about him. From a distance everything
about Chester Edding fit into the good-natured collegiate of
the Roaring Twenties complete with moth-eaten raccoon coat
and tweedy knickerbockers. Up close a second look told you
more. It was in his eyes; inquisitive, curious eyes. And in the
mouth; a sensitive, artistic, dreamy sort of mouth that slanted
up at one corner lopsidedly when he smiled. Kate had just
bolted her dinner at the cafeteria and was rushing back to the
darkroom; he was just arriving to eat his own quick meal.
He knew who she was and had watched her for almost a year.
The first time he noticed her she was walking across the campus wearing a live snake like a feather boa around her neck.
He hadn't thought her pretty. What he saw was an awkward
girl of uncommon looks and somewhat unfeminine character-
istics. She had a loping gait and stiff posture. Wisps of brick-
red hair escaped a drab cloche hat framing broad chubby

cheeks, and her clothes, ill-fitting and unfashionable, did little to hide her plump figure. She was reading a book as she walked and seemed to be oblivious to the stares and sidesteps around her. Indeed, the color of her hair and the snake were the only remarkable things about her.

He started looking for this strange apparition, but she seemed to have disappeared. He noticed she had missed a semester. She went away for the winter holidays and didn't return until the following fall. He asked around and heard that her father had died. The press of his studies and the constant activities of the school made him forget her. Then he saw her again, in the new term, just before dawn, when he was out running and usually had the world to himself, and all of a sudden he was interested again. She was precariously crouched on the roof of the Science Building before a wooden tripod, intently studying through the viewfinder of her camera the upside down image of the early light streaming through the tower on Willard Straight Hall.

"Say," called Eddie in concern, "do you need some help, miss?" Surely she was going to fall at any minute.

His call startled her and first one foot, then the other began to slip on the wet slates of the roof. She was sliding closer to the edge of the building. Then the tripod tipped over, and all of a sudden what had been a perfectly poised statue became a jumble of legs and arms and camera equipment scrambling for safe footing, which she just barely managed to do by jamming her foot in the gutters of the building. Eddie held his breath.

"Now you've done it," she said, turning an angry face to him, when she was sure of her balance. "Please go away and leave me alone." It was an imperious, dismissive demand, but rather than be annoyed, he was intrigued. A few inquiries and he found out that she was the photographer responsible for the dramatic photographs of the Cornell campus on display in the windows of the campus store. He tried to find someone who knew her and could introduce them, but he was a graduate student in engineering and she was an undergraduate in liberal arts, and except for chance meetings on campus, their paths otherwise did not cross. The only thing he learned was that she was pretty much of a loner and considered a bit freakish by the other undergrads. She had nothing to do with college activities and exerted no effort in making friends. But her photographs were stunning. Not just limited to buildings, either. Other students reported that she kept snakes and frogs and jars of insects in varying stages of the life cycle in her room. Her magnified photographs of larvae hatching, snakes shedding, and the chrysalis unfolding into a perfect butterfly exceeded anything Eddie had ever seen before.

Photographer, herpetologist, or plain nutcase, Eddie didn't care. He wanted to get to know her. So he looked for her photographs in the school magazine and the campus store, and he watched for her wherever he went. As the year progressed he noticed that, like the chrysalis, she herself was metamorphosing into a new and completely different creature. The layers of baby fat that had padded and insulated her had melted away, and now she was tall and lanky, possessed of an overgenerous mouth, widely spaced eyes, high cheekbones, and a body curved in all the right places. The ugly duckling had come together with startling effect.

Frank Goodfellow's death had left Kate with the gloomiest financial prospects. If he had been at all money-minded in his life, they would have been quite wealthy from patents on his inventions, but he had never been interested in money and had let his inventions go for small sums while he turned his thoughts to newer ideas. In order for her to return to college, she understood from the lawyer who read her father's will, she would have to work her way through. "The sale of the house, yes, would bring some income, but then the debts . . ." The attorney's voice trailed off. Kate stared at him with wide, intense eyes, and he felt himself slightly squirm in his chair as if it had been he, and not her father, who had not prepared his finances for such a day.

"Ah . . . Miss Goodfellow. Allow me to advise you. I did not know your father well, but he came to me on the advice of his employer, Mr. MacIntosh, who thought highly of him, very highly indeed. Perhaps he could . . ."

But he had no time to finish his sentence. Kate sprang up from her chair. "Capital!" she exclaimed. "I knew I should have to earn my own living, and I was just wondering what I could possibly do to engage myself, but you've solved my problem. I can't thank you enough. I'm sure Mr. MacIntosh and I can come to some agreement. He's a lovely man. And so are you. Thank you so much." She reached across the desk and pumped his hand and stared straight into his startled eyes with her own eager gaze. Then she gathered her things and, with one last wave of her hand, rushed out the door.

The prospect of earning her tuition for college did not scare Kate. Indeed, she was exhilarated at the notion of supporting herself. She'd fill up the emptiness and loneliness she felt with work, hard work, she thought with all the fervor of nineteen. She went home and immediately sat down and wrote her father's boss a letter. He, however, had no idea of how he could put an unskilled second-year student zoologist to work in a printing plant. Women in the workforce in 1925 were typists, teachers, or factory workers. College girls were supposed to get married. He sat for a moment thinking, the letter in his hand. Of course, it wasn't his concern, but he found himself wondering what would happen to such a girl. He thought of his own daughters in a similar situation but his daughters were pretty and well provided for, and both had young men queuing up to his door. They would marry without trouble, but this girl . . . he shook his head. He recalled the strange apparition that had accompanied Frank Goodfellow on his inspections of the printing presses. A tall, ungainly thing who lugged heavy photographic equipment and poked around for hours at a time in the noise and din of the shop. The photographs she and her father had made of the presses . . . quite good, he recalled . . . but who would be interested in the workings of a printing plant? Maybe . . . MacIntosh made a few telephone calls and within the week had secured Kate a position in an exclusive school for girls teaching photography.

Kate flew at her job with a zeal unheard of in private school circles. It was a quaint New England campus set in the rolling Berkshire countryside. Into this genteel setting Kate marshaled her students over hill and dale in a frenzy of photographic endeavor. The pay, of course, was beastly, but she discovered she could make a tidy sum by taking portraits of the students and of the surrounding scenery as well. By late summer she had perfected her techniques, saved enough to reenroll herself, and returned to Cornell a student once more—and a budding entrepreneur.

There were waterfalls on campus making Cornell one of the most spectacular campus sites in America, with fine old ivy-covered architecture and Cayuga Lake on the horizon. Boiling columns of water thundered over cliffs and down into gorges. She took dreamy photographs of the campus at night and of the surrounding landmarks. She would lie in wait for the perfect shadows and was fired up with the romance of stormy skies and the moon streaming through tower windows. These she turned into postcards; sales among the undergraduates were brisk. So brisk that she could not keep up with the demands of printing and still go to her classes. She took up portraiture. Students, mostly girls, flocked to her "studio," a corner she had carved out for herself in the commons room of her dorm. Kate had a gift for lighting so that even the homeliest girls could come away with a softly focused and very flattering photograph. Coeds loved her work but found it impossible to identify with this strange, aloof young woman who took her showers after midnight when the rest of the dormitory was asleep, who wore her hair pulled back into a tight bun, who was tremendously sincere but awkward and freaky looking.

Little did they know how much Kate longed to be one of them. As she took the pictures, she studied the girls in the same way she had studied her reptiles and butterflies, searching for just the right model to pattern herself on. She wanted to be one of the "It" girls, a term that had just come into vogue. To be "It" was to be popular, to be pretty, to be in a sorority, to have a smart comeback to everything that was said, to be a trendsetter who dared to bob her hair and wear stylish hip-hugging dropped-waist dresses.

College students everywhere were fueled by the activities and literature of a young Princeton dropout and his madcap wife. Jazz Age flappers and a garrulous drink-filled high life were the stuff of F. Scott Fitzgerald's books. He and Zelda were the darlings of all the smartest parties in New York, and suddenly it was terribly important to be restless and gay and jaded and to want more of everything—more fun in life and more drama. The girls posing in front of the camera talked among themselves about dances and liquor and men and sex. Kate, behind the lens, listened.

Kate had been unaware of her admirer—the older grad

student—but she was not unaware of the changes that had come over her. Often she worked through the night to get her photography work done so that she could attend her classes during the day. Meals were grabbed on the run or not at all. She didn't notice at first the fact that she was shedding pounds, but one day she needed a pin to hold up the drab black skirt that was almost her uniform. Another day a girl left one of the many pretty dresses she had brought for a sitting in Kate's room. It was a lovely thing, blue cashmere wool cut on a bias for a very slim figure. Kate tried it on and then stared mesmerized at her image in the mirror. The blue was just right for her pale skin and the deep red of her hair. She pulled her tumbled curls from her face and saw someone new. Gone were the chubby cheeks and in their place were sharply defined bones. Her face, if not pretty in the conventional way, was striking. She knew it. In one immensely satisfying moment she also knew she would never be a wallflower again.

Cutting classes the next day, Kate ventured into the local beauty parlor and had her hair bobbed. Then she went shopping. The saleslady at the Loom and Needle, a fashionable store frequented by all the sorority girls, was inspired. "Honey, in this sweater with your coloring, why you're going to be the belle of the ball." The short hair and collegiate clothes made Kate feel adventurous and independent. She was now a young woman to be reckoned with. Kate Goodfellow had grown up.

Now when Eddie saw her walking across the campus she didn't need the accessory of a live snake to draw attention to herself. He saw, with considerable irritation, that other young men were taking notice, too. He would have to move fast before the inevitable happened and the college swains moved in. That night he caught her between the glass walls of the revolving door of the school cafeteria.

He introduced himself and quickly asked her for a date. "Have dinner with me tomorrow."

Kate shook her head, no, but she was laughing at her predicament, trapped in a triangular space like one of the mice in her biology lab.

"Why not?" he persisted.

"Have to work. Let me go."

He spun the door around several times. "How about the day after or any other day of the week?"

"Couldn't possibly," said Kate, "I'll be in the darkroom every night for the next couple of weeks. Graduation is coming, it's my busiest season. Now can I go?"

He spun her around again. "Not until we make a date. Where are you going now?" he asked. "How about a walk? It's a lovely evening." They both laughed. It was raining hard.

"I'm going to work," she said, "and I'll be printing all night."

"All right," said Eddie, "I'll go with you and help. When we're done, I'll buy you breakfast."

Kate found his persistence and good humor irresistible. The fact that he was tall and good-looking and a little older than most of the boys she knew didn't hurt, either. Eddie made the tedious hours in the darkroom fun and they flew by. He was totally at ease, curious about the process of development, and impressed with her skill. He made her feel important, but most of all he made her laugh. It was this quality, more than anything, that made Kate fall in love with him.

"Tell me about yourself," he demanded. True to his word he had taken her to breakfast the next morning.

"Why should I?" she teased.

"Well, we're going to be friends, aren't we? I like knowing about things. I like facts."

"Can't we be friends without swapping biographies?"

Eddie smiled. "You're the first girl I ever met who doesn't like talking about herself. Is there some horrid secret in your past?"

"I wish there were." She laughed. "I'd like to be a mystery woman. The reason I don't talk about myself, where I was born, how I spent my summer vacation, and the latest campus gossip is because it bores me to death. I hate being boring. When I die I'd like to have this as my epitaph: 'Here lies the body of one who never bored anybody.' I like to talk about my theories and philosophies." Kate put her chin on her hands and looked at him. She was wearing a pale yellow tunic over her blouse. Her hair curled about her white face. Her eyes, which were wise and slanting, were gray—an odd green gray, like fog in an ocean harbor. And the intensity of her gaze was arresting.

Eddie felt a dull thud deep in his gut and a tightness in his throat, causing him to clear it before he spoke. "Tell me about your theories and philosophies, then."

"All right." She seemed pleased. "But first tell me what you're going to do with your life."

"Easy. I'm going to invent a rocket to the moon. I'm going to be the greatest aircraft engineer in the world."

"And I'm going to be the greatest photographer in the world." And they both burst out laughing. Hours later they were still talking. Kate, very sure of herself and expansive, and Eddie, quieter, easier but just as sure. They talked randomly about all the "meaningful" things that young people talk about when they are first falling in love. They talked about God. "I don't believe in God,' he said. "Nor religion. Nor any hereafter. When I die, I expect to be through, permanently and positively."

"Carpe diem," she agreed. "I want to try everything in my life, everything—however wicked or dangerous."

"What's wicked and what isn't? Who knows. . . ."

". . . Why do you think old people's eyes are sad? They're sad because they didn't do what they wanted to do. . . ."

"Freedom. That's what I believe in. In everything. Why should any other human being tell me what I can and cannot do . . . ?" "I want to go everywhere, and do everything, especially the things that women aren't expected to do."

That night Eddie appeared in the darkroom as if he had been coming there all his life, and Kate was happy to have him there. Eddie learned fast. Soon he began to regard the exacting standards of the darkroom as a challenge. He was happy. He had found a way to beat out the competition. He convinced her to do less portraiture and to get out into the world with him to do more architecture and landscape, working with the zeal of infatuation to make their expeditions as imaginative and exciting as possible. They chased over the countryside to view the perfect sunset, the most heart-stopping full moon, and they stayed up all night to catch the first rays of dawn.

The planets move at their own pace, and mere humans must wait for the perfect photographic moment, but in the waiting time there are minutes and even hours to be filled with kisses, cuddles, caresses, and other very pleasant diversions.

"Come on, Kate, I'm taking you out to lunch."

"Lunch! With all these prints to make? You're just trying to get out of helping me."

"No. I'm trying to get you out of the darkroom and into the light. It's a beautiful day and I have a surprise for you, so no more work." He was putting her coat over her shoulders and pulling her to the door. By now she was laughing and found herself propelled out into the brilliant sunny April day.

Eddie's car was something that never failed to delight Kate. It was ancient and it wheezed and coughed and groaned like a geriatric whenever he coaxed it into action. But coax he did, spending hours and hours of his spare time tinkering with the motor. He loved engines and though he often talked about the fancy cars he would own one day, Kate knew his real love was taking old, broken things and making them run again.

As she got in the car she spotted a picnic hamper. "A picnic, Eddie? What a wonderful idea. Should I bring my camera?"

"Not this time," he said and would not say more.

They drove from the campus to the edge of town. Then Eddie turned down a dirt road that led to an open flat field with a dilapidated barn. Eddie parked the car and grabbed Kate's hand.

"Close your eyes," he said, "and no peeking."

He put his hands on her shoulders and steered her around to the other side of the barn. "Okay. You can look."

Kate blinked. There parked next to the barn was an open two-seater biplane of the kind first flown in by barnstormers and daredevils who were known to crash just about as often as they remained aloft.

Eddie handed her a pair of goggles, a leather cap with chinstraps, and a long white scarf with a flourish. "Uniform for your first flight," he said, grinning.

"But, Eddie, can you fly this thing?" Kate turned a rather dubious eye to the machine. It had the look of something strung together with glue and a few rubber bands.

"Madam, you cut me to the quick. Fly it? Of course I can fly it! Like a bird! And she's not a 'thing,' she's got a name. See?" He pointed to the lettering on the side. "*Belle Aire*. You're not afraid to go up, are you?"

"Hey. Not me. Fearless Kate, remember?" But she was afraid. And excited all at the same time. A delicious feeling. In a minute she had allowed him to hoist her in the front seat, buckling canvas straps across her shoulders. She put the leather flyer's hat on, pulled down the goggles and twisted the silk scarf around her neck with aplomb. Eddie leaned over and kissed her. "Once we're up you won't be able to hear me. I'll touch your shoulder when we're going to turn."

Then he went up to the front of the plane and jerked the propeller into action, then rushed back and leaped into his seat like a pro. They bounced off in a crazy dance down the field, lifting a few inches off the ground, then bouncing down again, lifting, down again. Kate's teeth were chattering in her head and she hung on for dear life. Then, all of a sudden, the plane lifted and soared up into the denim-blue sky, its wings wobbling just a little as they caught the breeze. Kate didn't realize how tightly her eyes had been closed until she felt the new sensation of being aloft and opened them. What she saw made her shout in amazement. Below, the ground fell rapidly away. They cleared a clump of trees and sailed out over the valley. She could see for miles. The country became a series of patterns, furrowed fields and winding lanes and dark woods and tiny houses. Everything familiar was thrown out of kilter into a new dimension. In a second she had forgotten her fear, forgotten everything except the sensation of moving above the earth.

Eddie tapped her right shoulder and she looked to see in the distance the Cornell campus. All those familiar buildings, now in miniature. Eddie eased the plane down for a closer look, and the campus came rushing toward her, then he pulled back on the throttle and the plane arched upward again, and they were in the sky and of the sky, turning, dipping, gliding like the wind. Higher and higher and now her eyes stretched to a distant horizon she had never known existed. She could see the curvature of the earth, and suddenly she was crying.

All too soon it was over. Trees and grass and field pulling

them down like a magnet and the plane bumping and shuddering along the ground until at last they came to a halt not far
from the barn. For a few seconds they sat in silence. Kate was
too numbed to react, too overwhelmed to say anything. Eddie
jumped out and came around and started loosening her straps.

"Oh, Eddie," she gasped, "never, never in my life has anything been so wonderful. You're wonderful. Life is wonderful.
And"—she threw back her head and shouted as loud as she
could—"FLYING IS WONDERFUL."

After that day, each of them knew they had crossed over some
invisible line. A point of no return. They were young and the
world was beautiful. Now it was a matter of what to do about it.

CHAPTER TEN

IT WAS NOT easy to find a hospitable bed for lovemaking beyond slinking off to some hotel room with pretend wedding bands, and that would defeat their purpose. They were free spirits after all. And so it was decided they would carry a Navajo rug, a bottle of champagne, and a windup Victrola to their favorite spot, the top of a green hill overlooking the river. They would drink the champagne and consummate their love to Caruso singing "Vesti la giubba" from Pagliacci.

All started according to plan. The day, though cool, was sunny and welcoming. They arrived and spread out the rug. Eddie rather nervously opened the champagne, and Kate discovered she had forgotten the glasses. She too was nervous and chided herself because she knew this was going to be the most beautiful moment of her life. She knew all about sex and birth control from her mother, who had taught her from an early age that sex between two people who loved and respected each other was a fine event, but now she found she wanted to get it over and done with as soon as possible.

The record player was wound up, the record set in place. The hilltop air filled with the great tenor's voice, and after one or two swigs from the bottle they both began to relax. In no time the uncertainties buckled under the pressure of curiosity and excitement. Quickly they undressed. When the last button was unbuttoned, the last stocking ungartered, Kate lay on the rug, her red hair fanned about her face. For a moment Eddie could not move. She was so beautiful to him, like a painting by one of the Pre-Raphaelites. Her body was long and very pale. Her breasts were full and her nipples, exposed to the air and in the excitement of the moment, were hard pale buds. She looked at him through half-closed eyes, expecting and trusting. He groaned with pleasure and reached for her, the shock of their two naked bodies making any more restraint impossible on Eddie's part. He fell upon her in a whoop of love and longing. Kate, who wanted to feel the same abandon, instead felt herself all arms and legs and none of them doing what she wanted them to do. She closed her eyes tightly and tried to calm herself. Eddie was doing all those little things that before, in the dark, had pleased her. Now the nibbles on her ear, the hand trailing up her leg, the kisses were like an invading army for which she was totally unprepared. She had to relax. She loved Eddie. She arched her back and opened her arms, her legs, and her eyes to him. And then she screamed.

Eddie bolted upright in horror and confusion. Kate screamed again. There, so close they could feel the warmth of its breath, was an enormous beast. Kate rolled away from Eddie, and both struggled to get to their feet, sending the champagne and the record player skidding down the hill. Kate tripped over the hamper and fell, and Eddie leaped in front of her, putting himself between her and what he now knew to be a charging bull. "Run"—his voice was strangled in fear—"run for your life!" Eddie's eyes were tightly shut, waiting for the impact; instead, he felt Kate's arms go around his waist and she started to giggle. He opened his eyes; a fat brown cow chewing spring grass stared at them with wet saucer eyes. Kate was doubled over laughing, and Eddie, his breath coming in gasps, started to laugh, too. They howled with laughter. The cow gave them a rather weary look—perhaps she had witnessed this scene many times before—then slowly turned and ambled off, her tail twitching saucily from side to side over her fat rump. Still they laughed, getting weak-kneed and sinking to the rug. Oh, what a good joke, they gasped . . . did you see your face . . . you were so brave . . . run, run for your life . . . oh, Eddie, Eddie . . . and in the perfect moment of unendurable happiness, they came together as one.

Afterward they lay in the warm sun under their clothes.

"Does it show?" she asked.

"Does what show?"

"That I'm not a virgin anymore."

He propped himself up on his arm and peered at her in all seriousness. "Nope. You look mighty good though. Good enough . . ." and he made as if to grab her again, but she rolled over in the high grass, laughing.

"Imagine if it did, though. What if sex turned you green or made your hair fall out? Mother Nature might so easily have made this happen. There's a certain kind of beetle, very rare, that turns a bright red when it mates. I wish I would turn green or blue or all the colors of the rainbow. I want the world to know that I love and am loved." She stretched her arms up to the sun so that looking at her, at the freedom of her naked body arched in the grass, her red hair like a flag of independence, Eddie's heart filled with uneasy emotion. He had captured and now held a creature of mythical proportions. Something in her was set far above the ordinary restrictions and limits, he knew. At this moment he felt as if he were groping in the dark for something he could never quite have.

After that day Kate felt herself hopelessly and deliriously in love. She couldn't believe what a gift her body had given her—a gift of such immense physical capacity that she surely must have been reborn. She was a woman now and she carried inside her a pleasure machine that charged her every waking moment. Like young lovers everywhere, she truly believed that she and Eddie were unique. She experienced an almost unearthly joy in his arms, and quite often she sobbed after it was over, her happiness was so complete. The next few weeks they lived on the summit of love. They returned to their field as often as they could and fell to passionate lovemaking, never seeming to quite get enough of each other.

"Marry me, Kate." He held her tightly.

Kate felt her body stiffen. They had never talked about marriage.

"I'd make the world's worst wife," she said lightly.

"Oh, unquestionably!" he said soothingly, kissing her hair and her neck and the tiny place right under her ear that made her shiver. "But I'd be such a terrific husband it wouldn't matter." He laughed. Then sobered. "Well, I'd make a damn good husband now that I think about it. Because look! I wouldn't be jealous of your work. Or domineering. I wouldn't try to run your life for you. I believe in individuals, Kate. You're one—if there ever was one—and I'd respect that. Always. I'd respect your work and your time and your right to do as you chose. I wouldn't want you to cook or clean or grub around with housekeeping. You'd be free, do you see? More free than you are now because it's easier, I think, for a woman who is married."

Kate had gone very still. Then she sat up. "Are you serious, Eddie? I mean it sounds like you've actually thought about this."

"All I'd ask of you would be to live where I lived, and smile at me sometimes, and let me buy you flowers and pretty clothes. . . ."

"And help me in the darkroom," said Kate.

"And help you in the darkroom. Gosh, I'd buy you a darkroom and anything else you needed."

"Oh, Eddie. I love you. I love you so much," she said passionately, wanting to believe it all, wanting to want it as much as he did. But all she could think to say next was the truth. "I guess I'm not ready to think about this kind of thing. . . ." Her voice trailed off uncertainly.

"Just a thought," he said casually, but they both knew it was more than a thought.

In the weeks that followed, the marriage argument began to follow a pattern. Kate assured Eddie that she had never been so happy and yet so desperately torn. She could not reconcile her ambitions to become famous, to travel, to reach the top of her field as a photographer with her perfectly normal and healthy desire for love, marriage, and a family. The loss of her own family had left an empty place in her life, but weren't they too young to think of such responsibilities now? It was confusing and she did not like being confused. Not now anyway, when the world had suddenly opened up for her and lay stretched out like a limitless golden highway. Love had come too soon and too fast, she concluded.

Then one day Kate and Eddie saw something that galvanized their attention and in one moment sealed their bond. An exhibit of architectural renderings of skyscrapers was on display in Syracuse, and they had gone to see it. Eddie was fascinated with the engineering of tall buildings, and this meshed perfectly with Kate's love of architectural photography. Skyscrapers were new, exciting, heady stuff in 1926. Buildings taller than the pyramids, taller than the Tower of Babel—buildings soaring up to the sky shouting to all that American know-how surpassed even the great ancient wonders of the world. Both of them spotted the drawing at the same time. It struck them exactly in the same way and in an instant gave them a mutual goal and a reason to set off together after graduation.

The drawing detailed the Weston Steel Building due to begin construction the next year in Cleveland, Ohio. Something about its soaring tower, its needlepoint reach to the sky, its graceful lines, and at the same time its awesome power as it dominated the skyline of the industrial city, sent rivers of excitement over the two of them. Unlike New York, the Weston Building was not crowded by other tall buildings vying for space in that vertical climb to the sky. Cleveland represented industry, steel, progress—everything they admired. Cleveland was the new tomorrow, the future of America. They studied the building for a long time, and then went to dinner in a little Italian restaurant next door and talked about it for a long time more.

At the end of the meal Eddie pushed his plate away. "It's in the cards for us, Kate. I know it. If we were to get married, we could work as a team. We could start in Cleveland. It's just the kind of city where we could build our reputations. If we go to New York, we'll have years of hackwork and competition ahead of us, but a city like Cleveland is growing fast. What matters there is talent and willingness to work. We've got that, Kate. We can get to the top faster in a place like Cleveland. Then we'll take on New York. Hell, we'll take on the world."

Kate thought about it. Her own plans so firm in her mind—graduation with honors, research, photography, travel—had not figured on marriage, but then she had never reckoned on the power of love. If she had been a more sophisticated woman she might have noticed the almost manic edge to Eddie's insistence, but she only saw through her inexperienced eyes an ardent lover and heard in the increasing excitement of the moment words that encircled her heart. She fixed her eyes on something, nothing, on the table and twisted a match folder around and around in her fingers.

"We'd work together," he went on, as if reading her mind. "You and I will do it all together, Kate. Make names for ourselves. We'd go places and see things. Travel. Go to Italy and Spain and Paris. We'll be the amazing and much publicized Mr. and Mrs. Edding."

"Eddie," she said, suddenly sitting up straight, "what about children? Do you want them?"

"Well . . . sure. I guess I do. But only if you want them," he added hurriedly. "And not too soon, I guess."

"Oh, I want children. I really do. I mean, someday. Maybe three. I always wanted brothers and sisters."

"They can travel with us—the Edding Brats Abroad—or we can leave them behind with the nanny."

"Oh, no." Kate got very serious. "I could never leave my children to anyone else to raise. I want them to know what I know and believe what I do. Not that they won't have their own ideas. They'll have wonderful ideas and each one of them will be different. Part me and part you, but mostly they'll be themselves. That's what makes them so fascinating, don't you agree?"

"I do. I've even thought of teaching . . . I mean later on . . ."

"After we've traveled the world . . ."

". . . and gotten rich and famous . . ." He paused. "And when we've seen it all and done it all and gotten frightfully bored with too much living, then we'll come home to a wonderful house full of books, and great fat chairs, and firelight in the winter . . ."

He stopped. His eyes were seeing the room, the books, and the firelight. . . . He looked over at her. Her expression was rapt. Her eyes were seeing, too. And they were shining. All

over the restaurant people were moving, laughing, gesticulat-
ing, cutting their food with knives and forks, but the two of
them in the corner were very still. They were looking at the
future, listening to the echo of Eddie's words; it was as if they
dared not stir lest they lose it.

"Go on, Eddie," she said softly, "tell me more."

"We'd do it all, Kate. All you have to do is say 'yes,' and I
promise, I'll make it happen."

And so she did.

CHAPTER ELEVEN

THEY SET THE wedding date to coincide with graduation and wanted none of the usual wedding trappings, planning a small simple ceremony attended by just two or three of their friends.

"What about your family, Eddie? Your mother and father? Don't they want to come?" She had never met his parents, and Eddie hardly ever spoke much about his family.

He had told her once when she asked, "I have a mother and a father and a kid sister and a dog. I come from the most average family in America." Now, in answer to her question, he paused. "Of course they will want to come, but families have a way of complicating things. I wonder if we shouldn't just pay them a visit after the fact." His tone was light, but even with prodding he had little more to say. "I'll write then and tell them we're coming after the wedding."

Kate told Eddie about her father, about his inventions and her mother and the maps. He held her close when she told him about her father's death. "Oh, Eddie," she sighed, letting his warm arms comfort her, "it will be nice to have a family again."

* * *

They married two days after graduation. But even as she took her vows, Kate knew she was making a terrible mistake.

The day before the wedding Eddie's parents arrived unannounced. They had no intention of respecting the wishes of two foolish young people. Chester, *Chess,* Edding, Senior was much like Eddie, warm and friendly and outgoing. Mrs. Edding was altogether cut from another bolt. She was formidable in her appearance—the kind of woman who *ran* things, serving tirelessly on committees, her leadership never challenged, a pillar of the community. She was also the kind of woman who did not like surprises and odd behaviors. No sooner out of the car and after hasty introductions, she took one look at Kate, took her measure, and immediately took charge.

"I think my future daughter-in-law and I ought to get to know each other, don't you, dear? You boys can settle us into the hotel; Kate and I are going for lunch."

The hotel dining room was old and formal. Kate was unused to such surroundings and fumbled with the large, heavy menu and dropped her starched napkin on the floor. Mrs. Edding took this all in. Kate was confused by the elaborately scrolled *entrées* and ordered exactly what Mrs. Edding did. The waiter gone, Eddie's mother took no time to cut to the chase.

"Forgive me for being blunt, my dear, but that's the kind of person I am. Are you pregnant?"

"What? Am I . . . oh, no . . . no I'm certainly not. . . ."

Mrs. Edding sighed with relief. "Well, then, what in heavens name is the rush? You and Eddie don't need to marry in this hasty way. Why not wait a bit and come to Jamestown for the summer. As I said to Chess on the drive up, I'm sure you and Eddie don't mean to be unkind, but that's exactly what it is, my dear, a real unkindness not to allow me to see my only son married in a proper way."

Kate felt her cheeks flush. Where was Eddie? She had no idea of what to say, but Mrs. Edding didn't seem to think she should say anything. She was already planning the summer. For the next endless hour she talked nonstop between forkfuls of the chicken salad amandine and a rather greedy, or so Kate thought, helping of the hot club rolls placed between them in a little silver basket. Kate would, she effused, meet Eddie's old friends and get to know his hometown. Then, maybe in the fall, why, they could have a lovely wedding at the church where Eddie had been christened and served as an altar boy.

"But we've already planned . . ." Kate finally fumbled. "I mean, we've made our plans and . . ."

"Oh, posh." Mrs. Edding signaled the waiter for the check. "You can't marry like two fugitives on the run. A big wedding in Jamestown. That's what is needed. It would be the best thing for Eddie. A real welcoming home. And good for business, too. Eddie's been away too long. This graduate school was all nonsense if you ask me. But Chess was all for it . . . I don't know why. That boy has had his head in the clouds long enough, and you don't need fancy diplomas to sell dry goods. His father needs him. Jamestown is growing by leaps and bounds. Chess has been wanting to expand the business for years, and now it's time for Eddie to come home and take his place beside his father."

Kate stared at her. What in God's name was she talking about?

Far from the assuring man who had promised her the moon, Eddie was quiet, almost grim, two hours later when they were finally alone. Slowly the truth came out, in short, static pieces. Edding's Department Store was the family-owned business and had been for three generations. Under Eddie's father, it had become the leading department store in Jamestown. Edding's boasted a fashionable rooftop tearoom, a hair salon, a resident milliner, and a haberdashery shop along with all the latest fashions from New York. Coming of age in Jamestown meant Edding's suits for the boys and cotillion dresses for the girls, and no bride of any note got married in anything other than an Edding's bridal gown. "When I was growing up, no one ever asked me what I wanted to do with my life. They assumed, the family assumed . . . I guess even I assumed . . . I would go into the business. That's why I went to grad school," he confessed, "just to buy time. Get a better handle on things. And then I met you. All of a sudden everything I'd ever wanted and dreamed about came into focus. For the first time in my life I could honestly imagine being someone other than Edding's Department Store."

"But that's still true, isn't it?"

He paused. "The thing is, Kate, Dad's not as well as he looks. He has a bad heart. And I never really told them I wasn't coming home, so now I'm sort of caught off guard."

"But, Eddie, you never said anything . . . what about our plans? What about Cleveland and everything we talked about? Your mother is so sure. . . ."

"Shuhhhsh." He pulled her toward him. "Our plans are our own. We will get married tomorrow no matter what my mother thinks she has to say about it, and then maybe we'll go to Jamestown for a few weeks and my mother can give a big party, or whatever she wants to do. She's really not so bad, if you know how to handle her. Just let her think she's getting the last word and she's happy. Then when the time is right, I'll talk to Dad. He'll understand. He always has. Do you know I took him up flying once? He loved it! I just have to play the game for a while. . . ."

Kate listened and tried to believe, but her emotions ran the gamut from panic to fury. He had been using her and he had never told her who he was or what he was up against. She could see that Eddie was not himself around his mother and father. He felt guilty because he had interests and ambitions that were beyond their expectations. Then she began to doubt that he had ambitions at all. All their talk, all their plans—it seemed they were mostly about her. What was Eddie going to be doing when she was busy building her life? Tinkering with his old airplane? She said to herself, *I made a mistake. It's best to say it now before it's too late.* But even as these things whispered in her brain, her heart was shaken by a kind of spasm. She loved him. They were promised to each other. Tomorrow was her wedding day. Watching him talk, seeing the real pain and misery in his eyes, her heart began to win out. He was so clearly in love with her and so sincerely trying to do the right thing by his family that she began to rationalize. This setback was a problem, but hadn't her father always taught her that problems were made to be solved? A few weeks in Jamestown, hell, the whole summer, if that's what it took, to make Eddie feel less guilty. But then, their life was their own.

But it didn't work out that way. Oh, the wedding took place as planned, but somehow it no longer seemed to be about them. Mrs. Edding, her lips pursed, stood like a silent mountain of disapproval throughout the brief ceremony. Just as the minister pronounced them man and wife, there was a barely muffled sob from the front pew where they sat. Mr. Edding hugged her afterward and laughed a lot, but Kate wondered what he was really thinking. After a brief honeymoon at a friend's cabin on the lake, the newlyweds drove to the big, comfortable Edding home in Jamestown for the "few weeks" that were to last an agonizing year.

Eddie was different at home. His mother and father doted on him. His little sister treated him like a returning war hero. The dog was delirious. At the promised big to-do ostensibly to fete the married couple and introduce Kate to friends and family, Kate saw that she was hardly more than a footnote on the proceedings. Eddie had more friends than she thought humanly possible. A happy, young, well-to-do bunch with little aim in life except to clamor in and out of the house like a Broadway chorus line always coming from or going to yet another picnic, swim party, round of golf, dance, or "spin." A spin meant piling into someone's car and riding about town or out to the lake. Mrs. Edding took Kate shopping and bought her a wardrobe of clothes too frilly and girlish for her tall, lanky frame. Mrs. Edding taught Kate to play bridge, a game that made her fretful and nervous. Mrs. Edding gave afternoon teas and introduced Kate in a high, shrill timbre as her "dear daughter-in-law" to a bevy of elder women to whom Kate had nothing to say.

Kate found that she was actually afraid of Mrs. Edding, and no matter how hard she tried, she could not find a firm footing with this formidable woman. With every passing day Mrs. Edding seemed to grow more disapproving, more intolerant, more oppressive. And so Kate tried, really tried, to enter into the festivities offered by the young people, but it all seemed so empty to her. There was no one but Eddie to talk to, and he seemed so distracted by the social life and trying to be the good son that they hardly had two minutes alone together. One time she watched as Eddie danced with a pretty girl with rich dark hair and a flirty manner at one of the Saturday Night Cotillions at the country club. At one point Eddie leaned over to catch what the girl was saying, and suddenly he threw his head back and roared with laughter. Something caught in Kate's throat, not a bride's jealousy at the flirtation, but the beginnings of a growing bile of defeat.

They did not go to Cleveland in the fall. They did not go anywhere. "It's only for a year, Kate," Eddie pleaded. "We have to be practical, darling. In a year I can fix Dad's business so that it will run itself. I can train some eager young salesman to assist him, and in the meantime, I can earn enough money for us to be set for years. It's only a year, Kate."

So for only a year they rented a little apartment as far away from the Edding homestead and her draconian mother-in-law as Kate could manage. They furnished it with secondhand furniture, painted the walls, built bookcases, and, with Eddie's generous first paycheck, bought the biggest four-poster bed they could find. And there was a fireplace. All that Eddie had once envisioned.

Kate got a part-time job teaching botany in a private boys' school. She taught them how to use a camera and lectured them on the boundless glories of nature. She was a popular teacher because she was young and pretty and fun but became even more so when she introduced the boys to Eddie, who insisted on joining in on the nature excursions. Eddie was a natural and he soon began showing the boys how to fix old machines. His old heap of a car, which had now been replaced by a smart new roadster, as befitted the boss's son, was taken apart and put back together again a dozen times. Once he organized a trip to see an air show, driving the school bus himself with Kate trying to keep order among twenty boys unleashed from the rigors of school for one glorious day. Soon they were asked to chaperone the school dances, and Eddie thought that was just great. Even Kate preferred the dances at the school to the dances at the club. She loved to dance, and it made her laugh looking now on the young faces of the senior boys who cut in, remembering only a few years earlier her longing for such boys when she had been a senior in high school.

When she told Eddie the story of her prom, he had taken it so to his heart that he made a special point at these dances to make sure no girl stayed on the sidelines too long, even if he had to dance with her himself. Sometimes they would exchange twinkling glances with each other as Eddie danced by with some neglected little wallflower. And she loved him for it.

Still, it all seemed to be curiously unreal. It was as if she had suffered some sort of amnesia and come out of her coma years older. She was only twenty-one years old but was now treated as if she were a middle-aged woman.

The school had a surprisingly well-stocked library that became Kate's haunt. She pored over textbooks and periodicals. She found herself fascinated by the growing idea that photographs should replace line drawings as a means of illustration and talked enthusiastically to Eddie about her ideas. They made a project together: they took photographs of various insects, developed them to crystal clearness, then hand glued the photographs in the botany texts. They both found it very exciting.

"We could develop this idea, Kate. We could really take this somewhere, working right here from Jamestown."

"Mmmmm," she agreed, "someday, Eddie. But after this year we'll be in Cleveland, and there will be so many other more exciting things to photograph. They break ground for the Weston Building in the spring. . . ."

However, he seemed less and less inclined to talk about these kinds of things . . . things that could happen in Cleveland . . . and dropped the subject. But if the future seemed shaky, the passion between them was there. Often, they spent whole afternoons in bed making love, and these were the times of bliss.

Then one day in May the entire world was riveted by a single event, which captured everyone's imagination. At the school the faculty and student body gathered in the Commons Room to listen to the school's single radio. A voice crackled over the wireless.

This is Edward R. Morrow reporting from Long Island, New York. This morning I watched a sluggish gray monoplane lurch its way down Roosevelt Field, slowly gathering momentum. Inside sat a tall young man, his face drawn with the intensity of his purpose. Death lay but a few seconds ahead of him if his skill failed or his courage faltered. He was gambling for his life against a hazard that has already killed four men. And then slowly, so slowly as if by his indomitable will alone, the young pilot lifted his plane. It climbed heavily but steadily toward the distant trees. The spirit of unconquerable youth had won, and "Slim" Lindbergh was on his way to Paris.

The boys cheered and Kate cheered along with them. Somewhere out there alone over the Atlantic a young man was risking his life in a grand adventure. Kate felt her heart pounding. She rushed to Eddie's office to find him sitting at his desk.

He looked sheepish but resolute nonetheless. "I know what you're about to say, Kate. Don't say it. Let me talk first. The thing is . . . I want to stay here another year. I . . . I know it isn't what we planned, but—"

"Eddie, no. What about me?" Her voice was caught in her throat.

"Oh, now, be reasonable, Kate. This year hasn't been as bad as—"

"Eddie, listen to me. . . . Please listen to me. I agreed to this year because I love you, but this year is over and now it's time we got started on the life we planned. I have to get on with my own life, our life, out there in the real world. . . . I can't work here. I haven't taken a real picture in months. I want to be at the center of things, not isolated in this . . . this suffocating life. That's exactly what it is. I can't breathe here. I married you because we had a dream together, a partnership, and now you want to destroy the dream."

He was silent. Then he put his head in his hands, massaging the temples.

"Eddie, please, I need my life back."

Eddie lifted his head and spoke quietly. "I know you do. Let's go for a walk, Kate. Let's get out into the air."

They walked blindly for a long time, saying nothing until at last they were on top of a rise. The view was splendid and they could see all over the valley. She shivered a little in the spring air, and he instinctively put his arms around her and pulled her close.

"Did the boys listen to the news report?"

She nodded. "It's so exciting, Eddie. Oh, God, I hope he makes it."

His arm tightened. "Kate, I don't know how to say this except just to say it. I want to stay here another year because I want to teach. I never really knew what it was I wanted and now I do. I talked to the headmaster and he has an opening next fall in history. I can start an after-school program in mechanics, too. He's agreed to try it for one year. He wants you back, too, Kate. Don't you see . . . ?"

But she had shaken herself loose and was standing apart from him. "No."

"Listen to me. When I heard the news about Lindbergh, something in me became painfully clear. I'm not that boy. You made me believe that I was . . . or could be. But I'm not."

"What do you mean?"

"I'm not the amazing husband of the amazing Kate. I don't want my life to be one big adventure . . . an unknown. I like knowing the perimeters. You were the most exciting thing that ever happened in my life, and for a while I truly believed I could become the person you wanted me to be. But I can't. You're one of the rare ones, Kate. I'm just an average guy."

"No, Eddie, you're not . . . you're . . . you're . . ." but she really didn't know what to say.

He smiled sadly. "I know what I am. And I know I need this, Kate."

"And I need to go." The sentence hung in the air. Neither one spoke. Long shadows of magenta and orange and peach were cast over the landscape as the day came to an end.

"Yes," he said finally, and the way he said it—the misery of it and the simplicity of it—threw her off guard. For a long moment she could not even breathe, and she felt her heart pounding so hard it seemed to be trying to get out of her body. It couldn't be, she had done nothing wrong, and now he was letting her go. A flush of humiliation and panic welled up inside her.

Eddie tried to touch her, but she was frozen. She turned and walked away, willing him to come after her, willing him to stay where he was. She walked for hours until the stars came out and the sky faded to black.

They stayed together until the school term was over. The

departing boys said, "See you in September, Mrs. Edding."
And Kate nodded and smiled. Later that day, when Eddie
came home from work, she had already packed her bags. Few
words were spoken. Just before it was time for her to leave, he
handed her a box. "I want you to know . . ." he began, but the
words floundered. "Hey, just open it," he said softly. Kate fumbled with the wrapping, but once she saw what it was, she felt
as if she were paralyzed. Inside, packed in shredded wood
chips, was a long camera lens, the best there was on the market, the best ever made. It must have cost Eddie his salary for
a year. "I hope it comes in handy," he said softly. "I hope . . ."
But she was hugging him too tight for him to finish. They held
each other for a long, long time, her eyes filled with tears. She
had loved this man with all the explosive force of first love,
and she had believed in him. But now it was over.

He drove her in silence to the train station. Waiting on the
platform, they went through all the rituals of leave-taking.
Checking for the ticket, promises of sending an address just as
soon as she had one, making sure she had enough money . . .
until mercifully the train rolled into sight prompting a moment of pure spontaneity. They kissed and everything she
loved about him was there still. His rounded full lips, the soft
brown eyes now shot through with sadness. Then he stepped
back and she clasped his hand one last time. He turned without another word and stumbled out of her life.

Watching him, Kate knew, that to survive on her own
terms, she could never love like this again.

CHAPTER TWELVE

"Hey! Hey, lady! What the hell are you doin' up there? You're gonna git kilt." He was furious, the little man. His face had gone red; his eyes bulged out from under his watchman blue cap. Lord, God, why didn't this happen on the day shift? He was due to go off duty in an hour, and, sure, he was dozing, and why not, it had been a quiet night. Nothin' was happening until the 6:40 Super Chief from New York was due in. Jesus, Mother of God. And here was a dame hanging out over the rail trestle. Harvey Schmitt's eyes were popping, all right. Sure as he was living, there was a woman hunkered down on the wrong side of the railing on the overpass. And what was a woman doing up there anyway? This was the big yard. Every train from New York, Boston, Chicago, and points west went through the big yard in Cleveland. No trespassing in the big yard. Harvey's legs pumped to a run and he started blowing his whistle, though his breath was coming in short gasps. She was all wrapped up in something purple, and it looked like she was gonna fall off the ledge. He ran up the stairs as fast as his fat, short legs could take him and then started running even faster when he saw her wave to him. She was gonna fall for sure, and he could just hear the 6:40 coming off the main track into the yard. Harvey Schmitt thought he was about to die. "Hold on!" he shouted, but he was so winded he couldn't even hear himself. She waved at him again and then she was shouting at him.

"Grab my legs."

"What?"

"I said grab on to my legs. I've got to get out farther. I won't be able to get the right angle from here. Good God, man, are you deaf?"

Harvey clamored over the railing without thinking and flung himself down on the ledge and grabbed hold of two slim legs. He closed his eyes and held on for dear life. He could hardly breathe; he didn't dare look, but if he had he would have seen a young woman with her hair bunched up inside a workman's cap, dressed in slacks and a heavy man's plaid jacket, with a large black box gripped in one hand. Over the box was a purple hood. Her legs, thanks to Harvey, were flattened on the narrow ledge, her upper body was leaning so far down that she seemed to dangle over the tracks. The 6:40 screamed into sight, white smoke belching from its stack, the noise deafening as it roared toward the station. Harvey's eyes filled with smoke and the tears ran down his face, but they were more from fear and excitement than anything else. The whole footbridge shook and rattled so that his teeth chattered in his head.

And then it was over. The train hurled by and started to brake for the final approach into the station. Harvey didn't move.

"Okay. It's okay," a voice said. "Help me up." The legs squirmed and Harvey tugged and the legs found firm hold and the body twisted up into a sitting position. She had lost her hat, and her hair, red as the devil's, flew about her face. She was howling with laughter. "Wasn't it wonderful?" she gasped. "I got it. I know I did! There was only a split second just before the smoke took over, but I got it. "She bounded to her feet and climbed back onto the footbridge. She helped Harvey over the rail and even helped to brush him off, all the while burbling about her timing and the wonder of the big train. She acted as if nothing unusual had happened at all. But it had. Harvey Schmitt burst into tears.

Kate couldn't for the life of her understand why he was crying or what had frightened him so much, but she was very concerned. So much so that she insisted on taking him home in a taxi when he got off his shift. By then he had composed himself and he was almost sheepish, but Kate would not hear of letting him go alone on the tram. She had upset the little man and now she wanted to make it all right again. She took him home and Frau Schmitt insisted that Kate stay and share in the huge breakfast she had prepared for her husband. By the end of the meal they had all adopted one another. Kate promised to give them a print of the picture, and Harvey promised to introduce her to his son's boss, a tugboat captain.

From the deck of the tugboat, Kate saw a city in motion. If the America of 1928, the most progressive, prosperous year in the entire history of the country, was to have a signature image, it was here in the industrial strength of this city. Towers and construction derricks dominated the sky, smokestacks pumped white energy into the air, shrill whistles hooted and wailed through a cacophony of engines all competing against one another in the powerful rhythms of modern industry. All this Kate captured through the lens of her camera.

The tugboat captain, a big, hearty Irishman, had a brother-in-law who was a foreman in a factory. Here Kate found the machines and engines she had loved as a girl with her father. Machines manufacturing parts, assembly lines creating goods—these she began to see as more beautiful than pearls. She wrote passionately in her diary at night about the vitality of industrial life, the power of industrial forms. Why, they were like the finest masterpieces in art, she scribbled, and she, only she, could unloose their magnificence.

It would hardly take a novice in psychology to observe that this passion for the precise, functional form was an obvious antidote to the amorphous form of human emotion. Where love and heartache were concerned, make no mistake, there were no assembly-line solutions.

She tried never to think of Eddie, but in the sleeplessness of night, she could think of nothing else. At first the excitement and fun of getting herself settled in the new city and the new life before her kept her thoughts firmly focused on day-to-day needs. She had refused any money from Eddie, but his insistence finally wore her down and he had given her $2,000 with the promise of more just as soon as she sent him her address. That and the money Kate had saved from her teaching added up to what she considered a tidy fortune, but after six months with no income, she was beginning to worry. She never sent Eddie her address as promised, and she wouldn't for the very reason that he would see it as a call for help. The fact was, her marriage had been a failure. Her best and only friend was gone. The only way to make it come right was to make it on her own. But so far, it was not coming right at all.

It was not easy to be a woman in 1927 trying to break into a man's profession, which photography certainly was. Photography either belonged to the masters like Alfred Stieglitz, Edward Steichen, Ansel Adams, and Jacob Riis, or it belonged to the newsmen, generally a motley crew, but still, they were employed. Few women that she knew of had broken into the field beyond portraiture and fashion. Kate thought she had been prepared for the initial difficulty in being hired for commercial work, but she had underestimated the resistance the industry had toward women. On the worst of days she never got past the receptionist, on the best she got only a cursory look at her portfolio and perhaps useless advice to look for work in fashion or better still children's portraiture. The power and originality of her pictures, the intensity of her images, if anything, went against her. Men were uncomfortable around her—or lecherous.

Kate prided herself on her appearance and studied the fashion magazines for new ideas that she could adapt on her meager budget. Leaning as she did to bright colors and theatrical necklines, however, only made potential clients mistrust that such a come-hither bandbox could be relied on. She accepted invitations to dinner but quickly learned that promises made over cocktails were never honored in the cold light of day. She was on the fast track to becoming a joke.

She seemed unable to progress one iota toward getting clients. No matter how hard she worked, no matter how exceptional the portfolio she took around day after day, Kate Goodfellow could not find work. Corporate men saw little of the beauty of plough blades coming off an assembly line and train trestles and smoke pouring from chimney stacks. Production and dollars were their concerns. Who in the world would want to look at pictures of machinery?

One day after another discouraging round, tired and footsore, she sat herself down on a park bench near a public square. It was a cold day, damp and gray, as if the world had not yet invented its color palette. Even the pigeons (and there were hundreds pecking about on the ground) were perfectly cast in the uniform dullness of the scene. The square was empty and Kate was feeling sorry for herself. Things were not looking good. Besides, her feet hurt. She tried to wiggle her toes inside the high-heeled pumps she was wearing and stared for a long time at the two leather bows on her shoes, shoes that had been reheeled twice now. It was too early to pack it in and go back to her rooms, but the thought crossed her mind. She boarded in a comfortable old house, and she rather liked her Swedish landlady, who was big and tall and strong and looked every inch like one of those operatic divas in Viking helmets. Mrs. Gustafson would wonder why Kate had come home in the middle of the day and would want to feed her marinated herring or ludafisk or spicy meatballs or the contents of any one of hundreds of small dishes that filled her icebox. She liked to feed people and she liked to tell stories in a thick accent with a faraway look in her eye. Kate wanted to photograph Mrs. Gustafson nude—there was something wonderful about her bulk because it wasn't like your ordinary fat person. Her figure didn't sag and hang and look uncomfortable in any way. The flesh rose up from her body, not down, in proud peaks and rolling hills. Her bosom alone was in monumental defiance of gravity. Could she ever work up the nerve to ask Mrs. Gustafson to pose without her clothes on?

Just thinking about it gave Kate pleasure, and so she allowed herself to sink into one of her reveries. She was in a studio, the sign on the door proclaimed it THE GOODFELLOW STUDIO—BY APPOINTMENT ONLY. In her imaginings the room was large and white and spare punctuated by the dark shapes of cameras and tripods and industrial lights hung on rigid poles. Small, faceless assistants scurried about doing all those fussy little jobs that were so irksome to studio work. Off to the

side, in a little alcove, among overstuffed chairs, stood a bevy
of male admirers. These were the powers that could make all
things possible. Industrial barons who invited her to lunch,
scientists who vied amongst one another for her opinions, en-
gineers and architects and artists who stood in line to take her
dancing. And then she was dancing, round and round a ball-
room floor, a man's arm secure around her waist . . . her mind
racing ahead to a more intimate scene . . . a passionate scene
in which she and her lover . . . God, she missed sex. There he
was again, popping into her mind. Eddie. With her eyes closed
and her head filled with longing, it took her some time to
come aware of a voice nearby in the otherwise empty square.
A Negro preacher, quite old with a shock of white hair and
clothed head to foot in black, had perched himself on top of a
soapbox. In one hand he held his Bible, the other was raised to
heaven as he chanted and shouted for all to repent. Only there
were no "all"—only the pigeons pecking about his feet and
giving him no mind. Kate saw in a second that this was a sure-
fire photograph, only she didn't have her camera with her. She
cursed herself even though she knew it was impossible to lug
heavy equipment while she was making rounds.

Suddenly she spotted a camera shop just off the square and
down a narrow street, and getting up very slowly so as not to
disturb either the preacher or the pigeons, she tiptoed to the
edge of the square and then sprinted down the street.

Rolly Stebbins was about as unlikely a looking fellow as
you could ever imagine to work as a clerk in a camera shop.
He was only twenty-six years old but looked years older because of his muscular arms, his short torso, and his rather large
head. One would have taken him for a wrestler or, at the very
least, someone who should be doing heavy work in the outdoors, maybe a cowboy on roundup or a stuntman in the circus.
He had a short crew cut, which made his head seem far larger
than it actually was, and he wore thick horn-rimmed glasses.
Handsome he wasn't, and to make matters worse, he was shy.

It was no wonder that Kate took little notice of such a fellow as she burst into the shop and demanded that he lend her a
camera and a roll of film. He peered at her through his thick
glasses. Kate slammed her portfolio on the counter and urgently gripped the edge. She would have given the counter a

shake if it weren't so heavy and imbedded in the floor. Word-lessly he handed her a Graflex camera—one of the most ex-pensive in the shop. "The film's in it" was all he said. Kate grabbed the camera and was gone. The entire transaction had taken less than fifteen seconds. Rolly took off his glasses and pinched the place where they made deep ridges on the sides of his nose. Then, eyeing the portfolio, he put them back on. The leather was good, soft with hand stitching. The handles were worn and he liked that. He gingerly moved it to the far end of the counter and then went back to polishing lenses. All was very quiet.

Meanwhile, Kate rushed back to the square. Damn and double damn. The preacher was still there, oblivious to his surroundings, his arms punctuating the gospel, his voice soar-ing to the skies, but the pigeons had moved to the far end of the square. Kate stamped her foot in frustration. Then she re-membered a tiny grocery store next to the camera shop. She ran back and, fumbling in her jacket pocket for loose change, threw coins on the counter, grabbing a large bag of peanuts. Once back in the square she edged toward the pigeons, tossing the peanuts. The pigeons were happy to oblige her. They flut-tered and pecked and cooed their way back toward the preacher. A small crowd had gathered to watch the intense girl orchestrate her picture, a fact that did not go unnoticed by Kate. She braced the camera on the back of one of the park benches and began to focus. At one point she motioned to a man standing just outside the edge of her frame and, silently tossing him the bag, signaled for him to throw more peanuts. Kate steadied the camera and began snapping at the scene.

She was in a high state of exhilaration when, less than an hour later, she returned the camera to the shop. Her hair, never smooth at best, seemed to gain even more of an unruly wild-ness when she was excited. Her cheeks were flushed with suc-cess. She knew she had a good picture. Rolly grinned as she handed the camera back to him. "Why did you let me, a per-fect stranger, have this camera? Is it yours?" she demanded to know.

No, it wasn't, he admitted. Kate stuck out her hand intro-ducing herself. "Well, whatever made you do it, you saved my life and I thank you. I don't know what I would have done if I hadn't got it. It was wonderful. You know what I mean? When you have it, just right, when you close in on it, framing it, searching for just the right moment, smaller and smaller right to the heart and then, bingo. It's yours." Rolly nodded. Kate went on talking, and like most shy people, he was happy to let her talk. Besides, he liked what she had to say. In fact, Kate talked for a good part of the rest of the afternoon, and after he had made her tea from a hot plate he kept in his small apartment behind the shop, Rolly talked, too.

The shop and the building, he told her, belonged to a man who liked to tinker with photography. As long as the shop made enough money to pay the overhead and some small profit, he was content to let Rolly pretty much have the run of the place. Rolly had a darkroom set up in the back, and he took her there to show her what he was working on. Kate was fascinated with the things she saw being developed. He seemed to know just about everything about picture taking and myriad techniques for developing. He had papers Kate had never heard of and chemicals and equipment she had never seen before.

He offered to develop her roll of film for her, and she watched him, nervously at first and then with growing admiration, as he did so. His concentration was complete. The first few shots had been overexposed and Kate cursed herself, but Rolly was unruffled. Patiently he worked over the prints trying out different ideas and papers and chemicals. Rolly, Kate learned, could work miracles in a darkroom. The end result was nothing short of stupendous. He glossed her photo in a sheen, adding an extra dimension of light. It was at once realistic and poetic and it gave Kate a shiver of excitement. Rolly was not shy when it came to print work. He accepted her praise and they both peered down on the finished results like proud parents. A week later the Cleveland Chamber of Commerce bought Kate's picture for a brochure they were doing on the city. They paid her $10. It was Kate's first sale, her first commercial piece of work. Her luck was about to change.

For the rest of her professional life, Kate would wonder what would have happened if she hadn't found Rolly Stebbins. If ever there was a reason to believe in destiny, Rolly was it. She had needed Rolly, not just for the camera but for the change it brought over her work. He was devoted to photography as she was, he made her work better; he made it sing. He showed her how to keep her fingers moving while printing in order to dodge the deep shadow areas, how to burn through the highlights that were too dense in the negatives. He taught her that a photograph was a continuous creation, from its composition on the ground glass of the lens to the balance and elegance achieved in the darkroom. He had an uncanny eye for selecting just the right shot of a subject. Kate relied more and more on Rolly's expertise. She would explain to him what it was she was trying to achieve, and then out of a whole sheet or more of contacts he would select the one most perfect. It never crossed her mind that Rolly was in love with her, but he was—from the minute she had rushed into his shop.

At last! Recognition! The Chamber of Commerce entered her photograph in a contest. It won. This exposure brought in a number of business clients who were just beginning to experiment with photography in advertising. Kate's work was considered daring, sometimes even a little risqué. A perfume ad she created caused a mild sensation among art directors. In it she had taken a dozen sample bottles, which were long and thin with spire-shaped stoppers, and lined them up in a row in a top floor window of her landlady's house. From the window you could see the skyline of the city. For hours she had waited for just the right light. It had to be the last light of day, so that the shadows cast by the bottles matched the shadows cast by the tall buildings. The result was a photograph of sultry sophistication and not a little decadence.

The art director at the ad agency loved the picture and the pretty photographer who went with it. Kate went out with him. He made a pass. She turned him down but with just enough twinkle in her eye to wrangle introductions to other art directors. Sex was a new element in her business equation, and she lost no time in using it to her best advantage knowing exactly when and how to turn on the charm. Men adored her. She seemed so innocent and eager with an exciting edge of daring and humor. She was unpredictable, and in a time when most women were thoroughly predictable, Kate Goodfellow stood out. Soon she had all manner of advertising assignments—cosmetics, jewelry, shoes, hats—but art directors and perfume bottles were a far cry from the men who controlled empires. Her eye was on steel.

In the mammoth backyard of Cleveland stretching from the downtown office buildings to the swampy shores of Lake Erie, lay a sprawling cluttered area known as the Flats. The Flats were astir with masculine life. Tugs coaxed barges of iron ore around the river bend, locomotives pushed blackened coal cars, whistles blasted the air, and at the far edge of all this confusion, smokestacks raised their arms over blast furnaces where ore met coke and became steel. Weston Steel. If she could just break through this one barrier, she knew her career would be made.

Oh, to get inside, she dreamed as she stalked the Flats just outside the high wire fences that kept her at bay. She loved the tall thin towers belching smoke, imagined the heat and din of the scene inside like some descent into hell. Steel was the king of industry. Steel to build buildings, to span bridges, to frame the future of America. She had written to the president of Weston Steel but had received a curt answer from some undersecretary saying that Mr. Weston was not interested in photographs of his mills. She had tried to cajole the foreman into letting her if not in the mill, at least inside the fence but got for her troubles a lift home in the patrol car that had been summoned to remove her from the site.

The talk of Cleveland that year was the construction of the Weston Building now rising to glory over the skyline of the city. In New York the skyscraper had been born of necessity, on the tight little island that had to pile itself layer on layer upward if it were to grow at all, but in cities across America, the principal reason for building taller and taller buildings was for prestige. For that rare individual who could afford to build one, a skyscraper was the ultimate symbol of status. Jimmy Weston was such an individual. Up rose his building, soon to be higher than anything around it, dominating the city. Word was out, the architects were looking for a photographer to document the construction of the mammoth tower. Photographs that would say to the entire world that here was a building as modern as all tomorrow.

Kate, naturally, was determined to become that photographer. It became an obsession. The Weston Building was, after all, the very thing that had brought her to Cleveland. It was the reason she had married Eddie. Deep down, she equated the building with her marriage, and somehow, if she could conquer that building, she could conquer her feelings of failure and despair over Eddie. She had to do something to get the attention of the architects, but what? Nothing in her portfolio seemed quite right.

"You're not using your head," Rolly told her. "Show them their own creation. Get inside of it. Show them some sweat."

The offices of Simpson & Clark, Architects, were almost as imposing as those of the building they had designed. A few weeks after Rolly's remark, Kate entered the main reception room and with an imperious nod to the receptionist demanded to see Mr. Franklin Clark. The receptionist was polite only to the point of hearing that Kate did not have an appointment. "Mr. Clark does not see anyone without an appointment," she said dismissively.

"Well, then, I'd like to make one," Kate said, "right now." She retreated to the ultramodern reception area and sat down in a chrome and black leather chair uncomfortably low for her long legs.

The girl pressed a button and murmured something low into the receiver. In a moment she looked blandly over to where Kate was still struggling with the chair. "Mr. Clark has left for the day. His secretary suggests you leave your card and ring her in the morning."

Kate got up and was trying to decide how next to proceed when Franklin Clark himself came into the waiting room, on his way home after a long and tiring day. The receptionist half stood up and tried to signal to him, but he didn't notice because he was too intent on hoping his wife did not have plans for them that evening as she usually did. He wanted nothing more than a stiff drink, a hot bath, and sleep. Then, too late, he saw the girl waiting for him. He saw the portfolio. He saw the eager look on her face as she recognized him. He strode to the elevator and prayed one would come before she had gathered her wits and approached him.

But such was not to be. He was a polite man. He turned to

her with a polite if frozen smile as she delivered her pitch. He edged his way closer to the bank of elevators and stole a glance at his watch. He saw the hurt look on her face. He saw her numbly watch as he pressed the button again. For a moment she looked rejected, but then she squared her jaw and stood defiantly before him.

"Mr. Clark, as you and I can both see, the elevator is on the way down. We may have as much as a whole minute to wait for another one. If we stand here in silence, it's going to be embarrassing for us both. Won't you let me show just one of my photographs?"

She was pretty, he noticed. And he was trapped. He sighed and prepared himself for the worst.

Kate opened her portfolio to a portrait of two workmen standing on the girders of a building under construction. Behind them the sun glinted off the steel in an explosive halo effect around the two sweaty men, one wiping his brow with a large bandanna, the other shielding his eyes. Both looked upward, and the girders from the angle Kate had taken the photograph seemed to stretch to the heavens. It was a powerful testimony to man and steel, to blood and sweat, and it was beautifully rendered.

Franklin Clark was about to ask her point-blank if she had actually been the one to take the picture. It seemed impossible to him that a girl, a pretty girl in fashionable clothes, could have captured the masculine force he saw in the photograph, not to mention the blatant sexual impact, but one look at her face, at the intensity in her eyes, at the confidence in her attitude, caused him to think better of it.

He would learn that Kate had indeed taken this photograph along with hundreds of others. At first the foreman had waved her off, she told him, but she had gone repeatedly to the construction site. Finally, in frustration, she had burst into tears. She had to get a picture, she said. Didn't he understand? It was so important and she wouldn't bother anyone.

For a moment the foreman stood his ground against the barrage of tears that were, he hated to admit, having their effect. "No women on the site," he said. "Can't do it. It's too dangerous. Besides, the men take women to be bad luck."

She looked at him. "You're the boss, aren't you?"

"Hell, yes, I'm the boss," he growled.

"I'll wear pants and a hat. The men won't know I'm a woman."

In no time she was crawling all over the place. The men knew perfectly well she was a woman, but after a certain amount of gawking and innuendo they began to give her tips on what they would be doing next. She begged to go up high, but the foreman stood firm on that one. "No one goes off the ground but the crew unless you get permission higher up. No, sir." And he meant it.

Franklin Clark forgot his tiredness and took her back into his office. He looked at her portfolio and listened to her plan. She wanted to photograph the Weston Building from the top. "I want to see what the building sees." She wanted his permission to go anywhere on it. She would take full responsibility for her own safety and asked only for one man to show her the ropes and help her with equipment. Franklin Clark found himself nodding. He raised a few objections, but she had a rapid-fire answer for everything. She seemed to be equal parts wonder, enthusiasm, and determination. And Franklin Clark was no match for her.

At last she was free to move about inside the great steel structure at will. She was assigned a young man named Johnson who was a Sioux. The Sioux, she learned, were sure-footed and able to work at great heights. He had little to say but seemed, of all the men, the least anxious about her safety. It wasn't that she was not afraid, often she was, but her need to succeed outweighed her fear. Johnson took her up each day, showing her by his example how to ignore the heights and work one's foot farther and farther out on the girders. At first they practiced on beams with platforms underneath that could break a fall. Each day for a month she and Johnson climbed higher and higher until at last she was on the very topmost girder of the Weston Building. They were both very still. Then, at last, he gave her the go-ahead to try her footing on a lone girder sticking out into free air.

Kate nodded and prepared her camera. Now that it was upon her, she felt the old scary panic start to build in her gut. She fought it down and didn't dare to look at anything but the friendly, familiar black box in her hand. She checked it over unnecessarily. She could feel Johnson's eyes. Fear. The dreaded fear was creeping over her like a horde of killer ants she had read about once in a story. An echo from her past calmed her. *The only real handicap is fear. Be unafraid. Go right up to fear and look it in the face.* She remembered her father's last conscious moment before he died. That wink had told her that he had not been afraid even in death. She sucked in her breath and looked up at Johnson. His face was impassive.

Out on the girder, now two feet, now five feet, now eight feet away from the platform, Kate moved cautiously but steadily, repeating over and over Johnson's first rule—concentrate on the thing you have to do, limit your focus—don't ever get lost in the surround. Forget everything else but the job at hand.

Her camera was her foothold. The lens gave her balance. She had no idea of what Johnson might be thinking; in fact, she hardly knew what she was thinking. Thinking was something that either put you in the past or forward into the future. Up here, right now, breath, sight, the sound of air, pure air rushing past her ears, she felt a kind of ecstasy that was indefinable to her. As if some part of her was floating free of her body. She would never forget this moment. It was hers.

No one ever knew exactly who had tipped off the press, but they were perched on the roof of a nearby building. One floor down, from a large glassed-in room, another eye was pointed in her direction. It was the fifty-eight-year-old tycoon of Weston Steel. He had been watching the progress of his building for months now through a powerful telescope installed in his office, and now, all of a sudden, without his knowing about it, a girl was perched on a beam fifty-five stories above the sidewalk. Jimmy Weston rarely lost his temper, but he was mad as hell. Who had authorized such a display? What kind of woman would want to pull a stunt like this? And on his building! He hated tricks like this.

He adjusted the focus on his powerful telescope so that the girl's face came startlingly large and clear. He jerked his head back and squinted up without the lens. All he could see was a small dark hump on the massive steel girder that flashed in the sun. He took a deep inhalation and raised the glass to his eye once more.

This is what he saw. There, poised in a neat, head-hugging

cloche, on a girder so narrow it seemed like the tightrope of a circus aerialist, was a young woman. In both her hands she held a camera. Jimmy Weston held his breath. The girl inched forward on the girder almost to the very end of it, never lifting her head from the camera except once, and then, for a second, Jimmy thought he saw her register the danger she was in, but she quickly ducked her head back to the camera. That got him. He respected fear. Without it, you were not human in his eyes.

DIZZY HEIGHTS HAVE NO TERRORS FOR THIS GAL FOTOG said the Cleveland *Plain Dealer*. KITTEN ON A CATWALK headlined the *Chicago Sun-Times*. The photo they ran with it, the one that would get picked up by the wire services and flashed all over the country, showed an image of Kate gracefully kneeling on the girder at the moment her hat had been whipped from her head by the wind. With her hair streaming she seemed like a mythical creature wild and free.

She had presence. That was what he noticed first about her. It came out of absolute confidence in herself. She was not inclined to sit down, but strode about his office as if it belonged to her. Her portfolio lay open on his desk, but he had hardly glanced at it. Jimmy was enjoying her show much too much. He asked her if she didn't feel afraid dangling so precariously out over the city.

"Oh, I suppose so, but I feel secure with a camera in my hands. Danger doesn't bother me; it's a challenge I like."

"I see." He liked her breezy, offhand voice. She spoke in short takes. "And why do you think that is, Miss Goodfellow?"

"Kate." She stopped and smiled at him with a surprisingly sweet smile. "Call me Kate. If you keep calling me Miss Goodfellow, I'll feel like I have to behave myself."

"Not the proper young lady, I see."

"Oh, I can be proper when I want to, but I'd rather not."

Jimmy took that in. He glanced at her portfolio again. "Miss . . . ah, Kate. You tell me you've been trying for months to get inside my mill. Just what do you hope to find there?"

"Magic." Kate grinned at him. "I've been down on the

Flats watching your mill from outside the fence. You have, by the way, very determined guards. Nothing I've tried has persuaded them to let me in. But I've photographed just the same." She reached over, her arm lightly brushing against his for a brief instant, and flipped the pages of the portfolio. "Here. See?" The photograph had caught images of bright fire dancing away from the mill. She had taken the picture at night, and the effect was eerie, as if demons were at work.

"Slag," Jimmy noted. They both stared at the picture for a time, then Kate bounded away from him and resumed pacing.

"I have a feeling there's more beauty in your steel mills than you or even I ever thought possible. I want to go in with my equipment and see what I can find. You see, I think there is art in machinery and beauty in industry. I want to show people what I see. I want to excite people by taking something they've perhaps never thought about or looked at and make them look at it again. I can do that if you'll give me the time and the freedom to move about the mill."

She was wearing a tight-fitting wool jacket, quite masculine in cut except for the deep V of the neck. She wore no jewelry, but her hair curled on her shoulders and set off the fine, white skin of her neck, a very long neck that held up a determined head. Jimmy cleared his throat. "The last woman who went into one of my mills promptly fainted from the heat," he remarked dryly. "But even if you could manage to stay on your feet, why should I want photographs of the mills? I don't sell I beams like perfume ads."

"No, of course not. But there are two kinds of advertising. One sells a product and the other sells leadership. This is what I'm talking about for Weston Steel. I want to sell an image, an image that says quality and technology and power. When people can know and recognize that our top industries represent these qualities, it gives them confidence. That confidence is reflected on every level of American life. I don't want to sell steel, I want to sell Weston Steel, and I want to do it with images that will make the public stop dead in their tracks. My pictures will capture the strength and beauty and virility of steel. I guarantee, when people see my work, Weston Steel will be a name they will never forget."

"You really think you can do that?"

Kate leaned her arms on the edge of his desk. "I can do anything."

Jimmy raised one eyebrow. "You certainly seem to think so. Didn't it ever occur to you how dangerous that was out on that ledge?"

"I don't want a cautious life, Mr. Weston. I don't want security or safety. I want to challenge myself every day of my life and see if I can beat the odds. I think fear is a handicap. If ever I am afraid, I do something about it."

Jimmy cleared his throat to disguise the smile hovering on his lips. She was a knockout, this redheaded dynamo, and he liked her strut. So what if she was the biggest kook he had come across? He liked eccentric people. Wasn't used to them in women, but . . . he certainly wasn't against it.

He was used to the eager young men who buzzed around him whenever he ventured into the domain of the junior executive, but a girl, this girl, was something altogether different. She reminded him of himself in the early days. A boy without money or family or education. A boy who thrived on challenges. Jimmy Weston doubted that a steel mill was the right place to look for art and beauty, but he found himself agreeing to give her the chance to find whatever beauty she could among his blast furnaces. Then he asked her to join him for dinner.

Rolly was used to seeing Kate cry. She cried more than any woman he had ever known. When things didn't happen exactly like she wanted them to, when people turned her away, when it rained on the days she wanted sun, when the sun burnt through a perfect fog, when she overexposed her film—when anything happened that ruined her work, she wept copious tears. But even he had never seen her vent frustration to the extent she did over the steel mill. She was like a woman possessed. She went to the mill day and night. The foreman loathed her. She drove him crazy. He was sure she would get hurt if not killed the way she went about in the deepest recesses of the plant. Time and again she tried to take shots of the great ladle as it was pouring the liquid steel, but the intensity of the molten fire stymied her. Her camera blistered, the negatives melted and she herself came away with her face inflamed. The foreman begged that she be removed from the place, but Kate had her permissions in order. There was nothing he could do but stand back and curse the folly of old men and pray it would soon be over and this crazed woman gone from his sight.

Rolly grew to dread their time in the darkroom. She stood over him like a falcon watching the developing tray as if it were her prey. Time and again the picture came up dull, blurred, dead. The problem was light. They couldn't get their lights close enough to illuminate the brilliance of the sparks and the white light of the molten metal.

"Oh, Rolly," she said, her voice shaking through gritted teeth. "If I don't get this picture I'll die. It means so much to me." And it did. She could not admit defeat even though it had nothing to do with her or her skills. It had only to do with heat.

"Well, then, you will," said Rolly, but he was damned if he knew how it was going to happen. The next day a fellow came into the shop to buy film. A very ordinary-looking man, a traveling salesman with the gift of gab. It seems he was on his way to Hollywood peddling some new invention—flares. Flares? "Yeah. Sticks of light. Could use them on movie sets, ya know, if you're shooting on location. You light 'em like you would a torch, only they're made of . . ." Rolly stopped listening to the technical details. Sticks of light, bright light, bursting light that would illuminate for a few seconds, long enough to uncap and cap a lens. Kate and Rolly were beside themselves with hope and anticipation as they hurried the salesman into the steel mill.

"You see," explained Kate, "I want you to set off these flares at the precise moment when the ladle pours the steel. Can you set off more than one at a time?" The three of them huddled behind the camera equipment, sweating, their faces burning in the heat. "Now!" shouted Kate, and one, two, then three flares burst into light. When it was over, Kate looked at Rolly and nodded. "I think I got it." Then all three rushed back to the darkroom. Rolly made the negative and his heart sank. It was curiously blank. His look told Kate that once more they had failed. Numbly she stared down into the developing tray willing something, anything to happen. Suddenly a picture began to appear. "Christ almighty," whispered Rolly, "look at that." Then he started to dance up and down. What had looked like blank lines in the negative suddenly came up as a path of sparks. Kate had photographed the path of sparks that fly when the great ladle poured out its stream of molten metal. It looked like light from a plummeting comet.

CHAPTER THIRTEEN

"She'd make a damn fine piece of tail."

Jimmy Weston leaned forward and almost knocked over his water glass. Years of fine-tuned business dealings had trained him to keep emotion from showing in his expression, but he suddenly and quite violently hated the man who had just made that remark. J. T. Koontz, CEO of Erie Manufacturing, the largest manufacturer of rail cars in America, and on the boards of half a dozen of the prominent corporations in town, was known for his philandering. Koontz liked to brag that he could get any woman he wanted, and now as Jimmy watched J.T. watching Kate Goodfellow as she wove her way through the crowded club to the ladies' room, he hoped this wasn't true.

They were, the three of them, having lunch at the Century Club in downtown Cleveland. It was a masculine place given to solemn tuxedoed waiters moving quietly around dark, paneled walls and deep-cushioned green leather banquettes. Belonging to the Century meant belonging to the inner sanctum of the old boy network of big business. In a world where the average family income was $20,000 a year, here in this cushioned room, there was hardly a man worth less than a million and most were worth more. Women were not allowed in the Pump Room or the gaming rooms upstairs but though you rarely saw them, they were allowed in the main dining room. There were few ladies present today, and Kate, in her hip-hugging vibrant blue dress with its low loose neckline, caused not a few eyes to follow her path through the sea of dark, somber-suited men.

"You're a brave man, Jimmy. She's a firecracker." He grinned, leaning forward confidentially. "Am I right?"

"About what?"

"About the tail? Is she as good as she looks?"

"I wouldn't know, J.T.," Jimmy answered dryly, keeping his tone light. "That sort of thing is your department. I'm only trying to help her out. She wanted to meet you, so I'm introducing her to you. She's a damn fine photographer, I can tell you that. You ought to hire her or see that someone in P.R. hires her. She's got talent."

"Yeah, what was it she said she could do, 'wake up the beauty sleeping in a factory'? I like that. She can wake up what's sleeping in my factory anytime." J.T. winked at Jimmy. "Come on, old man. You're not going to tell me you're not sleeping with her. And if not, why?"

"Because I'm not. You know me better than that, J.T. And if I were, I certainly wouldn't tell you. You're worse than an old woman with your gossip. Ah, Kate . . . we were just talking about you. J.T. was just saying how interested he was in your work."

Kate beamed. When she smiled, Jimmy noticed, she seemed to light up from somewhere and it sparkled through her eyes.

J.T. cleared his throat. "Jimmy seems sold on your . . . ah . . . special talents. But I admit I'm a little surprised. How does a pretty gal like you possess this strange desire to photograph factories and machines?"

Kate laughed girlishly. She had heard that one so many times before it had become rote, but she responded to it as if it were the first time anyone had been so clever as to ask her such an original question. Smiling, she leaned toward him, allowing her expression to arrange itself into utmost sincerity, wondering all the while how a man so florid of face and inelegant of manner could be one the richest men in the United States. "I think there's a power and vitality in industry that makes it a magnificent subject for photography. Industry is the future. The process of taking raw material and recreating it into a functioning product is a fantastic tribute to American ingenuity." She looked from one man to the other admiringly. "It's all a matter of how you perceive things. When I look inside your mills and factories I don't see machines. I see forms I think beautiful because they were never designed to be beautiful. This to me is invigorating and inspiring. Business is our civilization. It is our character." She reached over and laid her hand ever so lightly on J.T.'s arm. "I believe the camera is the most important means of recording modern civilization there is, and the camera alone can show that beauty and mystery and eternal truths lay just as much inside your factory as they do in art." Then she stopped breathlessly and gave a charming little embarrassed laugh. "Well, I could go on and on, but maybe that has answered your question?"

Throughout this speech Jimmy had been watching Kate. Watching her turn on her magic, watching J.T. go from being a leering old fart to a quite malleable pawn. And now, why, he couldn't do enough for her, inviting her to meet anyone she wanted to meet, and, by gum, he assured her, there was no one he didn't know. *Good girl,* Jimmy thought. She could do anything she wanted with these men by simply expecting them to give her what she wanted.

Jimmy Weston had not meant to fall in love, but love was what hit him like a ton of his own steel the day she walked into his office. She fascinated him. It wasn't just that she was pretty and eager and unpredictable. It was more than that. She was like a rocket going off in his blood, and he wanted her like he had wanted no woman. He was used to getting what he wanted. He had built an empire on it.

J.T. might want to seduce her, but Jimmy wanted something more. He was not an old man, but he and his wife had grown old with each other. Theirs was not the flamboyant life of the rich but rather the solid life of the privileged. Mrs. Weston's name dominated the society pages of the local papers.

He had married her after making his first million, and he had married well considering his own humble background. In turn, she had served him well. She polished his rough edges and spent his money wisely. Their house on a hundred-acre estate was gracious and welcoming. A gray stone manor house with red brick terraces and an expanse of lawn sweeping down to the lake. Their two daughters were educated and poised. Even now they were in Europe with their mother for a grand tour, and soon enough they would marry. His daughters, like their mother, were cool-headed and conscious of their wealth and the responsibilities it generated. The years of marriage and childrearing in the Weston household had unfolded with propriety and good grace, and, until this moment in time, he had honored its supreme coda, "Thou shalt never cause a Scandal." Now he felt as if he were smothering in the heavy blanket of convention by which he surrounded himself.

He wanted her. He wanted her in ways he could not have fathomed only days ago. He wanted to harness her energy and drive and bring himself down on her and into her until he could catch her fire. He watched her for a week, unobserved from a high catwalk inside the mill, as she bent to the task she had set for herself. He wondered how her hair would feel to his touch, how the curve of her back would fit in his hand, how she would feel underneath him, on top of him. And then he struggled against these thoughts, but he failed and wondered again how her skin might feel; the long legs open to him, his belly against hers. No matter how much he had mired his nature in convention, his primal passions rose in wave after wave to the surface.

Since there was no one else on earth he could talk to about this sudden and surprising obsession, he tried to counsel himself. Would the mere act of seducing her be enough? Or would it only feed his passion and lead him deeper into an absurd situation? She was twenty-two years old. Only a few years older than his eldest daughter. A lengthy affair would surely have public ramifications, yet if carefully planned and executed, couldn't a man of his means have both? There had been other women in his life, but as he had grown older, the casual affair no longer interested him. Let J.T. behave like a randy college boy, let other men keep mistresses in discreet apartments;

Jimmy Weston was not the kind of man who did what other men did. Besides, this was not something he could imagine for this girl. She was her own mistress, anyone could see that. What then? Divorce his wife? Pursue the girl? Marry her? Throw away his good name and his family on a redheaded girl who dangled from buildings and took pictures of furnaces? Bah! It sounded like some cheap melodrama out of a dime novel.

He stared out over the city—his city. The steel skeleton of the Weston Building was silhouetted against a midnight-blue sky. But what did steel mean compared to human emotion? In the end he would grow old and die, and he would have known nothing of the kind of raw, earthy turbulence he imagined with this girl. He turned away from the view. He had to have her.

With his family away for six months, he had closed the large house and taken a suite at an exclusive hotel near his office. This was for convenience sake, but now such an arrangement seemed to play itself right into his hands. He would bring the girl there.

"Okay, Rolly. Now close your eyes and picture this. A magazine. Not a regular magazine, but a big, heavy, beautifully rendered photographic magazine devoted to business and industry. The camera, you see, will interpret business so that everyone can understand how important it is. The camera will go everywhere from the steam shovel to the boardroom, and the pictures will lead one through the whole process of industry. And I don't mean any pictures but really fabulous pictures, dramatic . . ."

They were sitting over the shop in a spare attic room that had taken Kate and Rolly a whole month to clean and paint and which now served as sort of a gallery for Kate's work. Not yet the studio of her dreams, but a place where her best photographs were framed and hung on the wall. She used it as a business address, a place to change clothes, and a work space. But mostly she used it as a place to dream her dreams, because in Rolly she always had an attentive ear. There was little furnishing in the loftlike space—at one end an old chaise that

Kate draped with a rose-embroidered black Gypsy shawl, a few metal industrial chairs lacquered in red and a low slung glass table. At the other was a long worktable with industrial strip lighting hanging overhead. The effect was at once daring and charming, bohemian and utilitarian. Kate and Rolly spent hours in the "studio" discussing the future.

Rolly stretched his legs and poured them each another glass of the homemade brew from the Italian grocery store around the corner. Prohibition, now in its eighth year, had spawned many a Mom and Pop still, and the Santinis, a large family, were happy to barter their concoctions for family portraits.

"Sounds like a pretty expensive proposition."

"Yes. Very expensive. But you see it's the only way to go. Look at the Weston Steel series. It's taken how long? Months to get those pictures into a booklet. And now what? Who outside of Mr. Weston's own investors are going to see them? And they don't need to see them because they're already sold."

"Who else should see them?" Rolly asked.

"Everyone. Imagine if 'The Story of Steel' were the lead article in a magazine. Imagine the impact it would have if that very same magazine was in every corporate reception room and boardroom in America. Don't you see, we wouldn't have to do anything but wait for them all to come begging for the same exposure."

Rolly had grown used to Kate's far-flung imaginings, but this idea had real possibilities. He had watched her go from art directors and P.R. men to the corporate magnates in so brief a time it made his head spin. She really could do anything, he believed, and suddenly he began to catch the fervor. A magazine devoted to good photographs of important subjects. A magazine financed by the corporations of Cleveland. The city was determined to outdistance all other industrial cities, even Chicago, and this was just the sort of thing that would create a stir. Nothing like it had ever been done before.

Ever since Kate had presented Jimmy Weston with the photographs from inside his mill, he had been most attentive to her. He had admired her work and offered her the princely sum of $5,000 for the series to be reprinted into a corporate booklet. Kate suggested they run some of the prints, including the one of the sparks of steel, in the rotogravure section of the Cleveland *Plain Dealer,* and he had agreed to that, too.

He had taken her to lunch at the Century to meet people he thought she should meet; then it became dinner and often a concert or the theater. He was careful to always see her in public places among people who knew him. He treated her like one of his daughters. He introduced her to his friends and their wives enthusiastically telling everyone about her work and her talent.

On one level they were both taking a basic inventory of the other, asking and answering careful, superficial questions about the other's life. Kate told him, as she had told Rolly, that she was twenty-two and just graduated from Cornell, erasing the year of marriage completely. And why not? Her success in Cleveland proved that she needn't admit to such a disastrous thing as a failed marriage. It was behind her—forever. She wondered how old Jimmy was, thinking perhaps sixty but maybe not quite. He seemed physically strong and he was certainly not unattractive. His hair was white, but his brows were as black as night and this gave him a rather dashing appearance. Deep lines ran to his mouth and that aged him, but his eyes were as sharp as a man half his age and his every movement deliberate and firm.

Kate was riding high and relishing every moment. Surely he meant to seduce her. She had caught the look in his eye on more than one occasion, and she wondered how long it would be before he made his move. Oh, delicious. A steel magnate wanted her.

Jimmy wondered if his ploy of escorting her about in public had fooled anyone, and he found he didn't care. He was hooked on her as surely as some men were hooked on drink or gambling. He looked on her with greedy appreciation—her gestures, the way her mouth moved, the whiteness of her teeth, the direct gaze, the luster of her hair and skin. She lent a kind of magic to the most ordinary places—familiar restaurants, the park, his office, even the streets. When he was with her, everything took on a kind of golden haze, and everything went well. The orchestra played not too loudly and chose tunes he liked, and people's faces looked soft and kind, and when he and Kate danced he felt easy and light on the dance floor just so long as she was in his arms. He grew confidential with her and told her many things. It was a love affair on his part—they both knew it—but Kate was too caught up in her own self-absorption and the newness of her power to realize the extent of his feelings. All she thought was—an affair with Weston Steel, why not? And never gave the consequences any thought whatsoever.

One night he invited her for the first time to his apartment for what he termed "a small surprise." Kate knew, just knew, he was about to make his move and decided to dress for the occasion. Rolly let out a long, slow whistle. "Where did you find *that* getup?" he asked, pretending to fan himself.

Kate laughed. "Oh, this old thing." She did a dramatic turn about in the studio. She was stunning. Her hair was pulled back in a smooth roll at the nape of her neck and she wore a gray dress, a demure color but of lines far from demure. It hugged her bosom and hips seductively and then fell in an uneven bias hem midcalf. Her shoes and stockings matched the gown, and the string of deep coral beads about her throat were the same color as her hair.

"Yeah, some rag."

"Actually, I borrowed it. It's for the model on tomorrow's shoot. Even the necklace. They'll never know it had its premier showing tonight."

"Before you go, Kate, come have a look at this." He led her to the worktable. On it, in a large blowup, was her photograph of the skyline of Cleveland. It was a study in smoke and clouds hovering over the city giving the print a feeling of movement, shifting winds and dramatic portent. There was a tension in the picture that lent excitement to it. Up in the left-hand corner of the page, Rolly had superimposed in block letters in bright red a single word: Power.

Kate almost cried. "Rolly," she breathed, "it's wonderful. Oh, my God. It's really wonderful. The name . . . everything . . ." She gave him a hug.

"Well, kiddo. It's now up to you. If your Mr. Weston is everything you say he is, if he really believes in your vision, then maybe, just maybe we can make a go of it."

Kate felt a twinge. She wondered just how far Jimmy

would go to back her. And tonight? How far was *she* prepared to go? It was one thing to allow herself to be seduced by a powerful man; it was altogether another if she wanted something for it. Her confidence in herself, to this point as large and galvanic as a powerful engine, now wavered. Gazing down on the image of her idea, she wasn't so sure. Her photographs were good, she knew that, but a magazine? A magazine required editors and staff and distribution and printing presses and . . . commitment, and wouldn't such a thing as that pin her down, close her off? She saw the glow and expectation in Rolly's eyes—dear, myopic Rolly, who truly believed in her. Well, what the hell. Who knew what the evening would bring? She gave Rolly a quick hug. "I'll be back tonight after dinner. Wait up for me?"

When she got to Jimmy's hotel suite, champagne cooled in a silver bucket and a table was laid for two in the small dining room adjacent to the sitting room. Jimmy greeted her with a chaste kiss on the cheek, poured the wine, and then led her to the large oak table in the center of the main room. It was piled with newspapers from all over the country, and in each one there were reproductions of her steel mill photographs. For once in her life, Kate was speechless.

"Are you pleased?" he said.

"Pleased as anything," she gasped. "Look at this—*The Chicago Tribune, The Atlanta Constitution, The Herald Tribune, The Kansas City Star* . . . thank you, Jimmy." She was shivering with pleasure. "Thank you for everything." And she flung her arms around him and kissed him full on the mouth. She felt his arms tighten around her, and the kiss, which she had meant as a friendly gesture, turn quickly to an ardent expression of love. Its depth and clarity were unmistakable.

When it was over, Kate laughed somewhat uncertainly, not knowing quite what to say or do next, but Jimmy took her firmly by the arm and led her to the sofa. He sat her down and then cleared his throat.

"Kate," he began somewhat formally, "I have something I want to talk to you about, and I want you to hear me through to the very end. These past few months have meant more to me than you will ever know. I have fallen in love with you. I want to make love to you. You must know that by now. But I'm not talking about a casual affair. I want more than that. I am married, as you know, and I don't want to hurt my wife or my daughters, but I find I cannot imagine going on with my life without you in it. I want you for the rest of my life. If you will agree, I will provide you with whatever you want—a house, a studio, photography equipment. We can sail to Europe and live in Paris for a while. You would like that, I know. You can take photographs to your heart's content, and I will see that they are exhibited—whatever you want. I can make the world a very comfortable place and give you all the beautiful things you should have. I can do all of this and more, and in return I ask only that you be there for me . . . as a lover, as a dear friend."

And there it was, laid out in front of her like a path strewn with diamonds. She stared at him.

"You don't have to answer me now. I want you to think about it. You're a young woman and I am not a young man, but I know I can satisfy you. Nothing matters to me but that I make you happy."

Kate had not taken her eyes from his face throughout this speech. She found she did not feel triumphant, as she had imagined she would; instead, she felt touched and flattered . . . and very strange. She reached out and took his hand with genuine feeling and a rush of emotion.

"Jimmy, kiss me again right now. I've been wondering how long it would be before you told me how you felt."

"You have?" He was surprised.

"Of course. What kind of woman would I be if I didn't know what an attractive man like you had on his mind? I will think of what you have just said, but now I don't want to think of anything else but you and me and the way we both feel right now."

She stood up and faced him squarely. He started to say something, but she shook her head and put one finger across his mouth, and so he drew her to him without another word. They stood together for a long time, not kissing, just pressing tightly against the firm length of the other's body. Then it was she who led him by the hand to his bedroom. It was she who drew the curtains against the night. She who turned on the bedside lamp so that the room glowed, and she who quite naturally, as if she had been doing this all her life, unbuttoned his shirt.

She came to him eagerly and without inhibitions of any sort. She was generous and open and passionate, matching his need with her own. They made love consumed with a lust that knew no barriers, no pride, no age, no ulterior motive. At last, in the early morning, exhausted, they slept.

Across town, in the loft, quite another scene was being played out. Chester Edding sat drinking coffee and talking quietly to Rolly Stebbins. Arriving not long after Kate left for her evening, Eddie was somewhat rumpled, pale, and tentative. Rolly was working late, and at first he thought it was just another one of Kate's suitors from the pool of art directors and admen who took her dancing.

"No, I don't live in Cleveland. I'm just passing through. I'm an old . . . friend . . . of Kate's," ventured the young man. "From college. Maybe she's mentioned me? My name is Chester Edding, but everyone calls me Eddie." He saw that Rolly had never heard the name. Eddie turned to go. "Don't let me bother you. If Kate's not here . . ."

Instinctively Rolly knew he should invite him in. Rolly was not used to playing host, and both men felt ill at ease for a few moments, but then Eddie started looking at the photographs hanging on the bare, white walls, and when they discovered they both shared an ardent appreciation of Kate's talent, they found they had hours of talk in them. Along about ten, when Kate had not returned, Rolly invited Eddie to share his dinner. Not much, he apologized. Soup cooked on a hot plate, but the bread was fresh baked and a hard salami came from the Italian store around the corner. Eddie leaped at the invitation and produced from his bag a bottle of bootleg gin.

"Bought it off a guy on the train," he explained. "I hope it's good."

Rolly allowed as how he didn't care, they could disguise the taste with the apple cider he kept in a keg down in the camera shop. An hour or so later, full of food and gin, they sat smoking and swapping stories. From time to time Eddie glanced at the door, and when he did Rolly would steal a

glance at the clock. It was midnight. Doubtless Kate would
not be checking in with Rolly tonight.

"So you two knew each other at Cornell?" Rolly ventured
when Eddie had looked again at the door. "Did you graduate
together last year?"

"Last year? No. I was in grad school but that was a couple of
years . . . well, it doesn't matter. Tell me about her. Is she
happy? Is she doing well?"

There was something in Eddie's voice that had an edge to
it, a sort of tension that made Rolly proceed carefully. He told
Eddie all about Kate's work in the last year, her dedication and
determination to make a career for herself. He told him about
the work she did for the ad agencies and the prize she had won
and the big coup with Weston Steel. He showed him the mock-
up of the idea for the magazine, and then he said after a pause,
"You know a year ago I never would have believed all of this,
but she has a way of making you believe. I don't think there is
anything that could keep her from getting what she wanted."
He saw the pained expression on Eddie's face and he looked
away. There was a party going on somewhere close by. They
could hear it filtering up the airshaft of the building—chatter
and laughter, the piano playing and voices singing, and somehow it was a sad thing, a sobering sound. Rolly ran out of
words and fell silent. Eddie stared morosely at the floor.

"You might as well know who I am, Rolly. You've been
very kind. I know she isn't coming back tonight. I . . . I just
hope, whoever the guy is . . . well, it's not my business anymore. You see, I'm her husband, or at least I will be until the
divorce comes through." And then the whole sorry story came
spilling out. Rolly got the feeling that Eddie had not talked to
anyone about this since he and Kate had broken it off. He listened patiently and quietly, wishing with all his heart that
Kate would come back. Rolly had trained himself not to mind
her affairs with other men, but now he wished they were not
quite so many and that she was not quite so smug about her
conquests. An affair with a man like Weston would have her
crowing for weeks.

At last in the small hours of the morning, Eddie stopped
talking. He had finally wound down and now stood and
walked about the studio. "There's a train out of here in about

an hour for Chicago. I've got a job there working for a settlement house for delinquent boys. I'm good with boys. I'm a good teacher. I've got an idea that education should be more about practical things—you know, like building and mechanics. That's the way to learn math and science. Get the kids out from behind their desks and into the life around them. Up to this minute I had hoped that maybe I could come back into Kate's life, sort of had a fantasy of scooping her up and taking her with me. I guess in a way I was hoping she wasn't doing so well so that we . . . could . . . oh, I don't know. I haven't been thinking very clearly I guess since she left. One thing I do know is that she doesn't need me in her life; she really doesn't need anyone, at least not now. Not when it's all ahead of her."

Rolly also stood. "I hope it works out for you, Eddie." They shook hands. "Do you want to leave an address for Kate? I'll tell her you were here."

"No. Don't," Eddie said with surprising conviction. "Don't tell her I was here. I'll write her after I get settled. Please . . . I would prefer it if she never knew I had tracked her down. It wasn't easy, you know." He laughed ruefully. "I'd just about given up, but then I caught her pictures of the steel mills in the Buffalo paper. That was only two days ago. I called Weston Steel and they gave me this address." He glanced around the studio one last time and then shouldered his canvas bag. "I'll take it back about her not needing anyone. She needs you, Rolly. She needs people who know how to work with her, not against her. She needs people who can help her to fly as high as her wings will take her." He smiled his half-crooked smile—and then he disappeared into the early morning light.

Kate woke up suddenly, not remembering for a minute where she was. She looked over at the sleeping form of Jimmy Weston, remembering now with perfect clarity all that he had offered the night before. Equipment, travel, entrée into the world of moneyed people and powerful influence. She could create her magazine, she could . . . She shut her eyes and tried to imagine this life of luxury. Jimmy could make anything happen—and it was all for the asking right here, right now.

She crept out of bed shivering slightly in her nakedness but went into the sitting room and pulled back the heavy curtains and stared out into the smoky dawn. In the distance she heard a long, mournful sound, and she knew from Harvey Schmitt that it was the early morning Super Chief on its way to Chicago. Thinking about Harvey made her smile. He and his wife were such good people. They worked hard and didn't complain. Work. She could hear her dad: *Work. Work for money. Work for love. Work for any reason. But work—that's what's important.* She turned and tiptoed back into the bedroom, silently retrieving her clothes from the small piles where they had landed the night before, and dressed quickly. Then she went to Jimmy's writing desk and extracted a thin gray piece of paper from the drawer.

He heard the click of the door and knew she was gone. A few minutes later he was reading her note.

I will always remember you as the first and greatest friend of my career. And I will hold in my heart forever what passed between us last night.

That morning Kate worked on a shoot for an ad agency that had been booked weeks before. By early afternoon she was exhausted and went back to her boardinghouse for a hot bath and then went to bed and slept through the night and into the next day in righteous soundness. In the late afternoon she felt so good that she decided to walk the few miles to the camera shop and take Rolly out to dinner.

The shop was closed and Rolly was not to be found when she let herself in. She glanced over the counter of the shop where a cup of coffee and the late edition of the paper lay side by side. No matter, she would go to the darkroom and work on the prints from yesterday's shoot. She was halfway up the stairs when she slowly turned back into the shop, retracing her steps. She picked up the paper and read the headline.

It was the twenty-fourth of October 1929. The stock market, after twenty-six months of the greatest boom in history, had collapsed.

CHAPTER FOURTEEN

THE JAZZ AGE. The Roaring Twenties. The Era of Wonderful Nonsense. Call it what you will, on that October day the carnival spin of make-believe, the reckless optimism of a country giddy with swollen profits, was over. The Great Depression blew in like a swarm of locusts intent on eating bare the prosperity of America.

In the weeks that followed, the pundits held that stock prices had stabilized and called the crash "wholesome," the outlook favorable. But nothing was the same no matter how much one tried to believe. The truth of the matter was that the economy was basically unsound; the middle class had embraced the boom-time zest for getting and spending. Savings were out and buying on margin was in. Banks and corporations were undermined by greed and fraud, the country's wealth lay in the hands of a very few people while vast segments of the society—farmers, coal miners, factory workers—lacked sufficient income to buy even their minimal needs.

The great god Business had stumbled and just about everyone else was stumbling along with it. Kate's prospects seemed to shrivel up and die overnight. Clients, who might have wanted to spruce up their annual reports with glossy industrial photographs, were in a state of confusion scrambling to close excess gaps in their budgets, concentrating only on the bottom line. Factories and mills and assembly lines were no longer working overtime to keep up with production. There were lay-offs now and worse, shutdowns. She watched all of her progress grind to a standstill as the weeks turned into months. How many times had she wanted to call Jimmy Weston and how many times had she stopped herself. His wife and daughters were back, she read in the paper. His empire was struggling to maintain balance.

The winter seemed longer that year. In March Kate began to worry in earnest. She resolved that if one more month went by without income she would break down and write to Eddie. Instead, Eddie wrote to her—or rather, his lawyer did. Eddie, she learned, was living in Chicago and had instructed his lawyer to finalize a divorce. She was overwhelmed with a panicky kind of emotion that seemed to open up the old wound of her failed marriage. There was no one she could turn to, no one to help her, and so she followed the instructions of the letter and on a spring day so lovely it seemed a mockery, she walked into a courtroom, signed a few papers, and walked out a divorced woman. She was truly cut loose now from all that had been. It was time to move on.

"Don't look so unhappy, Rolly. If it doesn't work out, I'll be back."

But they both knew it wasn't true. Kate was on her way to New York, and he knew (as did she) that given a taste of the city, she wouldn't be back. She hugged him. "I feel terrible. Maybe I should stay and tough it out, but . . . I think it's time for me to leave. Oh, Rolly, I owe you so much." Rolly had been footing the bills for them both for months.

Rolly shushed her. "You've got to do what you think is right for you. There's no work here and you certainly don't owe me anything. Believe me, you're the best investment I've ever made. Just make sure you're the best, Kate."

"Don't worry. I am the best." It was a perfect parody and they both laughed. "Just as soon as I get settled, just as soon as I find work, you're coming, too. Whatever would I do without you?"

"Lord knows." He smiled.

"After all," Kate went on, "you don't want to spend your whole life in the camera shop."

"It's a good enough business . . . even now . . . that is, if you can build a business on hocked cameras." Rolly shrugged. "But you're right, I don't. I've been thinking about it a lot lately. Every publication that's worth anything comes out of New York, and if there's work anywhere, it's there. Maybe, as partners, we could . . ."

The whistle blew and they both jumped, then Rolly hoisted her bags and handed them up to the porter. When he looked at her again, she was crying. "God, I expected the last sight I got of you would be a wet one. You cry more than anyone I've ever known. And you never have a handkerchief." He pulled one out of his pocket.

Kate blew her nose and kept on crying. And she cried until Rolly and the station and Cleveland were well out of sight.

As she walked under the high echoing dome of Pennsylvania Station and came out into New York, the heat of the summer day caught in her throat and dazzled her eyes. Surely no other city in the world radiated such heat as New York City in summer. The hot air bathed her face like a steamy towel. Buses lumbered by filled to bursting with heated, sweating people. Mothers dragged pale-faced children along sidewalks, urging them to keep pace, to hurry. Hurry along. Step lively. Move it. Taxies hooted and squealed and swerved and the traffic cop blew his whistle violently and truckers cursed in foreign tongues. The great current of humanity and excitement flowed through her and she was part of it even before she checked into her hotel on Thirty-fourth Street.

It was a city of streets, narrow canyons of pattern and light. She loved it. She walked everywhere and marveled at the mobs of people moving to and fro like the sea. The secretaries on the way to work, the Park Avenue ladies shopping at Saks, street peddlers, bohemians and Italians and artists in Washington Square, nursemaids pushing prams in Central Park. Tenements, townhouses, slums, penthouses, mews, lofts, walk-ups, doormen—it was profound, complex, and impersonal, and to Kate it was as exhilarating as if it were all an extravagant

•

theater piece orchestrated just for her. She loved it from morning to night. She got up at dawn all through the summer when
the air was clean and the moon was falling and walked to the
river to watch tugs gliding over the shrouded water like half-
apparent ghosts. She loved the rush hour when the city roared
and shook and shouted. She loved the late afternoon and the
sliver of sky like a blue ribbon glimpsed between walls. And
sometimes the sun set right at the end of her street.

"So you're the dame who climbed up in that skyscraper.
Where was it . . . Cleveland, right?" Kate allowed as she was, yes,
the very same dame.

"Yeah, we ran the picture a year back. Some gimmick. I always wondered if it was a one-shot deal. Someone told me
you were just a front for some guy who wanted the publicity."
He grinned. A cigar stub clenched in his teeth.

"That was no publicity stunt. I was hired by the architectural firm to—"

"Yeah? So what else ya got."

"Well . . ." Somehow Kate did not think her portfolio of
carefully studied industrial machinery and vaporous skylines
would impress the man she was now addressing.

New York, for all its promise and excitement, was proving
an even worse market for her work than Cleveland. And there
were no Jimmy Westons and lovely Century Club introductions to help her. She was on her own in a city where no one
found beauty in molten steel. In three months she had walked
more streets, ridden up, then down, on more elevators than humanly possible. Every ad agency, design firm, and magazine
in town all said the same thing. "We're not hiring." Until at
last at a midtown temp agency where she had thought she
might pick up some kind of office assignment, they had sent
her here. Here to this man who was chewing his cigar into a
nauseating pulp and near grimacing at her photographs.

His name was Ward Powell and he was the irascible and
terrible-tempered editor of New York's notorious tabloid *The
World Express*. Ward Powell's genius was that he was able to
make music out of murder, mayhem, and disaster. *The World
Express* was no ordinary tabloid. Its reporting was better,

sharper, more relevant to the chaos that churned daily in the
big city than any other newspaper like it. Powell hired good
writers and good photographers and sent them into the fray
with instructions to "go in over your head and not just up to
your neck." He was a man given to shrieking tantrums and dire
threats, and mention of his name in the press room's bar next
door brought on fits of heavy drinking, but he was in an amiable mood when he summoned Kate Goodfellow to his office.

History might look back on the 1930s as the Depression,
but thanks to a new innovation, the thirties also became the
era of the photojournalist. It was a crude career then, and pho-
tojournalists were considered the illiterate backhand of journalism. Hollywood had typed them well. They hung out in
police precincts, chased ambulances, and rudely elbowed their
way to the front of every disaster. In the movies, as they pretty
much were in real life, they were a rough and rowdy lot in
need of a shave, a pants pressing, and small change. They
drank cheap whiskey, played cards, dated waitresses, and
smoked butt ends of evil-smelling cigars.

It was a seamy profession noted for its low pay and ex-
hausting work, and yet it flourished. The public clamored for
pictures—the bolder, the bloodier, the more sensational the
better. Sensation in the popular press was nothing new, but in
1930, while the rest of the world sank to its economic knees,
news photographers were handed a much brighter forecast in
the form of the newly invented flashbulb.

Suddenly they controlled the light. Until 1930 news photographers were tied to dangerous flash powders or limited to
daytime shoots. With the flashbulb photographers could work
anywhere at any time, day or night. Indeed, the automatic
flashgun with its giant-sized bulbs became the trademark of
the archetypal tabloid photojournalist.

Flash! They swarmed wherever news was happening, the
large bulbs exploding mercilessly to expose the gruesome,
the grotesque, the forbidden, the *unthinkable*. To be good at it
you had to be crazy. Crazy enough to pull stunts and elbow
your way past police barricades. Crazy enough to sneak into
courtrooms and backrooms. Crazy enough to risk life and
limb for the best shot. All you needed was nerve—and a flash
attachment.

* * *

The window behind Ward Powell looked down Forty-sixth Street. A street of theaters, small theatrical hotels, and B-rated nightclubs; of little shops selling wigs and lingerie of the kind trimmed in black lace and pink ribbons. A gaudy street. Electric letters glowed above the sidewalk and horns hooted and men leaned against the larger-than-life playbills advertising Broadway shows reading the Racing Form.

Powell sat behind an enormous rolltop desk, its pigeonholes crammed with papers, telegrams, and letters. It was a crummy office, as down-at-the-heels as the street pageant it overlooked, but there was an aura about the place, a feeling that any minute a big story was about to break. Telephones rang, the Teletype machine clattered, men sat hunched over typewriters, wastebaskets overflowed.

He watched her now, sensing exactly her impressions of the place. He seemed bored. "You don't see many women in this game, ya know?"

Inwardly Kate sighed. She needed this job. She thought of the rent now weeks overdue. All that money she had earned in Cleveland gone on hotel bills and smart hats and imported shoes needed to impress employers. You can't eat shoe leather.

She had never thought she would sink to the level of the tabloids but sink she had; what's more, she was about to grovel. Work was work. She squared her shoulders and looked Ward dead in the eye.

"Children think the natural sphere of a parrot is in a cage because they have never seen it anywhere else," she said with more vehemence than necessary. "I'm an investigative reporter. I can go anywhere you want me to, do anything I need to. Don't underestimate what a woman can do."

"Hey. I like the fact that you're a woman. It's a gimmick we don't have around here. A gal like you ought to get by where these other schlemiels can't. Tell you what, Goodfellow, I'll give you a week to show me your stuff, and I'll even assign you to one of my best reporters. You two work as a team. Get there first. Get in fast and get your picture back to me before any other son of a bitch gets back to his paper. And honey—forget the 'investigative reporter' bit. You aren't bucking for a Pulitzer around here. You're working the deadline. Got it?" Ward Powell leaned back in his chair and surveyed Kate over the stub of his cigar. "Yeah. I like a woman fotog. Hey, Candy, is Larson around? Yeah. I think you and Larson ought to do just fine. Get me something good. Get an angle. Do something Weegee can't do." He waved her toward a door and then picked at random one of about six ringing telephones on his desk and started arguing into it. Kate waited for a minute, then realized she had been dismissed.

She backed away and headed for the door, both relieved to get away and excited. She had been hired—at least she thought she had been hired. The man they called Candy waved her over to his desk. "I'll find Larson for you, miss." He ambled off, squeezing his large frame between a series of desks that lined the room. Kate looked after him with some distaste and then looked down at his desk. It was littered with candy wrappers, stub pencils, cigarette ends piled high in an ashtray, and a yellow curled pad. She could see why they called him Candy—he gave Hershey's a bad name. She closed her eyes and tried not to breathe too deeply.

"Are you Goodfellow? I mean is that your name?"

A laughably young man stood looking up at her. He was short with a clean scrubbed face, a brush cut, and a lot of swagger. All he lacked was a freshman beanie. Kate's heart sank. Was this a joke?

"My name is Kate Goodfellow. And you are, no doubt, Larson?"

"Yep. Forrest Larson otherwise known as Woody."

"I should have guessed. So . . . Woody . . . have you worked here long?"

"You wanna know how old I am." He grinned. "I look about sixteen, right? Well, I'm not. I'm twenty-four. Probably older than you. I just have very young genes. The boss says you and I are to go out together. You ready?"

"Now?"

"Sure. Why wait."

"Do we have an assignment?"

"We sure as hell won't get one if we stick around here. Let's go over to the police precinct. It's too early for any action unless we get lucky, but it's a place to start. I'll introduce you to the chief. He's gonna love having a woman around." Woody winked and Kate was not at all sure the chief was going to love her at all. "Candy'll take you down to the shop for some equipment. I'll meet you in the lobby."

In no time they set off—a tall young woman in a smart suit and snap-brim hat lugging a ten-pound Speed Graphic camera, a flash attachment, and a canvas bag of bulbs and a short kid with his hands in his pockets, a wide-eyed grin, and a man's hat pushed to the back of his head—the Mutt and Jeff of the fifth estate. As they threaded their way through crowded Times Square, she learned more about her new boss and the work she was supposed to do. "The *World's* better than some of the tabs, worse than others. We don't just go for the blood, we go for the bigwigs, too. Ward loves to topple the high and mighty; it makes our readers feel good about themselves." Woody confirmed the rumors that Ward Powell was bad-tempered. "The only thing he said to me when I got hired was 'For Christ's sake, don't spell anybody's name wrong. A man will stand for almost any insult sooner than have his name garbled in print.' So naturally I go out and misspell some big-deal politician's name right off, and Ward practically cuts off my head. You haven't seen his shears yet. Keeps them in the top drawer of his desk. Don't go near him when the shears are visible."

"But how do we get our stories if we don't have an assignment?" Kate asked. "We can't just wander around looking behind garbage cans."

"Yep. We can. You'll see. There's always something going down in New York. You make the rounds—police station, hospitals. You make friends with detectives and plainclothes cops. You sit in the back room and listen to the police radio band and hope you get the first word on a breaking story. Then you move into action and beat the others to the scene. You'll see."

"Mr. Powell said something I didn't understand. 'Do something Weegee can't do.' Who or what is Weegee?"

"Come on," Woody said incredulously. "You never heard of Weegee? He's the best. Or at least he's the fastest photographer in the trade, and in this business that makes you the best."

"Fastest at what?"

"Getting to the scene of the crime. They call him Weegee because sometimes he gets there before the police do. Like he's got a Ouija board telling him the next headline. Get it? Ouija . . . Weegee."

"Oh," said Kate, feeling the competitive spirit in her bubble up to the surface. "Well, if he's figured out a way to beat the competition, I suppose we should figure out a way to beat him."

Woody shook his head. "Not me. I know how he does it. He sleeps in his car, which is equipped with a police band radio. When reports come in, he's ready to roll. He can deliver pictures to his paper before anyone else because he makes quick prints in a mini-darkroom he keeps in his trunk. Everything he does is on the run. Man, he doesn't even take the time to take a bath. This is one guy you don't want to get close to. Forget Weegee."

Kate wondered for the hundredth time what she was getting into. Chasing after violent crime in the wake of a dank-smelling man who slept in his car? Bumping along Times Square with a cocky kid? Avoiding her editor because he might threaten her with a large pair of scissors? She shifted the clumsy bag and camera and gritted her teeth, muttering, "Surely *World Express* readers want something more than unregenerate blood and guts spilled out to them on a daily diet? What about compassion? What about social issues? What—?"

"Naw," said Woody. "They don't. When you get to know as much about this business as I do, you'll find out that the common folk of the Western world want thrills and chills for their money. They don't want thoughtful articles on social reform, they want their emotions jerked. It's nothing new—think of those jolly old English beheadings, big day for the rabble. Think of the Roman games—hey, now, that was a family-fun afternoon of carnage. The tabs are just another bloodcurdling treat. Madam . . . ?" Woody stopped and gestured. "Here you see the famed West Forty-fourth Street Police Station. After you." He put his hand in the small of her back and ushered her up the stone stairs.

It was a large dingy room with windows so caked in grime that only a dim hazy light filtered in from the outside. The room was filled with blue-coated policemen and a variety of Broadway types. A drunk was listing at the rail in front of the

lieutenant's desk, a man was being frisked, a solicitous policeman was trying to calm a lost boy with some animal crackers,
an ambulance intern stood by while a belligerent bleeding
man argued with a bored cop.

Everyone eyed her; she heard a low appreciative whistle
from a plainclothes cop drinking his coffee. "Hey, Woody.
Looks like you got a tall order, there."

Woody laughed. "Hey. I like my women tall." Kate stiff-
ened. "Don't worry, Toots. Relax and have some fun. Nothin'
going on now anyway. It's after four. Anyone arrested after
four P.M. goes over to night court on West Fifty-fourth. The
judge sits as long as he has to, to clear the docket. Mostly it's
vagrants, petty hoodlums, prostitutes—anyone can be tried on
the spot, fined, jailed, or dismissed but sometimes you can
pick up some pretty good stories in night court. I got a scoop
on a suicide last week. Maybe you read about her? A chorus
girl, nothin' there, but I scratched around a little and found out
she was the daughter of some big-deal executive over in Jersey. What a break. 'They carried her out in a black wooden
box. Her body broken by the fall, her golden slippers still
strapped to her feet.' Maybe you saw it? Powell ran it big in
the late edition on Wednesday last."

Kate shook her head.

"Yeah. Well . . . it wasn't my best." He looked around one
more time. "Wait till midnight. Then we can go over to night
court and see what the action is."

He introduced Kate to a few policemen, then took her out
through a back door behind headquarters. Here a row of dingy
shops lined a narrow alley housing police outfitters and gun-
smiths on the ground floor. Upstairs were the "shacks."

"Offices," explained Woody. "There's no press room in
headquarters, so reporters hang out up here waiting for news."

Kate surveyed the room he led her to. It was bare except
for a few old battered tables and chairs, direct-line telephones
to various newspaper switchboards, a fire-alarm striker, short-
wave radio perpetually tuned to the police broadcast station
awaiting a hot radio call.

"No action this time of day. Usually there's at least ten
guys here playing cards or snoozin', but they head down to the
bars until the night shift comes on. Let's go over to . . ."

The high-pitched beep of the police-band radio sounded, and Woody stopped midsentence, all ears. Kate found it hard to follow the static and code number she heard, but Woody had it down flat. A bus filled with rush-hour passengers had run up on the sidewalk farther down on Broadway and plowed into a tobacco store. By the time they got down to the street, the emergency squad was rolling away from the curb and sirens were screaming in Kate's ears. Woody grabbed Kate's hand and they were flying down the street flagging a cab. There was a man ahead of them, but Woody pushed him aside and jumped into the backseat, Kate right behind him. "Follow that truck!" Woody shouted. He didn't look like a kid anymore. "Get your camera ready," he barked. His impatience and tension made Kate fumble with the bulbs, and he cursed her, just as she was cursing herself. "We're getting nowhere. Let's run." He threw some money at the cabbie, and Kate found herself running as fast as her high heels let her six blocks down Broadway.

The street was swarming with people. Over the tops of heads Kate could see the tail end of the city bus sticking out of what was once a small shop, now a shattered mass of blood and glass. The driver was still inside the bus, and passengers were walking around moaning and in a daze. The rest was a sea of cops, ambulances, crowds craning to see, fire trucks, and bedlam. Photographers were everywhere jockeying for position, rushing by her with their cameras held high and flashbulbs going off like small popguns. Woody was nowhere to be seen, so Kate started elbowing her way toward the accident. She made no headway at all. She backed off, looking up to see if maybe she could get up to a second floor across the street for a better angle. There were photographers already up there. Some of them perched outside windows on the ledges. She got pushed to the end of the block behind a police barricade along with all the other spectators. She tried to argue with a cop, but he wouldn't listen. She could hardly hear her own voice in the din. Then she saw two men running with a stretcher. They turned down a side street and disappeared into an alley. Kate backed out of the crowd and followed.

In the alley firemen were hacking down a locked door while

the medics stood waiting to get in. Kate sidled up behind one of the men holding a black bag. "Are you the doctor?"

He nodded. "Okay if I go in with you?" She gestured with her camera. "I won't get in your way." Before he had time to think about it, the firemen had cut through the door and they poured in, Kate included. The scene from inside was devastating. The front of the bus was crushed up against the counter of the shop. The shopkeeper, miraculously alive, was pinned to the wall. He was screaming in pain. The bus driver lay dead in his seat, his head smashed against the shattered glass. Kate did not think, did not plan, did not organize her thoughts. She lifted the camera and pressed the shutter. The room was suddenly illuminated in blinding light.

"What the hell . . ." A cop coming through the door grabbed her arm. "Get out of here, Flash, before I throw you out," and with that he unceremoniously shoved her out the door and back into the alley. Kate didn't care. She had her picture. Her heart pounding, she scooted out the alley and started back to the office at a run. Adrenaline licked at her body and left her tingling all over. It took her a half hour to get back to *World Express*. She raced in panting and found Candy lounging in his chair.

"Quick. Where's the darkroom, Candy? I've got something great."

Candy could move when he had to. He rolled his frame forward and began walking quickly toward the stairs. "Two floors down. I'll take you. Andy or Mike will print it for you. What's the story?" But she rushed ahead of him and down the stairs. She wasn't going to trust this shot with any other printer but herself.

Within hours Kate's picture was on the streets. Woody had phoned in his story minutes after she had watched the gruesome picture come up in the developing tray. *The World Express* had scooped every other evening paper in town. Ward Powell grunted his approval. "Beginner's luck," some said. "Only the beginning," said Kate.

They started calling her Flash. With the red hair and the pretty face and the flirty eyes, the name suited her. She became a favorite among policemen and medical examiners.

When the emergency squad rolled, she rolled with it. It might be a riot or a girl who turned on the gas; gunmen behind a barricade, a collapsed tenement, a gangland shoot-out, a murder. She liked the excitement. She liked the urgency. She liked the hours. She even liked the morgue. She grew totally inured to blood and death. She made friends with the crime specialists in laboratories and hospitals. She didn't wait for stories to happen, she created stories like walking the beat with a cop on a lonely waterfront where smuggling was suspected, or sitting with the plainclothes men in the back of a stakeout car. She developed a knack for turning her camera onto the human angle of the scene. Not simply another gang-war street murder but a group of schoolchildren seeing death for the first time. Not a fire but a heroic fireman carrying a kid and a puppy. Not a collapsed building but dispossessed tenants. She had an eye for the telling detail, the poignant human interest angle. Most of her ideas never got past Ward Powell, who seemed to be on a one-man crusade against sentiment, but a few did. And they were about to change her life yet again.

CHAPTER FIFTEEN

THE WORLD EXPRESS was an old newspaper started back in the days when the popular presses were called "penny dreadfuls." Newspapers selling for a penny had originally been started to champion the working classes until a chance sensational murder story involving a whorehouse and a respectable young scion of New York society caught the attention of the masses. The penny newspapers were happy to oblige curiosity by running lurid details of the murder. Sales trebled during the trial, and from that point on, sensationalism became standard editorial policy.

A few decades later, in 1875, a young man named Samuel Bennett immigrated to New York from Scotland. He was a shrewd fellow and saw opportunity in the cheap papers. Mainly, he understood like no one before him that the best way to sell papers is by entertaining the masses, not enlightening them.

Launching his *World Express* in 1880, he relied on new ploys as well as the old familiar circulation builders—to crime, scandal, and sensationalism he added lots of self-promotion, gaudy pictures, screaming banner headlines, stories about life in the city and how to live it; he pandered to celebrities like

Houdini, Sarah Bernhardt, and Buffalo Bill Cody, and he virtually invented attention grabbing exposes like cruelty in insane
asylums and fallen women of the streets. The "penny dreadful"
had now become the full-blown tabloid, and advertisers naturally flocked to the papers that headlined shipwrecks over the
shipping news.

As Bennett became a name to be reckoned with in the media, he championed the popular press as a great "palladium of
liberty" in which the private affairs and domestic doings of
every man, rich and poor, could be set down in good pungent
style. No one was spared the searing spotlight of *The World
Express*. Bankers caught in love nests, society girls on a fling,
politicians in league with mobsters, showgirls, con men, the
man on the street—they were all fodder for the tabloid mill.
Bennett grew rich and, like many of the newly rich, longed
to secure a respectable place in society.

When a prestigious newspaper in Philadelphia went up for
sale, he bought it, shed his tabloid image, and reinvented himself as a pillar of the fifth estate. He married and began his dy-
nasty among Philadelphia's up-and-comers. Two generations
later the Bennetts of Philadelphia ruled over a number of blue
chip holdings, having long since divested themselves of the
newspaper business, but out of some kind of sentiment or simply Scots tenacity, the family continued to own the profitable
World Express. The Bennetts had little to do with the management of so scurrilous a venture, handing the title of publisher
over to another clan, yet even after two generations, Samuel's
direct descendants held controlling interest.

In April of 1931 the publisher of *The World Express* died.
In June the newspaper on Forty-sixth came under a new management. Kate had been surprised to learn the history of her
paper—never considering it *had* a history. But Woody was, as
ever, a wealth of information.

"Yeah. We're the Bennetts' dirty little secret. Only it looks
like we're being let out of the bag. Your new boss is Otis Bennett. Ever heard of him?"

"Well, I've certainly heard of the Bennetts. Which one is
Otis?"

"The son. The one and only son. The Harvard son. He's
been up in Boston running a magazine he started called

something like *Business World*—catchy, isn't it?" Woody stuck a toothpick in his mouth. "I dunno, Toots, I figure we're about to see some changes around the old place."

They were all called into the city room a few days later and were introduced to three young men dressed in handsomely tailored suits. Otis Bennett was seated when they filed in but stood now to address the thirty or so people gathered. He was tall and thin and very pale with steely eyes and a shock of hair falling over his brow. He had thick black brows and there was something about him that reminded Kate of a picture in a book she had loved as a child. *Aunt Louisa's Animals of the Wild. The wolf is a crafty fellow and always moves with stealth.*

He introduced himself and his two colleagues. Fitzhugh Damian and Walter Lord. Fitz Damian was like a fidgety bird, small, trim, and full of movement. He put his hands in his pockets, he took them out. He scratched his head. He smiled. His eyes darted about the room, while Walter Lord lounged comfortably against a desk, long legs out in front of him, beautifully dressed, a handsome man, the kind you might like to see more of. The three of them together looked about as incongruous a trio to manage a tabloid as any could be.

Woody nudged Kate. "Look who isn't here." He inclined his head toward Ward Powell's office. The door was open, but sure enough, the large rolltop desk was gone. The office had been newly painted and appeared empty.

Otis Bennett was not a man given to speeches, although he was pleasant enough in a detached, distant way. After a few preliminary remarks he got right down to business. *"The World Express* will be called *The Express* beginning with next Monday's edition. From that day forward we will no longer be running shock-value stories. It is my belief that there are stories behind the headlines—stories about human endeavor and triumph that outweigh those about violence and crime. Don't underestimate the value of emotion. *The Express* will report the news as it happens, yes, but it will take the story in a new direction. In the next few weeks one of us will be talking to each of you about your work. Fitz will be assigning stories, Walter will be shaping them. Which one of you is Kate Goodfellow? Miss Goodfellow, please see me in my office at two P.M. Thank you."

That was all? Otis Bennett disappeared and everyone sort of stood around. Then Walter Lord stepped up to the bat. "What we're going for is a broader appeal. We've been following a number of the competitive newspapers, and they are all pretty much alike. The same story told with all the gory details. Our idea is not so much to change the stories but to tell them in a new way. Look for heroes, people who overcome handicaps, rags-to-riches, stories about animals and children. Touching stories about love or good works; informative stories about science; revealing stories about social wrongs; stories about the famous and the forgotten. There is greatness to New York—it's all around you every day—and *The Express* will come to stand as the chronicler of that greatness. It won't happen overnight, but the aim is to clean up the act first and then go for the heart of the city."

Kate was impressed, but Woody, along with most of the staff, had that "oh, brother" look, as if they had been handed a church bulletin to write.

Walter caught the general mood and laughed. "Cheer up, folks. We aren't about to kill the hen that lays the golden eggs. *The World Express* has been doing fairly well considering but we think *The Express* can do better."

At two P.M. sharp Kate was in Otis's office, which held no trace of the recently departed Ward Powell. It was clean and spare with two excellent large photography prints, one of the city skyline and one of the city slums, a large bare desk, and two leather desk chairs.

"I like your work, Miss Goodfellow. The photographs you did with the policeman on the beat were excellent. That's the stuff I want." He was silent and sat looking at her.

Kate waited. Was she supposed to say something? She cleared her throat. "Look, Mr. Bennett, I'm flattered you like my work and frankly I'm thrilled with the new philosophy, but it sounds to me like circulation is going to take a nosedive."

"Maybe. Maybe not." Again the pause. She would learn that Otis Bennett spoke in short, static sentences, as if words cluttered up the horizon. He was very decisive in his speech but there was an intensity about him as if he might explode at any minute. It was all very disconcerting. She waited, then started to say something, but he jumped up from his desk and walked to the window. "There's no reason to think that people can't enjoy something other than carnage. The paper has always been loftier than some. I just want more of it."

"Why the name change?"

"Ah . . . that's a whole other story. Later. Tell me something. Weren't you the photographer who took that series on the Weston steel mills? I thought so. For the past five years I've been publishing a business publication. Perhaps you've seen it. *Business Journal*. We featured some of the finest minds in our country. Scientists, inventors, politicians, professors . . . wrote at length about their topics and I published at length. It was an excellent journal read by leaders in industry, finance, even Coolidge read it, but few outside that elite group ever even knew of its existence. I wanted to expand the readership and to do so I wanted to publish photographs with it—big, important photographs glorifying leadership and the mind—but couldn't."

"What a coincidence! I had a similar idea just around the time I did those mill pictures. Only I wanted to concentrate on industry and business."

"What stopped you?"

She laughed. "I was stopped by the sheer lack of money and backers and maybe even my own unbridled confidence. What stopped you?" She looked at him expectantly.

"Ink." His voice was matter of fact. "No printer's ink can dry fast enough to reproduce quality photographs on high-speed presses." He looked at her as if weighing something in his mind. "You asked about the name change. I want to distance this paper from the name *World* because *World* is the name I want for my next magazine."

She waited again for him to continue. Then he was off. At first she couldn't follow what he was saying, but after a while she began to fall into his rhythm, his mind racing from one thought to the next, his abrupt silences, his words a kind of verbal shorthand so that you had to quickly fill in the gaps. Slowly it dawned on her what he was saying and her heart skipped a beat. Otis Bennett was talking about a new magazine, a big, beautiful, multifaceted magazine devoted to telling the news in photographs. "Not just any pictures but extraordinary pictures. Have you been to France? Germany? England?

You should see their magazines . . . filled with pictures . . . very exciting . . . effective . . . I will do that here. I have in mind a new kind of journalism. . . . I see words and pictures in the same context . . . equally . . . working together to create a new way of reporting. You see, Miss Goodfellow, photography is the key. Whoever controls the image controls the power."

"In the meantime, we wait for ink."

"Precisely," he said, "and at the moment we have a newspaper to get out."

Otis Bennett, she would learn, was consumed with a passion for reaching the public. To get the word out, to get it out in such a way as to excite and stimulate his readers, was all that he cared about. In the weeks and months that followed, Kate formed tight friendships with Fitz Damian, whom everyone now called Diz because of the frantic pace at which he worked, and Walter Lord, whom Kate had a mad crush on but who was happily married.

Slowly the paper made the changes Otis had prescribed. There was still plenty of mayhem in *The Express,* but it was balanced with human interest and photographs of faces, not bodies—the more photographs the better.

"Eugene Winslow, the poet?" Kate gasped. "Eugene Winslow is going to write for *The Express*?"

"Exactly." Diz had perched himself on the edge of Kate's desk and was busily rearranging her pencils and pens, lining them up according to size. "We need different kinds of viewpoints. Eugene Winslow is different. Besides, he's starving to death and can't feed his family. Our deal with him is he works for us until he earns enough to pay his bills for a year, then his time is his own. He can return to his pentameters until he runs out of dough again. Here, look at this." He fumbled in his pocket until a faded and creased news article was found. "It's about a factory up the Hudson that makes lightbulbs."

Kate looked blank. "Lightbulbs?"

"Yep. I thought you two might go up there and look around. You see, everyone who works there is blind. Thought it was interesting—blind people making lightbulbs." He winked at her. "Don't go falling in love with him. His wife is a terror. Mexican."

"Thanks for the tip," Kate said dryly, wondering how in the hell she was going to make blind factory workers look interesting.

She spotted him standing far down on the platform at Grand Central Station because he didn't look a bit like any of the other men waiting for the train. He was wearing a rumpled suit and a hat, and both looked as if they had just come through a war. His hands were thrust deep into his pockets and a cigarette hung from his lips. As she approached him, the ashes fell on his lapel, but he neither noticed nor cared. He had a kind of sleepy look about him.

"Mr. Winslow?"

He turned immediately but then stood staring at her as if she were not there. She said his name again, and slowly, then, as if coming out of a trance, he shook himself into a more alert stance.

"Ah . . . Miss . . . er . . . Miss . . ." He fumbled in his pockets, looking for what was probably a scrap of paper with her name. "Yes . . . yes, I have it. I put it in my wallet, but I don't seem to have my wallet. Now, that could be a problem because my money . . . the money they gave me is in my wallet. Good lord . . ." Now he was down on one knee subjecting his suitcase to a violent search, and suddenly the whole thing fell wide open, and wrinkled shirts and notepads and a toothbrush and underwear and pens and loose change began flying all over the platform. Kate got down on her knees to help him, and then the porter, too, who had been following her along with his cart piled high with Kate's equipment. Pretty soon a small crowd gathered, as they always do in New York, and people who couldn't be bothered to stoop themselves began pointing to various objects and directing the scene. "Over here, lady. Right next to the bench." "Hey, there's something over there." And then a second wave of spectators, attracted by the crowd, came over and wondered what the ruckus was.

"What's happening . . . is anyone hurt? Shall I call the police?" "Is he drunk?" At this point Kate started to giggle and then Eugene Winslow, who had found his wallet and was stuffing clothes back into the suitcase, started to laugh, too.

By the time a policeman actually arrived on the platform, the two of them were in gales, further confirming the notion that two drunkards were causing a disturbance at ten A.M. on a July morning in Grand Central Station.

Still laughing, they boarded the train and found their seats in the day coach. "Well, I must say, that's a fine way to set off," Kate said, "and by the way the name is Kate Goodfellow." She stuck out her hand and he his and she found herself looking into eyes the color of well-rinsed denim. His hair, a nondescript reddish brown, flopped about his ears in desperate need of a haircut, a smattering of freckles were on his cheeks, and many more freckles the color of cinnamon covered the backs of his hands. His whole appearance suggested a grown-up version of Huck Finn. Fall in love, indeed, she thought. Why Eugene Winslow could have easily been mistaken for any hayseed salesman from Kansas. In her mind she had pictured him lean and dark and hungry, with opium eyes like Edgar Allan Poe and generally quite mad the way poets were supposed to be. It was hard to see this seemingly mild and utterly pleasant-looking fellow as the man who had penned *The Spaniard,* the epic poem about the conquistadors and their plunder of Mexico. *The Spaniard* had made Winslow's reputation, and it was as dark and vivid and virile as its author, from all appearances, was not.

As they sped along tracks that hugged the Hudson River, they talked and it was all quite amiable and fun. He was a splendid listener, and Kate found herself exploding with conversation about the newspaper business, the Otis Bennett makeover, and her life in New York. But he seemed more interested in her photography and the equipment she had brought. "Oh, normally, I wouldn't be taking all of this, but before working for *The Express* I worked in Cleveland, and I specialized in industrial work, which is why I have this big camera and the lights and tripods. I don't know what pictures I'll be taking for the story, but I wanted to try using my old equipment again. I love factories and assembly lines and repeating patterns of products, but now I've grown to like faces, too." She shrugged. "I hope all of this doesn't bore you."

"Not me," he said expansively. "This is really fascinating. Tell me more about your work."

She found she was half flirting with him, and he seemed to encourage it. In fact, the more she looked at him, the more the hayseed quality faded and in its place was a very appealing man. After a bit they decided to go to the dining car for lunch, and as he started to fumble for his wallet, Kate put out a restraining hand. "Let's not go through all that again." She laughed. "I'll treat."

"You know, I'm not really this clumsy, it's just that I'm not used to carrying a wallet. My wife got this one for me because she said I'd lose my money if I didn't. She's probably right. Usually I stuff what little there is in my pockets."

Kate was walking just ahead of him when suddenly the train lurched and she fell back into his arms. For a second her face was only inches from his. She could feel his breath and the smell of tobacco and a nice soapy scent. Probably his wife had scrubbed him down in the bath, too. She wondered if he hadn't held on to her just a shade longer than necessary. When they settled into their chairs across from one another, a spotless starched white tablecloth between them, Kate asked him, "I've told you so much about myself. Now it's your turn. Diz Damian told me you were broke. Is writing for the populace a horror to you?"

"Horror? No . . . not at all. In fact, I'm fascinated by the idea of the popular press. And, yes, I'm broke, too. Of course, money makes anything go down sweeter. A couple of years ago I wrote jingles for radio advertising. Everyone felt so sorry for me and thought I must be at my lowest ebb, but I liked writing jingles. It reminded me of the songs my brothers and I used to sing in the backseat of the car when we were moving around with my folks. My boy loved it. He's ten. For once he could go off to school and report that his dad did something useful. So *The Express* is no horror. I'm interested in what goes on in the everyday world. I'm curious about people, especially when they're thrust into the limelight. And speaking of light, think about this story we're on. Imagine you are blind and every day you go to a place to make light. Now, if you've been blind all your life, what does that mean to you? What do you think about? What do you see or imagine you see in your mind? Bennett said all I have to do is write about what I see and what I think and then offered me the most outlandish deal to go with it. Now, that's a very good thing."

"I imagine your wife thinks so, too?" Kate said, hating the obvious casualness of her voice.

"Indeed she does. My wife likes to feed and clothe our children."

"More than one?"

"Three." He looked rather sheepish. "Twins the last go-round."

"Well, I guess that does take some feeding." She tried to think of something else to say about his family life but couldn't. She hoped he wouldn't start talking about his children. There was nothing that bored her quite so much as parental pride. Still, it often came in useful. Married men, if they were on the make, as many of them were, could always be cooled down when you got them on the subject of their children. Only now she found she regretted that Eugene Winslow was married and so tied to a family. They had planned to stay overnight in the up-state town . . . she leaned back in her chair and took a sip of her drink. She let her eyes linger on his face as he lit his cigarette.

When they arrived, they made their way to the electric lightbulb plant, where they were greeted politely but some-what suspiciously. The vice president in charge of public af-fairs had no idea what he was supposed to do other than escort them through the plant. What in heaven's name was he sup-posed to make of a duo from a daily paper in New York City? And such an off pair—the photographer dressed to the nines in a linen periwinkle-blue suit with matching shoes and a little straw hat, followed close behind by the writer wearing a baggy suit and a tie that had seen far better days. There were tiny cigarette-burned holes in it and even a coffee stain! It was not a cool day and inside the factory it was even hotter. In ad-dition, Kate's equipment was something to carry! Aside from her working camera, there was a large boxy camera that weighed close to 75 pounds with another box full of lenses, a sturdy wooden tripod with a massive tilt-top head, and a box fit-ted with lights and light stands. All this had to be lugged from point to point as Kate made her way through the plant looking for angles. In the meantime, Eugene chatted with the workers aimlessly about things that had little to do with lightbulb production. He seemed inordinately interest in everyone's life story, asking minute details until finally the vice president in exasperation asked, "Just what is this article supposed to be about?" And Eugene answered, "Oh, let's just say . . . the indomitable will of mankind." Which sent the man back to his office to reread the letter he had received from *The Express*'s managing editor.

Kate toured the plant in a happy state of mind. This was just the sort of thing she loved. She forgot about *The Express* and their story, she was after her own story now. "Something more is needed," she said to Eugene over and over again. "You see, it's like a puzzle and I'm missing a piece. Like missing the punch line." And then, all of a sudden, she found it.

He was an artisan, a giant of a glassblower, who stood high upon a pedestal, unseeing, his great face a blank, and with only the power of his lungs and the skill of his lips to guide him, blew golden hot glass nuggets into huge bulbs, streetlight size. Everything else in the plant was mechanized, but in the handmade streetlight was a craft as ancient as glass itself. Here one could turn back the pages of time and create a romance as lyrical as a painting, a story truly about the indomitable will of mankind.

The two of them left the plant in high spirits. It was getting onto evening and they were both hot and tired. At the hotel, which was an old boardinghouse, they parted, agreeing to meet in an hour for supper, but in less than an hour Eugene knocked at her door. When she opened it, she saw he was carrying a large hamper and a blanket.

"I got the landlady to pack us a picnic supper. It's too hot to sit in a café, and besides I've got directions to a creek with a waterfall. You game?"

Indeed she was thanking herself silently that she had packed shorts and a rather daring halter top.

"How perfect!" she exclaimed when they found the creek and the waterfall and laid out the supper. "God, I'm hungry and this looks wonderful." It was a simple country picnic—fried chicken and potato salad and fresh baked rolls and a blueberry pie—but there was plenty of it.

"Just like home," he said, handing her a crisp, dark drumstick and taking one for himself.

"Speaking of which, where was your home?" she asked.

"Didn't have one, really. I was born on the road, literally. My father was a land surveyor and my mother insisted on traveling with him. She went into labor somewhere out in Arizona, and I got born before they could get to town. We lived everywhere. We'd stop long enough for us kids to get some school, and then we'd push on. I lived all over the West, and then, when I was old enough to break away, I went down to Mexico. I had an idea I was going to be a cowboy down there, raise horses. When the war came, I wanted to join up. I lied about my age and pretty soon I was over there in France." He was silent a moment.

"Bad?"

"For a boy of sixteen, yes. It was pretty bad. I was one of the lucky ones, though. I got shot after a year, blew my guts all to hell, and they pretty much gave me up for dead. Spent seven months in a hospital. When I got out, the Armistice had been signed. I had Uncle Sam's money in my pocket, and I did what every red-blooded American boy should do, I went to Paris. Lord, what a time! I would have stayed on and been dead from absinthe within a month, but a very rich American widow lady picked me up out of the cafés and brushed me off and gave me the money to go to college. So I came back to New York and went to Columbia. That's about it, I guess."

"No, it isn't. You can't leave off there. My God, you're Eugene Winslow, the 'unofficial'—I quote *The New York Times*— poet laureate of America!"

He laughed. "Well . . . I guess there's a bit more. I only spent a year in school. My benefactress died and forgot to tell her heirs that I was on the payroll. I got work on a construction gang and eventually found myself back in Mexico. I started to write. Then . . ."

"Then you met your wife," Kate finished for him.

"Ah, well, no. Once I started writing, I found out I *had* to write. Writing was, to me, as harsh and demanding as the stomach is to food. I couldn't stop. After wasting a small forest of paper, I realized there were so many people I needed to know about and just plain needed to know. So I came back to New York. *Then*," he said with a flourish, "I met my wife."

"But I thought she was Mexican."

"She is. She was living in New York in the Village. She's a painter. Do you know her work? Her name is Malou."

"Malou Winslow?"

"Just Malou."

"I don't think so," Kate said slowly. "But that doesn't mean anything. Unless you artists and writers start murdering one another I probably won't know anything about you." She grinned but felt a little thrown by her lack of knowledge about the Village and its inhabitants. Malou, indeed!

"She's good. A good painter. A good mother."

Kate noticed he didn't say "a good wife."

"And is life in the Village all it's cracked up to be?"

He smiled rather indulgently. "Sure . . . when we get back, I'll take you to a little jazz club down on Sheridan Square. If you don't know the Village, this is the place to start. It's called the Café Metropole. The man who owns it used to be a shoe salesman in New Jersey. He wanted a spot to go where you could hear good musicians without the hassle of swank clubs and expensive checks. When he couldn't find that spot, he decided to start it himself. It's not fancy. It's down in a cellar, but most nights you can't get in. That to me is what the Village is all about. It's a place where people out of the mainstream come because there isn't any other place for them, not in this country, anyway. Village people need to push whatever it is that drives them to the limits." He looked at her and smiled, again a surprisingly sweet smile. For a second he looked all of twelve years old. He was adorable.

Kate, on impulse, leaned over and kissed him. At first she kissed him lightly, almost platonically, but he was having none of that. He reached up and pulled her down to him and his mouth devoured hers. She pulled away breathlessly. "Whoa."

"I've been wanting to do that ever since I first saw you."

"You have?" She was pleased.

"Yes. You know it." He started to pull her back to him, but she laughed and was instantly on her feet running from him.

"Ha!" He gave a shout, and laughing, too, he chased her and caught her. He pulled her to him and in an instant the halter top was off. They were both wildly excited. He kissed her again and then kneeled down quickly, undid the buckle of her belt and slid the white linen shorts down to her ankles and held them for her to step out. She was wearing the flimsiest of silk panties and he removed them and carefully laid them on the ground before turning back and pressing his face to her belly. Tiny white-hot flames licked at her body, but she ran from him again, and he chased her once more, this time tearing his own clothes off until he was as naked as she. They were laughing and whooping like two abandoned wood creatures. She nearly let him catch her, then fled once again into the stream, jumping at last under the water falling over a large rock that jutted out from above. There he caught her and held her, and she clung to him, feeling the cool, clear water and the heat of him all at the same time. With a furious haste he lifted her up and she wrapped her legs around him. It was clumsy, but it didn't seem to matter. They both came in an instant and glorious climax.

Afterward they fell upon the blanket pleased as anything at their behavior. There is nothing so invigorating as doing something you know you should not be doing with somebody else who should not be doing it, either.

True to his word, Eugene called about a week later and took her to hear some jazz at the Metropole. The evening was only marred by the fact that there was no place they could go afterward for sex. The women's hotel Kate lived in forbade male visitors upstairs in the rooms. Kate had never thought of moving, because she was just too busy to organize herself into an apartment. But now she did. A few days later she signed a lease on two rooms on the top floor of an old building on lower Fifth Avenue not far from Washington Square. It suited her taste exactly—the rooms were large square spaces with fancy Victorian moldings and a fireplace, bricked up, but a fireplace nonetheless. She had the floors polished and everything else painted white. And then, rather like the studio loft in Cleveland, she bought only the most minimal furnishings, hung black-and-white photographs, hers, on the wall, and bought a large bed with an iron bedstead.

It was here that she and Eugene repaired every chance they could. Eugene, experiencing steady money in his pockets, was inclined to spend it. He knew haunts and speakeasies and jazz joints. They ate well, they danced, they went from club to club, listening to the wail of horns and blues singers.

Kate loved it. An ardent lover, the bohemian night life, rooms of her own lifted her to the top of the world. Add to that her growing reputation at work, offers from other newspapers, ad agencies seeking her out, and you have the ingredients for a much inflated ego. She began to preen in the office, treating her peers like assistants and her assistants like peons. The secretaries loathed her. Even nice Walter Lord, to whom she turned whenever the least little thing bothered her, had begun to reach his limits. No one quite knew how to deal with such a prima donna.

Kate became blasé about her married lover, naively assuming that either his wife did not know or did not care. Certainly, she never discussed it with Eugene, because compassion for others and concerns for such trifles as infidelity played little part in her self-styled life as a modern woman. To be modern, of course, meant unrestrained sexual freedom. You moved fast, you drank too much; you danced all night and lived as if you cared for nobody. Love was passé, but sex was altogether another matter.

On his part, Eugene Winslow was delighted in his eager lover. She wanted it all the time and so did he. He declared he had never met a woman as uninhibited in bed as she, likening her passion to that of a great locomotive coming full steam into the station.

And so it went for more than two months.

That year, 1933, the biggest news story in New York was not about the fact that one out of four Americans was out of work, that breadlines had become normal facts of everyday life, that Hitler was made Chancellor of all Germany, or that Prohibition after ten long years had ended. No, in New York the story that rocked the headlines for months was about a pretty housewife from Queens named Ruby Barnes convicted of murdering her husband in a thunderously publicized "love triangle" involving a handsome, smooth-talking ladies' lingerie salesman named Jed Smyth. For months every tabloid in town had followed the trial and photographers had chafed at the bit because they were banned from the courtroom. Whenever Ruby or Jed were transported in and out of court, photographers hung from windowsills to try and get a picture of the two lovers. Mostly they had to be content with blurry images and hats held over faces that satisfied no one.

Every raw, flaring word of the trial had been eaten up by the readers of the sensational press. In due time, Ruby and Jed were convicted and sentenced to die in the electric chair at Sing Sing. As Ruby's date with death neared, the rare spectacle of a woman being put to death sent the tabloid press into a feeding frenzy. At *The Express* it was only moderately less of a frenzy. Otis had challenged Kate to get an exclusive, and so Kate had tried everything she could think of. Time was running out. If only she could get in to see the condemned woman before she died. Kate had written Ruby notes throughout the trial and sent her small personal presents in the weeks before the execution, but Ruby had never responded. Kate knew that other photographers and reporters had worked every angle available to influence the warden to let them have one last go at Ruby, but he was unmoved, and so Kate decided to write directly to Ruby one last time, asking her, woman to woman, if she would request Kate's presence with her in the final moments before being led to the death chamber.

"They will not allow a woman reporter in the execution room," Kate wrote. "Only men. If I could photograph you one last time before you go, then perhaps it will soften their final words about you that these male reporters will send out across the country to their newspapers." Her answer came on the morning of the day before the execution. Ruby Barnes had asked for Kate Goodfellow.

Kate crowed, strutted, and preened, her insensitivity matched only by her triumph. "Think of it! A woman's final thoughts and words just before she is clutched in the deadly snare that sears and burns and KILLS," she parodied the headline. She was so taken with her performance that she didn't notice the deadly quiet that settled over the normally buzzing city room. Suddenly a hand slammed down on her desk and in one swift motion it swept the clutter to the floor. Kate was instantly on her feet and sputtering.

"What in the . . ." But whatever she was about to say died on her lips. She found herself staring into a face quivering with hatred. If eyes were bullets, Kate would have already been dead.

It was a woman, a dark and earthy woman, a strong woman with a face contorted in its passion. It took Kate only a second to register the face and less than that to know to whom it belonged. Malou! She was as startling a human as Kate had ever seen, larger than life with a sharp bloodred mouth and enormous black eyes outlined in black pencil. She had entered the office dressed in black trousers, a black sweater, a purple scarf tied around her head and a great woven shawl thrown about her shoulders. She seemed to glide into the room like a jungle cat. Her heavily lidded eyes and the prominent nose quivered with the vibrations of her rage.

"You bitch." The voice was firm and steady and deadly. "You fuck my husband. You take his money. You take a father from his children. Let me tell what I will do to you if you ever see my husband again." Malou leaned over the desk. Kate was so astonished that she couldn't move, caught like an animal in the headlights of an oncoming car. Malou's eyes held hers for another long moment, then, in a voice that was low and almost conversational, yet so clear and deliberate that everyone in the office, riveted to the sight, could hear everything said. "Pig. Have you ever seen a pig slaughtered? Bleeding from a slit to the throat?" Her hand slowly mimed a slice to her throat— hands that were, Kate saw, strong with long spiky fingers like steel spiders. "They suffer much. They are afraid before they die. I do this to you in my dreams. You understand, redheaded woman? I swear on the life of my babies, you go near my husband again, you pull down your silk panties for him, you laugh with him, you kiss, you fuck him . . . I will slit your throat while you squeal in fear." Kate's mouth dropped.

Walter Lord stood in the doorway to his office. He was enjoying this immensely and was almost moved to applaud, as if the whole thing were some perfectly rehearsed, perfectly enacted stage vignette. With a final penetrating look at Kate, Malou turned and swept by Walter Lord, not giving him so much as a glance, and then she was gone.

There was a moment of silence, then Walter started laughing. "Wow! Some performance! Well, honey, I guess you . . ." but he didn't finish the sentence. Kate was bawling like a baby. Great heaving sobs and gulps came blubbering forth, and for a second he thought she was going to fall over in a

faint. One of the secretaries rolled her eyes and strolled over
to the water fountain to get Kate a glass of water, but Kate was
too distraught even to notice. She could not stop crying. She
could not. She was angry and humiliated and embarrassed.
She was all of these things and more. Walter took pity on her,
and because he could think of no comforting words, he took
her by the arm, grabbing her coat, and firmly propelled her out
the door and down in the elevator, across the street to the bar
where they all hung out. There she willingly got as drunk as a
lord.

The next afternoon, feeling like sin, she boarded the train
to Ossining, New York, for the final interview with Ruby
Barnes.

They gave her less than ten minutes before Ruby was to be
led from her steel cage down the corridor to the execution
room. Before taking her to Ruby, they allowed her to look in
that room where the instrument of death was housed. It was as
obscene a contraption as Kate had ever seen, with sprawling
oaken arms and a steel helmet with electrodes dangling from
it and worn-looking leather wrist and leg shackles. Ruby would
precede her lover, Jed, and be the first to die in this unholy
embrace of the law's ghastly ritual of justice. Kate dutifully
took a picture of the chair. Then she was led down a small corridor to Ruby's cell.

The door was unlocked and slid back so that Kate could
enter. And suddenly there she was, face-to-face with Ruby
Barnes, once notorious lover and killer, now a small, frail, and
utterly alone human waif. The papers had sensationalized this
mildly attractive housewife beyond all recognition. She and
her dapper little salesman had murdered the dull transit-
worker husband for the insurance money and to clear the way
for a continuation of the affair. It was hard to imagine the now
haunted pathetic form Kate saw huddled in the cell, throbbing
with a passion so intense that she might murder for it.

Two matrons stood beside her in the small room. Ruby was
dressed in a white blouse and gray prison smock. Her feet
were in slippers, the kind old men wore. One section of her
hair had been clipped to the skull so that the electrodes could
be attached. But even in the shapeless smock and unattractive
slippers, one could see the girl that had once been. A girl who

wore ribbons in her curly hair to match her dresses. A girl who loved to dance and who wanted excitement and romance. Now her face seemed to be made up of lukewarm water instead of blood. She was utterly devoid of emotion, and she looked at Kate in a detached way.

Kate faltered. Nothing in all that she had done before affected her so strongly. She had not known what to expect, but somehow she had not expected this. The lump in her throat and hands cold and shaking signaled something far more profound than a hangover. Her camera was outside in the corridor because she had wanted to talk to Ruby first, but now she could not open her mouth. Ruby, who in the whole of her twenty-eight years had probably never had an ounce of dignity, seemed now, in the last minutes of her life, to rise to that degree. She stared unblinking at Kate, and then a ghost of a smile hovered on her lips.

"Thank you," she said, "for the presents you sent me." Her voice was soft, even with the traces of her broad borough accent. "I never had stockings from Saks Fifth Avenue before." They both looked down at her legs. She wore black cotton stockings, the right one of which was rolled down to her ankle. It was a shapely leg with smooth white skin. "I wasn't allowed to have them once I came here."

Kate nodded. Her heart was pounding. This was wrong. So terribly wrong. One could not think about what this woman had done, only what was being done to her. "Ruby. I don't want to intrude on you now unless you want me to. If you allow me to take your picture, it will be in my newspaper, maybe newspapers all over the country. It will be the last picture ever taken of you. I can understand if you don't want to have anything more to do with the press. The newspapers have not been kind to you, but I promise I don't want to exploit you anymore. I want only to bring this whole tragedy to some sort of dignified close."

Ruby didn't say anything for a long minute, then that ghostly smile again. She nodded. "I'd like that."

The picture Kate took, and she only took one, showed a small, thin, pale human being, sitting erect on a low backless stool. Behind her there was a high barred window. It was now night and the sky showed inky black. For Ruby there would never be a chance to be out in the night air again. In a few minutes she was going to die. It was the simple and ugly truth of it. She was alone. The shutter took all of this in, in a split second. Ruby did not move or jump or shield her eyes in the blinding flash of the bulb. Perhaps her senses were telling her to wait for the hot blast of the electric torrent that was soon to sear through her body.

The priest arrived and Kate was told to step out into the corridor. Kate could hear Ruby's responses to the prayers. It was the sound of a child's voice, such as one that could be heard in the streets of the city, a small child lost from her mother and among big, strange men—the warden, the guards, the priest: her keepers.

Now it was time. The priest came first and then the others. Mostly they shielded her body from view, but Ruby paused for only a moment and turned her head to look at Kate. She looked at her, and in a fleeting beat of the heart, her eyes registered trust, then her face went blank and the guards closed in around her once more. The last thing Kate saw from where she stood were the tiny feet shuffling in the slippers as Ruby turned the corner and entered the electric chair chamber.

Kate left the prison moments later. That night she turned in her picture and her story, but *The Express*'s exclusive was upstaged. What appeared the next morning in a rival paper stunned even the most hardened tabloid reader. It was a riveting full-page photo of Ruby Barnes being electrocuted in the death chamber at Sing Sing. Using a miniature camera he had secretly strapped to his ankle, the reporter had snapped the picture at the instant the lethal current surged through her body.

Kate sat silently at her desk, the picture in front of her in all its horror. Then, leaving her camera and press pass on the desktop, she walked into Walter Lord's office and quit her job.

PART THREE

1935

". . . nothing to fear but fear itself."

CHAPTER SIXTEEN

SEVENTEEN MILLION PEOPLE out of work, dust storms hanging like a black scourge over half of the United States, and everywhere people on the move, foreclosed from their land, out of work, out of hope. Riots, violence, poverty, despair, revolution, suspicion, fear—these were the bywords of the day. Everyone scrambled to keep head above water, to eat, to survive. And there was no end in sight to the Great Depression.

Frightened and hungry, the story of millions could be told in the space of a few short minutes in the Relief Office on Lower Broadway in New York.

"We're out of food. My husband hasn't worked in over a year. I've got four children home in bed. I keep 'em there so's they won't get such big appetites. . . ."

"Sorry. We can't do anything for you."

"What do you mean, you can't do anything?" She was a small, thin woman and now her voice quavered. "They told me to go see Relief. They said you could help."

"I'm sorry, madam. The city has temporarily run out of money. We're turning down 700 families a day."

"I don't care about them! I have four kids to feed and I got to get help!" She was becoming hysterical, and the man behind the desk signaled to the policeman stationed at the door. "Don't tell me New York's too broke to help me. I won't leave until—"

"Lady, you heard what he said." The officer took her arm and eased her out of the office.

And all across America it was the same. Thousands of young people roamed the country, drifting aimlessly from city to city, riding in freight cars, walking the roads, and begging for food. Families moved in with one another, or split up, and everyone was looking for work, any work, anything at all.

However reluctantly the world got pushed around the corner into the meager thirties, history was brewing enough social ferment to keep writers busy for years to come. And no writer had benefited more than the author of a book titled *The Road to Nowhere*. Privately its publisher worried that such a depressing and grim book would find few readers in an already depressing and grim world, but it was the work of one of their most promising and popular authors, and Nautilus House was inclined to take the risk. Unlike the author's first book, a titillating and lusty view of small-town life, which had topped the best-seller lists for thirty-six months, then gone on to become one of the longest running shows on Broadway, *The Road to Nowhere* seethed and boiled in the sordid details of America's most deprived citizens. Set in the Deep South, the book centered on a family of sharecroppers who by sheer strength of will boost themselves up the ladder into the security of jobs in the textile mills of North Carolina. Here, life proves a worse hell than it ever was tilling the land. The rapacious mill owners ultimately destroy their own mills in an orgy of decadence and indulgence, and the workers are set adrift. There is no returning to the parched land, no other employment anywhere. They turn in on themselves, cannibals of mind and spirit—and body. It was a lusty, bold, and shocking book.

To everyone's surprise, the book surpassed sales of every other novel in print that year. Its title became the battle cry of workers, farmers, the poor, the disenfranchised, and the disillusioned. The author's bleak portrayal of the hopeless and apathetic life among the Southern poor was beyond imagining.

Even so, it seemed to provide the bewildered victims of failed capitalism a pivot on which to turn and face the enemy, making the author a sort of literary statesman for the underdog. Critics said the book sold more for its prurient passages than anything else, but this was nothing new to the author. His work had been banned before. Sex, he said, was a metaphor for the most basic truths of mankind. Indeed, he seemed to have such an affinity for human despair that upon meeting him for the first time, people were openly astonished at the charming figure before them. He was the antithesis of all that he wrote about.

Healthy, robust, and a prodigious lover of the good life, Hopper Delaney was part of the small centripetal group that set the social tone in New York City. He cut a playboy swath on Broadway and was a favorite in Cholly Knickerbocker's daily column, where his name was coupled with any one of a half-dozen beautiful women. With two best-sellers to his name *and* the Broadway show, the Depression had not hurt him in the least—and for Hopper Delaney, that was a problem.

Looking at him as he was on a certain day in early spring of 1935, one might not have noticed anything out of the ordinary. The day had started out in a perfectly normal way. It was his habit to get up before the first light and write until late morning. Then he bathed, dressed, and by one o'clock he was usually at lunch with someone. He rarely worked in the afternoon. He went to the track; he poked around his favorite haunts—bookstalls off Fourteenth Street, coffeehouses in the Village, offbeat neighborhoods, sometimes chess or even bocce in Central Park. Some days he just walked. Today for instance. He had lunched with Norma Kingsley at "21" Club. Normally a lunch with Norma followed with an afternoon in her bed. She was a woman who demanded such attention, and he was happy to oblige. Norma Kingsley was a star and carefully cultivated her image along the lines of the great stage personalities—supremely glamorous, divinely elegant, and terribly refined—but behind closed bedroom doors, she was a bitch of a girl from Chicago's South Side, big, lusty, blond, and demanding. She had also created the leading role in his long-running play *Belle*.

Norma was soon to take the Kingsley look, the Kingsley hair, the Kingsley laugh to Hollywood, where she would play his notorious boyhood heroine on the silver screen. Norma *was* Belle, his Belle, and the Belle for whom he was justly famous.

How she had physically managed to take Belle from a girl of eighteen to an old woman in three acts was still a mystery to Hopper. She didn't resort to makeup or a succession of wigs but rather altered her speech rhythms, redefined her postures, and played tiny tricks with her voice. In the final scene the audience was held spellbound for five stunning minutes as she silently circled the stage, drawing closed the curtains of her house, seeming in the process to wither into a geriatric posture of defeat. Out of this frailty, she then turned back to the audience for the final soliloquy, and in some masterful illusion that could not be explained, she grew taller, then taller still until, in triumph, she dealt the final, caustic truth—the denouement of the play. Night after night as the lights faded to black the audience felt themselves witnessing a once-in-a-lifetime performance. She never failed to bring them to their feet in thunderous applause. Every actress in Hollywood had fought for this role, but the studio producers in an unusual casting turnabout had gone with the Broadway star. "Those movie queens are sitting like vultures," her agent said, "hoping to pick you clean."

"What the hell," growled the deep, gravelly, cigarette voice, "if a South Side girl can't fight vultures, she has no business being on the streets." Today, Norma had an important interview on the radio, and they had parted after lunch with the fleeting brush of almost lips on each cheek. They both understood whatever had been between them was over.

It was a perfect spring day, warm and soft. Not his favorite time of the year. Spring was too ephemeral for his taste. He did not like seasons in transit. Long, hot, unrelenting summers were the stuff of his blood. Winters with their short, gray, bitter days stimulated his mind. Spring was a girl with a flower in her hair, a tease, a flirt, and far too young to interest him. It was a habit of his, this walking the streets of the city, often whole days of walking as he pondered plots and characters and stories. He loved the city. It had been good to him. It had fed him and entertained him and made him its favorite son.

Today was a day for reflection. He was thirty-six years old. He was in excellent health. He lacked for nothing. He had money, fame, friends. Women adored him and he them. His whole life had been about women. They swirled in and around his work, they perched in his memory banks, they comforted him and seduced him and petted him. Lucky Hopper. But luck had a disarming way of changing. There was good luck—the kind that had taken an eager, ambitious kid and swept him through the portals of success. And then there was bad luck . . .

"The life of a writer is just ten years, after that it's all repetition." Where had he heard that? Maybe he hadn't heard it, maybe he had said it. He'd been quoted as saying a lot of things. Ten years ago he had been in the first flush of fame. Ten years was a remarkably short time.

Hopper had been walking downtown all this time through the busy garment district and then the freshly scented flower district into a sort of no-man's land where all the buildings seemed to have given their souls over to permanent grime and defeat. Here were novelty stores and sewing-machine repair shops and wholesalers of dusty merchandise, and he wondered who would buy such things and why. Coming to Fourteenth Street, he turned crosstown just short of the Village and kept his pace steady. He was at Union Square now, a junction alive with a mob of women in S. Klein's struggling in and out of cheap clothes; ill-kempt Communists shouting from soapboxes; the jobless leaning on the iron fences; the astounding blond mannequins circling in the upstairs windows of the Alaska & Hudson Fur Company, and in the square, old men sat playing checkers. Where had they been at his age? At work? Having kids? In love? Unaware, like most, that time would one day run out and deposit them here, to await the end with a lot of other old people. Back home when he was a boy the old men had sat on the benches in front of the courthouse as old men did all over the South playing pinochle or whittling wood down to smooth slivers to pick at teeth and massage old men's sore gums. Some, he remembered, were without arms or eyes or legs, veterans of the Civil War, or the Spanish American War; men who sat and talked and watched the smart

young kid who rushed by them delivering medicines in brown
parcels to ladies over on Fillmore Street, where the big white
houses were. Hopper could see them etched clearly, undimin-
ished by time and distance, in his mind's eye. For a second he
thought of sitting down next to one of the men on the benches
of Union Square. He liked talking to strangers and had a
knack for drawing people out, hearing their stories. But today
he didn't break his stride. He had too much on his mind.

He was not thinking about what had happened in the ten
years of his great good fortune but of the misfortune of everyone else. All over America there were people starving, people
destitute, but nowhere was it so hard as in the South. Sometimes it seemed to him the South had always been poor, certainly it had always reeked of an underclass. Even in its
heyday the South had built its prosperity on the backs of the
poor and enslaved. Yet it had been, no denying, once the seat
of American civilization—its surface, a mannered, gracious
world, all but disappeared in the five long years of war. In the
decades that followed, the rest of the country moved on, but
the South had seemingly faded from the American consciousness to little more than fodder for Tin Pan Alley songs and
ladies' romance novels. This, of course, was an extreme point-
of-view. Southerners themselves took pride in their heritage
and preferred isolationism over Yankee progress. This insular
life created a land and people as rich in mysterious, magical
lore as it was in poverty and racial brutality. Hopper's books
and views had not made him a popular son of the South. Indeed, he had been denounced from pillar to post, but there was
no mistaking his devotion to his homeland. He had left the
South in order to get beyond the weight of regional solipsism,
only to find he couldn't get the region out of his head.

The image of himself as a youth kept popping to the forefront of his mind. Yet Hopper Delaney, small-town boy of the
South, and Hopper Delaney, famous international author,
seemed on this soft spring day in 1935 to have no relationship
to each other. First he had been the one, and then, as if a magician had tapped his wand, he had become the other. He had
been turned inside out, or was it outside in? He wondered.

* * *

To say that young Hopper Delaney had burst upon the publishing scene of the 1920s was as true physically as it was artistically. Mallory Harwell often recalled the story of the young man who had accosted him at the ballet. Harwell loved the ballet. It was for him something out of time, and out of this world. It removed him from the profession of books and words and authors and agents, a profession in which he was lionized as publishing's preemptive editor, and gave him a respite in muscle and grace, in form and precision and wordless expression. He had season tickets for every Wednesday—tenth row, two seats on the aisle—and he was there, with his wife or another guest, without fail. Wednesday, Mallory said, was his midweek fix.

On one particular Wednesday in April of 1924, Anna Matveyevna Pavlova was dancing. She was on the final leg of her American tour, declaring that it would be her last. The great Russian ballerina was, that year, forty-three years old and wished to retire at the peak of her powers. Tickets were impossible to get, and yet here was Mallory alone, the seat next to him vacated by the onset of one of his wife's habitual migraines. As he came down the grand staircase at intermission, he was in a trance of deeply felt pleasure over a performance which was sublime. So he did not notice a young man at the bar, a young man improperly dressed for such an occasion, a young man who suddenly stood up straight, fixed his tie, rubbed his hands on his trousers, squared his shoulders, and made so bold as to approach.

"Mr. Harwell?"

Mallory looked at him in bewilderment.

"I hope you don't mind my introducing myself, but I wanted to meet you. You see, sir, I am a writer, and I've been trying to get in to see you, but . . ."

Mallory's eyes glazed. He did not take lightly to eager young writers who demanded his attention without an appointment. He particularly did not like being accosted at the ballet during intermission, when all he really wanted was a glass of champagne while the images from the first act were fresh in his brain. He was a precise man with precise habits and strict professional manners. It was just this sort of precision and finesse, of course, that made him the kind of editor he was. Gifted writers in Harwell's hand achieved peaks of shimmering brilliance.

". . . I've tried everything, you see. Your secretary is pretty fed up with me. I even took my lunch in one day and sat there for the whole afternoon, but you never came out of the office. Or maybe you weren't even there, but I really must show you my work, sir. . . ."

It might have been the audacity of the young man, his ill-fitting clothes, his drawl, his boldness, but Mallory allowed him to finish his speech.

He took a long moment and then spoke with an audible sigh in his voice. "My dear boy, in a few moments I am going to return to my seat to witness the pinnacle of human beauty and achievement. You say you have a manuscript for me to read. Does your manuscript approach in any way the performance we have seen thus far?"

Hopper shrugged. "I can't say for sure. I haven't seen the performance. You see, I . . . I sneaked in. I read that you came to the ballet every Wednesday. I took a chance."

Mallory paused again. Here was a cocky fellow—raw, fresh, and new. A budding talent? He doubted it. As Harwell had grown older and infinitely wiser, he had grown jaded on the subject of raw, fresh, and new. Now he trusted only seasoned writers, those who appealed to his intellect and astute critical powers. He most certainly did not trust the unstructured emotions of the young. Young people all thought too well of themselves. He weighed his options.

"I happen to have an extra ticket for tonight's performance due to a last-minute cancellation," he said slowly. "I will offer you that ticket on the condition that you watch one of the greatest performers of all time and try to imagine your manuscript, your talent, in just such a league. Afterward, if you still feel confident, I'll see that my secretary gives you an appointment."

In the second act Pavlova performed "The Dying Swan," her beautiful signature solo piece to which the audience went mad with a full twenty-minute ovation. Mallory himself was so taken, he did not notice the disappearance of the young author. Just as well, he thought on the way home. Just as well he get a dose of the truth now.

The next day he received a note. "Please tell your secretary I can meet with you at your convenience." Signed Hopper Delaney.

He presented Mallory with a suitcase filled with more than a thousand single-spaced typed pages, his shoulders hunched with the weight of his tome. Harwell allowed the young man a few minutes of his precious time, and eyeing the suitcase in horror, he nevertheless agreed to read a portion of it. It had happened before to be sure. Once in every decade a book is written that causes a sort of mass public hysteria. Delaney's book was to be such a book.

But that all came later. First came lunch, where Mallory was able to penetrate the ferocity of the young man, who, it seemed, was not only in need of an editor but of food. Between ravenous bites of steak and potatoes and bread and pie came the first bits and pieces of the story of Hopper Delaney, the itinerate preacher's son from Mississippi. And later still, after weeks of sifting through a daunting stack of manuscript pages, Mallory Harwell took him to one of Gaby Leigh-Bell's parties. Of course Mallory claimed to have discovered Hopper, but Gaby was the one who nurtured him through the early days and led him triumphantly through the labyrinth of the New York fame game.

"Well, my goodness!" said Gaby. "Who goes here?" She saw two burning eyes, and she saw a beautifully shaped face. She saw a square chin that one day might be called "rugged" but now retained the softness of youth; she saw also that his ears were big, and that was endearing; she saw his brows were dark and thick, and that his black hair needed cutting, and that his mouth was full and young. All this she saw in one split second. "Hello and welcome," she said, smiling warmly at him. When Gaby smiled, her whole face seemed to shatter and collapse, and her eyes became like tiny, merry eyelets. What Hopper saw was a friendly soul, a cheerful fat lady, well-meaning and good-natured, and he needed that.

"Hello," he echoed, adding, "ma'am" in his slow drawl. Gaby roared with laughter and took him by the arm and pulled him into the din of the party.

"Ma'am! I like that. Whereabouts in the South?"

"Oh, you've probably never heard of it. . . ."

"Don't be so sure. I am a daughter of the Confederacy myself. You'd never know it, would you, but I used to have as much mush in 'ma mouf' as you do."

He laughed. "I guess I do sound pretty full of grits, don't I? Mr. Harwell sure has a hard time understandin' me."

"You look good when you laugh. Do that some more. Now, where was it you're from?"

"Corinth, Mississippi. It's not far . . ."

"From Memphis. See now, I do know it. Corinth's as pretty a town as ever I've seen. Why, honey, we would have been neighbors except when I was young, you weren't even born. Now, if this isn't a real coincidence. I used to live in Oxford. My daddy was a professor at Ole Miss. He loved walking the old Shiloh battleground near Corinth, and then we would have an early dinner at the Waldron Hotel. We moved to Louisville when I was just thirteen, but I remember Corinth. 'Deed ah do, Mistah Delaney.'" She gave him a little sideways glance, lifting one plump shoulder up to her many chins in a mock parody of a coquettish Southern belle. Her imitation was hilarious, and Hopper found himself laughing as if they were old friends. "Now, look here, Hopper, honey, you are not to leave, do you understand, even though we might get separated, you are not to leave my house until I've had a chance to talk to you. This bunch won't clear out until dawn, and then we'll have breakfast. I mean it. I want to talk to you. In a few minutes an entire chorus line is coming from the Cotton Club to do the shimmy for us. You'll like that." She was shouting into his ear now because the sound of talk, music, and laughter had reached a high decibel level.

She left him after another minute or two, but not before making sure he had a drink and introducing him to a pretty girl named Puff. He had never seen anyone quite like Puff. Her blond hair fell in three thick commas that seemed glued to her cheeks and forehead. She had dark, bored eyes and a vivid petal pout of a mouth. Her dress, cut to her waist in the back and held together by the barest slim straps, was covered in beads that seemed to jiggle and dance all to a rhythm of their own. She made little effort to talk to Hopper, said "how amusing" once or twice, and then was gone. Hopper didn't mind; like someone who has been on the outside so long looking in, to be suddenly and without warning inside and welcome was enough for him. He wandered the party, his eyes and ears taking in all he could. He was in New York at last, and he was in the best place in New York, although he really didn't know how good it was at the time. He just felt like, no matter how much a stranger he might appear to be to this swaying, laughing throng, he belonged. He had never really belonged before.

Hopper Delaney's South was not the old romantic South of vine-covered verandahs and mint juleps in the heat of the afternoon. His was a dusty, itinerant, rootless South, where poverty scratched itself in the red dirt and people eked out a minimal existence on small cotton farms or in shabby mills that ran day and night crushing cottonseed into oil for use as a lubricant in the factories up north. Hopper's father was an ordained Presbyterian minister who could have made a solid and respectable living for himself and a stable life for his family if he had not preached so vigorously against injustice and inequality. He was drawn to those who suffered the most grinding poverty—sharecroppers crowded into ramshackle cabins, and millworkers in the squalid shantytowns on the far side of the railroad tracks. To his all-white congregations he delivered blunt sermons on the brotherhood of man but, not surprisingly, his outspoken racial liberalism brought him open hostility. Christian brotherhood most definitely did not extend to "people of color," and Pastor Delaney was not welcome long in any given pulpit. He was a restless man and never minded moving on, while his wife, who had come from a comfortable, middle-class home in Virginia, grew increasingly withdrawn and discouraged. The Delaneys moved about constantly from place to place, tent meetings mostly, hospital ministries, and sometimes he would preach to gatherings of country people at fairs just like a sideshow act. They relied on providence and often out-and-out charity for shelter and food until they discovered their son was too smart not to have a more serious and steady education. So the boy and his mother settled in the little town of Corinth, Mississippi, tucked in the northeast corner of the state just across the Tennessee line. Corinth, it seemed, had a superior high school where Latin, and even some Greek, was taught along with the world's classics. His father had then continued on without them, returning once every three or four months to be with his wife and child for a short spell before the restlessness moved him back out on the road. When he was home, the best times for the boy, he talked long hours to his son about the Bible, about God and his people, about Jesus and His message of love, about the power of love, about the meek and turning one's cheek in the face of hatred and injustice. His daddy was a born storyteller, and the stories he told were the passionate, virile stories of the Bible. To the impressionable ears of his son, these were the most extraordinary stories ever told, filled with unspeakable hardships and everlasting truths.

He was a funny guy, his father. He didn't look at all like a preacher. Tall and gawky with freckled hands and a large head, the years of travel and sun had left his face deeply parched and wrinkled far beyond its years, but he had the gift of talk and anyone could see he was kind. Hopper inherited his father's height and the slightly gangling walk with his arms thrust forward and the large, expressive hands. From his mother he got his dark hair and eyes and the moody, troubled nature. From her also came his love of reading. She worked at the Corinth Library, a musty old house with a rambling porch and wicker rockers where he sat long afternoons with an icy cold Coke and stacks of books. The library also served as the town's historical museum. Mostly local memorabilia of the Civil War in old, scratched glass cases—cannonballs and bullets and tattered remnants of uniforms—with a smattering of old arrowheads from Indian days. It was a place that smelled of leather and aging paper in the humid Southern air, a smell so dear to Hopper that in later years when he came into a secondhand bookshop on a rainy day, or poked around dusty curio shops, he would stop and inhale in a rapture of fond memory.

When Hopper was fourteen his father died of a hemorrhaging ulcer. He bled to death alone in an old rundown boardinghouse on the Gulf some three hundred miles from home. Hopper and his mother went on the train to bring the body back for burial, a ride that had taken them four days round-trip, what with sidetracking while the express trains came through and the stopovers. He remembered most (funny what you remember) the box of beaten biscuits his mother had packed for the trip; biscuits hard as tack, with slabs of fat, greasy, cold sausage and sweet butter spread in between. They were so good washed down with the cold lemonade or iced tea sold by country women who came down to the station to meet the trains hoping to make a few extra pennies. The boy had thought it a feast for the gods, and all the while his daddy rattled around in a wooden box in the baggage car behind them destined for the Henry Cemetery.

Corinth was as pretty a town as ever one could imagine. Its main residential avenue was wide and lined with magnolia trees, apple trees, and a profusion of azaleas. Brides who married in May rode in carriages on carpets of apple blossoms. By June the air filled with the heady scent of magnolias. Corinth's old families lived in houses given to large porches and breezy, cool-looking drawing rooms with long, graceful windows and wide-slatted shutters that could be closed midday against the brutal heat and sun. These were the people who owned the bank and the local cottonseed mill and the town's only department store; they did the doctoring and lawyering and judging. Their wives went visiting and attended teas and book clubs and planned parties presenting to all the world an aura of gentility raised to near perfection. Behind those slatted windows, however, was often another story. Like small towns everywhere, Corinth had its fair share of gossip and scandal. Neighbors could hold grudges for generations on business dealings gone astray and family insults. Sheriffs could be bribed, girls were seduced, wives drank in secret, and husbands often wandered. But the town held itself together and most people born there stayed there. In the main, distinguishing oneself in the world at large didn't seem to be a big part of the scheme of things.

Beyond its beauty and gentry, Corinth held few distinctions, but it was a good place for a boy with an ear for a story to grow up. There were stories about Indians and the Civil War. There were still trenches on the edge of town where the Confederates had turned for one last stand after the retreat from Shiloh. There were old men and women who remembered the battles, the all-day roar of the cannon, the wagonloads of wounded coming into town. The ladies' book club, which met every Tuesday evening at the library, was a treasure of stories and gossip especially for an unobserved boy out on the porch next to an open window; there were stories over in the colored part of town told from front stoops, and there were stories told over the soda fountain counter at the drugstore. Hopper lived in the stories and never tired of hearing them—even the ones he had heard many times before.

There was a solid middle class who ran the shops and clerked for the various professions. The Delaneys fell into this stratum. It was Mrs. Delaney's salary as a librarian and Hopper's after-school income on which they depended. As it turned out, Hopper had a knack for making money, and the variety of the jobs he devised for himself exposed him to every segment of life in a small Southern town. He spent hours riding all over town on his bicycle collecting odd pieces of junk and discarded bits of metal which he sold to the junk dealer for sometimes a whole dollar a load. Then, he hit on the notion of buying laundry bluing direct from a wholesaler and selling it to the Negro laundresses for half of what the grocer charged. He soon became a fixture over in colored town and was greeted with friendly waves and cries of "Here come Mr. Blue Man." As a teenager he grew into a disturbingly handsome young man with dark, observant eyes and a forest of tangled black curls. The girls might consider him a rare catch, but he had no time for sports and no spare money to take girls out, and so, for the most part, he was outside the mainstream of youthful life in Corinth. He spent a great deal of his time alone but he was not lonely. Working after school as a delivery boy for the drugstore, he was privy to another sort of life in town. A delivery boy went in and out of back doors and stood patiently waiting while the mistress of the house found a coin for a tip. The mistress might further detain him to help her with some household chore or to simply sit a spell to while away the long afternoons. A delivery boy who was smart and in possession of a beguiling smile could learn a lot about life from going in and out the back door.

His mother insisted he go to college but because he was never able to keep up with the tuition from one term to the next, he would have to take months off to work. A lot happened to him in those years. He rode boxcars all over the South, finding work on the docks of New Orleans, in saloons and pool halls, as a chauffeur on a military post driving the top brass to and from the local whorehouse. He learned to play cards with the girls between tricks and once joined a magician's sideshow and learned illusion. He even sold pots and pans door to door and was so charming he fast became the company's best salesman, but when they offered him the job of regional manager he quit, because he didn't care to advance himself in the cookware business. Like his father, he was restless and preferred the insecurity of the road to settling down. He met all types of people in all sizes and colors. He heard their stories and their troubles. He got quite good at gambling and pretty soon made most of his money from cards and, for a time, fancied the gambler's life, buying himself flashy clothes and slicking his hair back with expensive pomade.

When he was twenty-two, his mother died and Hopper came back to Corinth for her funeral filled with a youthful swagger. Then something happened that set him down to becoming a writer.

It's not often that a single knock on a door can change a life. The door in question belonged to an old, gray fortress-like mansion that stood on the outskirts of town and it was here that Hopper Delaney found the infamous character that fanned the flame of literary inspiration.

They called it the Castle because it certainly looked like one. It was a large, ungracious stone house with rounded corner turrets surrounded by a spiked iron fence, red with rust, the yard parched from heat and neglect. Most of Corinth's children idled their youthful days speculating on just what it was that went on inside the forbidding, sinister-looking place. All they knew, all anybody knew was that its owner was a woman who almost never went out, and then, if she did, it was at night and in a closed car, her driver, a Negro not of local origin. They said she still had red hair (dyed of course) and that her house was done up all in red with ornate velvet chairs and flocked paper that had come from France. The woman's name was Alma Wydell, the very mention of which made boys snicker and mothers give severe looks. In Hopper's novel he had kept the red motif but changed Alma's name to Belle.

Alma was Corinth's Madam. The Castle, built soon after the Civil War by two bachelor brothers by the name of Caldwell, was even then considered an eyesore. The brothers moved farther South, and for twenty years the house stood empty. Then one day Alma Wydell arrived in town with papers that said she owned the house. She moved in and it soon became pretty well known who and what Alma was all about. They said she'd won the deed off Mr. Caldwell in a whorehouse on Bourbon Street. For some time the ladies of Corinth tried to have her run out of town, but Alma was smart. She had gotten to the men first.

Alma was a tough businesswoman; she knew what her clients needed and wanted and she gave it to them—some said for a price that would make you choke. Her girls were often seen about town, dressed in bright colors with faces painted like garish carnival dolls, but never Alma. Her only daytime trips were to the bank. She grew very rich. About the time Hopper was growing up in Corinth, Alma closed her house and curtained herself off from the prying eyes of the town. Her Negro servant was her go-between for groceries and other needs, and she owned cats—seemed like hundreds of them. From the street you could see them peeking out of windows or coming and going from the basement stairwell. Word got out that Alma had made her will and was going to leave all her money to her cats. People shook their heads, but by this time Alma was so much a part of the fabric of the town that nothing she might do really shocked them.

Hopper called his book *Belle*. It was the story of a young man who, like all the boys in town, grew up wondering what presence lurks behind the curtained windows of an old, gray house. He becomes obsessed with meeting the woman who resides inside. His obsession grows, so, too, his boldness. One day he ventures up to the front door and rings the bell. It echoes deep within the house, but no one comes to the door. Again and again he comes to the door and waits. At last, one early evening in spring, the air already touched with the humid summer to come, he sees a shadowy figure lit in candlelight in the front hall. The door is opened and the boy enters the house with its pungent scent of cats and its red, red walls.

The young man, who has no name in the novel, meets the notorious Belle, and as the book unfolds so, too, the conceits, lies, and wickedness of small-town life. The people of the town are presented in the full dimension of their lives, their corruptions and secret drives. Belle sees all, tells all, reveals all. Not the very least of what she reveals is the art of making love. In probably four of the most sensual pages ever written on the subject of a woman's desires, Belle instructs the boy with astonishing sexual candor.

All this and more Hopper told to Gaby that first morning they spent together. He wasn't by nature a confessional sort, but Gaby knew how to draw people out. She sat in her small study opposite him, smoking many cigarettes through a short ivory holder and drinking quantities of hot black coffee, which she sweetened lavishly with saccharin tablets. "Thinning," she explained, then she would reach for the rich pastries she had brought in from the little French bakery in the Village. She didn't talk to him so much as make him talk—whenever he ran down, or grew self-conscious, or for any other reason became suddenly laconic, she asked another question and that would set him going again. And thus she found out about his life—how he had left Corinth for good and come North to write. The only rent he could afford landed him in Hoboken across the Hudson River from Manhattan. From here he could see the city from his window and could feel the ache of wanting to belong to it. Often he would spend whole days in New York, walking the endless furrows of those parallel streets absorbing a parade of images, feeling the energy and vibrancy of this strange society wherein even the most humble element acquired its own luminous quality. *Someday,* he promised himself, returning to the fifth-floor walk-up. As drawn as he was to the world New York had to offer, his attachment to the insular place from which he had come was even more profound. From the room in Hoboken, he could peer, as if through a telescope, at the carnival of characters he had known, flamboyant and sad creatures jostling among themselves and jabbering at him to get on with his work, to sing their song and rest their souls.

Gaby watched the young man's face. Now he was telling her about his next book, the one yet unwritten, and she listened less to his words, heavy with images of Southern sharecroppers beset with all the ills of ignorance and dire poverty, but more to the passion in his voice. There was an enigmatic quality to this handsome young man and she found the inconsistencies totally to her liking. People were so often predictable and half the people she knew she regarded as nothing more than a nest of bogus bohemians. But not this fellow. She fervently hoped that Mallory, who had brought so many writers to the forefront, would not fail this one.

"You see," he said, his eyes fixed on some dusty back road embedded in his mind, "every good thing that has happened in this country has passed the sharecropper by. They are the truly forgotten Americans. My daddy tried to fight injustice by standing up in front of a tent meeting, but I'm going to fight it with books. Books that all Americans will read."

Gaby leaned forward and patted his knee. "Do you realize we've talked through the night and most of the morning? All this saving the world from injustice had better wait for another day. I'm going to send you upstairs to the little room just off the second-floor landing. Have yourself a rest and then we'll talk some more. I declare, it's almost lunchtime."

Hopper stumbled up the stairs as instructed and flopped across a soft little bed all dressed in gay pink ribbons and lace, and there he slept clear through to the next day. When he came down again he was considered part of the household.

The house was in the section of Manhattan called Chelsea on a pretty tree-lined street. Its exterior, twin to all the other four-story brownstones on the street, looked smaller than it actually was, having more depth to it than frontage. Still, it was not large, considering the prodigious amount of people it housed. Inside Gaby had cleverly knocked down many of the walls on the parlor floor to allow for her parties. Otherwise, there was nothing really spacious about the house, but to Hopper, the fact remained, that in all his years of familiarity with Gaby's house, he would always recall it in his mind as a towering, floor after floor, skyscraper hotel of a house. There was no other way that everybody could have fitted in. Hopper never exactly moved in to Gaby's, but he had a room there and he was always eating there, so he might as well have moved in. Seems like others had the same privileges, too.

That first day, coming down after his long sleep, he met twenty people. Half of them proved to be daytime visitors; the other half were inmates—some temporary, some eternal. They included relatives of Gaby's, people from Europe, people going to Europe, out-of-work actors, rich girls from nice families in need of introductions, an aging impoverished Russian aristocrat, musicians, and freeloaders. There were even two children who Hopper assumed were some relation to Gaby but turned out to be the children of a dance team who had taken their act on the road. It took Hopper several visits to sort these people out, and by that time there had been changes in the ranks and they were mostly not the same people he had started off with.

That was the way it was at Gaby's. There was a floating population that defied any census; it varied with the seasons, with the ocean liner sailing schedules, with the state of things in show business, with the way the horses ran, and inevitably with the national prosperity. But no matter how many or who, the atmosphere was always that of a perpetual party.

Hopper's book, *Belle,* was published in 1925 and hit the bookstands like fireworks at a funeral. Critics hailed Delaney as a new literary force; preachers and politicians denounced him; librarians refused to order his work; and booksellers kept it behind their desks and out of sight. Young people passed dog-eared copies amongst themselves and regarded his book as the best sex manual ever. In no time, he earned the reputation of being America's most banned writer.

Gaby was as proud as a peacock. He was now at the center of her parties, not on the fringe. The Russian count, with some prodding from Gaby, agreed to take Hopper in hand. Hair was cut, clothes were tailored, an apartment befitting the number-one best-selling author was found and furnished. Stylish women took notice. He moved easily in the frenetic Roaring Twenties. In 1929 *Belle* was adapted to the stage. It, too, was a hit.

Americans thrived on success stories. Herbert Hoover was in the White House and there was a chicken in every pot. Amelia Earhart was the darling of the day. Detroit had just seen the largest business merger ever. The stock market was trading at such a rate that overnight it created thousands of instant millionaires. America was on the go and so was Hopper Delaney.

Then came the crash. Like everyone else, he lost a great deal of his money. Strangely this did not bother him. In a curious way the sudden tumble of his finances gave him back an edge that had disappeared in the boisterous circus of fame and prosperity. In his desk were countless drafts of the book he had once promised Gaby he would write. It was not easy for him to write about poverty and hunger when he himself was dining at El Morocco. It was even harder to conjure up tar-paper shacks and shoes fashioned from old tires and tied on with rope when he walked in comfort on hand-sewn English boots to parties in penthouses. More and more this youthful voice, the voice that had stayed up all night talking to Gaby, nagged at him. He was a writer, a powerful and controversial writer. He needed to find his voice again.

He went South and traveled the old railroad routes he had traveled as a young man. Only this time he rode in the splendor of the Southern Railway's finest Pullman. From his window he watched the landscape go by and when he felt like it, he would get off the train and spend the night in some small town and walk out into the country and talk to people. A new version of the book began to take shape in his mind. *The Road to Nowhere* put to rest any literary speculations that he was a one-book writer.

This, then, was the man who walked downtown on a beautiful spring day wondering why he had failed. Failed to achieve his one goal in life—to make a difference. He had once said he would change the world with his books, yet the words he so passionately believed in had changed nothing. Thousands of people had read his books, and most of them considered the characters exaggerated, the situations overdrawn. He was no more than a sideshow—and the underdog he sought to champion was still the underdog. He knew this because he had gone to Washington some weeks before to testify at a congressional hearing on poverty. "Do you know what it's like to be so hungry you'll eat snakes? Do you know that in this country there are children who are deformed by malnutrition and women who dress in rags and beg for pennies? This is not India or China, this is happening every day in Mississippi and Georgia and Alabama. While the rest of the country suffers today, the rural South has been suffering for decades." He talked passionately, filled with articulate rage and heartfelt empathy. They listened; they did not believe him. When the senator from Georgia rose up from his seat and denounced Hopper Delaney from the floor of Congress as "untruthful, undignified, and unfair," Hopper had tried to rebut. He pleaded with the Senate to send a delegation down South to see with their own eyes. "Hell, yes, it's undignified," he said, "starvation and hopelessness always are." But no one cared to listen. The words had failed. Now he must find another way to show them what he knew to be true. Fiction was not the answer. Hopper wanted to write about the South as a journalist. He wanted to retrace the hundreds of miles he had walked as a boy with his father and document what he saw. He wanted to experience his people and his homeland in a way that no fictional accounting could. He wanted to dispel the notions of the South as a place of dueling oaks and wilting, flowerlike women and toe-tapping darkies picking cotton and playing banjos and replace them with truths about dire poverty and untreated illness. He wanted the rest of the country to see the brutality of chain gangs and racial violence.

His new book would make them see. He had an idea that had been fermenting in his mind for some time; a plan to bolster his case by illustrating his words with the most convincing, most expert witness of the decade. He would prove he was not writing fiction through the powerful medium of photography.

CHAPTER SEVENTEEN

To those New Yorkers out on that same spring day, the sight was probably just a passing curiosity, but it was a magnificent sight. A knight, his armor gleaming in the soft morning air, galloped on a chestnut horse across a mist-filled stone bridge. King Arthur himself couldn't have wanted better.

"Great! Perfect! Just perfect!" came the disembodied cry of a woman's voice through a megaphone.

Virginia York held her clipboard to her chest, closed her eyes, and said silently to herself, *Let's do it one more time to cover ourselves.* As if on cue, the voice, which came from a position somewhat lower than the bridge, called up again. "Let's do it one more time to cover ourselves." Virginia signaled to someone else unseen who was hunkered down in the middle of the bridge. He stood now and waved acknowledgment before kneeling once more out of sight. Rolly Stebbins pulled a cord and almost immediately the loud sputtering of a machine was heard and great clouds of smoke began to billow up into the air. The knight and his horse had turned and were riding back at a much slower pace to where Virginia stood.

"Hey, lady" came the muffled moan from somewhere inside the metal casing, "this friggin' thing is torture. I can't do it again, I tell you. I'm bleedin' to death in here."

Virginia sighed. She had no doubt it was torture, but there was nothing she could do. "Just one more time, Mr. O'Banyon. I can't tell you how much it would mean to us if you could just do it one more time."

"Yeah, tell me, lady. How much . . . Jesus, mother of God . . ."

He was trapped in there. She knew it and he knew it, but she supposed she could finagle the budget to allow him a small perk. "Mr. O'Banyon, I'm going to add on an extra hour to your fee. Would that make doing it again a little easier?" She knew money talked loud and long these days.

There were no more sounds from the armor. Virginia raised her arm, the man on the bridge raised his, somewhere down on the rocks at the edge of the lake a woman dressed in jodhpurs and boots, her hair bunched up under a black beret, was busily adjusting focus on a large camera perched on a wooden tripod for what seemed an interminable time. Then the signal came back to go.

The newspaper ad campaign calling for a fully armored knight to gallop through Central Park in the morning mist was some local bank's idea of a way to attract nervous depositors. How it was to achieve that, Virginia was not quite sure, but this was not her concern. What had been her concern was getting the whole thing together. She had researched all possible sources of armor in New York, from theatrical costumers to the props department at the Metropolitan Opera. To her practiced eye, these were inferior and unworthy. Then she visited a museum in Brooklyn and found exactly what she wanted. "Genuine full-plate, sixteenth-century metal armament," the curator informed her, "complete with helmet, visor, beaver, breastplate, gauntlet, *and,*" he pointed out proudly, "lance rest." Could she rent it? For an advertisement? Why, no, never, absolutely not. Rent, indeed! huffed the curator. Virginia was used to this sort of obstacle, and she was very good at circumventing obstacles of every sort. It was part of her job.

For every job that came into the Goodfellow Studio, it was she who translated Kate's inspirations into props, models, locations, and permits. On the day of the shoot, she had to help in the actual taking of the pictures, hold lights, smooth clothes, cajole people, reassure the client, run out for sandwiches, hot drinks, cool drinks, supply aspirin, get written releases from the models. There was very little Miss York couldn't do and few who were immune to her persuasive, reassuring powers. The museum curator was no match for her, and soon she had secured the armor.

Finding a man small enough to wear the suit who could also handle a horse was her next task. A riding academy close to the park and a willing rider in the form of a retired racing jockey soon provided the solution. Willing though he was, the horse, who had learned nothing of knight errantry during its lifetime beat around Central Park, was terrified when the jockey tried to mount in his heavy amor. He reared; he charged; he beat his hooves into the stable doors so that one broke clean from its hinge. The jockey meanwhile had already started to complain about discomfort from deep inside the metal suit. Rolly was all for giving him a hip bottle of rye whiskey, but Virginia was afraid he would get too drunk to ride. At last she found the solution for the horse; she had him blindfolded. And she relented somewhat on the jockey; she allowed him one slug of the rye. For a brief moment everyone quieted down. Up went the jockey onto the beast, off came the blindfold, and to everyone's astonishment they looked splendid against the trees and sky of Central Park.

Virginia looked at her watch. Kate had no time to go back to the office and change clothes for the lunch immediately following this shoot. Today she would have to change in the back of the cab. This was not at all unusual. Kate was a hurrying sort of person always in motion. Before her taxicab had reached the curb, she had the door open and was half inside while wheels still moved. She could change outfits quick as a wink in backseats, washrooms, broom closets, and behind doors and emerge looking every inch as if she had stepped out of a fashion magazine. Virginia picked up the small suitcase containing Kate's new soft gray poplin suit, the hat, a small pancake with just a touch of whimsy in the form of a small fan of feathers (something of a trademark for Kate), and the lovely white and gray spectator pumps delivered from I. Magnin's late yesterday afternoon. The entire ensemble, while in the very latest style, was nonetheless subdued. Kate attached great importance to appropriate costumes for each event in her many-faceted day and often changed her costume several times to suit her shifting schedule. Virginia, who had no such problems, wore without fail one of three suits purchased on the layaway plan from Best & Co.

After Kate had been bundled off in the cab, Virginia and Rolly began breaking down the equipment into valises. The rider had been freed from his torture chamber and sent on his way with a bonus. The precious suit of armor was wrapped in muslin to be returned to the museum. Virginia and Rolly worked quickly, not needing much conversation because they worked well together. Then, too, they were both quiet people, reserved and not given to idle chatter. Once Rolly was packed into the van, Virginia hailed a cab for herself.

"The Chrysler Building, please." She checked her hair and lipstick in a compact mirror. Akron, Ohio, was due in this afternoon. Virginia smiled to herself. They spoke of Akron, Ohio, as if it were a person, but in reality Akron, Ohio, was the Safety Tire Company and their biggest client to date. The photo campaign, set to run in every major family magazine in America, not only glorified the rubber tire in living color, but it infused it with supernatural powers. Safety tires appeared to stop automatically before running down helpless pedestrians. Oh, the darling little children who tripped on their roller skates in front of an oncoming car. The housewife (Virginia herself had posed for that one) flinging herself over and over in front of cars, spilling a veritable cornucopia of groceries: potatoes that rolled madly about, eggs that smashed, milk that sloshed. The Safety tire saved their lives every time.

Virginia flipped open her steno pad and checked her list. The caterer, the flowers, the few well-chosen models to sprinkle the party, Kate's cocktail dress, a piano player, an excessive selection of liquor—yes, all was in order, as she knew it would be. Satisfied, she settled back in the cab and gazed out at the fine spring day.

Circumstances had made it clear to her at a very early age that careful planning, perfect attendance, attention to detail, and conservative appearance were the things that would carry her through. Three years ago she had stood on the corner of Forty-ninth and Lexington Avenue, her hand holding her hat firmly on her head as she craned her neck backward to stare up at the Chrysler Building. Going on this particular job interview was just about as daring and spontaneous a thing she had ever done. She could not see the top from where she stood, but like most New Yorkers she knew that somewhere sixty floors above, steel gargoyles were keeping a falcon's eye over the city. Who on earth would house a photography studio up there? Who indeed but a woman named Kate Goodfellow who was in need of a secretary?

For a brief moment the sensibly dressed, suitably coiffed Miss York had qualms. It was hard to imagine working for a woman. No one she had ever heard of had worked for a woman. The agency had known little about the position, only that a secretary was needed, that the hours would be erratic, that office management experience was mandatory as well as the usual typing and shorthand skills. All this Virginia possessed. Her efficiency and her skills were excellent, and she could probably have had, despite the Depression, almost any secretarial job in the city. Why, then, was she applying for a job for a company about which she knew nothing at a salary that was well below her earning capacity?

The suite of rooms she found on the top floor of the Chrysler Building was almost empty of furnishings. Everywhere were packing boxes, books stacked on the floor, cardboard boxes, and bits and pieces of photography equipment. A wooden door propped up on two sawhorses made for a makeshift table. The telephone sat prominently in the middle of the bare wood floor.

"Hello?" she called, peering from one room into the next. There was no answer. Virginia checked her watch. It was the right time and the right place. A sign on the door declared this to be the Goodfellow Studio. She stood in the middle of the room. The view from the windows was breathtaking, and she walked over to one that was open to see better. What she saw made her gasp in horror. Outside, perched these sixty-three stories above ground on the head of a giant stainless-steel gargoyle, was a woman. She was kneeling with an enormous black camera balanced in front of her. At that very moment the woman turned around, and spotting Virginia, she waved and shouted, "Hello! Listen, I need the big lens. It's over by the door in the black case. Can you get it for me?"

Virginia backed slowly away from the window, fearing that if she looked away the woman might fall. There was no black case of any kind near any door that she could see. Her eyes searched the room frantically and then lit on the open door of a closet. Inside—voilà, a black case, but unlatching it she saw many lenses, big, little, fat, thin. She reached in and grabbed the fattest and heaviest and rushed back to the window. There was no one there. Virginia's hand flew to her mouth.

"That's it! You're a genius." A hand fluttered in the window from the ledge and after taking the lens from Virginia deftly screwed it on to the camera. Then one leg followed the other back into the room. "Never thought I'd need this, but you just can't tell. I love the big lens. Makes all the difference in a long shot—sort of brings things into focus without distorting the drama, you know?"

Virginia didn't know. "I thought you had slipped and fallen."

"Oh"—she laughed—"not me. I have a God-given sense of balance. When I was a little girl I used to walk to and from school on the thin edges of fences."

"But . . . you're sixty-three stories up in the air!"

"I know. A Sioux Indian gave me a valuable rule for heights. No matter how high up you are, make believe it's no more than eight feet. Then relax and enjoy yourself. The problems are really the same."

"They are?" Virginia felt slightly light-headed . . . Sioux Indian?

"You're here about the job? Great. Let's see now. I suppose I should ask you things, but I really don't have time right now. I just got a last-minute booking at *Vogue*." She stepped back and eyed Virginia as if she were a bug in a jar. "Do you read *Vogue*?"

"Well . . . yes and no." There was certainly no reason for Virginia to read *Vogue* magazine, which was about expensive clothes and fashionable gossip, but of course she was familiar with it just as everyone was. Slick and glossy, *Vogue* reflected in its pages the absurdities and luxuries and snobbery of a world to which Virginia had no access.

"You're a fashion photographer?" Virginia queried.

"I'm anything I can get," Kate said with a tight smile. She turned now and was shuffling through a stack of photographs on the makeshift desk, plucking some out at random and fitting them into a large leather portfolio. "Look. I don't have to tell you that this is probably the worst possible time to be starting a business of any kind, least of all something as ephemeral as a photographic studio, but this is what I'm doing. At the moment I have two clients. *Vogue* magazine, for which I do portraiture and pack shots for products like shoes, stockings, accessories, and cosmetics." She held up a portrait to the light and then showed it to Virginia. "You like?" Fay Wray, the star of this year's hit movie *King Kong*, was draped in white chiffon and posed against a formal staircase beautifully lit so that elegant shadows played against the walls and floor. But what was arresting about the picture was that Kate had widened her shot to reveal the phony set. Tips of lights and tripods, a paint-spattered rung of a ladder, a corner of a makeup table—she had, in effect, destroyed one illusion and instantly created another, more exciting one. It was a delight.

Virginia was impressed. "Why, it's wonderful," she breathed quite sincerely.

"Yes," said Kate. "It is. And they'd better like it over in editorial because I'll be damned if I'll do one more sitting with that bitch. You know what they say about actresses? It's true."

They were both silent for a moment contemplating whatever it was that was said about actresses.

"And the other?" Virginia asked.

"The other what?"

"The other client . . . you said you had two. . . ."

"The Express."

"The tabloid?"

"Exactly. Only I don't do news stories. I do inserts. A series of photos printed separately from the regular news on some human interest story. Maybe you saw my piece on the World's Fair in Chicago?"

No, Virginia had not seen it for the very reason that she did not read the popular press. Her newspapers were the ones read by her former employers—*The New York Times* and *The Wall Street Journal*. Sharpening pencils, icing the water, polishing glasses, and laying clean crisp copies of these two tomes on the conference table had been part of her daily duties.

Kate inserted the photograph she was holding between two stiff sheets of paper. "Now, let's see. I suppose I should interview you, shouldn't I, but . . ." She impulsively reached over and grasped Virginia's arm in a wholly spontaneous and friendly gesture. "Tell you what—you're hired." She then snapped the portfolio shut and turned to reach for an expensive-looking fingertip coat thrown across a chair as if all was settled.

"But . . . but you don't know anything about me," Virginia stammered. "Don't you want my resume or—"

"Listen, we won't know if it works until we try it. I can tell you're organized and that's all I need."

"You can?"

"Sure. Those employment agencies have been sending people to see me for the last three weeks, and they've never fully grasped what I've been looking for. I've had a steady stream of gum-chewers, girdle snappers, and every miscalculated shade of Clairol blonde. I can tell right off you're different. You're wearing a linen dress and a string of pearls. I've always been impressed with anyone together enough to wear linen clothes. I have one or two linen dresses in the back of my wardrobe that I can never find the time to iron so anyone who has them actually ironed and *on* must be organized." All the while Kate was preening in front of a small mirror and adjusting a green felt hat on her head. When she looked up, Virginia saw that three green feathers dyed to match the felt were curled in a delightful fashion under her chin—very theatrical and utterly chic. She grinned at Virginia, a big, eager confident smile. "Like it? It's one of the perks I get from working for *Vogue*. Unfortunately, cock feathers won't pay the rent. They tell me there's no money out there for photographers, but I'm going to prove them wrong. There's money enough if you know how to go after it. Advertising, for instance. All those captains of industry I've flattered up one side and down the other by making their greed look patriotic. They all advertise somewhere. Why shouldn't I get the work? That's where you come in."

"Miss Goodfellow, I think you should know I don't know anything about advertising or photography."

"Good, then you won't be tempted to tell me how to run my business. I get the clients and do the shooting. Rolly, Rolly Stebbins, he's the technical end and you're, hmmm, I guess you're the calm and efficient and . . ." She eyed Virginia again and Virginia shivered slightly under the penetrating, intense gaze. ". . . well-pressed end. You will keep the books and handle the clients on the phone and keep me on track with appointments and juggle shooting schedules and . . . oh, I don't know. You'll simply manage things. You're good at that, I can tell. Now listen, I'll give you the quick tour before I go and you take all the time in the world you'll need to decide. It looks rather bare, I know, but I haven't the money yet to decorate. We spent every last penny on equipment and rent. Rolly said he thought we were crazy to take on this place, but I couldn't help myself. It was the gargoyles. When I saw them I said there was no other place in the world I would rather have than this for my studio. Up high where I can breathe."

"Do you live here, too?" Virginia asked, peering around. They had walked from one near empty room into another, but she could see that the closet was filled with clothes.

"No." Kate sighed. "I wish I could, but only the janitors can live in the building. I applied to be a custodian, but they turned me down. Still, it doesn't matter. I can do everything else here, and I can work all night long if I want to. Rolly and I often work all night long. I like working at night. Do you?"

Virginia allowed as how she didn't mind working at night.

"Good. I plan to do a lot of entertaining, too. It's the only way to get those execs to take notice. Parties. I've got two terraces. This one"—she flung open double-glassed doors onto a terra-cotta terrace which ran impressively on two sides of the studio—"will be for entertaining." A smart, cold wind almost blew Kate's hat off, and she grabbed the door and hastily pulled it shut. "And this one"—she marched Virginia through yet another room which was dominated by a large fish tank to another door—"is where I keep my pets."

Two very unpleasant-looking alligators about four feet long lay in a shallow trough blinking in the brilliant sunlight. "A friend sent me the alligators from Florida. I keep turtles, too. They remind me of my college days. I majored in herpetology."

Virginia looked blank.

"You know, reptiles and amphibians. Do you like reptiles? Watch. This is so fascinating." Virginia watched as Kate produced a large slab of red meat from a little cooler in the corner of the terrace and tossed it to the alligators, who promptly sprang into action and began tearing the meat from each other's mouths with vicious carnivore gusto. "Astonishing, isn't it, how they respond on top of a skyscraper exactly as they do in the wild."

"Astonishing," echoed Virginia.

"Then it's settled. Can you start soon? Tomorrow?"

Virginia hesitated; she had never in her life encountered such a situation.

"Look." Kate paused as if trying to think up just the right enticement. "I won't kid you into thinking we're solvent. We're not. But I know we can do it. I know I can get the clients, but I need someone to run the office and do the follow-up after I've made the contacts. If you'll just say yes, I promise you a desk *and* your own telephone extension. Then, when we've got some money coming in, we'll fix everything up. I see it all very simple—glass and aluminum and natural wood. Very plain, very spare, ultramodern, don't you? So, what do you say." Virginia saw that they had completed the tour of rooms and were back at the main door. Kate turned and took her hand warmly. "I'm not hard to work with. You will come on board, won't you?"

Virginia took a deep breath. "Yes."

"Good girl. You won't regret it. At least, I hope you won't. Now I have to run. We'll see you tomorrow morning at ten sharp." She shook hands once again and then picking up her portfolio, gloves, and handbag, she scooted out the door.

Virginia took a moment to catch her breath. The whole thing was so absurd it made her laugh. Imagine offering a desk and telephone as fringe benefits. She looked around the studio. She could do without the alligators and she doubted very much that Kate was easy to work for, but for a woman who had quit one of the highest-paying secretarial jobs in the city in the middle of the Depression, she felt she had rather landed on her feet. Or maybe, as she again took in the vast panorama of the city, she had sprouted wings.

She had graduated top of her class at Katherine Gibbs and had gone straight into the offices of Allerton & Sims on Wall Street, where she had worked for the past six years. Everything about Virginia exuded propriety from the modest makeup to the neat navy blue dress with its crisp white collar. She knew she looked almost as if she were in uniform and she liked that. Uniforms suited her. She had worn one since she was twelve. She wondered if she was the only graduate from the Fairfield Preparatory School for Girls to work her way up through the typing pool to the very top secretarial echelons on Wall Street. Probably she was. More likely still, she was probably the only graduate from Fairfield who had ever held a job. Girls who went to schools like Fairfield almost always married as soon as they had completed their debutante season and perhaps a year abroad. But not Virginia York.

Her mother had been the secretary to the headmistress, a fierce old woman whose pedigree eclipsed all other high-ranking Virginia families. Mrs. August Jefferson Blount III could and did trace her lineage to the Norman Conquest. At seventy she ruled the Fairfield School with an iron hand.

Virginia and her mother lived in a small suite of rooms on the ground floor of the dormitory right next to the dining room. There was no Mr. York, at least not in Virginia's memory. He had died soon after she was born, or so she had been told. He was never mentioned, although her mother was firm about being a widow. "I am a widow," she said, "and must work to support my child." Virginia was nine when the job offer came from the exclusive Fairfield School, and though it meant moving out of the apartment she and her mother had lived in all her life, it also meant a first-rate education for Virginia. In return, they lived on a pittance meanly doled out by the austere Mrs. Blount, whom they both feared. Still, if she worked hard, a diploma from Fairfield might mean a scholarship to college.

Virginia was a good girl, the kind others called "nice" and "sweet," but she never really made close friends among the others. Still, she was elected class secretary three years running and was on one occasion invited to visit a classmate over an Easter holiday. This she found difficult. She didn't have the right clothes and the boys lost interest in her when they found out she was a "nobody." Maybe if she had been vivacious or even fast she might have succeeded in the smart prep school set, but she was none of these things.

In her senior year her mother died. Virginia had always known about the drinking and had been good at covering for her mother, who, being small and thin and pale, looked as if she might really be stricken with all the illnesses Virginia concocted for her, but as the years progressed it had gotten worse, even to the point of the girls snickering quite openly at her mother as she sat swaying at one of the school dining tables during dinner. Mrs. Blount began to issue dire warnings about dismissal if things did not get better. But things had not improved—they had gotten worse. One Sunday morning at the end of her senior year, while the rest of the school was in church, her mother had gagged on her own vomit and choked to death. Mrs. Blount, who was not altogether unkind, nevertheless felt the disgrace would mar the otherwise happy festivities of graduation, and so Virginia was not allowed to march with her classmates through the arched canopy of daisies wearing her white graduation dress. She was given her diploma early along with a check. This and an insurance policy left to her by her mother covered her expenses for three years at Katherine Gibbs.

For six years she had worked for Allerton & Sims, Attorneys at Law, the last two of which she was executive secretary to Mr. John Sims Hamilton, nephew to the senior partner. The dignified old Wall Street firm suited Virginia to the core. Rich in furnishings as well as clients, the polished wood-paneled walls and soft thick carpeting became her safe haven from the world outside. A world of cafeterias, subways, and a shared apartment.

At Allerton & Sims poise and skill were *de rigueur* for secretaries. Virginia's boarding school demeanor and cultured accent gave her an edge, so that when John Sims Hamilton arrived on the scene fresh from Yale Law School, and handsome as a movie star, he picked her out of the typing pool to sit in his front office. She was in love with him from the start and set about making herself indispensable to him. They were a team—his brilliance interwoven with her skill—until they formed a seamless partnership. Only somehow the team had detoured to one hotel room and then another, and the bounds became confused.

She was too naive to understand how one-sided the relationship truly was and too reserved and miserable to make a fuss when his engagement was announced in the newspaper. Day after day she had sat in the outer office fielding his calls, making his appointments, typing his letters, brewing his coffee. Now she booked theater tickets, ordered flowers, made reservations in elegant uptown restaurants, reserved the stateroom on a ship bound for Bermuda for his wedding trip. When the office staff had thrown him a party two days before the wedding, she had raised her glass and drunk the champagne along with the others. On the day of his wedding she lay on her bed in the small apartment where she lived on West Seventy-ninth Street and wept until she knew she would never cry like that again. Then she had gotten up, typed her resignation, forfeited her two weeks' severance pay, and started looking for another job. That had been two months ago.

"Excuse me. Can I help you?" Virginia, a million miles away, twirled around and gasped. Rolly Stebbins was so startled he dropped the case he was carrying, which broke the clasp, and suddenly hundreds of small peanut bulbs were rolling every which way across the floor.

"Oh, dear . . . I'm so sorry . . ." she said to his equally flustered and awkward apologies, and then the two of them were down on the floor scrambling after the bulbs. When at last they seemed to be all safely squared away again in the case, Virginia smiled and extended her hand. "I'm the new secretary. You must be Rolly." She found herself looking into the kindest brown eyes she had ever seen.

Rolly grinned shyly. "Welcome aboard, or maybe it's welcome aloft." He gestured to the sky outside. "Miss . . . ?"

"York, but please call me Virginia. I . . . I'll have to tell you I'm a little dizzy from all this. I mean Miss Goodfellow just left and I'm not altogether sure what I've agreed to. I mean I've never done anything like this before."

"Oh, that's okay," said Rolly kindly. "Neither have we."

*   *   *

Less than a month had gone by since Kate's call brought Rolly to New York. He had managed to come out of the crash with $10,000 intact. Enough to pay the rent for six months; enough to build a darkroom; enough to buy the enormous studio lights, lay the fat cables, build backdrops, print calling cards, and hire a secretary. When that $10,000 was gone, there would be no more. Kate and Rolly simply had to make it. They studied the ads in print. She knew she could do better. She and Rolly spent hours experimenting with lighting and chemical baths. They would cough and sputter in the fumes and Kate's fingernails turned brown because she could never be bothered with the delicate dabbling with print forceps. Rather she plunged in with both hands, rubbing the surface of the prints with her fingertips to get just the tone she wanted.

Building a portfolio, she started making the rounds, only this time with all the moxie of a New York insider. She had never worked so hard in her life. It seemed she was always running, dressing, going to meetings, lunches, dinners. At first it had been fun working with models and art directors and big corporations. Nobody bled on your feet or smelled bad or knocked you down to get ahead of you. No one ever started sentences with "Say, what's a pretty gal like you . . ." And the money one could make in advertising was fun, too. Men on Madison Avenue appreciated a well-turned-out woman. Rolly's investment had also paid for new clothes and hats and an expensive leather portfolio. They might have to skip a few meals, but when Kate went on a sales call, she looked like a million bucks.

Virginia settled in as nicely as a hermit crab in a stolen shell. She sorted, filed, arranged cocktail parties, juggled clients, and kept Kate's schedule running in peak form. Sometimes Virginia would schedule two lunch dates in a single day. Then there were cocktails, dinners, the theater, and late-night dancing. All of these engagements seemed to be with potential clients. Men in flannel suits carrying important briefcases often appeared unannounced in the studio. When this happened Rolly and Virginia would enter into a kind of frenzied charade of office work. The telephone would start ringing, photographs would be bundled and marked for messenger delivery, champagne and whiskey were offered up in the finest crystal glasses from a sophisticated mirrored bar that had once been a coat closet, and Virginia and Rolly would rush about the studio in a parody of overwork. In reality a friendly secretary twelve floors down was enlisted to ring their phone on cue from Virginia, the messenger service never materialized, and dregs from the generous and free-flowing drinks were always siphoned back into the bottles after the client left. Everything was orchestrated to appear as if the Goodfellow Studio were humming with activity.

What Kate did in the after hours to lure clients was not something Virginia cared to speculate on. Men came and went. Men of the hour. Clever executives on and off the Avenue, magazine and newspaper men, football heroes, showbiz people, agents, publicity men, fashion photographers—men who could help her, give her jobs, introduce her to other potential clients. Once when Virginia was unpacking a camera case after Kate had gone on an overnight trip to bid on a job in Pennsylvania, she found a round rubber object.

"What's this, Rolly? A new lens cover?"

Rolly had turned beet red and snatched it out of her hand before it dawned on Virginia what it was.

Inside of a year the phones rang without the help of a secretary twelve floors down. Inside of two years the Goodfellow Studio had achieved a certain status by Madison Avenue standards and Kate Goodfellow was a name to be reckoned with. Her signature was in dark shadows and sharp edges, vivid contrasts and brittle surfaces, the kind of slick style that went down well in the deepening days of the Depression. She was a perfectionist. She would stand over Rolly in the darkroom checking print after print, and often Rolly would print hundreds of versions from a single negative. Virginia became an expert at picking through the negatives and finding the best. Even so, some would not be good enough for Kate.

"No, no, no. That doesn't look like silver. I don't care if it is silver, it photographs like pewter." And so they would coat the silver with lacquer and bounce lights from screens until it met Kate's approval. If the subject was soup, it must out-soup any soup ever dreamed of, with fragrant fumes seeming to rise straight up from the page. Achieving these effects became Kate's specialty—and Virginia's nightmare.

The food ads were the worst. In the first place, food never stood up well to the heat of the lights. Cakes, puddings, gelatin salads all slipped and slid into gooey masses within minutes under the glare. Real food could not be used. Virginia often wondered what readers of the women's magazines would think if they knew how the foods pictured in glowing color were handled, squeezed, patted into shape, glued, propped up, mauled, and varnished. The most delicate, frothy, featherlike dessert topping would be hard as a rock if you went over and tapped it.

Kate built her romantic needs into the texture of her working life, and she went after lovers the way she went after jobs. The more, the better. She moved easily from affair to affair. Sex was merely another tool in the strategy. Men seemed to come and go in a steady stream, and after a while, at least to Virginia's mind, they all seemed to blend together. She was astounded at how Kate treated them. She accepted their gifts with delight only to recycle them on as her own gifts to someone she needed to impress; she flattered, cajoled, used men to meet other potential clients, and accomplished all of this with the greatest of ease and elaborate show of affection. Yet, Virginia observed, the eager smile, the enraptured face completely evaporated when Kate turned away, as if a light had gone out. It was as if the man of that hour was not even there.

Kate simply expected the world to give her what she wanted on her own terms and, when it had, she could be astonishingly blunt and cruel. The trail of frustrated suitors stretched from the corporate heads of industry to flying aces to social scions. It made no difference. The shell was impenetrable. It was only the work, and recognition for the work, that counted. Any man who knew her should know that.

In the last two years she had lived on train timetables and mail and messages and flowers and appointments and shooting schedules. But none of this made her happy. Kate sat back in the cab and mentally reviewed the shoot with the knight. Now that there was nothing she could do about it, she began to find flaws—maybe there had been too much mist, the early light had changed so quickly, the angle might have been better

from . . . It seemed the more she worked the more exacting
she became. There was always something more that was
needed. She was exhausted. She was always running, and the
more she ran the more it felt as if she were staying in the same
place. There was a strange flatness to her life. She felt impatient
and preoccupied and she couldn't help the feeling of emptiness that hovered just outside the edges of her consciousness.
It was times like this that she wondered about the dream. That
great dream of success that had been hers when she had first
started out. She remembered the vividness of that dream better
than all the things that had happened to her in the years between
and yet the dream eluded her even as she became more and
more successful.

As she rode now in the taxi, she thought about an enormous 8×8 box of putty, sand, and clay representing Anytown,
USA. Through it ran an imprint from the grids of a giant tire.
It was perfect. The imprint of the tire in the putty looked impressive. Kate herself had spent hours on her knees with
tweezers placing the last little touches to make the miniature
town look as real as could be, complete with tiny roadside
signs, toy automobiles, and little miniature houses, fake trees,
matchstick swings. Fake made to look real. The mock town
and its tire sat in the middle of her studio awaiting approval
from the Akron men.

It would be hard to explain the trouble they had gone to for
the ad. Ordinary sand would not stand up under the lights, so
they experimented and found a way to make mud look like
sand by kneading together putty with clay and mud, but then
they found that a tire, a real tire, couldn't make a clean imprint
so they had to have a tire hand-carved from wood at considerable expense, the tread sculpted extra deep so that the photograph would show the crispest, most convincing tire track the
nation's motorists had ever seen. And all the while, in Akron,
a bloody battle had been going on between the tire workers
and Safety Tire's management. Some two thousand men had
taken to the streets and had been beaten back with clubs and
sticks. They were paying her $1,000 a photograph to glorify
the rubber tire, and these battered men in the streets of Akron
were striking to get wages up to $26 per week. That was real.
In the real world an eight-year-old girl worked a twelve-hour

shift in a textile mill—and who cared? A ragged, gaunt-faced family stared at the sun-parched wasteland that was their Oklahoma farm—and who cared?

Well, for starters there were artists and writers and photographers out there who did care. Cared enough to devote their talents to documenting the upheavals of the world. Americans were awakening to the urgencies of their times and breaking out of provincial, regional boundaries. They wanted information and they demanded explanation. Photographers joined the ranks of painters, writers, and performers as they turned their art toward documenting the struggle of the great masses. Ansel Adams, Paul Strand, Edward Weston, Dorothea Lange, and Walker Evans were focused on the worker and the plight of the plain-suffering human being. Social concerns became a dominant artistic theme. While Kate tweezered miniature weeds into fake roadsides, other photographers were concentrating on migrant workers, the laboring classes, and the forces of hatred and evil hammering at the gates of civilization. Kate, sitting in her ivory tower, knew she was missing out. Social ferment was everywhere; other photographers were exhibiting pictures of immense power; she was glorifying the rubber tire.

"Mr. Bennett, for you, Kate. Shall I tell him you'll call back?" Kate had just arranged a total of twelve models in a circle with their hands arranged on a drape of velvet. Twenty-four hands in all, two hundred and forty perfectly manicured fingernails. In the center of the circle was a tall, slim bottle of nail enamel. The lights had been set and reset a dozen times and now appeared to catch a small light from each nail. The models could not sit or lean against anything and they had been standing at an awkward angle for most of an hour without a break.

"No," said Kate after a moment's hesitation. "I'll take the call. Don't anybody move."

The models groaned and shot Kate murderous looks. Rolly ducked his head in frustration, and Virginia handed Kate the telephone without comment.

Kate tucked the telephone in one hand and began a series of infinitesimal adjustments to the focus on the large camera.

Pleasantries were not exchanged; they rarely were when Otis Bennett called. Both he and Kate seemed only interested in talking business, and the business they talked was photography. Otis had not given up on his plan for a magazine devoted to photojournalism but was no closer to its fruition than he had been four years earlier when he had taken over *The Express*. The problem was still the same. There was no ink on the market that could dry fast enough for mass-marketing a magazine the way he envisioned it. But that had not kept him from pursuing the vision. *The Express* now boasted a regular insert feature of newsworthy and human interest pictures fashioned after the success of many European newspapers. The readers loved it and Otis had gotten more and more national in his pursuits. Social issues had become his primary focus. Now, as he talked, Kate's expression began to show more and more interest at what was being said to her on the line. Within minutes she had hung up. As she bent her eye to the camera lens, she told Virginia to call the airlines and book her a ticket to Topeka, Kansas. Then she pressed the shutter and two hundred and forty lacquered fingernails were captured on film.

CHAPTER EIGHTEEN

"IF IT RAINS . . ." These three little words had suddenly become the most melancholy in the national lexicon. This was the year that the Dust Bowl made its full-blown debut. America's breadbasket, they called the Midwest, only now the drought had destroyed millions of dollars' worth of wheat crops, killed tens of thousands of herd animals, and forced untold numbers from their homes as if in a Biblical plague. Western Kansas, Colorado, Wyoming, and nearly all of Texas were paralyzed as dust piled up in houses and schools, stopping traffic and causing businesses to close. The land, thousands upon thousands of miles, was swirling into powder and rising like funnels of grit into the air.

In time people would recall 1935 as the blackest year of the drought, especially the early spring months from March through April. Everyone back East knew about the overgrazed, overplowed Plains farmland, yet no one seemed able to visualize it. No one had actually seen what the devastation looked like.

"This drought is affecting everyone," Otis told Kate. "I want to do a story, a real story, on what's going on out there.

I want you to go. I want to run the story in next week's editon. Think you can do it?"

She did. Two days later she was in Topeka pacing about the small office of Ernie Wing.

"Don't you see, ma'am, no one rightly knows where to tell you to go. What exactly is it you want to see? Maybe a dried-up riverbed? How 'bout that?"

"No, no—nothing so obvious," she said impatiently. "I want to really get out there and experience the drought. The way the farmers do. I want the effects of the drought. I want to get at the heart of it. Kansas is one of the most hard hit areas and here you are sitting right in the middle of it and you're telling me you don't know where to send me?"

"Well, now, I sure don't." Ernie Wing leaned his chair back and propped one foot on his desk. Confound this woman. She had been pestering him for hours. Lands in Topeka with ten bags of gear and says she wants to hire an airplane to take her to "see the Dust Bowl" like it was a national monument or somethin'. Red hair flyin' and wearing pants to boot. Another one of those city reporters and damned hard to understand. Ernie was kinda enjoyin' it all the same.

"Well, I'm not taking that for an answer," Kate said and promptly sat down opposite him. "Don't you understand, I've got five days to deadline. Five measly little days to really capture what this thing is all about. All I want is a little cooperation. You're the manager around here. Why can't you just try and find me a pilot and a little information?"

"Look, lady, I don't care who you are and what you've come to get, I can't just point you in one direction. Hell, er . . . excuse me, ma'am . . . heck, you're talking over a thousand miles of territory. I haven't got those kinds of planes. We hire out crop dusters here, strictly local hops. Why don't you just go on down to the hotel and get yourself a room and cable those folks back in New York . . ."

He was having himself a good time and Kate knew it. "A crop duster would be perfect. I need something that can fly low and a pilot who knows the terrain. And I don't know what I want to see until I see it. Why don't you just try to help me?" Her eyes were beginning to fill with tears. This was so damn frustrating. She had forgotten how impossible people could be. She pulled a map out of her handbag. "If we've got a thousand miles to cover, I need an airplane and a pilot right now. Won't you just find me one pilot I can talk to?"

There was a laugh from behind her and Kate turned with some annoyance.

"Hey, Ernie, how about Stony? He's just come in." The fellow in the door jerked his thumb toward the small, dusty window.

"Aw, she don't want Stony."

Kate was on her feet. "I don't? Sure I do."

"Ma'am. Stony is crazier than you are. Why, that crate he calls an airplane was obsolete before you or I was ever born."

Kate grinned. "Stony sounds like my man." She shouldered one of her smaller bags and made for the door.

"Are you a pilot?" she asked a tall, thin man dressed in faded jeans and boots. He was just about to wrap the front part of his plane in a burlap sack.

"Could be."

"Stony? Is that your name? Okay, well, look, Stony, here's what I want. I want someone to fly me over this whole territory. I'm on special assignment from *The Express* in New York—do you know it?—well, it doesn't matter. I've got five days to put together a photo essay on the effects of the drought. I don't know exactly what I'm looking for, but when I see something I want to photograph, I don't want to hear about how I can't or shouldn't. I want to take pictures from the air and the ground. Can this. . . . ah . . ."—she gave the airplane a quick glance and saw at once that it was indeed an old model—"flying machine of yours land on open ground or do you need an airstrip?"

"I can land on anything you want except water, but that won't matter 'cause there's no water out there to land on."

"When can we go?"

Stony pushed his hat to the back of his head. "I didn't say we could."

"Look, I can pay double your fee. I can pay more than that, but we have to get going. I've been talking and talking to that man, that Ernie, in there, and he's been as obstinate as a mule. Please say you'll be my pilot, I can't wait any longer. I just have to get up there. Please." Her eyes filled with bright tears.

Stony looked most uncomfortable. He chewed on his lower lip, then took his hat off and scratched at the back of his head. Then he looked up at the sky. It was a clear day, maybe five hours till dark. Then he looked back at the pleading face of the woman from where? New York? Shit.

"Takes me about half hour to gas up and get supplies, ma'am."

"Oh, good," Kate gushed. She stuck out her hand and grabbed at his, giving it a firm shake. "And don't ma'am me to death, okay? My name is Kate. Do I pay you now or later?"

"I'd wait to pay later, ma'am." This was said by Ernie, who had followed her out onto the tarmac. "'Cause then you probably won't have to pay at all. Last feller that tried to land in the middle of the Dust Bowl is still trying to dig out." Ernie thought his joke was so good, he slapped his thigh.

For the next three days they flew over a thousand miles. Kate was stunned at what she saw. She had never seen landscape like this. Blinding sun beat down on withered crops, creating a ghostly patchwork of half-buried corn. The rivers, once free-running streams, had all dried to sand. Fine-blown dust rose up in sinister spouts, and as far as the eye could see were colorless acres which should have been green with crops in April but now were carved in aimless dry ripples. Here was the Great Plains, America's breadbasket, a crucial source of food for the country, a way of life for hundreds of thousands of people. Here was the land that had once inspired Willa Cather to write of meadowlarks on the wing, clean white curtains dancing in the breeze, wild verbena and lilacs in bloom, and cold fresh water coming up from the well in the bucket. But no more. Below her 100 million acres drifted in aimless circles of dust and dirt.

All day long from earliest dawn until the very last possible rays suitable for taking pictures, Kate and Stony flew over the devastation. She was fascinated with the patterns of the parched earth and with the drifting sheets of dust. More than that, she was fascinated with the potential of aerial photography. Stony had never seen anyone so excited by the view from 5,000 feet. Sometimes she had him strap her on the wing and fly at full tilt so that she could get the picture she wanted. Her best moments were his worst. Stony knew the limitations of his airplane and the dangers of the dust storms. Kate didn't care. She seemed impervious to the finely filtered dust that blew everywhere, turning the sky to a coppery gloom.

The first two nights they settled into hotel rooms in towns with names that mocked the reality of the situation—names like Harmony and Promised Land. She and Stony would sit in the worn rockers of threadbare lobbies and talk to the locals. She learned how hard it was to get the dust out of the gutters, how it filtered through keyholes like a fine, soft talc, how carpets and draperies and tapestries were so dust-laden that their patterns were indiscernible. They advised her to take a wet washcloth to bed to keep the grit out of her nose as she slept, and "best try to lie still," they said, "because every turn stirs the dust on the blankets." At night the wind moaned in the eaves, and by morning they would have to shovel a basketful of dirt to get at the plane.

Most of the time she sat in a single seat behind Ernie with the door open so she could get a better view. Their food, water supplies, and her equipment were stuffed into every nook. She rode with a large black changing bag in her lap in which her busy hands kept unloading, boxing, and reloading her film holders so that she would be ready for whatever they might meet. With the wind whistling at high pitch she couldn't actually talk to Stony until they landed, but they had fallen into an easy sign language. He knew when she wanted to circle, land, or go on. Increasingly, she shook her head in a gesture that bade him try somewhere else. Something more was wanted.

On the third day, a day surprisingly clear with blue skies and a brilliant sun revealing the parched land, after flying for about an hour on their way to a settlement in Oklahoma they'd heard was particularly hard hit, Kate saw something below that looked interesting and signaled to Stony to land, but he shook his head. She waited for a few minutes, then she nudged him again. There was no way to talk because of the noise from the motor and wind, but she sensed from the hunch of his shoulders and the concentration in his eye that something was wrong. She had gotten used to the little antiquated plane. It felt cozy in the back tucked up with all the supplies and the clear view of the earth rushing below her through the open door. She had immense faith in Stony's abilities as a pilot.

He'd flown over Germany in the war and then come home to be a barnstormer, earning his livelihood stunt-flying at country fairs. His airplane was every bit as old and extinct as Ernie Wing had said, but Stony flew it like it was the very latest model. Now, having grown accustomed to its rattle and shake, she could discern nothing new in the racket it made. Suddenly Stony turned halfway in his seat. Through the din, he yelled something at her and reached back and pushed her head down onto her lap. She saw the ground rushing up to meet them and then she realized they were crashing.

In reality it took less than a minute for the tiny plane to come to a stop in the soft dirt, but it seemed like an eternity. They bumped, tilted, bounced along the ground. She thought they would never stop. She heard a ripping sound and a series of loud shots, like pistols being fired. She held her head in her hands but reached her arm out to hold down her camera bags and the precious film already exposed. At last another series of bumps and then the little plane came to a halt, its nose dug into the ground like a pig rooting in the dirt. Then there was silence.

Kate looked up. Stony was hunched over in his seat. She could see blood coming down the side of his face. "Stony? Are you all right?" She pushed herself up to a sitting position and pushed boxes and containers off of her. "Stony?" He didn't move. Dear God, was he dead or just passed out? Her leg seemed pinned down and it took her a long time to dislodge it from the cramped space, but at last she wiggled herself free, all the while calling his name. He didn't move. Kate dragged herself from the plane, and had to steady herself for a minute when her feet touched the ground. She was dizzy. Then she looked around her. It was desolate. They were in a field, just as dry and patched as every other field she had seen. Tumbleweeds rolled and danced by her and the wind moaned. She noticed that there seemed to be a lot of birds around them, fluttering and chattering nervously, but she thought this might be due to the plane crashing. Other than that it was quiet. She turned back to the airplane and the slumped figure and as she did she exclaimed out loud. There, not a hundred feet away, was a farmhouse! She started toward it for help and then quickly turned back and in a reflex reaction extracted her camera case and film. At that very moment she heard a groan from Stony and she breathed a sigh of relief. He was alive and there was help at hand.

"It's okay, Stony. We landed in a field behind a house. I'm going for help. I don't want to move you without help."

He groaned again and struggled to say something to her although he did not lift his head. She leaned down to hear him better. His breath came in gasps and twice he tried to lift his head. She got a canteen of water from the back and wet the back of his neck and then doused her scarf and wet his mouth. He lifted his head then, and she saw that his mouth was filled with grit and dirt. Carefully she reached into his mouth with her finger and pulled out what she could, then she wiped his mouth. All the while she kept reassuring him that the farmhouse was nearby and she was going for help. She couldn't understand why he would not let her go.

Finally he swallowed hard and whispered, "It's a black blizzard. I saw it coming in the distance. No time . . . no time . . ."

Kate whirled around. Now she saw what Stony was talking about. There were more birds arriving every moment as if fleeing from some unseen enemy. Then, on the north horizon, a towering black wall was moving toward them; there was no sound, no wind, nothing but the immense black wall.

Kate's jaw dropped. For a second she was too disbelieving to react. Stony was coming awake now and had struggled out of his seat. "We've got to get to the house," he gasped. "Grab what water you can. We've got to move. Now!"

But Kate was walking away from him. In an instant she had pulled her camera out of the bag. It was a picture of a lifetime. It was THE picture. No one would ever believe this. She knew she had maybe ten seconds to get it. She steadied the camera and focused, her hands trembling a little. She could hear Stony fumbling in the airplane telling her to hurry, hurry, but she was like a sleepwalker. She took a deep breath and pressed the shutter. Quickly she extracted the film pack and inserted another and then another. She got five pictures, each focused on the deadly wall of black cloud coming nearer and nearer at a terrifying speed. At last she grabbed on to Stony's arm and the two of them rushed to the farmhouse.

The storm struck seconds later. It filled the room, like a thick, dank fog. "This must be what it was like at Pompeii," Kate said, gasping for air. Outside, the sky was black; inside, silently and steadily a thick, charcoal fog settled on everything, including the two figures who sat against the wall. The door and the windows were shut tight, yet those tiny particles seemed to seep through the very walls. She wrapped her scarf around her nose and mouth. Still the black dust penetrated. She could feel it in the back of her throat; she could feel it fill her nostrils. She felt as if she were being buried alive. The storm lasted for three hours.

When it was over, the sun came out again, shining in a rosy hue. All round them the dirt was piled high, drifts of it against the fences and sides of the barn. The farm was abandoned but serviceable enough for Kate and Stony to decide to stay the night before seeking help. He seemed almost fully recovered and was embarrassed at the fuss Kate made over the gash in his temple. Still, he submitted to her ministrations and first aid.

Together they dragged supplies out of the airplane, and by nightfall they had made quite a cozy nest for themselves in the farm kitchen where Stony had built a fire in the stove and was heating up a can of beans.

Kate gave up trying to sweep the dust outside and wandered from room to room with a flashlight. In a closet she found a pretty pitcher sitting in a large china bowl.

"I wonder why they left this?" she asked.

"Who knows. They take all they can load onto the back of a truck and move on. Maybe it was just one thing too many. You want to wash?"

"Do we have enough water?"

"Well, not for a bath." He smiled. "Enough to wet down."

She nodded and when he had filled the pitcher, he walked out on the porch for a smoke. Kate watched him from the window and then peeled off the jacket she had been wearing and then the shirt and underclothes. Oh, God, it felt good, the cool wet water against her skin as she dipped the cloth and let the tiny dribbles run freely down her bare torso. She vowed she would never take water for granted again. She rubbed the grit from her face and neck and then decided to strip down completely so she could run the wet cloth all over her body. There was something so haunting about this place, so removed from the world, so isolated, that it was as if she and this tall cowboy were the last people left on earth. The thought made her acutely aware of Stony as a man.

Stony walked to the far end of the porch, and she could see the small, burning end of his cigarette. He did not seem to her like a man given to wild emotion and that excited her. She pulled some fresh clothes out of her haversack and luxuriated in the feel of being clean. Then she went to the door and called to him.

"Any water left?" he asked, and she thought she detected a small look of approval at the much improved Kate.

"Oh, yes. It's all in the pitcher. I didn't use much."

He surprised her by walking to the basin, stripping off his shirt and splashing water on his face and over his chest. His back was lean and muscular. His jeans were hung low on his hips and she could just detect the line of his buttocks. She must have looked as ravenous as she felt because he turned around quickly and saw, without mistake, the look on her face.

He grinned. Kate walked over to him and in an instant he had pulled her to him and she felt the rough mouth on hers and the dry stubble of his beard.

"God," she gasped when they pulled apart, "I want this." He threw down a blanket and she kneeled and unbuckled his trousers until at last she could reach her hand in to caress him.

He groaned with pleasure. She liked that. She liked having this control. At last he could stand no more of her teasing and was on her and Kate gasped with surprise. They tumbled and rolled together, rocking measure for measure until at last she could feel herself climbing to the outer limits of sensation, and she gasped out to him that she was coming. He was ready. They both ground together and exploded in hot wetness.

Afterward, lying next to him, their bodies naked in the stream of moonlight that filtered through the grimy windows, Kate watched him as he smoked another of his hand-rolled cigarettes. She felt a satisfaction she had not felt in years. The events of the day had left her exhilarated. She had her picture. Tomorrow she would get more. Stony had fallen asleep now, and as his breathing fell to deep steady inhalations, Kate, too, drifted off. Great unfriendly shapes rushed toward her, threatening to run her down. As they drew closer, she saw that the shapes were cars on giant rubber tires. They were moving in a menacing, zigzagging course, their giant hoods raised in jagged alarming shapes as though determined to swallow her. She began to run, but now she was in the desert and her feet sank into sand and dirt and she could not escape. The muck was all around her and the giant grid of the tire began to roll over her. She awoke with Stony's hands on her shoulders, shaking her into consciousness.

The story she brought back to New York was a shock to everyone who stood around the desk staring at her pictures one after another in silence. No one could quite believe it.

"I talked to as many farmers as I could. One man told me that for six months it was unusual to see clear daylight from dawn until dusk. Another said he had been at the movies when the dust storm hit Dodge City. Here, I wrote down what he told me." She handed the crumpled slip of paper to Walter Lord and he read,

> "When I walked outside, it was as if someone had put a blindfold over my eyes. I bumped into a telephone pole, skinned my shins on some boxes and cans in the alleyway, fell to my hands and knees and crawled along the curbing until I could see a dim house light. Lady Godiva could have ridden through the streets without even the horse seeing her."

"I heard terrible stories," Kate went on. "I talked to a woman who had lost her son. He was seven and he wandered away in the storm and was lost in the gloom. Later a search party found him, but it was too late. He had suffocated in a drift.

"One storm alone lasted twelve days, they told me, and wiped out one half the wheat crop in Kansas, one quarter of it in Oklahoma and all of it in Nebraska—five million acres blown out in a single storm. Livestock and wildlife went with the crops. A rancher told me that in a rising sandstorm cattle quickly become blinded. They run around in circles until they fall and breathe so much dust that they die. Newborn calves suffocate in a matter of hours, and the older cattle grind their teeth down to the gums trying to eat the dirt-covered grass. Horses and cattle climb over fences buried in the dust and wander away trying to get to places where there's still water in the riverbeds. Most are dry, but those that still have water are putrid. The dust covers the surface and the fish die. Everywhere—everywhere there is death."

The Express ran twelve of Kate's pictures and the prints were exhibited to mixed reviews at the Artists' Congress. Critics claimed her work was not equal to the gravity of the situation, that she had failed to portray the staggering human tragedy of the Midwestern farmer; yet they all agreed that the drama of the devastated landscape was fascinating and that there was energy and originality in the photographs beyond any seen so far. The exhibit drew crowds, and while even Kate could admit that as far as social documentation was concerned, she was still an outsider looking in, she didn't care. She was proud. Proud in a way she hadn't been for a long time. She knew now more than ever that she wanted to move her attention to the ever-deepening hardship and sorrow of the Great Depression. The Dust Bowl had taught her one of the most valuable lessons of her life—you can never do anything better than what is real.

CHAPTER NINETEEN

OTHER HOSTESSES TRIED to analyze what made Gaby Leigh-Bell's parties so much fun, but it was impossible. Gaby, when asked, merely shrugged and said, "A really good party is like making a wonderful soufflé: Timing is everything." But it was more than timing. Gaby's secret was to fill her parties with carefully orchestrated elements of surprise. A surprise guest, for instance, or unannounced royals, or maybe the lights might go out at midnight, leaving the guests in candlelight. She abhorred the idea of allowing her guests to do what they wanted to do. "Everything must be done for them," she said, "but the effects of the party must appear just to happen." She was a genius at mixing people and often invited warring factions to help set an edgy tone. Above all, Gaby loved a theme—always subtle and sometimes known only to herself. Something exotic like gangsters, something religious like a Buddhist, something warm and fuzzy like a litter of kittens. Gaby said a good party should occur in one room only, and that room should always be too small for the number of guests invited.

The party given that night in early spring of 1935 was no more, no less than countless parties given by Gaby in the past, yet there was excitement in the air. It was right to be gay and

outrageous when the whole rest of the world was teetering toward the edge of disaster. Hitler had gained control of Germany, and only last month newsreels showed German troops
marching in the streets of Berlin for the first time since the
Great War. There was a sense of here-it-is-again, a feeling of
inexorable repetition—of living in the past and in the present
simultaneously.

Oh, but tonight was for singing Cole Porter's latest, "Anything Goes," and drinking and falling in love. Tonight, the
room glittering with mirrors and lights was full of people intent on happiness however long it could be sustained. Gaby
moved easily through her party, her chins wagging on top of
the bright length of orange that went for an evening gown, her
plump hands weighted down with rings, a tiny hat decked with
wobbling veils and roses perched on the raffish burst of hair,
and a whopping silk flower pinned at the shoulder with a paste
diamond brooch.

"Good evening, whoever you are," she said gaily to a group
of people as she passed. "I've met you all, but I have no memory for names, not since I got so nearsighted."

"Ah, names," said a young woman with jet black hair and a
desolate expression. "I sometimes forget my own name, especially in a bank . . . it always happens in a bank. I suppose it is
because we have no money."

Gaby laughed and moved on. She was looking for Hopper
and he had disappeared and she had wanted him to meet . . .
now who was it? Well, it was somebody. . . . It was always
somebody . . . ahhhh . . . there he was and wouldn't you know
it, captivated by the femme fatale in the black velvet dress.
Gaby changed course. She wished she could remember names
better. Faces always, but never names. Now, who was that
woman with the red hair?

Kate would remember this night for the rest of her life. The
haze of smoke and a dizzying flood of blue-white lights, and a
tattoo of talk, punctuated by occasional screams of laughter.
She always remembered everything—names and faces always
matched, dates never eluded her, things like the clothes she
had worn or what she had said, the smallest details of her life,
even the most trifling, were catalogued in her memory ready
for instant recall. But in the years to come, for the life of her,

she could not remember why she had gone to that party or whom she had gone with. And that was odd because it had been the most important night of her life.

"Hopper, good to see you . . . do you know Kate Goodfellow? Kate, Hopper Delaney."

And there it was. Kate Goodfellow lifted her head and met Hopper's gaze.

"Kate Goodfellow." His voice was surprisingly soft for a man so big and the Southern drawl just enough to make her smile. He took her hand in both of his and held it for a moment, looking down at it curiously. "I should know your name," he said with real concern, "I should know you."

She could not help herself. She was flattered, as he had meant her to be. He let go of her hand and she was sorry. He turned smoothly to her partner. "You don't mind if I steal her away, do you?" And then, without consulting her, he took Kate's elbow and propelled her to a small alcove where his large frame blocked her view of anything else but him.

"Do you always behave this way?" she demanded to know. "As if I were waiting and ripe for the plucking?"

He smiled again, a lazy smile, and spoke in a soft drawl. "Always when the spirit moves me."

"That would be rather often, I should think. You seem very practiced."

"You seemed deeply interested. Don't forget that."

"I don't know what you're talking about."

"Yes, you do. Cigarette?"

She shook her head and then watched as he cupped his hand around the match and inhaled the blue smoke.

"You had the most alarmed and searching look just now when you turned around to see if I had come to you. Did you think I might not?"

"I simply don't know what you're talking about."

"You lie, Miss Goodfellow."

Kate heard herself saying coolly, "I knew you'd be insufferable."

Hopper laughed. "I've been called insufferable before but never with such conviction."

Kate laughed, too, and then she began to relax and to enjoy this chance meeting. He was looking at her now through half-closed eyes, and she felt her skin tingle in a delicious way and wondered if he might be thinking exactly the same thing she was thinking. She leaned back against the wall, glad she was at the right party wearing the right dress talking to the right man. It all might have gone exceedingly well had not Mallory Harwell clapped Hopper on the back and thus in-advertently and disastrously altered the delicate balance of wits between two bold egos.

"You're a photographer, Miss Goodfellow," said Mallory after exchanging the usual pleasantries. "I've seen your work . . . at the recent Artists' Congress exhibit? I guess Hopper's boring you with all the details of his next book . . . wants a photographer with him when he revisits the South . . . yes, a book, and nonfiction this time about all those things he wrote about in *The Road to Nowhere*. High time those . . ."

Hopper stirred uneasily. He had not known she was a photographer and he was sorry now to hear it. He watched the look on her face swiftly change from polite interest to alert attention. Like a jungle cat who smells a kill, she turned those intense green eyes on him once again, and he saw with dismay that she was ready to pounce.

A book! thought Kate. Such a book with Hopper Delaney would push her career exactly where she wanted it to go. On her own, it could take years to earn the kind of artistic credibility she now wanted, but with a name as big as Delaney's she would go straight to the forefront of the current documentary movement in photography. He was a hero in social reform.

"I'd like to show you my work, Mr. Delaney," she said, and he mumbled something about how he would like to see it. . . .

"When?" she demanded.

"Miss Goodfellow," he began wearily, "I'm not ready to make any commitment now. . . ."

She persisted. "I've thought of doing a book myself," she pressed, "because I have a great need to further engage my work in the social ferment. . . ." Hopper groaned inwardly. She was an amateur. He said he would think about it . . . he would let her know . . . perhaps at some later time. But a polite Southerner is no match for an ambitious Yankee. In the end he agreed, reluctantly, to meet with her again and to consider her for the job.

From that moment on she barraged everyone she knew to put in a good word with him. Otis Bennett, Mallory Harwell; she even wrote Eugene Winslow, anyone she could think of in publishing and the literary world who might further her cause. Hopper got stubborn—"Christ! She's in advertising!"—and sent word via Mallory that he didn't care for her brand of photography. She sent word back that neither did she and would he please look at her current work on the Dust Bowl and when could they meet again to talk. And because her work was good and because he could think of no other excuse, he agreed.

Now, waiting for her to arrive at his flat, Hopper Delaney was having severe second thoughts. The truth was he was reluctant to work with a woman. As if on cue, a vision of red hair appeared in his brain. She swam into his mind, filling it as if a sea wall had burst open. He did not want to work with anyone who made him feel in such a way. He did not like her. He did not trust her. In these past weeks she had made him feel uncomfortable, and Hopper did not like feeling uncomfortable with women. It was not what was supposed to happen. He had been attracted to this woman from afar, but up close he found her ambition and aggressiveness abrasive. Career women such as this Kate Goodfellow always made him nervous with their sharp edges and brittle talk. The idea of actually traveling for two months with such a woman was unthinkable. How could he parade her through the rural South? An unmarried man and an attractive, dynamic female traveling together? Would he have to eat his meals with her? Wouldn't the very fact of her being a woman and a Yankee antagonize the very people he was hoping would trust him enough to let him come into their lives? And yet for all of his misgivings he knew, without knowing outright, that this was predestined. He glanced at the clock. She was almost an hour late. Time and appointments were critical to him. Drifting to and fro in heedless disregard of obligations was the most annoying of professional habits. He fidgeted with a drawer stuck in his desk but gave up on it and wandered over to the large windows in his study and stared miserably out into the day.

Hopper lived in one of those nineteenth-century townhouses facing Gramercy Park; the kind of house that harkened back to a less hurried and more genteel New York. It was the perfect writer's lair—the furnishings comfortably shabby with a clutter of photographs, prints, paintings, memorabilia perched on the mantel and shelves and tables of the crowded room, some even propped up on the floor for lack of any place else to display them. Bookcases defined the space; an old desk and an even older Smith & Watson typewriter dominated the study. The light from the windows facing onto the gated park filtered through the air, musty from the slight blue haze of tobacco his tobacconist blended for him. A leather chair and a shaded Tiffany lamp completed the scene. The room reeked of the literary life.

Kate, whose notion of decor ran to severe modern design and then as little of it as possible, took in the clutter with one eagle-eyed sweep of her head and then made a little too much of a show trying to find a place to lay her coat. She shook his hand with a firm, single, purposeful shake. She was not inclined to sit in the chair he drew out for her, preferring, so she said, to stand.

"I think better standing," she announced. "Actually I think best of all when I'm moving about but"—she gave one more sweeping glance around the room and then shrugged—"please, you must sit." Hopper felt thrown off and annoyed. He sat himself firmly down behind his desk, where he at once felt safer from the locomotion of this woman. She seemed even prettier to him in her well-cut suit with a flat pancake of a hat perched over one eye than she had at the party. Her red hair calmed somewhat and rolled in a soft twist at the nape of her neck made him want to reach over and pluck out the tortoise hairpin so that it might fall free. It was all very disconcerting.

He offered her coffee, tea, a sherry? She declined. Then he said, with exaggerated politeness, how much he admired her work. She said nothing but nodded her head slightly in agreement with his assessment. This renewed his annoyance. Changing tone, he got down to business. Nevertheless, she must agree that her experience, despite the work she had done on the Dust Bowl, which, when all was said and done, rarely equaled the gravity of the subject and surely she knew, did not qualify her for the seriousness and scope of the project he meant to undertake. After all, commercial photography and tabloid photojournalism were her strongest suit and did not, he felt, qualify her to convey deep human emotion and social comment. Nevertheless . . .

He was maddening, thought Kate. And pompous. He seemed immune to her charms and stuck on his own urbanity. Nothing about him suggested the fire she perceived in his work, which was mystifying. It wasn't until later that she would learn that the very mildness he displayed was all part of his act. A disarming quirk in which he would fade, blend into a background of dullness, where he remained almost invisible until he had heard what he wanted to hear or experienced what he wanted to experience. She had never in her life come up against a man so hard to handle.

"Of course, I'm not expecting the photographs to carry the book," he droned on, "merely back up my observations, still . . ." Hopper stopped talking. She had turned away from him and was staring at something so intently he thought it might be a snake. Instinctively, he got up from his desk and came around behind her, his eye following hers to a stuffed raccoon placed under a table and so alive-looking that it seemed ready to scurry out. The raccoon was one of the few boyhood treasures he had brought North and something he had grown to regard as his mascot and good-luck charm. "Oh, don't mind that little fellow." He laughed. "That's my touchstone. Why, he's seen me through more writer's blocks than I can count. An old Negro gave him to me when I was about ten and said he had magic in him. I swear I think he does. . . ."

Hopper was just warming to his story, but Kate pirouetted around, one hand on her hip. "Mr. Delaney, I have another appointment at four and I haven't much time." His face darkened. "I'm sorry," she said with instant sweetness. "I'm sure it's a lovely story and I'd love to hear it some other time because I want to hear everything you can tell me about the South. I just want you to know I am more excited by the prospect of this book than anything I have worked on for the past four years. I'm ready to wholly devote my time and talent to social documentary. I have a very deep desire to enter into people's lives with the camera. Perhaps we could talk about scheduling? I understand you would like to spend two months? I can clear my calendar for July and August."

"Ma'am, it is obvious you've never been in Mississippi or Georgia in July and August. You can cut the heat with a dull knife." She was going to exasperate him, he could tell. *Her* time, *her* scheduling?

"You can? It sounds perfect for our purposes. We want the Deep South in all its torrid torment. The hotter, the better, I say."

We? Our? Whose book was this anyway? "I think we should talk this through, Miss Goodfellow—"

"Please." She leaned toward him so that suddenly and quite surprisingly he found he was only inches from her face, staring into gray-green eyes with yellow speckles in them that bounced light as if they were tiny stars. The scent of her so close filled his nostrils. She smiled brightly. "Don't you think we might get on a first-name basis? If we're to be partners in crime, that is?"

"Why . . . why yes, of course. Please call me Hopper . . . most of my friends call me Hop . . . whatever . . ." Damn. Why was she making him stutter so?

They held together for a moment, caught in the narrow space that was actually no space at all. She forced herself to remain bland. Poise was a thing she had developed, a thing she could wrap around her like a shawl. She refused to look like a woman whose heart had nearly jumped out of her chest. Other women might melt, she would not. "Okay. Where were we . . . July?"

"June and July." He snapped on his professional mantle and returned to his desk. He was definite. "I want a clear two months. I don't want to hurry this thing, but I'm fairly certain of where I want to go and what I want photographed. We'll be traveling by car and you'll have to travel light. I warn you, conditions can be pretty crude. I expect stamina. There will be no fancy frills. I'll want to see your work from time to time, so you'll have to figure the logistics on making prints or contact sheets or whatever it is you do so that I can see. I don't know how you photographers work, but that's not my problem."

Kate's face was impassive but mentally she was grinning ear to ear. He had forgotten he did not think her qualified for the *seriousness and scope of the project he meant to undertake*. As far as she could tell, she was on. She saw that he regarded the book as his, her contribution only an adjunct. Well, okay, she would let that pass for now. He looked quite adorable sitting there behind his desk with his stuffed raccoon.

"No. It is certainly not your problem," she said, reaching for her coat to signal it was time to go. "I'm looking forward to working with you, and, trust me, you will be very happy with my work. I have a feeling about this book, a strong and good feeling." She swept the coat over her shoulders before he could come around from behind the desk to hold it for her. The hand she now held out to him was warm and the look she gave him was also warm. Hopper relaxed with the familiar ease he always felt when the opposite sex had been won over. There was no reason why this shouldn't be a very interesting summer—just so long as she knew her place—and apparently, from the shift in mood, she did.

CHAPTER TWENTY

It was a mistake from the beginning and Hopper knew it. When he got to the hotel in Clarksdale, Mississippi, the designated meeting point, some fifty miles south of Memphis, there was a telegram stating she would arrive a week later than planned. He was furious. There was no explanation, no apology. Peggy King went immediately to the hotel operator and got her to put through a call to the Goodfellow Studio. The girl at the switchboard with the very long, pink nails and the name Flora emblazoned on the lapel of her seersucker dress went into a dither, having never placed a call to New York City before. To make matters worse, the New York operator couldn't understand a word she was saying.

"Ah sed," said Flora for the third time, "Ranlandah fo-uh, nan, seban, fo-uh . . . no, ma'am . . . that's Ran-landa . . . fo-uh . . ." In exasperation Hopper grabbed her headset directly off her head and shouted the name and number down the mouthpiece in so loud and rude a voice that the New York operator hung up on him. Peggy led him outside. It was an old hotel, and like hundreds of old hotels in the South, it was graced with a sagging front porch with large wooden rocking chairs on which to sit and view the dusty Main Street.

"Sit here, Hopper. I'm going to get you a cold Coke from the drugstore. I'll be right back."

"Damn her" was all Hopper had to say to that.

Peggy King was Hopper's answer to traveling alone with Kate Goodfellow. She was signed on as secretary, but in reality she was his shield. The third person at meals, the buffer where accommodations might be less than private. Peggy had been a short affair when he had been in Washington for the Senate hearings. She was a no-nonsense sort of career gal from West Virginia, had worked on Capital Hill and knew her way around the labyrinth of government. She had been immensely helpful to Hopper in his quest to reach the ears of the Senate over the plight of the poor in the South and downright maternal when his voice had all but been drowned out by the Southern politician who declared, "Mistah Delaney has a big imagination. Folks in my state get along jes' fine if you leave 'em alone and don't go stirrin' 'em up."

Well, here they were sitting on the steps of a run-down hotel on a hot morning in June, and nothing was "jes' fine" at all. Peggy, who would have admitted, if anyone had asked, that she was more than a little bit in love with Hopper, had a pretty good idea that a working partnership between Hopper Delaney and Kate Goodfellow would be a tough mix. She knew about Kate from various sources and contacts in business, and, frankly, she didn't like the sound of her at all. Of course, a lot of that had to do with the fact that Kate was just the sort of woman that other women loved to hate; independent, on the fast track to success, men rumored to fall all over themselves just to touch the hem of her skirt. Peggy soothed Hopper, saying all the right things about it must be some dreadful problem, that he mustn't jump to conclusions, that very likely . . . blah, blah, blah, all the while secretly enjoying the fact that her words were having little effect on Hopper's temper.

Kate was not in her studio when the call from Clarksdale finally came through. She was in the lobby of the Loew's movie theater on Broadway, having investigated every fountain in New York and decided that this one was the most suitable new home for her collection of turtles (the alligators having been sent to the Central Park Zoo). At the very moment that Hopper was shouting his frustration down the long-distance wires into Virginia's ears, Kate was stalking the grandiose three-tiered replica of an Italian Renaissance palace, waiting for a moment no one seemed to be looking. The moment came, she hurried up to the splendid fountain, and slipped in her reptilian trio. And then, tears in her eyes—for she had loved her turtles who had lived under her desk, bumped into her legs, and taken lettuce leaves from her noonday sandwiches for the past year—she hurried out into the lovely June day.

Only a week before she had given notice to the management of the Chrysler Building and that morning signed a contract with *World* magazine. Somewhere in New Jersey an inventor not unlike her father had finally come up with a fast-drying ink that would revolutionize halftone printing on high-speed presses. While this accomplishment might not have made the headlines, or even the footnotes, in *The New York Times,* it had galvanized Otis Bennett. At long last he was finally to realize his dream of a photography magazine for the populace, and Kate was one of four photographers signed to his staff.

It was a heady moment for both of them. There would be no constraints on her. The magazine would cover news and human interest with equal fervor. There had never been anything like it before. The first issue would roll off press some six months hence. In the meantime, she would close down her studio and fulfill the commitment to Hopper Delaney. To do this in one week was already taxing her levels of efficiency to the hilt, and she was stunned with indignation when finally that afternoon Hopper's ire caught up with her.

"But what are you so angry about?" she wailed into the phone. "We made our agreement two months ago. So much has happened—surely I can make you understand. You see, Otis is moving ahead with his new magazine and he's moving fast. I've signed on as a staff photographer—exclusive. I'm closing the studio . . . now, wait, just hold on a minute . . . there are a thousand details I have to see to, and I simply couldn't leave New York without clearing up my affairs. It wouldn't have done you or me any good. I want to come to the book project with a sense of serenity so the ideas can flow without me worrying over niggling details." She listened to more sputtering on the other end.

"How could I explain all that in a telegram? For goodness' sake, it's just a week! What . . . ?" Kate suddenly sat down, she was so shocked. "Why, what in the world are you saying?"

What Hopper said, his words icy with disdain was "It's all off, Miss Goodfellow."

"Off? What do you mean 'off'?"

"Precisely that. At least it is off until some other time when it would be more convenient for all parties." His words dripped with sarcasm.

It was Kate's turn to be furious. "Now, you listen to me, Mr. Hopper Delaney. I can't believe I'm hearing this. I've been planning for this trip for eight weeks! I've been reading and studying and talking to anyone who will talk to me. I'm ready to go. My bags are packed, and then suddenly Otis Bennett decides to move ahead on his new magazine and . . . oh, for goodness' sake! What have I done wrong? It seems to me not unreasonable that a date made months ago could be just a little bit elastic. You can't wreck an entire plan just because of a postponement of a few days! Be reasonable."

"I consider myself very reasonable" came the answer over the wires. Then there was a long silence. "You have three days to get here. That's it." His voice was brusque—and then the line went dead.

Kate was beside herself with frustration and anger. *She* did not take orders. *She* was not spoken to by anyone in that tone of voice. Did he not know whom he was talking to? Did he think he could get along without her? His precious book would have no impact at all without her photographs, of that she was sure. She wished he weren't a thousand miles away. She wished she could stand right up to that arrogant bastard and give him a piece of her mind. Reasonable! Three days wasn't reasonable. It was an insult. She paced about the studio, already in chaos with packing boxes and three temporary clerks working under Virginia trying to file and mark her equipment and papers.

Within minutes she started to calm down, reasoning with herself. There was no way she could let this project slip through her fingers. It was just too important to her plan. Of the four photographers on staff at *World,* the other three were men, all of them exceedingly experienced in photojournalism. Two had come from Europe, where they had been working for similar magazines for years. The third ranked among the most artistic and talented in the profession. All three were names to be reckoned with. If she were to insure that she would not be given the "women's" assignments, she needed the prestige of a book. This alone would verify her expertise in issues of social importance, despite her experience. Everything depended on her collaboration with Hopper Delaney. She could not bear to have such a brilliant idea die stillborn. She had no choice but to get herself down to Mississippi in the time allotted her. Well, okay, she would grovel and obey orders—but only once. She would do whatever it took to get her photographs into his book, and then she would see about Mr. Hopper Delaney. Oh, wouldn't she!

They met on the porch of the hotel exactly three days later eyeing each other like two bull terriers. Then Hopper asked her if she would like a cup of coffee. She nodded and followed him into the lobby. It was a hot day, and the steamy canopy of heat settled over everything like a cloying blanket. The only stirring in the humid air was to be found under the overhead fans in the hotel lobby, but to Kate there was magic in the heavily scented air. The hotel itself had seen its best days in a bygone era. Now it emitted the romantic ambience of sultry decay. It was like a stage set, she thought, a set right out of Hopper's play, complete with the scent of a flower she couldn't name. She was aware of the stares she got from the bellboy and the telephone operator, and she treated them to a wide and open smile. Kate was dressed head to toe in white linen, as if she were traveling in the tropics. Hopper sat down on the counter stool of the coffee shop and ordered two cups of coffee. Staring straight ahead, he drank the black liquid down to the last drop, then he looked at her.

"I don't like arguments."

She nodded meekly. There was a silence, then, "When do we leave?"

"Now." His hand came down on the counter with command. She grinned and was happy to see the faintest smile hover on his lips.

When they walked outside again, a soft damp breeze touched her like a moist palm, making her sleepy and pleasurably aware she was somewhere else. And she was. Mississippi was alien territory; a land with a smell and pace and character all its own.

"What's that scent?" she asked, stopping at the top of the steps to breathe deeply.

Hopper, a few paces ahead stopped, too, perhaps taking a moment to fall under its exotic spell himself. "Jasmine."

Jasmine. She thrilled to the sound. It was all around her, clinging like a vine, enchanting her senses.

The enchantment was almost immediately broken. She had not reckoned on Peggy King. Hopper left her on the porch to bring around the car, and suddenly there was a female voice and an outstretched hand. Peggy was enjoying Kate's surprise and chagrin. "I've heard so much about you and your work, Miss Goodfellow—or shall we go to first names right off since we'll all be together for such a long time? Agreed? Good. I see you calmed the beast down." Peggy said this with just a little bit too much possessiveness, and Kate's eyes narrowed in annoyance. "He's really wonderful to work with. I know." Again the cozy familiarity. "Goodness, but you do have a great deal of luggage."

They both looked at the mound of cases and leather bags that were piled on the edge of the porch. Indeed she had. The townspeople from one end of the short main street to the other had all gathered to see the largest stack of assorted baggage they had ever known to be packed away in a single automobile. As soon as Hopper came to a stop, Peggy took charge. She supervised a small squad of Negro boys as they tucked valises, cameras, lighting equipment, film, and tripods into every inch of the car except the front seat. She made sure there was a nook in the backseat amidst the towers of baggage. It suddenly dawned on Kate that someone was going to have to sit back there, and from the smug look on this Peggy King's face, that someone was meant to be Kate herself.

Hopper got into the driver's seat and then, just as Peggy was about to climb into the front, Kate blocked her way and said, "No. You sit in the back. I have to talk to Hopper. We have a lot of planning to do, and it won't do for me to be shouting from the rear." And with that she pulled the seat forward and indicated with a regal wave of her hand for Peggy to climb in. Peggy bristled, but one look at Hopper told her he was no match for Kate, and so she elbowed one of the cases roughly away from her and wriggled into the tiny space she had allotted the backseat passenger. They set off in stony silence and a cloud of dust, leaving behind the fine citizens of Clarksdale, who would, no doubt, talk about this for weeks.

The route was to take them south along Highway 1, passing through small "blink" towns, anonymous down-on-their-luck affairs filled with shotgun shacks, low-slung bungalows, and sagging porches. Men, mostly colored, in overalls, either sat or stood in clusters at local feed stores. Mules hitched to wagons were everywhere. There were few women to be seen except the old grannies shelling peas in porch rockers and children hanging over tire swings in dusty junk-strewn yards. The Mississippi River did its snaky shuffle behind a continuous line of levees, with bayous and lakes formed by the past indirections of floods. The plan was to head south hugging the river roads, then turn east and cut across the middle of Mississippi, through Jackson toward Alabama and Georgia. Along about nine in the evening, Hopper stopped in Yazoo City at a hotel that looked almost exactly like the one they had left behind. Kate would learn that almost every hotel in the South looked as if it had been designed and built by the same man—a sort of Johnny Appleseed of hostelry.

By the next night, her romantic notions and enchanted feelings were beginning to crumble like the fallen-down ante bellum mansions she saw dotted along the route. The monotony of cotton fields in the Delta gave way to the monotony of scrub pine and dusty farms in the interior. It was hot, that was for sure, and there were precious few gentle breezes. The car was not new, but it was comfortable. It was a deep blue roadster with soft, tan leather seats. They rode with the top down until the high heat of the day, during which they either parked in the shade of a tree or abandoned traveling altogether for a hotel verandah and lemonade. The plan was to have no plan—to just go and see what there was to see. Peggy wore a light traveling suit, high heels, and a hat, which was the usual and proper attire for a woman. Kate wore something that looked like a cross between a safari costume and a riding habit. She had tied a purple bandanna around her long, slim neck and on her head she wore a vintage British pith helmet that looked delightfully absurd. Hopper caught on very quickly that she liked people to stare at her—and stare they did. The effect of this little entourage—one man and two pretty women, one of them looking more suited to the back of an elephant, a car piled with luggage, on the dusty back roads of the rural South—was a mind-boggling sight to the destitute sharecroppers and field hands along the way. When the group stopped to interview people and take pictures, they were regarded with awe and wonder.

Everything Kate saw she wanted to photograph, but Hopper dismissed most of her ideas. When they did stop, invariably the light was all wrong or the sense of what they had stopped for escaped her. After four days Kate realized she was in trouble. Things were not going her way—not at all. For one thing, though she asked a million questions, she couldn't get the answers she wanted out of Hopper. He answered her questions, and quite politely, too, but the point of the project remained an enigma. She had to know how he saw the broader outlines of the book before she could begin to realize the visuals. Working with someone else was not an easy task for her—in advertising as with *The Express,* she had been the star and everyone had bowed to her expertise. To her credit she kept her mounting frustration and irritation under wraps. Besides, she didn't want to give smug Peggy the satisfaction of knowing just how very worried she was, so she tried to relax and absorb what was going on around her. She saw broken-down cars and broken-down people. She saw colored children in the cotton fields, some still in diapers. She saw mule-drawn carts and stiff redneck farmers going to market. She saw women behind the plow dressed in tattered cotton dresses and wearing bonnets fashioned from newspapers. Mostly she saw a defeated people trapped in the confines of their shacks and shanties. Nobody smiled much—only the children, who by the grace of God were as yet unbeaten by the hardships, giggled and pestered her with their naturally inquisitive nature. They wanted to touch her equipment or stare up at the fire-haired lady in the funny clothes.

What she came to realize in the first week was that Hopper was moving through his natural element. The eroded red-clay earth and the ravages of hungry human beings was territory he had known since he was a child. She, on the other hand, was on strange turf. She needed to probe it and discover it for herself, but this she was not allowed to do. Hopper had planned his book precisely. He knew exactly what he was going to say and had a strong inner vision of how it should be illustrated, yet no matter how hard she tried, she could not get him to translate his thoughts to her.

When she made suggestions, he would listen to them politely and then maddeningly say, "That's not what I'm after."

When she demanded to know what it was he was after, he would say, "I'm not the photographer; that's your job." And so she would take pictures, hundreds of them, hoping that out of sheer quantity would come the quality that both of them were looking for. Peggy was, needless to say, no help.

Only that morning they had stopped and Kate had been encouraged by what had taken place. Quite excited, really, because at last she had been allowed inside one of the tenant shacks and the man, the farmer, had given permission for Kate to take pictures of his wife. It had to be just right. She took out her large camera—a beauty of a thing in a polished wood box with gleaming brass fixtures, and screwed in onto the heavy tripod. The camera lens was too wide, so she unscrewed it and placed it back in the velvet-lined case. Then she took out a smaller lens from a similar case and screwed it on. After placing the tripod and camera inside the two rooms that comprised the whole of the house, she began to experiment with composition. Light was a problem. She taped a piece of muslin over the window so the sunlight filtering through was not so harsh. She moved the tripod inches to the left and readjusted the legs. She lowered the camera five inches. Now a few inches to the right. She set the aperture and held the light meter to the woman's face. Something was wrong. Kate stepped back again and peered through the lens. The woman stared at her impassively, her expression never changing. Kate stood back and squinted her eyes at the scene once more. Then she reached over and deftly moved the objects on the dresser behind the woman, repositioning a cracked mirror against the wall so that the objects were reflected in it. It was that simple. The broken perfume bottles, the comb with its chipped teeth, the tattered doily; now they were mirrored, and the effect was even more poignant. Kate adjusted her light reflectors. Perfect. Kate smiled and told the woman not to move, although it was not necessary. She had not moved once since Kate had asked her to stand in front of the dresser. She bent her head once more to the viewfinder. She fine-tuned the focus. Now she had exactly what she wanted and she pushed the plunger of the shutter release.

She was elated, but an hour or so later, after they had driven away, she knew something was wrong. Hopper looked grim. Kate tried talking to Peggy about the shot, but Peggy was as unforthcoming as Hopper.

"What's going on here?" Kate finally said, peering from one sullen face to the other. "I'd like to know why you're both so moody."

Hopper was silent. He was always silent in the face of her demanding tone.

"Look, I can't work this way. It's like working in a complete void. I've done something you don't like, but you won't tell me what it is. Tell me what I need to know. Talk to me."

"All right, then," he said mournfully, as if he had been expecting this all along. "From now on I'll tell you what to take and when to take it. I've watched you work, and I think you're missing the whole spirit of this thing."

"Please explain that." Kate could feel herself bristling.

"Hell, if I have to explain it to you, it isn't worth it."

"You're upset and you won't tell me why. The picture I just took is brilliant. I know it. I can feel it."

"And what do you feel? A posed study of a woman's face isn't what I'm after. I'm looking for the truth and the truth of that woman's face is dignity in the midst of futility. You're scaring people. You're bossin' them around. Making 'em pose this way and that, then staring at them like they were bugs or something. The whole thing feels like one of your ads."

Kate flared. "What do you think good photographs are? A snapshot on the run? A picture doesn't just happen. You have to wait for it, look at it from the point of view of the light and the composition."

He let out a breath of impatience and gripped the wheel of the car even tighter. "Now, there's a word—*composition*. Christ almighty, you take an old, tired-out sharecropping woman who's picked cotton since she was four years old, who's never had anything in her life but sickness and hard work but who, by sheer force, has kept the barest flame of her feminine nature alive by collecting a few cheap gewgaws and put them on what passes for her dresser. And without asking that woman, you move those broken bits of china and that cracked mirror and bottles filled with colored water this way or that way because you've got to get COMPOSITION!" He was so angry his face had gone to a dangerous red. He jerked the wheel and pulled the car to a stop. Then he turned to her, and Kate saw that there were tears in his eyes. "Don't you see? Those were her things. Maybe the only pretty things she's ever had. She's arranged them the way she wants them arranged. You've altered her ways to suit yourself. There's no truth in what you do."

The silence that followed was painful to them all. For once, Peggy didn't relish the discomfort Kate was in and Kate was in real distress. What had she done! What had she done! Why, she had done nothing but put the tall glass bottles to one side of the woman's head. Placed in such a way they caught the light that filtered in through the waxed paper windows so that it spilled across the dresser in a million tiny fragments. The woman had watched her in silence, but so intently that Kate had said, "There now, I think this looks better, don't you? You see, it makes the composition so much better." And it had! She knew the picture was going to be good. The light had been just right. It had taken her an hour to set up her reflectors inside the small, dark room because she had to light the back of the woman's head so it wouldn't come out flat and dull. And the dresser was behind her and it had to be just right. He didn't understand photography. That was the problem.

"Come off it, Hopper. You're a writer. Do you write cold copy? No. You write and rewrite. You compose and edit just as I do. The big difference is you go off to a room somewhere by yourself and you are left to yourself to manipulate your words. And you have all the time in the world to do so. I don't. I'm out there on the firing line with everyone looking on while I try to get at the heart of it. Listen. I understand what you're saying, but I'm not trying to please that woman back there.

What she thinks or doesn't think isn't the point. I'm trying to wake up a sleeping world to the issues of poverty and despair. If I think I can do that better by rearranging a woman's dresser, then so be it."

He looked at her hard. "You take over."

"Of course I take over. I have a vision. I make things fit to what I see in my mind. There is an energy in what I do. A power that takes over. Art is not replicating; it's creating."

"I'm not going to sit here and argue with you. Our work is over for today." And then, in a supremely masculine gesture, he drew himself up and stonewalled the expression on his face, threw the car in gear, made a U-turn, and headed back to town.

Kate could barely talk. She sputtered. "I . . . I don't understand you at all. I feel locked into some struggle for control, and I don't see why it has to be this way. After all, we are two professionals and we've both got the same purpose in mind—to make an important social document. Isn't that what we talked about? From the very first night I met you, we talked about the importance of such a book. You said this book was going to shake up the country. Well, fat chance—if I can't do my half the way I see fit." They rode in silence all the way back to the hotel, which was, as usual, no different from the others, but at least Kate had a large front room with a huge shade tree just outside her window. She went immediately there, undressed, ran a cool bath, and tried to calm down.

The bath, and the sweet-smelling salts she put in it, served to relax the tension of the day. Breathing a sigh of contentment as the muscles in her neck uncoiled, she closed her eyes so that she could review the situation. She organized her thoughts in a neat grid in her mind, beginning with how right she was for the job. She was one of the best photographers in the business. Otis Bennett thought so. The Artists' Congress thought so. That ought to lend a little weight with Mr. Holier-Than-Thou. She loved this job, loved the idea of it, wanted to succeed at it. Conclusion. The problem was not her; it was him! What, then, was *his* problem? He persisted in putting her down. Why? Was it only because they had gotten off on the wrong foot, or was it some deep-seated male prejudice that didn't want a woman meddling in his work? Or maybe it was just a supremely inflated ego that couldn't stand a shared spotlight. Well, she had been putting up with the male ego all her life, and over the years she had learned how to deal with it. She had learned to listen to them talk, hang breathlessly on their words, rapt in attention, to flirt without promising too much. And she had learned that armed with a few of these techniques and a good face and body, she could do pretty much what she pleased with men. Still, it was frustrating to have to play games. It wasted her time. She sighed. Hopper Delaney, like all men, would have to be handled.

Maybe Peggy King had something to do with her problem with Hopper. Kate sank down lower in the tub and lazily ran soapy hands across her breasts and down her tummy. Why was Peggy along anyway? Yes, she took notes when Hopper talked to people, but he had an uncanny memory for conversation. He could, at the end of the day, recite verbatim whole chunks of conversation and dialogue. His ear was as fine-tuned as the most delicate of musical instruments to shifts in accent and colloquialism. Peggy was excess baggage. Were they lovers? Were they, even now, in his bed down the hall? Was she comforting him and shoring up his high opinion of himself?

She let the drip from the faucet fall between her toes. It tickled. She remembered one time when she had been so tired at the end of a particularly difficult shoot and Eugene had made her lie in a hot tub while he rubbed her feet with cream. She had never known how sexually tuned the feet were. Eugene had told her that the Chinese considered the feet a sexual organ, the main sexual organ. And he had proved it.

She sank still lower in the tub and allowed her hands to trail over her body under the water now silky with the scented salts and soap. It was nice to be tall and slender. It was good to have skin that only needed light cream and hair that looked best when it was loose and free and not permed and done up to look like a doll's wig, like Peggy's blond hair that was crimped and waved. There was no other woman on earth she wanted to be but herself, and that was nicest of all.

A sharp rapping at the door shook her from her reverie. Hopper announced himself from the other side of the door and instantly Kate was out of the tub. He didn't want to disturb her, he said, but he needed to talk to her. Kate grabbed at a towel and called out that she was just getting out of the bath and could he come back in a few minutes. There was a pause before he agreed. She could hear his footsteps going back down the hall. She shook her head in swift and sudden revelation. This man and Peggy were not lovers. If she knew anything, she knew when two people were having an affair. Theirs was at best only a lukewarm friendship. What would solve her problem? Get rid of the odious Peggy and make the collaboration work in harmony? What would turn this ogre into a lamb? What indeed! It was so simple a solution she laughed out loud.

A few minutes later, when Hopper was allowed to enter her room, Kate was in bed with a filmy silk nightgown held up by only the barest shoestring straps. She had closed the shutters and the room was pleasantly cool and dim. Hopper stood for a moment and then, acutely uncomfortable, apologized for disturbing her and turned to go.

"Oh, no, you're not disturbing me," she said quickly. "I just wanted to lie down after today. I'm so sorry for upsetting you. I shouldn't have spoken to you that way. I was upset, too, but I've thought about what you said and I see that you're right. It's just a new point of view for me. I want to learn from you. I really do. I think you're an excellent teacher."

"I'm no teacher, Kate. And I don't intend to become one. Now that I'm here I think I should say what I came to say. What happened today was only one of a series of things I've found that are jeopardizing the work. It's not that you're wrong, it's that you're wrong for this project. I don't think we're getting anything accomplished, do you? Certainly with all the squabbling we're not. I want to stop the project for now, maybe rethink the whole thing." His voice was very soft and gentle, but Kate heard the steel of it underneath.

"No." She felt her throat constrict so her words came out more of a gasp. "I can't let you do this. Don't you see how much this all means? I don't think I've ever worked on anything that meant so much. If I haven't done what you want up to now, please don't abandon me. I can do anything, I will do anything you want. I . . . I'm so used to doing things my way, that I've forgotten how to listen. But I will, I promise you, from now on."

"I'm sorry, but my mind is made up." He wouldn't look at

her. "You and I don't have the kind of temperaments that jibe. It hasn't been right from the start. When we first met, you said, 'Tell me about the South. I want to know everything.' That's the problem. I can't tell you about the South. I can't tell you what to see. You have to feel it inside. You have to know in your gut what it's all about. I've felt like a tour guide just showing you around."

"But don't you see that's good?" The strap on her nightgown fell down, but she didn't seem to notice. "Our book is going to have to show people what it's like down here. Most of the people in this country, like me, don't know. You've got to make me feel about it as you do. You've got to work with me as if I were the whole rest of the country. This is your territory and the rest of us *are* only tourists. This is our opportunity to do something worthwhile and you can't"—she had started to cry—"you can't end it."

Hopper looked distressed. He walked to the window and stared through the wide slats of the drawn blinds. Kate was out of bed in a flash and by his side. She just stood there, and then she reached up to touch his shoulder. "Oh, God. What can I do? What can I do to change your mind?"

He turned. For a moment he seemed to resist her, but she was so close to him, and in an instant he had pulled her into his arms. He was surprised at the feel of her—soft, so soft like a kitten—and warm and sweet-smelling from the bath. He could feel her nakedness in his arms with only the thin satin gown between his fingers and her flesh. Her body was surprisingly round and full of curves. This he had not expected. Her face was so angular that he had imagined her body the same way—hard and sharp and aggressive—but it wasn't. Her breasts felt full and round like the ripe summer melons of his imagination. Her waist tucked in just above a wonderfully round expanse of hips and buttocks.

"My God," he breathed. "You're a woman after all."

"Did you ever doubt it?" came a teasing answer.

He gripped her tighter. Come to think of it, he had never doubted it. He had been thinking of her this way all along, only he hadn't admitted it.

Kate gave a small breathless laugh and pushed away from him so that she could look him in the face. The question still hung in the air, but the look on his face told her what she wanted to know. She moved back to him, smiling, a little like a cat about to lap a bowl of cream.

Things were moving very well. Up to that moment things were moving exactly as she had envisioned. She liked him, liked the strength in his arms and the passion in his eyes. She allowed her head to fall back so that he could kiss her, and she wanted him to kiss her. She wanted him just as much as he wanted her.

"Look at me," he growled. "Open your damn eyes."

She did, a little surprised. "Now listen to me." He shook her a little as he said this. "I know all about you, and I know all about flimsy nightgowns and perfume and crying to get your way. This isn't about having your way or my way. This is about something else. Understand?"

"Wait a minute . . ." she sputtered, pushing at him hard, but he didn't budge. "You think I planned this? You've got the most inflated, horrendous ego I've ever encountered. What's more, you're . . . you're . . ." She couldn't think of anything mean enough to say to him.

"I'm what," he said roughly, the briefest smile hovering on his lips.

They kissed and kissed over and over again. It was all sensations—liquid and fiery sensations that moved inside and drove them on. She reached her arms around his neck and fought to hold him as tightly as he was holding her. He felt good. It was good. She felt the walls she had built around her come tumbling down, not realizing until that moment how very strong and very high she had built them. He picked her up and carried her to the bed. She watched him as he took off his clothes. His chest was broad and strong as if he was some sort of trained athlete, and he was surprisingly slender, something his clothes and the broadness of his shoulders had disguised. His eyes were black with intensity and his hair fell over his forehead as he came into her arms once more. He held himself just above her and moved against her chest and belly with infinite grace and strength. She was trembling all over with pent-up need and something else—a fantastic desire to lose all control, to give of herself in a way she never had. She raised her hips and he came down hard inside her.

She was on fire with him and she felt something stir deep like a shiver. This was not like the kind of sex she had ever had before. It did not seem to be about playing clever games or scoring conquests or falling in love or having a good time. It was about something old and primitive. It was about a longing so deep that until now she had had no idea it resided in her body or mind. Being here with this man was about finding a place, about finding out about something she needed but never knew she wanted. And she wanted more.

Over and over again her body rose to an explosive level, but he would not let her have the relief she desperately wanted. His control over her was complete, and she realized that this was all part of what she wanted, for she could not fully surrender herself without trusting his control. He was waiting for her trust. At last she was beyond thinking about anything except the two of them and the edge which they clung to before the tremendous leap into space.

They did not speak for a long time afterward but lay in each other's arms heavy in the aftermath of passion, in the heat of the late afternoon, in the dim light. Overhead the fan made languid circles, throwing small, steady puffs of air on their bodies, drying the sweat and sending tiny, tingling shivers scurrying over the surface of the skin. Through the slats at the windows, a golden light fell on the dark wood floors and crept ever so slowly across the room as the sun sank outside. She could hear stirring from the hotel kitchen out back and someone singing and the soft accents of men and women calling to each other as they headed home for the evening or greeted each other on the verandah below her window.

"What do we do now?" she asked in a hushed, reverent voice.

Hopper rolled over and lay on his back. "Do? I think we can do anything we want to. We can sleep. We can talk. We can smoke. We can dance a jig on the windowsill." He reached down to the floor and felt around for his trousers. "I'm going to smoke. You?"

"I don't smoke. I've tried it over and over, but it makes me choke. I used to think to be a true woman of the world you had to smoke. My mother smoked. She had the most delicious way of plucking the tiny bit of tobacco off the tip of her tongue. I used to sit on the floor when I was little and watch her, waiting for just that moment. I think that was my very first experience of waiting for the perfect visual moment."

"That's funny. I don't think of you as having a mother . . . or a father. You're Athena burst full-grown from the head of Zeus, red hair streaming in every direction, your camera as your sword."

Kate laughed. "I like that image."

"I do, too. It suits you. And in many ways your camera is like a sword. You can smite the enemy with it better than any sword."

"What's this? A plug for photography?"

"Sure. The camera is the most convincing witness to what ails the world. The trouble is seeing it in just the right way. You can't photograph the thing itself, you have to see the in-betweenness of things. A human face holds very little unless you know its history. You have to start by knowing what a man holds in his heart—or what a woman believes to be true."

Kate propped her head up on her hand and turned to face him. "But how can I know all that? That's the writer talking again. Seems to me a writer's strong suit is the ability to work over a period of time, honing his skills, researching, dredging his memory, going after things like a miner prospecting for gold. A writer has time on his side. But a photographer doesn't. That photograph of the black blizzard . . . it came out of the sky, it was there, I was there, I grabbed the camera and shot."

"Fair enough, but let me ask you this: Would you have been capable of getting the pictures you did afterward of the cattle dying and the women digging out the school and the funeral for the boy if you hadn't experienced the blizzard yourself?"

"Yes, of course. I agree that to understand the human condition, you have to understand what forces brought on that condition but there's also a simple matter of gut reaction. The heart has eyes, too."

"To see is not enough," he said, stubbing out the cigarette. "You have to know how to look."

"I disagree . . ." She sat up. The color was beginning to climb in her cheeks. "There's such a thing as the natural instinct. I know when something is right. I know it! There's something that happens . . . when I'm looking through the lens something else starts to happen. It's like the whole world slips away and it's just me and the thing I'm going after. It's almost . . . like sex. It's that intense. It's . . . it's . . ."

He had pulled her to him again. "Like sex. Like this." He was teasing her with his hands and his kisses. She resisted, wanting to talk, wanting to make him see, understand, but it was no use. The edges of her points no longer held and she couldn't remember what was so important about it in the first place. Sensations flowed over her like waves. She caught her breath sharply as she felt his fingers on her nipples—strong, square hands cupped her breasts and she cried out from the pleasure of it. The sensations became more and more jumbled—his tongue, wet, everywhere—her neck, breast, down her belly—her thighs parted and a huge wave caught her up and lifted her to the crest so that she begged him to enter her. He was hard inside her, and they rolled and plunged until once more she exploded into a thousand tiny fragments.

Afterward they both felt a little sheepish. "Do you think we made a terrible racket?" Kate whispered. The hotel walls were thin and the bedsprings groaned at the slightest movement.

"Fearful," he confirmed. "Most likely they're going to run us out of town for disturbing the peace."

"Good. I haven't seen anybody running since I got down here," said Kate, and Hopper roared with laughter.

"Lesson number one on Southern living: keep the pace slow and real lazy like. We're going to turn you into a Magnolia Blossom yet."

They never went down to dinner. They talked late into the night. The next morning they went downstairs hand in hand. The manager came over to them, and, not looking at Kate, he handed Hopper a note. It was from Peggy. It read, *Dear Hopper, Looks like three adds up to too many. The backseat was crowded enough as it was—good luck. Peggy.*

"Your friend checked out real early, Mr. Delaney," said the desk clerk. "She caught the 5:08 to Atlanta."

"Oh, dear," said Hopper.

"Oh, dear," echoed Kate with a satisfied smile.

They looked at each other and laughed. It was the laugh of two people who shared a secret. Two people who stood on the brink of an adventure and the adventure was themselves.

CHAPTER TWENTY-ONE

AND SO THEY proceeded on their own down the dusty back roads of Mississippi, Alabama, and into Georgia. Kate discovered that rather than a man of silence, Hopper was a great talker. His stories seemed to overflow. He was a happy man, a pilgrim come home. He told her about himself, the ways of his people, his favorite foods. He told her ghost stories and legends he had grown up with. They talked about religion and books and art. They talked about food and sex and told each other secrets and were astonished and tremendously pleased when the other confessed to the same weakness or sin or wicked cynicism. He called her Magnolia and she tried every nickname she could think of but could never come up with one that fit. So she called him Hop just as all his friends did, but somehow made it hers. Sometimes as they drove they sang, both of them, at the top of their voices with the wind whipping their hair.

As often as they could, they bypassed the towns in favor of the backwash of the rural country and would often go for full days without seeing more than a sagging country store with a gas pump. She saw sights she had never seen. Once they were shot at by a guard when Kate got too close to a chain gang with her camera, and once they climbed in the window of a white revivalist church where the congregation writhed on the floor while the preacher held hissing snakes in his bare hands. Mainly, though, she saw poverty of the humblest sort. She discovered that Hopper was a kind man, willing to accept and find charming or sad or endearing human traits she found utterly infuriating. "Why are they so passive?" she complained of the farmers. "Why don't they fight back and demand something better?"

"The average sharecropper is a man who owns as near to nothing as any man in the United States," he replied. "He has no mule, no farm tools, no land. He has nothing but the labor of himself and his family. A sharecropper may live on the same plantation all his life and will get no rights outside the terms of his contract. The landlord stakes him to his seeds, a mule, tools, and food. He gives him the meanest of shacks to live in, as you have seen. At the end of the year a sharecropper earns about two hundred dollars for the whole year's work—not for the man alone, but for the entire family. Out of this, he must pay rent to the landlord on the shack and the price of the seeds for next year's planting. He and his family, and his family before him, have taken a beating by this system for so long a time now." Hopper shrugged. "Only pain and indignity remain. These people are thin on hope as they are thin in body. Hell, they eat cornmeal and molasses and pig fat. They go into the fields when they're six and chop and hoe and pick until they die. Fighting back is the last thing on their minds."

"It's positively feudal," Kate muttered.

"Worse than feudal. In the Middle Ages, serfs had, by law and custom, rights and dignities unheard of here."

"But why doesn't someone do something about it?" Kate demanded, her anger burning.

"Well, honey, we are."

And Kate beamed.

Whether he was aware of it or not, Hopper introduced Kate to a whole new way of working. His quiet, completely receptive approach showed that he was not only interested in the words a person spoke but in the mood in which they were spoken. He would wait patiently until the subject had revealed his personality, rather than impose his personality on the subject. Kate watched and learned.

Hopper had a gifted ear for regional accent. He could pick up every shade and nuance of characteristic in every state and county they traveled in. This was particularly useful, as they were first seen by country people as aliens and treated with appropriate distrust. The people they were seeking for pictures were generally suspicious of strangers. They were afraid they were going to sell them something they didn't want or fearful they were taking pictures to ridicule. Reassuring them was a very important part of the operation. When they saw a scene that interested them, they would roll up to the farm and Hopper would emerge from the car, stretch and scratch his head and push his hat back and wipe his face. Then he would amble over to the farmer and lean on the fence and make some comment of the "nice day" sort or ask a bland direction, eventually easing into telling the man what he was up to through a series of remarks issued every few minutes or so. The farmer, leaning on his hoe, would respond in like frugality. This "conversation" was mysteriously productive. Kate would wait in the car until a barely perceptible nod from Hopper came her way, and then she, too, would amble out, careful to stay in the background with a small camera, not stealing pictures, exactly, but working on general scenes and locales. Kate, to whom no amount of doctoring could alter her Yankee speech and ways, was always referred to as someone "Down South on her vacation." Once the farmer and Hopper had reached some kind of rapport, Kate could close in quite freely for portraits. Sometimes, not often, they would be invited inside tiny two-room sharecropper houses. Kate met the women and children there. Women who eyed her bright hair and fancy clothes and never let on what they were thinking. Children were bolder, lured by the camera equipment and the fancy people who had swooped down on their otherwise stern and plain ways. Kate was often surrounded by a solemn ring of pale, washed-out eyes, transparent like marbles, their gaze fixed on the shiny hinges and locks on her carry cases.

Always, after a shoot, Hopper would drive away in silence. He never took notes but there was, in that silence, the power of the scene imprinting in his mind. And months later, when words had to mesh with pictures, it was impossible to imagine that the two entities had not been created by one person—the vision was so perfectly matched.

A man and a woman stand in the doorway of a shack. They are thin, the cords in their necks strung taut, the hollows in their throats deep enough to hold a jigger of liquid. He wears overalls, she, a worn flour-sack dress. Her cheek is gaunt, though a wisp of curled hair touches it; his ears stick out, which might be comical except for the expression on his face. You will see no softness of hope in their faces. People don't expect much when they've farmed cotton all their lives.

Soon the work, the travel, the conversation, and the love-making began to take on a kind of flow that was unlike anything Kate had ever experienced before. Though surrounded by poverty and distress, Kate felt in herself a joy that was complete. It was all so natural, like breathing, this life she was leading on the road with her man. Had anyone ever loved so completely?

For his part, Hopper—who considered himself a worldly man, especially when it came to women—had not reckoned on this restless, alert, vibrant female who was so alive with energy, intensity, and sexual appetite. He had never known another woman to equal her drive and passion. Not just in bed but in every aspect of her daily life. Of course, the work was intense, but there was a fire in Kate and it burned in every particle of her. The way she moved. Her speech. Her silence. By God, he had never known a woman who could listen more intently than she did. She would fix her eyes on him and truly listen not only with her ears but with her whole being. She could draw him out and follow his thoughts to such a fullness that it was often as if they were one mind. In bed she was like a wonderful, well-oiled machine filled with a strength and capacity for pleasure. She understood her sexuality and had no qualms about demanding—and getting—what she wanted. Hopper thought of her as a magnificent Thoroughbred who might be paced and controlled for much of the race but when the finish line was in sight, held back nothing. The effect on him was powerful.

Kate had been too long without a real love in her life. All the others, the passing flirtations, the brief interludes, the affairs, however long or short, had lacked one essential ingredient—love. She had forgotten what it had been like with Eddie—to be in love, delirious and completely in love, but all that she had experienced with Eddie was now lost in youth and inexperience. They had been like puppies playing at something that was so much more than they could possibly know about. With Hopper it was altogether different. She was different. She was a woman who knew what she wanted. She had willed herself not to fall in love with anyone after Eddie until experience had taught her a few things. Now she was ready for a man like Hopper Delaney, and it scared her not at all to give herself over to loving him. In this swirling, random universe they had found each other, and now that they had, they were free to plumb the depths of their feelings without fear. She was a woman whose feet had left the ground, and she intended to allow herself the full measure of her happiness.

"It's so hot I can't move." Hopper gave a half-grunt, half-sigh from under his hat, which was covering his face. They were lying in the shade of a giant tree in the heat of the early afternoon somewhere in Georgia. Kate reached over and nudged Hopper's foot. "It's so hot I can't eat or sleep or even think."

"Now you're talkin' like a Southerner, honey."

Kate moaned and sat up, shielding her eyes and peering out into the hazy, white heat that engulfed them. "Oh, Lord, for a nice cool ocean to jump into. How do you stand it, Hop? How can anyone live in this heat? No wonder this place is so backward."

"Well, honey. Getting all agitated won't help. Here, let me show you something my granny taught me when I was little. See, you take a rag and dip it into ice water. . . ." He took a clean handkerchief from his pocket and wet it in the cooler they had brought, which held a large melting block of ice. "Now you put it here on your wrist . . . and here on the back of your neck. . . ." He turned her over on the quilt they had spread out on the ground under the tree and pulled up her perspiration-soaked cotton blouse. "And here, up and down your spine."

Kate gasped. The cold, wet cloth was a shock, but it brought an almost instant relief from the suffocating heat. Hopper dipped the cloth into the ice water again. "Sit up and take your blouse off and let me give you a good soaking."

Kate did as she was told, undoing the buttons and then her shimmy underneath. She lay back down again on her stomach, but Hopper rolled her over once more and positioned her arms above her head. The icy cloth sent shivers through her, and a bare puff of a breeze brought goose bumps to her skin. He stroked her tummy and under her arms with the cool dampness and then her neck and finally her breasts.

"Hmmmm," she sighed. "I sure do like your granny."

"Yeah, well, I have a feeling I've gone beyond Granny's remedy here." He bent down and brushed his lips to the nipples of her breasts. Then rolled back again on the blanket and pulled his hat over his eyes, and the look of her contentment swam before him in the darkness.

She lay motionless, still feeling his soft lips, her eyes lazily half-open tracing the flow of the trunk of the tree up through the branches. The tree was an old one, its trunk gnarled and sturdy and comforting in its stalwart strength. The branches reached far into the sky, shrouded in the deep green foliage. So many forks in the road, she thought, so many possibilities but all connected to the trunk. A sense of well-being flowed through her. The leaves moved in the soft damp air, and the sound of their rustling was as pleasurable a sound as she had ever heard. The tree, the air, the hum of nature going about its eternal business were suffused with her own iridescent joy. Everything seemed part of one great wholeness.

She moved closer to Hopper, who was sleeping soundly, his face in total repose, his mouth relaxed and slightly puffed up like a child's. She laid her hand on his cheek, and he nuzzled it ever so slightly from the depths of his sleep. She loved him then more than ever she could have thought possible. Why had it taken her so long to learn that there was nothing so easy and so uncomplicated as love?

Late that afternoon they drove by a Negro congregation gathered by a creek. They were clapping and singing as one by one new converts entered the creek to be baptized by a great burly preacher. "This is wonderful," Kate whispered.

"I've got to get this. Look at the light on the water. It's perfect." She started to get her gear together, but Hopper put his hand on her arm. "No. Let's just listen," he said. "They're lining. The lead singer sings out a line, then the others repeat it." It was a happy song filled with references to the River Jordan and joyful washing in the blood of the Lord. As the bodies swayed and chanted in unison, both Kate and Hopper fell under the spell of it as the sky overhead turned to a brilliant fuchsia pink.

When it was over, the preacher approached the car, and Hopper got out to greet him. Kate had long since learned that the colored communities were much less suspicious of strangers than the whites. They were invited to come back to the churchyard for a picnic.

The church was not a proper church but an old wooden pavilion with no walls. Under the roof, planks had been laid over benches and set with bright tablecloths. A feast of collard greens and potato salad and biscuits and fried catfish stretched down the tables and over to one side a whole pig roasted over an open pit. They stayed through supper until the moon rose up, and then someone brought out a banjo and more jubilant, hand-clapping gospels filled the damp night air.

Hopper said very little, but Kate could see by the expression on his face that this all meant something very dear to him. The people seemed to accept him; they let him listen and would have let him talk if he had wanted to, but he had no desire. Nobody asked them any questions about themselves, where they were from, why they were here, but after a while the preacher turned to Hopper and asked, "Do you sing?" Then everyone fell silent and Hopper said, "Sometimes. Not very well."

There was a long pause, then the preacher said, "Be nice to hear a song." And Hopper said, "Then I'll sing you one." Kate began to see it was a sort of ritual. "This was my ma's favorite song. She had me sing it to her at night after we had gone to bed—me on the little bed on the porch and she in the big bed just inside the door. If I've forgotten some of the words, someone help me out." Hopper stood up and the firelight caught his face. He closed his eyes and then he sang the oldest and dearest of the spirituals, "Swing Low, Sweet Chariot." He had no trouble with the words, and his voice, maybe a little hesitant in the beginning, got stronger and richer as he sang. Tears gathered in Kate's eyes. ". . . comin' for to carry me home. . . ." His voice rose above the crowd, above the smoke from the fire. She knew he was singing for something long gone in his life, not just a mother or a father but for the peace and beauty of his once home, the simplicity that was lost, the red sunset on the water, and the voices, the voices of his youth all gathered now around a fire on a dusty back road in Georgia. ". . . swing low, sweet chariot . . . coming for to carry me home." His voice was low but strong, and it carried the last note out to a hum.

"You're mighty quiet, Magnolia. What are you thinking?" They were in the car one afternoon a week or so later. The trip was almost over; in two days they were booked on a train out of Atlanta.

"Oh, I don't know. I guess I'm thinking about going back to the city. In a few days all of this will be over."

"Not likely. We've got to put this book together, you and me. I want you to help me write the captions. You're so much a part of this, you're not going to run off from me now, are you?" His tone was light, but both of them had been wondering what would happen when they got back to New York.

"Don't get your hopes up," she kidded. "I'm not easy to get rid of."

"Have you heard more from Otis about the new magazine?"

"Well, it's all systems go. The first issue is scheduled to come out next January."

"Are you excited?"

"Yes, I am. I just don't want this to end. Hop . . . I want you to know something. Something about me. When we get back to New York, I'm going to be very busy. I believe in this magazine and I believe it's right for me. I have this feeling that everything I've ever done in the past has been building to this moment. I have to work. I need to work. I don't exactly know why this is; I just know it is. I guess I'm trying to say I'm defined by my work. It doesn't mean I don't care for you. It's just something inside me. Without work, I'm nothing. But . . ."

He looked at her and grinned. "But what about us? Is that what you're saying? Listen, Magnolia, you've come to the right man. I don't know why I'm a writer. All I know is that it's a compulsion, something I must do. So I understand. Honey, there is no way I would stand between you and your work. I want for you whatever you want for yourself. Believe that. Besides, I'd sooner wrestle with a greased pig than try to hold you down."

They rode along in silence for a while, both of them wrapped up in the warm cocoon of the car. They were riding through a particularly destitute region, and as always her eyes were searching for a good subject. Suddenly, up ahead, she saw it.

It was a house that had all but disappeared under huge billboard posters advertising painkillers, automobiles, foodstuffs, and face creams. She was used to seeing magazine pictures used for ornamentation inside a house but not an entire house encased with them. It struck her deeply, having just left the advertising world. She made Hopper stop the car and go to investigate. In a few minutes he came out and waved her up onto the porch.

"Honey, come in and meet Miss Ida."

A woman, very old and tiny like a shriveled-up walnut, smiled from a rocker and beckoned her in. Inside the effect was bizarre. The wale of the walls and the ceiling were papered in colorful advertisements carefully cut from magazines. Kate was afraid to look too closely, afraid she might see one of her own vapid ads from the land of plenty, but Miss Ida was clearly proud of her house. Hopper looked around, nodding his approval.

"It's very practical, you know. The paper is good insulation from the heat and the cold. It's clean and it can be replaced for nothing."

Kate took the old woman's rough and gnarled hand. "Miss Ida, I'm a photographer and I would like to take your picture. Would you mind?"

"Mind? N'm, I don' mind." She smiled a big, toothless smile. "Make yo'sef to home."

Outside, a crowd began to gather as Kate unloaded the car. Men wandered up from the creek bottom with fishing poles, women came down the dirt road and up paths with babies on their hips, and children, a sea of them, crept closer and closer to the strange-shiny contraptions that were now placed on a blanket on the ground. One little girl, bolder than the rest, marched right up to Kate. "Me, too," she said boldly and pointed to herself with a big smile. "I want my picture taken." Her head was a mass of tiny pigtails jutting out, each one tied with a bright ribbon.

Kate laughed. "Okay. But first you have to be my helper. My name's Kate. What's yours?"

Her name was Roberdean and she was quick and bright as a dollar. Kate asked her how many brothers and sisters she had, and she giggled and said, "Oh, I gotta a heap of them. I sure do. I can't count 'em all. But I got me a twin, too."

Another little girl, not so happy and free-spirited, was jerked by Roberdean out of the crowd to meet Kate. She, too, had the little pigtails, but there were no ribbons in her hair, and she hung shyly behind her bolder twin. "This here's Geraldine. She don't talk." Standing together, the two girls were identical and Kate was enchanted. She asked them to pose inside the shack with Miss Ida, who turned out to be their great-granny. As she set up the shot, Kate talked to Roberdean. It seemed that she and her sister went to school on alternate days because they only had one school outfit between them— one pair of shoes, one "good" dress, one coat in the winter. Kate listened and kept busy fiddling with her cameras, but all the while she could feel an anger start to burn in the pit of her stomach. Framing Roberdean's wistful little face was a background display of the affluent world's goods. Roberdean and her shy sister could look their walls over and find a complete range of shoes and dresses and overcoats, but would they ever get a second set of clothes that would take them both to school every day? And would the school teach them how to get out from under a world in which papered shacks served as houses and prejudice and poverty were the norm? Kate had the uneasy feeling that the answer to her questions was a resounding "no."

They lean against their granny's old rocker, one on either side—one smiling happily straight into the lens as if she has been having her picture taken every day of her life; the other ducks her head. Granny's old, hazy eyes cannot see what the girls see, but they know the road does not stretch long or far for any American of color. The land of the free is white.

Kate waited and then pressed the button. A second's blinding flash illuminated a scene that would change her life forever. From that moment on, everything shifted in her eye, in her mind, in her heart. To see things was not enough; to understand was everything.

CHAPTER TWENTY-TWO

THEY WERE RADIANTLY in love. When they looked at each other, others could barely stand to watch, envious for their glory in each other. It wouldn't last, said his friends, people of urbane wisdom, whose jaded bright eyes were surprised at nothing, awed by no one. These things, they said knowingly, never last. When a month had passed, they gave it until Christmas. After Christmas they shrugged . . . she was too ambitious . . . he was too traditional . . . they were too much in love. This sort of mooning and sighing over each other might go down well in the movies, where passion had its place, but in real life such behavior was not normal.

But then it was 1936 and everything happening that year seemed contrary. It was the year that began with Edward VIII's succession to the throne and ended with his abdication to marry Mrs. Simpson. It was a year for relaxing the hip and letting the gams fly in a new beat called swing. It was the year of the Berlin Olympics, when Hitler called Negroes an "inferior race" and then watched Jesse Owens take four gold medals in track and field. It was the year that seven General Motors plants shut down, adding thousands of more names to the list of Americans out of work; the year the Spanish Civil

War erupted; the year Germany, Japan, and Italy formed the Axis.

It was also the year that *World* magazine made its debut.

Early in September, Otis Bennett surveyed his staff and laid out the entire premise of the magazine in his usual succinct style. "Our magazine is about quality. Our photographs will be the best ever produced in a news format. We are attempting each issue to capture a week—no more, no less. Our stories, our content must be the very essence of that week. A week is a short time and yet something about each issue must not only resonate with our readers but should echo through the decades to come. Who can know what the future will value. It could be a major news event, it could be something seemingly trivial. That is why each of you will be called upon to do many assignments—some in the forefront of the news, others on the simple goodness of daily life. Make no mistake, both are equally important. Both reveal who we are and what we care about."

Kate's eyes slightly narrowed. She was worried that being the only woman reporter was going to land her on the light side of the magazine. Simple goodness, ha! She knew from her days at *The Express* how passionate Otis was about his "good, clean, common decency" stories. What were the others thinking? It was a room full of talent, and she could feel her competitive juices deep in her gut. Her eye caught Rolly looking at her. He winked. And Virginia next to him. Who ever knew what Virginia was thinking? She was glad Otis had agreed to hire them. Well, he should. They were the best. Her sweep of the room finished on the three other photographers—all male, all with impressive, solid, seasoned credentials. Well, watch out, guys . . . *she* was going to break first from the starting gate. *She* was going to get the first cover.

With the January deadline looming, the office by November began to take on the look and feel of a war zone. Photographs were everywhere, story ideas, hundreds of them, were scattered among file drawers, trashcans, and pinup boards. Diz Damian's desk overflowed with memos and tear sheets and old, yellowed bits and pieces of things that had once been letters and clippings. His mind, deeply focused on about twenty different things at any given time, gave him the appearance of the prototypical absentminded professor, the sort of man who needed his wife to set him on a straight course out the door each morning and a secretary to keep him going throughout the day.

Diz as editor-in-chief of *World* had given up any semblance of normal working hours. He all but lived in the office, having dispatched his wife to Michigan to visit her sister, sleeping on his sofa and eating, when he remembered to eat, food his secretary brought in from the local restaurant. Mainly he guzzled Alka-Seltzers.

"So far this magazine is a veritable stew of picture journalism," he wrote his wife in Dearborn, "fresh ingredients, leftovers, salt, pepper, and a dash of Worcestershire. We're running a story on New York debutantes, Japanese schoolchildren in San Francisco, a report from Ethiopia and the Italian invasion, a sports story on amateur golf, a Hollywood story about the Marx Brothers, and a series about the oldest cattle ranch in America. Guess where it is? On Long Island. But I still haven't got my cover story and less than a month to go."

"Come on, Diz. This is me, Kate, the can-do girl. Give me a lead . . . anything. I want the cover, Diz."

"Kiddo, everyone wants the cover. I can't hand it to you on a silver platter. I don't know what it is."

"Well, then, tell me what you're thinking. What are you looking for?"

Diz reached out and made as if he were grabbing at something. "Grab. That's what I want. The cover has got to demand that the reader sit down and look at the entire issue and learn something. I want a story that has impact, but I don't want to get too heavy . . . something big in size and scope . . . something that fascinates . . ."

"Big? I can do big. Skyscrapers . . . oceans . . . airplanes . . ." This eager assault went on daily until at last Diz called Kate into his office late one December afternoon.

". . . so that's the scoop. Otis wants something on the new dams being built out West."

"For the first issue?" Kate demanded.

"Depends on what you get. We don't want anything too political. If we run something on the dams, we're really giving a nod to Roosevelt and the New Deal. That's okay and not okay, if you know what I mean. But we'll see . . . what do you think?"

Kate eyed Diz. "I have a feeling you're trying to tell me something."

"Don't get excited, honey. We're sending you to Montana, to photograph the dam at Fort Peck. It's the biggest dam in the world, and we want you to do it big as only you can do. Get me the same thing you got in those steel mills and factories. We want power and American know-how and 'look at us, ain't we grand'—that sort of stuff. This first issue has got to sell Americans on America and sell it big. I want you to take large-format cameras, lighting, the works. I've got a newspaper pal out there who's lining up some assistants." He paused and kind of raised one eyebrow. "But now, listen." He started fishing in his pockets. Out came paper clips, mints, pencils, a notebook, and a few tattered and ripped news clippings. He rummaged through these and at last handed a small, frayed clipping over to Kate.

She squinted at it. "'Boomtown, USA. New Deal, Montana,'" she read.

"Yeah. Boomtown. I like the sound of that. Sounds different, like the old Wild West. Like the Gold Rush. Upbeat, you know? See what you can sniff out. Maybe a story . . ."

Kate understood. Get out there and *find* a story.

A month later 200,000 copies of *World* rolled off the presses and were delivered to newsstands across America. They sold out within hours. Distributors cabled New York for more copies, sold those out, and cabled for still more. On the cover was the portrait of a dam, an arresting arrangement of monolithic concrete shapes, strongly composed and given even more strength by the two tiny figures standing dwarfed at the bottom. All over the country, work relief programs were breathing new life into a wilted populace desperate for work, but no one knew whether Roosevelt's New Deal could pull it off. This photograph seemed to shout out that the country was going to survive. If America could build a structure of this magnitude, why, America could pull itself out of the Depression. But the dam, however magnificent, was not what sold the magazine.

Something new and fresh was happening inside the issue and, as it turned out, something far more significant.

Boomtown, USA, was the story of a dusty, rawboned, false-fronted shantytown—the wildest Wild-West town in North America. Here was a new American frontier, a place of construction workers, gamblers, taxi dancers, roustabouts, honky-tonk bars and opportunists. In the shadow of the great dam you could almost smell the whiskey and feel the brawling life with its rough edges, few illusions, and no amenities. The main street looked like a hand-painted set for a Western movie thriller. Houses were built of tar paper, tin cans, and old boards. Taverns opened at eight in the evening and ran until six in the morning, and no one seemed to care that Montana had banned drinking and gambling. Kate had a field day—she entered into the melee of drunken men, dimestore girls, and get-rich-quick entrepreneurs, dance halls and bar fights with characteristic zeal. There was no end to where her camera went and what it took. The crowning picture, the one that *said it all,* so to speak, was the final picture in the essay—a baby perched on the bar of a roughshod saloon.

Diz and Kate and Rolly had created the first photo essay. A story in photographs. A series of pictures on a single theme that had a life all its own. There were captions and a short lead in words, but the story read in pictures. The public loved it. They had never before seen such a thing—a magazine about images. Every detail, every expression could be looked at in part and as a whole. It was dramatic, immediate, and important. It was like being there, they said. *World* magazine gave you something to think about.

Subscription orders poured in, and every available press in the country was employed to handle the weekly run. Otis's dream had come true. He had his picture magazine for the masses, and along with it, his rising star, Kate Goodfellow. The more outlandish the assignments, the more attention she got. She rode with a posse hunting down a gang of outlaws; she went down in the coal mines of West Virginia; she appeared at the picnic the Roosevelts threw for the visiting new King and Queen of England; she wooed herself into the good graces of a big city boss, then exposed his corrupt government from the inside. She crisscrossed the country at an alarming speed, taking her camera behind doors and into places no woman, often no camera, had ever gone before.

She got used to the telephone ringing in the middle of the night. "Kate, there's a flood in Louisville, we've got a plane waiting for you. . . ." Hers was the last plane into the most disastrous flood in twentieth-century America. Most of the city was inundated and the downtown was like a beleaguered castle, surround by a moat. She thumbed a ride on a rowboat and was not seen again for three days. As always, it was the small, telling things that caught her eye—a café dispensing hot coffee to rescue workers only everyone was standing on the countertops; a pet store, the owner and animals huddled on the second floor; a funeral parlor, the undertaker standing waist high in muddy flood waters performing the last of all human services.

Women looked for the story by Kate with every issue. To them, she was a heroine. So few women had been able to enter the workforce and fulfill the dream of an exciting and bold career. But dream they did and Kate became their symbol—their flag. The women's magazines clamored for her story, fashion designers sent her clothes, letters came weekly begging her to speak at various civic functions or to appear on radio shows telling about her daring exploits.

Other photographers studied her pictures and tried to analyze what made them so good. Admirers talked about intensity and framing and an uncanny knack for being able to see three or four levels all at the same time. Detractors said she posed people, and anyway, it was all darkroom technique. What everyone said was true. She did pose people, like the time she snatched a baby out of one woman's arms and put it in another's as they stood in a relief line. The surprised woman, who had never seen the child or its mother before, stared in distress at the now crying bundle in her arms. It was exactly the effect Kate wanted.

She insisted that no photograph of hers ever be cropped. "Print to black," she demanded, which meant each negative was printed full so that the black area showed around the edges as proof that the images were just as she shot them. And woe to layout if they cropped her pictures to fit page allotments. Her fits and tempers and demands soon became part of the working week at *World*. With her red hair caught under stylish hats, her signature slacks and tailored jackets which made her look sexy and assured, she was catapulted right up there in the minds of the public with their favorite movie stars—she was a tomboy and a woman of the world all scrambled into one. She loved it.

Kate brought Hopper to the office, clearly enjoying showing off her trophy, and Hopper, who normally would have minded very much being put in such a position, minded not at all. Kate led him from office to office, and he nodded and smiled and even signed a few autographs for some of the younger secretaries. Kate beamed. Hopper basked. She was so beautiful, so perfect, so utterly vivid in his sight that she could have asked him to do a tap dance and he probably would have done it.

They were everywhere in the fast lane of New York life—El Morocco, the Rainbow Room, "21" Club, weekends on Long Island, dancing in and out of the Central Park casino to Eddie Duchin, in and out of limousines, front row center, lights up, thundering applause. He, the writer. She, the photographer. They, the golden couple of the hour.

She has the gift of excitement, he told friends. *He has irresistible charm,* she told colleagues. When a female reporter asked him if Kate liked his books, he replied, "Darlin', she likes everything." And the way he said it was a scandal and got quoted and distorted, which pleased them immensely. They behaved like two spoiled children on a spree. Cholly Knickerbocker reported on their antics with almost obsessive regularity, and he bemoaned Kate's frequent out-of-town assignments almost as much as Hopper did. The year flew by.

CHAPTER TWENTY-THREE

"CONFOUND IT," HOPPER grumbled. He was struggling to get to his feet from one of the low-slung metal and leather chairs in her apartment. "First, you can't get in these things, and then when you do, you can't get out. What kind of inquisitor invented these torture chambers?"

"The same one who invented the hammock," Kate replied, laughing at his predicament. "Look at me, Hop. It's a matter of rolling your body out, see, like this." And she promptly plopped herself into the matching chair and with her long legs and agile body demonstrated an artful and graceful exit. Then she grabbed his hand. "Come on, old man. I'll help you up." But he pulled her down into his lap, ignoring her protest that he was mussing her gown. "This is crazy, Kate. I spend half my time coming and going from this place. Come live with me. I can't stand all this modern discomfort."

"Live in that musty old mess? Where would my clothes go? Where would I go? Come on. We're very late." She struggled to free herself, but Hopper was having none of it.

"You're going to sit still for a minute. I have a surprise for you, but you have to promise to sit still and calm down. . . ."

"Sit still? I thought we were due at Mallory's an hour ago."

"We were, but now we're not because I called and said we both had the flu, and since we don't we're going out together tonight just the two of us to a dark little restaurant that no one knows about and we're going to celebrate."

"Ah. And what are we celebrating this time?"

Hopper reached inside his vest pocket and drew out an envelope. He handed it to Kate. Inside was a check. Kate looked at it.

"Twenty thousand dollars! Hop, what is this?"

"The most beautiful money in the world, Magnolia. Royalties."

"Our book?"

"Yep. Funny, isn't it? A book about poor people makes other people rich."

Kate stared at the check. She had never been handed so much money in one go. It was dazzling.

"It reminds me of a time when I was a kid," Hopper went on. "My father had friends up in the Northern churches, and he wrote telling them how much his congregation needed clothes. He was preaching in one of the most depressed backwaters you could imagine, down in Georgia, and soon enough a box arrived. To his great disgust the box contained a handsomely tailored tuxedo, and this was supposed to be handed over to some man who never owned a whole pair of britches in his life."

"Now, Hop, don't you get all misty-eyed and Southern on me." She wriggled free. "Now I feel guilty. I'll tell you what, let's give the money away."

"No. Let's be unregenerately guilty. Let's buy ourselves a house."

"A house?"

"Sure. I saw a nice little house down in the Village on my walk the other day. A love nest. Just for the two of us."

Although Hopper was careful to mask his feelings, it had become most important to him that he and Kate live together. Her constant travel was beginning to wear thin, and he was lonely without her. He wrote her long letters when she was on the road telling her he wanted her beside him, that she was

missing all the fun. Besides, he reasoned, they needn't give up
their respective apartments. He would use his as an office and
she could use hers for entertaining. It would be worth every
penny, he said, even with their variant schedules, even with
the long days and weeks in between their meetings—a place
all to themselves.

"No friends, no work."

"Why no friends?" she asked.

"May I remind you that you have no interest whatsoever in
my cronies?"

"I certainly do not. All they do is drink bourbon and wom-
anize and go to the track."

"And your friends . . ." he trailed off. He really couldn't
abide her magazine associates and the constant talk about
leads and scoops and the latest techniques in the darkroom or
the competition for space in the magazine.

"Why not, Kate? Why not?" And Kate, who loved him
more than she ever thought possible, agreed to look at the
house on Cherry Lane.

It was a gum stick of a house sandwiched in between two
others, on a street both crooked and quaint. So narrow, there
was only one room on each of the three floors, all of them
connected by a crooked little staircase. It was enchanting, just
like a playhouse, and she agreed instantly on buying it. They
went about decorating with childlike intensity. The living
room had an open fireplace and oak rafters, the walls lined
with bookshelves and a huge leaded window facing a minus-
cule back garden. An artistic salon made for creative people,
they thought. The kitchen was not much more than a closet
adjoining the living room with a two-burner stove, a porce-
lain sink that Hopper said looked like an overgrown soap
dish, and a red painted icebox only three feet high. Kate pronounced the kitchen charming and cunning because she did
not cook, and kitchens were merely places to keep ice and
hors d'oeuvres. But Hopper grumbled. He supposed he might
manage omelets in such cramped space, but that was all. Onto
this floor came an oriental rug, an easy chair, a pretty little Ed-
wardian settee, and a pair of five-feet-tall baronial wrought-
iron candlesticks. The middle floor was for "stuff"—books,
clothes, things, and more things. The top floor was the bed-

room, so chosen because of an enormous skylight. They had specially made for them a rolled mattress, which they laid down on a bare floor painted a deep burgundy. They dressed the bed in black satin sheets and bought dozens of silk cushions from Chinatown with kimonos to match. Here they were as contented as could be.

Kate was not allowed to give out the telephone number to *World* magazine. Only Virginia knew and she was instructed to call only when absolutely necessary. Their happiness was made up of little things. Breakfasts on a painted tray found while poking around the little curio shops on Bleecker Street, the sun shining in from the skylight to warm them. Midnight talks by the fire and candlelight in the shadowy living room, where they sat side-by-side and close together on the rug, their backs against the velvet settee's edge, their feet stretched toward the fire. Thinking aloud and telling each other what had happened to them in the other's absence. Raids on the little icebox just before retiring. A French ice-cream parlor on the corner. Little intimate jokes, secret nicknames and code words. Cheerful scuffles for possession of the bathroom mirror or the last chicken leg or a particular section of the newspaper.

Hopper read aloud to Kate from books she hadn't read, and she rubbed his neck and massaged his head to ease his cramped shoulders and neck pains. She saw that writing was a grinding business and that stringing words together in a creative sequence was a lonely piece of work. He saw that days and days in the field and hour upon hour in the darkroom was a tenuous labor at the mercy of layout, cropping, and, worst of all, a last-minute "kill" if something more relevant came in. She was demanding in her work and he liked that. He was exacting in his, and she loved him for it.

And always they made love, never growing tired of each other, longing for each other, passion seeming to grow deeper the more they were together. Every time they finished, one or the other would murmur, "It can't get any better than this." And then they would laugh because it was a silly thing to say, never, of course, doubting for a moment that it would only get better and better. From their black satin bed they would hold each other far from the turbulence of their lives and watch the night sky over Greenwich Village. When it rained they were ecstatic. When it snowed they were reverent. The night of the snow, watching the big fat flakes, Hopper said, "I wish this were it. I wish we were the only two people in the world." And Kate said, "We are. We are the original man and woman."

A perfect, perfect life—for a while. Sometimes at night, when Kate was away, Hopper would lie awake looking at the stars through the skylight trying to sort through his feelings. It was as if he was living in a passionate dream in which only Kate was real to him and everybody else was unimportant and a little vague. Before Kate, he had surrounded himself with people, amusing people, gay people. People to whom things like home and family and the sense of living one's life in pursuit of harmony and contentment were scorned as old-fashioned and suffocating. Now these things seemed important somehow, and there was growing in him an urgency to acquire them. It all had to do with her.

She had a hold on his heart that baffled him. It wasn't that he had never been in love before, but built into each of the many serious relationships he had experienced was an unfailing sureness of having the upper hand, the control. With Kate, his emotions had become far too tangled. At first, of course, the joy of her, the excitement generated by her energy and intensity and sexual appetites had thrilled him, and he had entered into the affair with all the assuredness of the man of the world that he surely was. Kate had not then attained a rank to challenge his own, but such was certainly now the case. They were equals and he was proud of her, he said to himself. Of course he was. She was magnificent . . . but he wondered where it was all taking them.

Sometimes he resented the time allotted to him. Like a jealous lover, he was beginning to loathe *World* magazine. He accepted that fame was an integral part in Kate's career plan and self-promotion an integral part in her character. He didn't want to change her; he just wanted more of her. He tried to remember what he had felt in those first heady days of his own success, but that time was lost now in all that had happened to him over the years. Writing had become progressively more difficult in the face of his fame and the expectations of his peers. The complex struggle to change the world had narrowed down to a far more simple and deadly struggle of just keeping his passions for such youthful ideals alive.

Lying in bed alone, he found that these things weighed on him as he felt the pendulum slowly shift. It was a subtle thing, hard to pin down, and he would have been the last to think that it was he who had to have the control between them. It wasn't control over her, but maybe it was control over himself. As she went from strength to strength, it left him feeling unsure of where he stood. "I've been waiting for this all my life, Hop," she said happily, referring not to him but to her job. "Freedom. Freedom to do what I want to do, to experiment, to explore, and finally I cannot only do these things, but I can do them without everyone making such an almighty fuss over the fact that I'm a woman."

"Yeah. And what a woman." He pulled her close.

Little things started to creep into their precious time together. She accused him of being moody. She called it the "white storm" because, she said, his face would go pale and his eyes would cloud over. Usually she could cajole him out of these moods but not always. They were brought on often by something so small as an ill-timed party comment about her latest exploit, or a simple observation she wanted to share with him stemming from an assignment, and, worst of all, a call from Virginia telling her of some late-breaking event.

Kate worried about Hopper and his moods. Hopper did not enjoy his tempers, but in time he began to rely on the attention she gave him when he was under the spell of one.

When it came right down to it, what brought them on was not the fact of her rising fame, of her work, of the sporadic time together, of all the leave-takings. It was that she wanted to leave. A new assignment was for her like the very deepest nourishment. He couldn't stand to think of it.

In the best of times, of course, he admired her greatly. He loved her aliveness, her alert, tense restlessness. She was lively, witty, filled with vigor, and all of these things excited him. She adored him. When they were together in public, she deferred to him, in private she praised him, and it was all very sincere, even touching. But then she would say something like how perfect they were for each other because above all the men she had known, only he was so mature and secure within

himself that she could be sure he would never raise emotional
obstacles to her work.

Damn her work!

It occurred to him that he had been so willing to live in the
fast lane with her that he had given her an entirely false impression of himself. Her job picked her up and put her down
erratically. She thrived on it and assumed he did, too. But he
did not. In a few months he would be forty, and for the first
time he began to consider his age and the things he really
wanted from life. He had often characterized himself as a sort
of vagabond bon vivant. All those hackabout years scratching
at money as a young man, jumping trains and taking work
where he found it. Living in a cold-water flat in Hoboken, his
mind drifting and sifting through a million images and words,
searching and never resting for long. Then the recognition, the
success, which made him a vagabond of another sort. Money,
especially when you've never had it before, almost certainly
kept you a vagabond. It was so easy to spend, there were so
many interesting people who beckoned once you stepped inside the inner circles of power and success. There were so
many fantasies to satisfy.

What he wanted now, what he needed most in his life, was
some stability, the kind that came from knowing that in the
whole godforsaken universe there is one other person who
loves you as much as you love them and who is willing to lay
themselves open, unconditionally, to that love. He reflected
that throughout his life, he had never known this, never even
felt the need for close friends, content with jolly good times
and sporting buddies and lovers who arrived in his life with
their own built-in expiration date. The realization of his aloneness intensified his love and need for Kate. It also scared the
hell out of him.

She, on the other hand, had never felt less alone. Work embraced her like a large loving family. The early days of *World*
consumed everyone who believed in the magazine, and it was
exciting, absorbing work, in a great cluttered room full of
shirtsleeved figures, typewriters that chattered like a million
teeth on a cold night, air filled with smoke, stacks of photographs on metal carts, layouts, ideas, jokes, decisions. It was
alive, frantic, breathless. From the very first day Kate had

only to enter the editorial room to feel her spirits soar. It was a refuge and a resort, a place where the little aches of two selfish lovers were forgotten in the mighty creation, week by week, of a *Thing*.

Early that summer they quarreled. It started as most quarrels do, over nothing. Kate had arrived home from an assignment on the West Coast early on a Sunday morning. She was leaving again that night. It was a matter of throwing old clothes out of the bag and fresh ones in before returning to the airport. He didn't even know where she was going. He had long since stopped asking. However, he did know where she had been—Hollywood—because she had been chattering about it ever since she had come home. "You should see Beverly Hills, Hop. House after house, each one trying to be as grand as the next. A Moroccan palace right next to a white-pillared Southern manse, and all of them with great imposing front doors and circular drives. We went to a party at William Powell's. He was wonderful, very debonair and glamorous, just like the characters he plays in the movies, but his taste in décor was ghastly. The interior was all white with *fur* carpets! Everything out there is so luxurious . . . everything. English butlers and swimming pools in all sorts of sexy shapes and champagne coming out of fountains and women with white minks over their bathing suits . . ."

She went on and on about the people she had met and the parties she had gone to and the story she had shot on the back lot of MGM and how sweet and kind everyone had been and ". . . guess who I ran into?" She didn't wait for him to guess. She didn't even notice that he had said nothing for the past half hour. Indeed, he hadn't even looked at her but stared at the tray of breakfast he had fixed, most of which had gone untouched. "Your old flame, Norma Kingsley. I can't believe you gave her up for me. My goodness, but if she isn't the most glamorous movie queen out there! She looked fabulous. Well, she should. She certainly made a success of herself in your movie. She said . . ." but he didn't listen to what Norma had said. He was too caught up in the fact that Kate had not noticed his morose mood. Was she blind? She had not asked him once about himself, about what he had been doing alone without her for these past weeks! He had missed her terribly. New

York seemed empty without her. The weeks had dragged on, and there was no purpose to existence, and nobody of all the people he had seen amused him much. But she didn't care. She had stopped loving him.

She was now pacing about the room in that frenetic way he hated because it meant her mind was away from him, a thousand miles away. Maybe with someone else. Maybe in some other man's arms. Well, why not? A woman like Kate probably had all sorts of lovers when she was away from him. The thought made him ill.

"I'm going to take a bath and pack now, I think," she was saying. "That way we can have the whole day and maybe go out to dinner tonight before I leave." She opened the closet and was rummaging around. "Darling, did you remember to pick up my dress from the dry cleaners?" It was an innocent enough remark, but he decided not to take it that way. His voice filled with weary scorn.

"Pick up your dress! No, of course I didn't pick up your dress. What do you take me for? Your personal maid?"

She turned around slowly and looked at him. "No. I would never do that. But it's Sunday and I need that dress and you seemed glad enough to do that for me when I called you."

"Well, I didn't pick the damn thing up. I forgot. I do have other things on my mind besides your wardrobe, speaking of which is crowding us out of these midget closets."

Her eyes narrowed in annoyance. "I need that dress, Hopper. I have to travel light, and it's the only one I have that I can wear in the day and then out to dinner if I have to. I would have asked Virginia if you couldn't do it, but you said—"

"I don't care what I said," he exploded. "I don't care about whether you can wear something out to dinner or not. I don't care what you wear or when you wear it."

She could see the color drain from his face, his eyes small darts of anger. Kate crossed over to the dressing table and sat down. She put her head wearily against the back of the chair. "Please don't ruin our time together. Not this time, Hop. Listen to me a minute."

But Hopper would not listen. He was exceedingly angry and it felt good. He bolted from the bed and in doing so knocked over the tray of coffee and eggs and toast and the three tiny pots of imported English marmalades. It clattered and splattered onto the bare burgundy-colored floor. "Listen, hell!" he shouted. "What do you think I've been doing all morning? Do you think I want to listen to all that drivel about Hollywood stars and fur rugs? Do you think I'm one of your *many*"—the word dripped with sarcasm—"fans, someone with nothing better to do than to hang on your gay little tales of how ostentatious two-bit actors are? Why don't you talk to me for a change? About something, anything of substance."

Kate was angry, too. "May I ask one question?" she said coldly. Hers was a still and frozen anger, not like Hopper's. "Did you not pick up my dress on purpose?"

"Would you shut up about that fool dress—"

"Don't ever tell me to shut up."

And then the fight began in earnest. They said much to each other in the next hour, until the original point of the dispute was lost in the chaos of utterances, until they forgot altogether how it was that this frenzy had started. Now they quarreled over Hopper's jealousy; over Kate's work; over Hopper's attitude toward Kate's work, which Kate maintained had been "dishonest" from the start. Violently they hurled slights and innuendoes and imagined deceits dredged up from memory; long ago incidents made grievances, *pro tem*. There was the dinner they had gone to with Diz Damian where Hopper leveled a disproportionate degree of hostility over a discussion of words versus visuals that had shamed Kate for weeks. There was the incident of the handsome young assistant who often traveled with Kate and whom she had tried to integrate into their social life.

"And why not?" spat Kate. "Do we have to spend all our time with those conceited literary snobs, those middle-aged sots you call friends?"

"Those snobs, those *sots,* just happen to be some of the most gifted writers of our time. Unlike you ambulance-chasers who think the whole world revolves around the flashbulb."

Kate said Hopper had no zest. That he had listened to himself saying "a writer has only ten good years," that his ten years were up, that he hadn't worked on anything new since their trip South, that he only cared about sitting around the house mooning because she was out in the world seeing and doing. Hopper, stung, because she had hit dangerously close to the mark, struck back with statements to the fact that Kate only cared for her own fame and glory at the expense of all else and that she was letting everything that mattered, really mattered, love and respect and caring between two people, go to rack and ruin.

Kate's reply was the inevitable one. "Well, if that's the way you feel, you know what you can do."

So Hopper did. His exit from the house was spoiled by the fact that he wasn't dressed. Such exits should be instantaneous to make the most dramatic point. But he dressed with as much dignity as he could and then strode down the tiny staircase past the living room where Kate stood facing the window, her back to him. He reached inside the closet for his jacket and his hat, jammed said hat on his head, yanked open the door, heard its shattering bang behind him, and, on the whole, felt better than he had in months.

He went to Gaby's. There he cooled off in spite of himself. No one could stay hurt and angry for long at Gaby's. She was throwing a "small" lunch party for friends from Paris, a rather maddening English woman named Raine Farrington, her brother, Henry, and two French women, both very chic and beautiful. Later, he learned they were lovers. About fifteen other people were there as well. The talk flew about the room inspired by Raine, who appeared to know just about everyone of the artist/writer/international crowd and was filled with amusing news and gossip. Talk of this sort usually bored Hopper, but today it seemed riveting. He drank two soothing bourbons and by lunch found he was not only enjoying himself but was fully prepared to forgive Kate. After all, she hadn't meant what she said; he knew that, he could see it in her eyes. Underneath the anger he had seen in them suffering and incredulity that she was saying such cruel things to him. She had not meant them any more than he had meant what he had said. His feelings now were downright cozy. A lovers' quarrel . . . clear the air . . . something to chuckle about in the weeks to come.

After lunch the talk turned to politics and the room started to fill with the blue haze of cigarette smoke. Henry Farrington, who had remained fairly quiet during lunch, turned out to be a rather interesting fellow. He was a journalist and was closely connected with Winston Churchill. It seemed that for years Churchill had employed a whole battalion of young men to travel throughout Europe for him, to be his eyes and ears during the long years of retirement from Parliament. Henry was one such man. He had been in Spain, in Austria, in Germany. He talked knowledgeably about Hitler, about the inevitability of a European war, about Hitler's rise to power and the recent taking of Austria. Henry had just come from Czechoslovakia and reported German troops of over 400,000 massing at the border. Czechoslovakia would be the next to fall, he said, into the maw of German assault. And then? England was not prepared for war. Would America help them? Talk went late into the afternoon.

Hopper left Gaby's sometime after five feeling sobered. Of course, one read every day in the newspapers about Hitler and was horrified, but the concerns of the Americans were still so nationalistic. There were strikes and riots, and unemployment still hovered at eight million people. He, like most Americans, while not ignorant of what was happening in Europe, was essentially uninformed. And he was more informed than most—or so he had thought. Listening to this Farrington fellow, he wasn't so sure. Still, it was Europe's problem. The age-old rivalries and hatreds coming once again to an ugly head. America would stay out of it . . . but who could ignore the brutality and cruelty and butchery of the Nazis, no matter whose war it was? It was time to come out of the hole. It was time to pay attention.

He wanted to see Kate. He wanted to apologize. He wanted to get out of his doldrums and start writing again in earnest. The world was falling into a dark abyss, and what was he doing about it? He had to get back to the little house on Cherry Lane before it was too late, but when he got there, it was dark—and she was gone.

He hailed a cab. A half hour later he was running across the tarmac at Idlewild. Kate was standing there talking to one of the crew, supervising the loading up of her photographic gear. Her head turned. His hand shot up. She broke into a wide, happy smile and rushed to meet his embrace.

A week later, upon her return, they agreed to go on a much needed vacation together. Hopper had a friend who offered his house on the coast of Maine. To his surprise, Kate agreed to come with him for the entire month of July.

CHAPTER TWENTY-FOUR

IN YEARS TO come she would forget how the arrangements had been made or how she had managed to take so much time away from her work or the anticipation she felt, but she would always remember the first moment they had stepped out into a bright blue day from a chartered seaplane and onto the launch in Bar Harbor, Maine. The air was like champagne.

Waiting at the dock was an antiquated, wood-slated Ford station wagon with rattling curtains and a steaming radiator cap driven by a gangling youth in a white shirt and a stiff collar, no tie, a derby hat, and khaki pants. His name was Tommy McGrath. He was to take them some twelve miles to the house on Northwest Cove. Tommy was a kind of errand boy for everyone along the route, and the procedure of his vehicle through the countryside was as sociable and leisurely as if by horse-drawn buggy. They ambled along the rocky coast, weaving at times inland to where farmers were working fields, and you could smell the fresh earth and the spruce trees and pine lumber intermingled with the mud marshes and the tang of salt air. They stopped often to deliver news and goods, to take a package of seeds from Mr. Billings at the General Store over to Mrs. Torrey at Torrey Farm, to pick up a cradle from Mrs.

Eaton and see that the Winnepauw family got it for the new baby. At one farmhouse they waited while cream was skimmed from milk and bottled. The farmer's wife, Mrs. Foss, was a friendly sort and gave them a cup of tea. Mrs. Foss, it seemed, had many daughters, and each and every one of them would be glad to come and clean or cook or "do what needs doin' for yer missus." Kate and Hopper agreed to send word back with Tommy after they got settled.

They were the only passengers that day, and as they rode they talked to Tommy, who was an enterprising boy and quite taken with his status as tour guide of the area. He told them how and where to get fresh fish and lobsters, the farms that would deliver eggs and vegetables; he knew of bicycles they might have for the month and said he would find them a small sailing boat if they liked. At long last the old car turned off the main road down a rutted lane, and there in the clearing stood the house owned by Hopper's friend, a Swedish poet who had imported a craftsman from Sweden to build his seaside lodge.

The exterior of the house appeared to be a simple rectangle of natural wood. It was surrounded by a dark forest on three sides. If they had felt the slightest disappointment at the plain exterior, they both gasped in amazed appreciation upon entering the house. It was truly a work of art. The wall facing the sea of the large central room was a series of large glass panels. The house was perched high on a cliff, the ground falling quickly away so that it seemed almost as if one could take flight over the panorama of sea and sky. The interior was a high-ceilinged, beamed room divided in the center by a stone fireplace. On one side was a large, heated pool sunk into the floor. It was fed by a trickling waterfall which fell the full height of the two-story room over a series of gourds and metal plates so that soft, melodious sounds filled the air. On the side that looked out over the vast expanse of sea and sky was a brightly woven rug, giant cushions with movable armrests and low tables. Rolled mattresses and hammocks served as beds, and there were all sorts of nooks and crannies beautifully fitted with shelves and cupboards.

"Look!" Kate exclaimed. "It looks like fairy land." She was pointing to a view of a stone garden with rocks covered in moss, trees twisted into fantastic shapes molded by the prevailing wind, footpaths and a wooden bridge leading to stairs at the cliff's edge. Below they discovered a small crescent of sand beach. Everything about the house and the surround delighted them, and they spent the whole of the next few days exploring as if castaways on a deserted island.

Before leaving New York, Hopper had made extravagant arrangements for food and wines to be sent ahead of them on a specially chartered seaplane. The house came well supplied with jazz and classical recordings with an enormous old Victrola to play them on. Music and cooking were two of his favorite pastimes, and he entered into the planning of their enjoyment with enormous zest. Kate, for her part, was contented to be fed and pampered. She was exhausted from her eighteen months on the road, and more than willing to put herself completely into his hands.

There was a wooden heated sauna on the beach from which they would run sweating and naked into the icy sea, screaming and gasping and howling before tearing up the stairs and into the warm, scented pool inside the house. The weather was perfect, hot during the day and cool at night so they could curl up together around the great open fireplace drinking wine, eating, and talking. Twice a thunderstorm filled the night sky with jagged lightning and wind moaning in the eaves, thrilling to watch from the comforts of their divans, and with the fire blazing they held hands, eating popcorn, watching as if in a movie theater, the spectacle of nature's tempest.

"We are alone in the universe with each other," Hopper said one night, stroking her head, which lay in his lap.

Kate snuggled up closer to him and murmured, "I sometimes feel I have always been alone. My parents both taught me to be alone, stand alone, in order to truly know who you are."

"Ah, but now you are talking of independence. Stand on your own two feet, set your own rules, follow your heart, and all that."

"Well, then, what do you mean by alone?" she asked, sitting up and holding her empty wineglass to him. He picked up the bottle and poured. "Look at that, Magnolia. Look how red it is with the fire shining through it." She held her glass up and for a moment they were silent. The wine was a deep ruby color which, when held to the fire, seemed to have a life of its own.

"What I mean," he went on, stroking her hair and marveling as he always did at the intensity of the color, "is not a sense of independence but the sense of surrendering your will to the awesome infinity of nothingness. I remember one summer when I was twenty-two. I was living down on the Gulf working on a shrimp boat, but I had already started writing my first novel and I knew my life was going to change. I was saving money to go to New York and I was so eager to leave even though I knew I would be giving up everything I had ever known. It was September. I decided to hitch my way back to Corinth for one last look and then get over to Memphis to take the train north. I figured, even if I had to walk most of the way, I wanted this one last feel of the South because I knew even if the novel never came to anything, I would never be that boy again. Well, I guess I did walk it at least half the way. Not many country people had cars or trucks, and sometimes it was just plain faster to walk than ride on the back of a mule wagon. In any event, it took me weeks to get up to Corinth. I picked up jobs for a room and a meal when I could, or I played cards for it, but one night I had no place to stay. I found a pine forest and I lay down on the pine needles for the night. The stars were out like nothing I had ever seen before, and there was a meteor shower going on and the sky was alive with rockets of light. It was an awesome sight and so beautiful that I cried to see it. I hadn't ever remembered crying like that before. I cried because I knew, most certainly, that I was alone." He fell silent, staring into the fire.

Kate reached up and stroked his cheek. "Don't stop talking, Hopper. I love to listen to you. It sounds like an awful moment, though. Really frightening."

"No, not really. It was more inspiring than anything else. You see, out of that sense of aloneness, I came to understand something that has been, I guess, the driving force of my life. I realized that our purpose here on earth is to love. To find something or someone to love because love is the only way that we are not alone." He made a wry face. "I forgot all about my night with the shooting stars in the years that followed. I was so busy being a success. This business of success has a way of taking on a life of its own. You want something so badly and you do everything to get it, but then success grabs hold of you and you forget what it was you wanted from it in the first place. I was content with the life swirling all around me. I did not allow myself to dwell on such matters as love; I was having too much fun. The point of my life was living it to the hilt. There was the work and there were the girls, beautiful girls, wonderful girls, and for a long time I was satisfied. But the day I met you at Gaby's, my memory was jolted and I was reminded of that boy again crying under the tree. That was why I was so difficult. I knew you were going to be important to me, but I was frightened of having to change again. I was scared as all hell itself."

"Why, Hop, you never told me. I thought you thought me quite a silly dolt. You made me feel like everything I had done up to that minute in my life was useless."

"It wasn't anything we said or anything I felt toward you. In fact, I think I did think you rather a dolt. But there was something in you that jumped right inside my body. The day you came to my apartment . . . remember? You were so sure of yourself and I was fit to be tied. After you left I walked all over the city cursing you, cursing the book, and cursing anything I could get in my head to curse, but by the end of the day I knew what it was I had to do. I had to change again. I had to find that boy and take him down yet another road."

She reached up and laid her hand against his cheek. "No wonder you were so angry with me." Then she leaned forward and kissed him. It was a long kiss, not without passion, but passion of a different sort. Then she pulled away and put her head back in his lap. "Keep talking, Hop."

"It was like dying and coming to life again. I was no longer the boy crying under a tree, but a man crying out. I had found you." He stroked her hair again. "So in a sense, I've always been alone—until now."

Kate rolled over and propped herself up on her arms and looked at his face. "When I first met you I had the idea that you were someone who had had everything he had ever wanted. You were so overwhelmingly tall, staring out at the world with a kind of imperious boredom straight over my head. I knew all about you, I thought, but I was filled up with clichés and gossip. I wanted nothing more than to show you up. I wanted to take your book away from you and make it mine. I wanted to be just as sassy and obnoxious as could be. And I was."

He laughed. "Yes, you were."

"But what changed everything for me was the way you felt for those people. You weren't going after something the way I was, you were feeling it. You changed everything for me, Hop. The way I see, the way I work. We make a great team, you and I. We should work on something together again."

Hopper never stopped stroking her head, but something in what she said was not right. He had been, only moments before, relaxed the way good wine and wonderful food and human warmth can relax the mind and body. Now, however, he felt a twinge of caution. "Am I loved because of how I fit into your work, Kate?"

"No, and don't you start all that again." Kate wriggled over and buried her head in his chest, her hand automatically beginning to stroke his back, beginning its familiar journey over his body. She felt his resistance and refused to acknowledge it. She knew what gave him pleasure. She loved this body, she loved feeling his rising excitement and her own.

He pulled her to him, his eyes black pools. "I can't get enough of you. I want every bit of you, every part of you." He massaged her back, her neck, her buttocks—his hands touching her skin as if it were a rare and precious cloth. All of his interest, all of his attention was focused on her so that not a gesture, not a tremor was lost. He studied her and explored her, and she opened up to him as she had never done before. "Remember this," he said, with a sudden and terrible urgency. "Keep it forever."

The days stretched into two weeks. They made love, bathed in the ocean, soaked long hours in the pine-scented pool rubbing oils on each other, eating and drinking like hedonists. Hopper was an excellent cook. Eating well, Hopper instructed her, was one of life's supreme pleasures. He was appalled by her lack of sophistication when it came to food and wine. "All that running around the country got you nothing but stodgy diner food—fried, flipped, and mashed." He took it upon himself to educate her. He alternated his quite extensive culinary repertoire with simple, local fresh foods from the farms and sea. They ate lobsters wrapped in seaweed and buried in hot coals, sitting cross-legged on the beach, cracking open the lobsters with rocks. They ate corn wrapped in its husks and grilled in the embers of the fire. Once he planned a Turkish dish called shashlik meant to be served skewered on a flaming sword, but at the last minute found there was nothing in the kitchen resembling a sword on which to cook it on. He searched the house and garage and finally came back with a pitchfork. This he scraped and scrubbed until the tines were clean and then speared the cubes of lamb and beef, onions, shreds of liver, mushrooms, and tomatoes. The three-tined pitchfork had a suggestion of medieval banqueting about it, and so they played madrigals on the phonograph, and Kate fashioned a crown of flowers for his head and for hers. They roasted the shashlik in front of the open fire and ate the succulent meats with their fingers. They wandered down to the tiny village of Northwest Cove and sat on the docks talking to fishermen, buying fish for chowders right off the boats.

I get the old sense of harmony here, Hopper wrote to Gaby. *The days are handed out like monumental gifts, each one bringing with it some new discovery, some natural treasure. Kate is ecstatically happy—you can't imagine the change in her disposition . . .*

Mornings they left each other alone. Hopper worked as he had always done, and Kate, who had kept her promise to bring only the smallest and lightest of her cameras for pleasure shooting, ventured into the natural setting. She loved walking through the forest with the sound of the sea beating against the shore rocks and the gulls calling overhead to distract her. She loved the trees, dark blue spruce, black cedars and tall pines that soared to the sky. She searched the forest floor for wildflowers—columbine coming up through cracks in the rocks, maidenhair ferns, and jack-in-the-pulpits peeking up from heavy shaded crevices. She experimented with various exposures against the changing light in the forest and marveled at how long it had been since she had just taken pictures for the joy of it—no assignment, no deadline, no jockeying for space. With Hopper sequestered in a small room away from the main room, she felt content knowing that he was writing, sealed for those few hours in his own planet away from distractions. She knew she was his greatest distraction and she worried about it. She loved him, yes, and more than she had ever thought possible, but at the same time she knew she loved with caution.

The past two years had been amazing. Everything she had ever dreamed of, she now held in the palm of her hand. Out there, the world was large and beckoning and always was that next assignment, the next test, the excitement of the new and unknown. Work was her balm. The fame was exciting, even heady at times. Walking into a party, watching the heads swivel toward her, listening to the undercurrent: "That's her . . . there she is . . . that's Kate Goodfellow." And there was the love she had with Hopper . . . and yet by some capricious quirk of fate, her love for this man and her work did not mix. Hopper seemed to want to barricade himself from new experience, something she could not fathom. Worse, he had an almost pathological attitude about *World* magazine, as if the magazine itself was some evil seducer. She was desperately in love and she needed love, but she needed work, too, and perhaps just as much. The pressure of his love was becoming too much for her, but she knew she could not break from him. There was something in the force of his need that kept her devoted to him, adoring of him. There was something in her that wanted to make him happy. She was in deep with Hopper. One part of her said "no," but the greater part said "yes."

All these thoughts drifted through her mind sitting with her back against a log one morning in the soft sand on their own little crescent beach. The sun was warm and there was no breeze. The gentle sea made a lisping noise when it came in. Gulls lay quiet on the water, like children's toys in a bath . . . all was serene and hushed. She had the eeriest feeling that she was somewhere in-between, not conscious or unconscious but floating like the gulls on an eternal sea. So she wasn't at all aware she was being observed until she heard someone coming down the stairs from the cliff above. She turned and couldn't make out who it was because of the way the sun fell, but he waved and she waved back, feeling as if she were coming out of a long sleep. As he got closer she saw it was

Tommy, and she also saw in his hand the unmistakable yellow
and black envelope of Western Union.

After a midday swim in the ocean, Hopper came up the path
to the house, invigorated by the cold seawater. Today he was
going to cook a Portuguese shellfish stew, distant cousin to the
great French bouillabaisse. He had planned the meal as a surprise and frankly had gone to a great deal of trouble about it.
For days he had been down on the docks talking to fishermen
about the variety of fish he wanted. From the chef at the Bar
Harbor Yacht Club he had bought two bottles of Meursault
wine and a bottle of Chartreuse. The dough for the authentic
Portuguese bread was even now rising in a great bowl covered
with cloth. As Hopper envisioned it, the meal would start with
the bowls of rich, garlic broth and a platter of fish and shellfish
heaped in the middle. This would be washed down with the
chilled Meursault. A salad and a mild goat cheese would follow, then the meal would end in the French tradition with rich
coffee and a glass of green Chartreuse into which he would
grind black pepper. Hopper, justly pleased with himself, whis-
tled as he climbed the stairs and then rushed onto the deck,
throwing off his robe so that he could plunge into the heated
pool.

The house was full of people. Two men were packing and
unpacking camera equipment from an endless array of valises
which were stretched end to end in the main room. A woman
stood near them checking things off of a list. Another man,
who turned out to be the driver of the car outside, leaned
against the large painted Swedish cabinet smoking a cigarette.
In the midst of all of this Kate was bent over a large map
spread out on the dining room table. She had on slacks and a
jacket, her traveling outfit.

"We brought you the best we could find in the time we had,
Miss Goodfellow," said the girl, holding up a dull green military parka. No one seemed to notice or care that Hopper Delaney was standing in the doorway stark naked.

Kate began rooting around in a large bag near her. "It
doesn't matter. If I get cold, I'm sure I can buy something
there. A sweater . . . or something." The girl turned away and

spotted Hopper. She gasped and then started to giggle.

"Hopper!" Kate whirled around. "Oh, darling . . . I have to tell you . . ." but then she stopped too and started to laugh. The more she laughed, the more she had to laugh. Hopper didn't move.

"What the hell is going on here?"

"Darling, don't you think you should—"

"No. I don't. Get these people out of my house."

"I can't. I mean we haven't any time. Don't you see . . ." She gestured at the mess on the floor, as if that explained everything. "Diz sent me a telegram yesterday, but Tommy . . . well, he had 'errands' to do. So they were already here by the time I got it . . ." She saw his face and hurried on. "It's the Arctic Circle, Hop. They want a story on the new governor-general of Canada who's gone off to explore the outer regions of Canada. Imagine, the Arctic Circle! The magazine didn't know a thing about the expedition until a few days ago. They've been trying to make arrangements, trying to find me, trying to get all this equipment up here . . . really, it's been extraordinary. These people have been driving for two days. It's going to be terribly exciting. . . ." She paused because she could see the look in his eye. She started toward him.

"I said get these people out of my house. Do you hear me?"

"Of course I hear you, you're shouting and you don't have to. I haven't time to argue. The plane leaves from Bar Harbor in less than an hour. Please, Hop . . ."

But he had grabbed her arm and had jerked her out onto the deck. The drama that took place was for the people inside like watching a movie with the sound turned off, for no one could hear through the thick glass. They could see plenty, however.

Kate twisted and turned in his grip, but he was stronger than she was. "How long have you known about this, Kate?"

"I told you. Diz sent a telegram—"

"You told him not to contact you unless it was an emergency. I heard you."

"I consider this an emergency, don't you?" She jerked her arm free and rubbed her wrist.

"You're going to go?" His tone was incredulous.

"Hop . . . please. This is my job. I have to go. Stories like this don't wait for my convenience . . . or yours, for that matter."

"Let someone else go."

"No." Her voice was measured and cool. "Why should I? You can't possibly think I would turn down a chance to see the Arctic Circle. Why, no one except explorers have ever seen it. Diz had a terrible time chartering a plane. No one flies that far north. It's exciting and important and—"

"—and what does that make me? Us? Something that passes the time until a more *exciting* ticket comes along?"

She looked at him with wide, uncomprehending eyes. "Why are you doing this? Why are you reacting so violently? I'm going out on an assignment. This is what I do. This is my work. What did you think? That we were going to remove ourselves from the human race forever? Hopper, I'm sorry I have to cut it off, but we've had the most wonderful two weeks. Please don't spoil it. I love you, but you can't take me away from my work. You should know that about me by now."

He let her go with a catch in his throat that startled both of them. It was a cry of pain. For a second he could not speak because he had no words and perhaps not even the ability to speak them if he had. His emotions were suddenly and so vehemently tangled up that he was thrown into a state of confusion. He stood back from her and tried to find in her face the woman who had kissed him awake only this morning with a flower in her hair. Instead he saw the look of someone impatient to get back to her chores and into her car and onto her next bloody hell *assignment*. He felt an icy stillness seep into his body and he shivered. She reached down and picked up the terry robe that he had thrown so buoyantly to the ground only moments before.

"Put this on," she said, not in kindness but with a slow, measured voice. "I think we've given the audience a good enough show for now. I'm going back inside and finish what I have to do." She turned to go and then looked back at him with an expression that now showed some glimmer of confusion, too. "Please don't be this way, Hop. I didn't know this trip was coming. It doesn't mean anything more than a few weeks . . . a month maybe. I'll be back and we can—"

"Where do I fit in your life, Kate?" he asked quietly. "Am I just one more scheduled event? Do I have to fit neatly between shoots and assignments?"

"Hopper, don't do this to me!" She raised her arms savagely and her voice shook with a vehemence that struck them both momentarily dumb. Startled, staring unblinking, they faced each other. Hopper's lips were parted for speech, but he closed them and felt his teeth click and his jaw harden. He was suddenly tired. He had trusted her. He had been wrong.

Kate's eyes were now swimming in tears, but Hopper took no notice. He pulled the robe around him and stalked off.

CHAPTER TWENTY-FIVE

HE CAME BACK to a hot and gritty city where there were few left to console him. Most of his cronies had decamped to the cooler shores of Long Island or retreats in the Adirondacks, and while Hopper could have had any number of invitations to stay, he chose to nurse his wounds in the gritty heat generated by steel and concrete. His emotions ran the gamut from fury to anguish to despair to bitter fury all over again. Worse than the anger was the sense of futility that set in. This scared him. He was living on the edge of his life for the first time, and he saw how helpless he was. It was not pleasant.

As the days dragged on into weeks, he determined to isolate himself from everything and everyone until a curious little incident occurred. In and of itself it was an insignificant thing, but it left an impression on Hopper. He found himself one afternoon on the Upper West Side, not an area that interested him much, but he had been walking through Central Park and decided to wander over to Broadway to an Italian restaurant he knew of—a big, dark wooden eating hall where he could count on a cool drink and anonymity. Because of the heat, the side streets were mostly deserted, but he found himself watching a young girl, maybe she was ten or eleven, playing

with a ball in a fenced-off school yard. It was an intricate soli-
taire game in which the ball was thrown up against the wall and
a series of moves had to be made before catching the ball
again. One—throw the ball and catch it. Two—throw the ball
and clap twice before catching it. Three—clap three times and
twirl. Four—clap, twirl, bounce. And so it went. She was good
at the game—agile, confident, and totally engrossed. Enter a
gang of boys. At first they watched her, then they started to
tease her and jeer. She paid no attention to them. Clap, twirl,
jump, bounce. The boys seemed more and more agitated until
finally one boy ran and pushed her off balance, grabbed the
ball, and threw it over the high fence into the street. Laughing,
they wandered off. What stayed with Hopper long after was the
expression on the girl's face. She had not been scared of the
boys, probably she knew them. Nor had she been angry. It was
the look of resignation and acceptance that got to Hopper. As
if, even at that young age, she had no illusions and knew that
no matter what, the ball was going to be snatched from her
and thrown away at the whim of the dominant male hierarchy.
He forgot about his drink and walked for many blocks before
hailing a cab to take him home.

Tweedledum and Tweedledee. That's how she came to think
of them—His Excellency, the Governor-General of Canada,
aka Lord Dumfries, and a full-fledged bishop of the Church
of England, Archibald Tweed, aka Archibald the Arctic. This
unlikely duo was steaming the waters of the Arctic Ocean on
board an old tug of a supply ship otherwise known as the S.S.
Diligence.

It had taken Kate almost a week to track the *Diligence* and
its illustrious entourage somewhere out in the wilderness,
and during that time she had been so busy giving chase that
she had had little time to reflect on the scene she had left in
Maine, but make no mistake, she was angry. He was unreasonable, possessive, and selfish. She had been a fool to think he
understood her. Her work was like a religion to her, and it
would always come first. Men could never understand this in a
woman. They never listened, and if they did, only heard what
flattered their utterly inflated high opinions of themselves. She

had expected it from lesser men, but not Hopper. His behavior was childish and vain and utterly stupid. She forced him out of her mind and concentrated on the work at hand. *Work, Kate. Work for pleasure, work for love, work for necessity—but work.* The words of her father comforted her now. Her father alone among men understood her, and he had given her so much. He had trusted her; shown her beauty where no one else had known it existed, taken her to places no girl had ever been and treated her with respect, encouraging her in every way possible. Why couldn't she find that kind of man again? It never occurred to her that built into the noble equations of her father's life was a wife, who devoted herself to her husband. And that which makes a perfect father, does not necessarily qualify as a perfect husband or lover.

The seaplane that took her so briskly away from Maine deposited her in the far north of Canada in a town called Churchill, the last commercial harbor on Hudson Bay. Once there she was on her own. She had to find a pilot to take her to the barren lands bordering the Arctic Ocean where tiny settlements were awaiting sustenance from the *Diligence*. This was not easy. The only experienced pilots flew the Royal Canadian mail to the outposts and these pilots could only take on limited charter work. Any passenger had to be prepared to give priority to the delivery of goods and mail. This meant said passenger could find herself stranded in the bleakest of waysides waiting weeks for passage on an irregularly scheduled airplane.

The pilot Kate eventually found soon earned her utmost respect. As they flew out over the last town of any size, all signs of human life and civilization seemed to disappear. And yet, without warning, after hundreds of miles following the lazy curves of a river and hours in the air, he would circle what looked to Kate like nothing more than a patch of trees and swoop down on a tiny settlement. He seemed to be able to fly with his fingertips over terrain that had never been mapped because it disappeared under a great ice load ten months of the year. All outposts relied on their radio equipment and the bravado of these mail pilots—flyers who could also act as medics, mechanics, and, once, Kate's pilot told her, he had stuffed a whole pack of yelping protesting dogs into the tail of the plane to fly them inland to a trapper.

Air travel exhilarated her and she was at once immersed in gathering as much information as she could from the pilot. How warm was the summertime in the Arctic? How light is the light of the midnight sun? Would the flashbulbs stand up under salt air and damp sea conditions? Rolly had made some shrewd guesses as to the photographic supplies and packed her accordingly. This attention and care had, unfortunately, not been applied to the gear they had sent her to wear. The summer air in the Arctic, it turned out, was cool and damp. Like a rainy spring day, the damp air soon seeped into the bones, and Kate wondered how well she could survive the persistent chill in the only parka the *World* researcher had been able to muster in the sweltering heat of New York in July.

That day her pilot put down in a small trading camp hundreds of miles from nowhere, and as he refueled, Kate went into the tiny clapboard Hudson Bay store in search of a sweater. The dark, musty interior was overflowing with merchandise— enough canned food for several winters, blankets, thermos jugs, Bunsen burners, woodstoves, gloves, and fur hats. There was even an old dusty but unused hand-crank Victrola and a stack of aged records. Seeing it she thought instantly of Hopper and Maine and the evenings by the fire wrapped in each other's arms. She fought down the tears and pretended intense interest in a heavy knit sweater on one of the counters. As she did so, she came aware of a small, dark man staring at her from over one of the counters piled with long johns. He stared at her so intently she started to feel edgy. What in heaven's name was the matter? Had she suddenly turned green?

He came around the counter pulling a large trapper's fur cap off his head, which he pawed and pulled in unbearable discomfort and embarrassment. "Excuse me, miss," he stammered in a heavy French Canadian accent, "but I stare at you because my wife, she is same shape of you." This burst out in a rapid-fire sentence so that Kate could not at first understand him. When at last he was made to say the same sentence over again, she could think of no suitable reply to this fact. It was only then that he began to tell her his sad little tale. It seemed his wife was from one of the Canadian provinces. He had left her to seek an income in the north territory trapping furs. Soon enough he had made enough money to induce his wife to come north. In preparation, he had arranged for an Eskimo woman to make her a hooded fur garment they usually made only for their own girls who were about to marry. The trapper's wife arrived, took one look at life in the far north, and promptly returned to the comforts of Manitoba. The coat had been lying ever since on the back shelf of the trading post because the trapper had not known what to do with it. He was determined that this redheaded woman, right here and now, should have it.

Reaching behind the counter, he came back with the garment lying across his arms. It was made of the smoothest caribou fur, trimmed in white reindeer. Like a dress, it hung midcalf, complete with hood edged in wolverine fur. "It's beautiful!" Kate exclaimed. It truly was one of the most beautiful things she had ever seen. "I couldn't take it, really, you must keep it for when you marry again." She thrust it back into his arms, but the little man shook his head. He kept gesturing for her to try it on. When she did, the trapper, the storekeeper, and now, the pilot, all stood back to admire her. Aside from being a most flattering garment, the fur framing her face and setting off her pale skin and red hair in a most dramatic way, it was warm as toast.

Something about the warmth it gave her and the face of the trapper whose marriage had met such an unhappy demise softened Kate's heart. A wave of forgiveness came over her. Hopper could be so gentle, so thoughtful and warm. She recalled how he liked to wash her hair, the two of them in the tub like kids and the games they had played. It was all so silly, splashing each other and . . . He had encouraged her, hadn't he? They collaborated on the book, equal partners in every way, and he encouraged her work then. He was a complicated man, a lonely man. More than that he was a needy man and not used to coming second. Dashing off at a moment's notice was great if you were the one doing the dashing, but if you were the one left behind, it must be very hard to bear. She hugged the caribou parka around her and right then and there sent Hopper a telegram via the radio transom.

One more day of flying and they spotted the boat on which His Excellency and his party were traveling. The crew and passengers of the S.S. *Diligence* were most surprised to gain a

passenger, what's more a lovely one outfitted in Eskimo wedding furs and carrying what seemed an excessive amount of
luggage, but she was made very welcome. They had already
been at sea for three weeks, so a new arrival made for much
festivity. Kate found that the passenger list, in addition to the
governor-general and the bishop, also included an aide-de-
camp, a cook, a valet, a secretary, and an English travel writer,
Percy Saunders, deeply engrossed in a book on the Dominion
of Canada. Everything possible had been laid in by Lord Dumfries to make the journey as comfortable as possible, and
now with the addition of the attractive magazine photographer, it was a surprisingly jolly party that cruised the Arctic
waterways.

The *Diligence* managed to get in two trips per year during
the summer thaw to deliver goods to the far north before the
great freeze sealed the tiny missions and trapper camps away
from the world again. Her deck was crowded with chickens
and pigs in crates, a tractor, assorted agricultural implements;
canned goods, clothes, and boxes piled high with other items.
In the midst of this the bishop sipped tea, the writer pecked at
a portable typewriter from a makeshift desk of two planks
stretched across crates, Kate set up her tripods and light reflectors, and His Excellency dictated notes to his secretary. Four
meals were served daily by the excellent chef—breakfast,
lunch, tea and dinner, and all of this was laced with the most
fascinating conversation.

Lord Dumfries, while exceedingly polite and hospitable,
was nonetheless a rather formidable character. It was extraordinary to Kate how he had managed recreate on board an old
steamer tug, in a land so remote it had never been fully explored, all the niceties of the gentleman's life. His clothes
were impeccable, his servants prompt in their ministrations,
and his daily schedule as ordered and punctual as if he were in
the center of London.

The bishop, on the other hand, was a cozy old sort and
given to much to-do over his drink—sherry before lunch,
whiskey before dinner, wine with dinner, and a large snifter of
brandy before bed. He was a large man with white hair and a
pink, jolly face of the Santa Claus persuasion. He loved talking and was genuinely interested in Kate and what she had

been sent to accomplish. He had been to the Arctic before. Once every other year it was his duty, he explained, to travel to this most desolate and remote corner of the world to minister to his communicants. Seasoned as he was, he was full of small tidbits of information about the Eskimos and life out on the tundra. Kate was most amused to find that it was a custom for a bishop to take the name of his diocese as a surname, which explained why this bishop was known as Archibald the Arctic. "But you must call me Archie, my dear, everyone does except my wife. She calls me Tweed."

And so Tweedledum and Tweedledee and Percy, the writer, and Kate, the photographer, and the whole lot of them resembling something of a real-life mad tea party set forth through the ice floes farther and farther north to the pole. Kate disagreed with the bishop that they were in a desolate place. No, she exclaimed over and over, it was stunning! The few short months of summer caused the ice to melt just enough to create arctic ponds—water that sparkled in the sun and formed extraordinary patterned rivulets over the vast expanse. Here and there were clumps of trees and swaying grasses, and fields of lichen of the palest green against startlingly blue ice formations. On her second day on board, the captain, a Mr. MacKensie, called out, "Polar bears off the starboard bow!" And indeed, a mother and two cubs stood staring at them before ambling off. Seeing such magnificent animals in the wild set Kate on a frenzy of animal photography. People assumed there was no wildlife in the Arctic, but there were walruses and caribou and whales and seabirds and even hares.

Percy attempted to amuse them in the evenings with facts about early explorers and animal habitats. He was an unusual looking fellow, pale as a ghost, tall and gawky like a stork, and his awkward appearance unfortunately carried over into his speech. Lord Dumfries, ever polite, appeared to listen, and the bishop out and out snoozed more than once during these "lectures," but Kate was riveted. This was the stuff of her college zoological days and to Percy's delight (few had ever shown him so much interest) they spent hours in deep conversation discussing the mating habits of polar bears and the migrations of whales.

Beyond wildlife, there was a vista so vast and awesome,

Kate wondered if there was a camera big enough to take it all in. Once, as she waited to catch the sun's rays coming through an ice formation, she took a deep inhale of breath—*how many people on earth have seen what I am seeing?* she thought. It was right that she had come. This was important. It was as if she was moving through a dream with nothing to distract her but the sheer sense of being alive. The loneliness of the land-scape, the colorless, unending tundra, the cliffs of towering ice and the black, rocky islands untouched by human existence—here on top of the world, it was a kind of perfection she had never known and she wondered why everything else was so complicated.

The *Diligence* traveled at a leisurely pace stopping in tiny set-tlements along the way to deliver their supplies and give the governor-general the chance to make a speech. This he did with great ceremony. It was always the same speech followed by a short tour of the community ending with Holy Commu-nion led by Archibald the Arctic looking grand in his white surplice and four-cornered cap.

At every stop Kate took the opportunity to send another cable to Hopper.

> PLEASE CABLE STOP I LOVE YOU STOP I MISS YOU
> WHAT CAN I SAY STOP YOU ARE A BEAST STOP I CAN'T
> LIVE WITHOUT YOU IF I COULD ONLY GET ONE WIRE
> FROM YOU

"Archie," she said one night after dinner as the two of them sat out on the deck bathed in the half-light of the midnight sun. "You must have to counsel people on all matter of things in your work. May I ask you something?"

"Of course, my dear. But I warn you, if it's about matters of the heart, and I think it must be because no one seems to want advice on anything else, I warn you, I have few answers."

"Fair enough. Maybe there are no answers. But how does one know what to do? What guides other people? I've never really thought about this before because I think I'm a pretty smart girl when all is said and done . . . but what do you make of another person whom you love and who loves you but . . . who makes it all so difficult? Oh, I don't know . . . I can't make up my mind no matter how hard I try."

The bishop was silent for a long while, and Kate thought maybe she had stepped over some invisible line of propriety, but then he said, "Love, true love, is not worrying or wondering or resisting. To be truly engaged in love is to be free of all that. It's a matter of letting go and accepting the other person as he is, and when you do, the difficulties simply go away. It's all very simple, really, but we persist in making it so difficult."

"You're married. Has it all been so simple for you?"

"Ah. I am sixty-eight years old. I met my wife when I was twenty, a long time ago and a different world, I'm afraid. A different century. I was a student and my wife was my second cousin. We had few expectations. We were both traditionalists. By that I mean we were not inclined to wander outside the confines we were born into. I had no reason to think about what I felt or if it was right or whether there could be something more. We married. We have four children. We have shared interests—our dogs, the garden, the children and their children, of course. I never had doubts about my calling, and she has been a good wife to that calling. But not so long ago, maybe twelve or fifteen years or so, I was pottering about in the garden, and my wife was coming down the lane outside our house in Dorset with the dogs. She couldn't see me, but I could see her and I watched her walking toward me for some few minutes. There was nothing unusual at all about the moment except I was inexplicably filled with an overwhelming feeling of love. And at the same time of letting go as if I had been holding on to something all those years. Blocking something, I suppose would be a better way of explaining it. I suppose it could have gone the other way. I could have been filled with remorse or disappointment or—perhaps I might have felt nothing. But instead I was blessed with a rare moment of the most blinding love. It was all so quick and simple and yet very profound. Mind you, we were then in our fifties, far past the age for these emotions, but I have been blessed, I think, to have had this moment."

He was silent again and Kate felt let down. His transcending moment, however wonderful for him, didn't seem to hold any relevance for her. Yet, mulling it over later that night in her bunk, the message was loud and clear. She needed to let go of something inside herself, some barrier that kept her from him.

They had been traveling for two weeks and the settlements were few and far between. Soon they would be turning back for the long journey home, but that day the *Diligence* put in at a very, very small post—little more than a shack with an anti-quated radio system. The radio operator asked permission to come on board. He was all grins, and spotting Kate, he approached her with mock formality. "We have been searching all over for someone who fits this telegram," he said, "and we decided you are the likeliest candidate." Kate looked at the cable he handed her. It was addressed to MAGNOLIA BLOSSOM, ARCTIC CIRCLE. Kate read the message, aware that everyone was looking at her with concern. Then she burst into tears and laughed all at the same time. The message read: COME HOME AND MARRY ME.

For the final week at every outpost someone would climb aboard asking for someone named Magnolia. Kate learned that in the entire Arctic region, news and messages were relayed from post to post via radio. Everyone naturally listened to everyone else's messages, resulting in a sort of over-the-back-fence communications system. Hopper's proposal and Kate's affectionate replies were followed and enjoyed throughout the Arctic zone as if they were a radio soap opera.

When Kate cabled Hopper that she was coming home, someone thought to tip off a news reporter in Toronto, who sent the message along to someone in Chicago, where Kate was due to change planes for New York. At Chicago's Orchard Field she was aghast to find herself surrounded by news photographers who seemed to know every bit as much about her personal life as she did.

"Are you going to marry him, Kate?" "Set a date yet?"

"What is this?" she demanded to know. "What are you talking about?"

"Aw . . . don't give us the runaround. So what's your answer going to be? I hope it's yes. You gotta put that poor guy out of his misery."

Kate looked around at the sea of grinning men and found she was unreasonably annoyed at being on the other side of the cameras. Just then, through the din of the airport, she heard her name called over the loudspeakers and turning to go to the counter to get her message, she bumped headlong into the beaming smile and open arms of Hopper. A blaze of flash-bulbs went off in unison.

CHAPTER TWENTY-SIX

A TRIP WEST; a marriage on top of a mountain in a ghost town, a renewed and passionate desire to make it work. It would work, Kate vowed. She would make it work. Her plan was simple. So simple, it had, in the moment she thought of it, lifted a heavy cloud of doubt, and though it wasn't quite as dramatic as Archie's dazzling moment, it was good enough. They would work together. She spoke to Otis and Diz. "Together we're a perfect team," she insisted. "Oh, I don't expect him to cover every story with me, but any big story, important story, you've got a ready-made pairing here."

Diz nodded, smiling. "Sounds good, kiddo. I sure don't mind putting the name Hopper Delaney on the roster and the husband and wife angle is great." Diz was as sanguine as ever.

Otis, however, frowned. "It occurs to me that Hopper is not exactly pounding at our door with enthusiasm. What makes you think he wants to write for *World*? Magazine writing isn't really his line."

"He wants to be with me." Kate was very sure of herself. "He's not going to write about teenage slumber parties, but put us on something with guts, something like what we did in our book. Hopper won't care what he's writing for just as long as it's about something meaningful. Think about it, Otis."

It was a time of contentment, new hope, and of such intimacy that neither one of them would ever forget it. They bought a farmhouse in Connecticut. She tried to make his study just like the one in Gramercy Park but at the last minute found some amusing wallpaper with the alphabet running all over it and put that up instead of the wood paneling she had planned. He arranged with Rolly to have a printer make giant blowups of her photographs of the forest in Maine, and these were fitted by seam into their dining room. They acquired two Maine coon cats. Kate discovered a domestic side to herself that she had never known. She loved fine china and linens and her table settings were always perfect, as if they were layouts in a magazine. He was happy poking through country barns and antique shops for odd pieces of furniture, and once found two big pieces of a black walnut tree trunk, which he carted home and deposited on the doorstep. "What on earth . . ." she said. He shook his head. "I don't know, but aren't they beautiful? Look at the double pattern of concentric circles." Kate's solution was to have a slab of heavy clear glass cut to the size of a dining room table. The tree trunks became the table stands so that the entire room took on the aura of an enchanted forest. They were both so pleased.

The letters that flew between them when Kate was on the road were close and loving. That Christmas they sat on the floor with the cats in front of the fire and drank hot rum and opened scads of presents to each other—silly things, like a Lionel electric train because he had always wanted one as a boy and funny little hats for the cats, who refused to wear them. Hopper tracked down first editions of old botany books with beautiful hand-painted illustrations which she wept over as if finding old friends again.

And they talked about having a child.

"It would change everything for me," Kate said quietly.

"One life is not better than another, honey," he said. "It's just a different life. You're wonderful with children. I've seen you. You pay attention to them, make them feel their opinion is worth something. Children give back so much more, I think, than ever we give them. You could draw from them, do photography for them, do books . . ."

"It must be a fascinating thing to watch a growing child," she replied dreamily. "To absorb his expanding world."

"A child, our child, would be a wonderful thing. You'd make a wonderful mother, Kate . . . like your own mother."

She didn't say anything, but she looked very pleased. "I've always wanted to have children," she told him. This was true, but . . . was there ever a right time?

Certainly not in the winter of 1940. Who could believe it? That loud little man with the Charlie Chaplin mustache was the master of all Europe. Hitler seemed unbeatable. Swastikas flew on the Champs Elysees, and war rallies in Berlin dominated the picture magazines and front-page stories in the news. Poles, Czechs, Danes, Norwegians, the Dutch, Belgians, Yugoslavs, and Greeks were now the unwilling constituents in Hitler's "New Order," many of them sent to death camps or forced to work as slave laborers. To the West, Britain stood alone. To the East, Russia lay like a giant bear. Americans watched the newsreels and picture magazines in dismay as London burned in the Blitz. Night after night hundreds of German dive-bombers and deadly *Dorniers* and *Heinkels* roared over the English Channel, most at night, dropping their cargoes of death. In one night alone there were 1,500 separate fires in the city of London. Bombs fell everywhere—on the East End slums, on Buckingham Palace, on cathedrals, on parks, on landmarks as old as the old city itself. Americans saw fires and skeleton walls and sidewalks buried deep in rubble and children being evacuated and crying women and homeless dogs, and roads clogged with frightened, desperate fleeing refugees.

The world had tumbled into a nightmare, and a journalist had no choice but to pay attention. That year in early January the screen version of Hopper's novel, *The Road to Nowhere,* was released. Though the reviews were excellent, the box office was a disaster. It seemed Americans had a different view of their country now—more patriotic than critical, and where there had been despair, there was now pride. Diz wanted Kate and Hopper to go out into the heartland and report on the new state of mind in America. Hopper was enthusiastic. Traveling about America was appealing to him. A whistle-stop tour felt just right. Kate agreed with reluctance. Somehow this was not the glorious assignment she had meant when proposing that the two of them work together, but she couldn't refuse and so they went.

For a time it seemed as if they were recapturing some of the excitement and discovery they had found in the trip South, and on Valentine's Day they sent out a photograph of the two of them sitting atop a train plying typewriter and camera. But after a few weeks Kate had had it.

"This is wrong!" she exploded. "Don't you see, Hop? We're in the wrong place at the wrong time. Winston Churchill is talking about blood, sweat, and tears and we're trying to drum up interest in the fraternal lodge picnic in Boise, Idaho. No one cares about that anymore—least of all the Americans themselves. They care about what's happening to people in bomb shelters. They care about what's going to happen to their sons. I don't want to be stuck out here in Idaho, I want to go to Europe."

Once she had said it, Hopper knew it would be useless to try to dissuade her. It was true what she said; the eyes of the nation had turned inexplicably abroad. They discovered that the whole country had an air of marking time, and everybody said *we'll-be-in-the-war-in-three-months,* or they said *we're-in-it-now-but-we-don't-know-it,* or they said *it's-not-our-war-and-we'll-never-get-into-it.* Everyone had an opinion—and emotions ran strong. America was like a ticking time-bomb waiting to go off. More and more boys went off to training camps, and there were uniforms everywhere looking new and spruce and awkward on these boys, so young they looked as though they were playing dress-up.

World magazine had three reporters in Europe, and more and more the pages of the big, glossy publication were reporting war news. But wanting to go and going were two different matters.

"You've got three guys over there, why not me . . . and Hopper, too. I know I can find stories that are different. And if America gets in it, I want to be there. I want . . ."

Diz put his hands on her shoulders and made her sit down. "I hear you. Listen to me and don't interrupt. Last week we had a very interesting communiqué from the Soviet ambassador in Washington. No one, least of all the Soviets,

thinks Hitler will hold to his nonaggression pact with Stalin.
Hitler is going to move on Russia, and he's probably going
to make his move soon. He'll want it over and done with before the winter sets in. Otis wants to send someone into
Moscow."

Kate leaned forward. "Russia? No one from the West has
been inside Russia in years. What makes you think they'll
let me in?" It was true. Russia had been closed to all Western
correspondents for over a decade. News, photographs, everything came only from their government-controlled news
system.

"Well, the fact is, they won't let you in. But . . ."

"But what, Diz?"

"But, according to the ambassador, they would welcome
their great hero Hopper Delaney. And, yes, his wife as well."
Diz winked.

"Hopper?" Kate was confused. "I don't understand."

"Honey, they adore Hopper in Russia. They love his books.
The Road to Nowhere is one of their bibles—oppressed underclass in a capitalist society, et cetera, et cetera. The movie may
have been a flop here, but in Moscow, it's standing room only.
If Hopper will agree to go, he will get the red-carpet treat-
ment. You will go along as his wife, and maybe through him
you can get permission to respectfully take discreet photographs and, incidentally, get a bead on the German assault."
He paused looking at her closely. "You're awfully quiet,
Kate."

Kate blinked. "It's great, Diz. It really is. I just need a
minute to take it in."

In less than a week visas had been arranged and preparations
made, yet it would take them over a month to reach their destination. With the occupation of France, Poland, and Czechoslovakia, Hitler's armies had all but closed every possible
route through Europe. There was no choice but to travel the
other way around. They traveled by ship to Hong Kong. Then
by plane deep into China skirting the Gobi Desert to enter
Russia through its southeastern door. They traveled with five
cameras, twenty-two lenses, four portable developing tanks,

and three thousand peanut flashbulbs. Their luggage weighed in at 617 pounds, of which 600 was Kate's.

It was a miserable trip plagued by typhoons by sea, sandstorms by land. The airplane provided them in Hong Kong was old, too old for the war being waged between China and Japan, and broken engines waylaid them several times in dreadful outposts. Nervous exhaustion set in. More than once Hopper threatened to abandon the mission and take them home where they belonged. Kate cajoled and begged and pleaded with him. He had to go, his books were more popular in Russia than in America; if he was a great writer now, this trip would make him a great hero as well. By the time they got to Moscow, she had him convinced that he alone could save all of Mother Russia.

But despite all her best efforts, Hopper was ill at ease. Foreign travel was not his métier. All the traits she had witnessed on the trip through the South—his patience and easygoing manner, his concern for humanity, his curiosity—were nonexistent on Russian soil. For the first few weeks Hopper stayed in their room at the American embassy and refused to venture out. Kate, however, thrived. Her reporter's temperament propelled her into the streets. Moscow was like an untapped gold mine, and she set about finding its hidden treasures with zeal. Children, shops, shopkeepers, subways, fashions, schools, parks—anything that took her fancy. She knew she was being watched but no one ever stopped her. Even the day she went into a church and found services going on. The West had been led to believe that religion had been forced underground, but no, here it was just waiting for her eager lens.

Day after day she rushed back to the embassy filled with delight at all she had seen. Hopper barely paid attention. He stayed holed up pounding out stories on his typewriter—stories about home. "But these are about poor blacks and whites in Georgia." Kate held up a raft of papers, incredulous. "There's a whole new world out there, and you're sitting here writing about this?"

He was furious with her for that, and he stayed furious with her. "Look, Miss Star Reporter, it's because of me you can take these pictures in the first place."

Diz had not exaggerated. Hopper's books had sold in the

millions. Themes of the downtrodden in a capitalist society went over big in a Communist country. The powerful Soviet Writers Union put pressure on the Cultural Relations Committee to recognize Kate Goodfellow as a meaningful ally in the Russian cause. For once his influence was greater than that of *World* magazine, and he was unabashedly smug about it.

Kate simmered but acquiesced. After all, this was the fruition of her dream—that together she and Hopper would form a grand partnership, that between them and ahead of them lay a broad highway of books and articles, that together they would meld into one perfect union of collaboration. She never said another word about his writing or his barricade against the Russians. Instead, she admired the stories and brought him back amusing bits of news and observations at the end of each day as if he were a convalescent. After a few weeks he emerged from his shell.

June 22, 1941. Three huge German armies had massed on the Russian border. Everyone agreed it was only a matter of days before the Germans would attack, yet when it happened, everyone seemed unprepared. The Germans moved suddenly and viciously with tremendous force. At the end of the first day they had destroyed over eighteen hundred Russian army airplanes in the greatest victory of a single day's battle in the history of military aviation.

The Germans surrounded Leningrad in the north, and were heading for Stalingrad in the south and Moscow in the center. "Russia is broken!" shouted a jubilant Hitler. "She will never rise again!" In Moscow the city began a massive evacuation. Kate and Hopper were summoned to the ambassador's office.

"Don't talk too much," Hopper cautioned. "Let the ambassador feel he is doing his duty. The less we argue, the better chance we have to stay put."

Kate squeezed his arm. This was her Hopper. This was the man she loved. She knew he could handle people better than anyone alive.

The ambassador greeted them gravely. "No one knows how soon Moscow will be bombed, but when it begins, the loss of life and destruction are bound to be terrible. It is my duty to protect the lives of American citizens." Kate and Hopper said nothing.

"I have secured two tickets on a train bound for Vladivostok; from there we can, I feel sure, promise you safe conduct across the border. It might be your last chance to get out of Moscow." Still they said nothing.

The ambassador leaned back in his chair. "However," he continued, after a meaningful pause, "if after thinking over the perils to which you are exposing yourselves, and if, after seriously weighing the dangers involved, it is your considered decision to stay, our embassy will help in every—" He had no chance to finish because in the next instant Kate was around the desk and the United States ambassador found himself landed with an exuberant kiss.

That afternoon they were moved over to the National Hotel, where the ambassador saw to it that they were installed in a corner suite overlooking the Kremlin. It was an ornate room given to gilded cherubs, crystal chandeliers, tables loaded extravagantly with pretty objects and bronzes, and an immense bed covered in silks and embroidered satins. A grand piano and a white bearskin rug completed the decor. The manager was puffed up with pride over the splendor of the room, but Hopper and Kate momentarily forgot their manners and went into peals of laughter so that the manager thought them both quite mad. Regaining their composure, they forced attentive faces as he pointed to the balcony in the room, the *very* balcony on which Trotsky had addressed the trade unions. Stepping out onto the hallowed space, he proudly pointed to the view of the Kremlin, Lenin's tomb, and Red Square. Kate breathed a sigh of bliss. It was a photographer's dream. The German Luftwaffe would no doubt head straight for the Kremlin, and in doing so, directly toward the lens of her camera.

She knew she was facing the biggest scoop of her life; the biggest country in the war was about to enter the biggest war in the world, and she was the only photographer on the spot representing any Western publication. She carefully put the developing trays and chemicals in the bathtub. Hopper was as galvanized as she. Two blocks away CBS radio had succeeded in setting up a broadcast unit after three years of red tape and negotiation with the Soviet government. Whether or not they could commence to broadcast was contingent on whether Hopper Delaney was the broadcaster . . . if he would consent, then red tape could be cut when it wanted to be. His job would be to send eyewitness accounts over the airwaves into Europe and ultimately America.

The Germans were expected to begin bombing Moscow that night. Hopper insisted on staying with Kate. Then, when the all clear was signaled, he would make his way to the radio unit. All was in readiness. Three cameras were taped to the balcony, each aimed in three different directions. She planned out her shots by daylight. When the bombing started, she hoped the incendiary light would be enough to show what was happening.

Then, when all was ready, the two of them sat on the bear rug as delighted with themselves as kids at a birthday party. Their taut nerves and expectant energies gave them both the same idea at the same time. Kate leaped up and pulled her slacks off as fast as she could. Hopper never bothered to do anything but unbutton his trousers. She lay down on the bear rug and he came into her with a lover's mighty desire. It had been a long time since they had made love like this. Now it seemed new, as if they had never known each other before—the danger, the monumentality of what was about to happen, the strength and power filled them up until they exploded into each other with a force neither one of them expected. They couldn't talk—not then. When she finally got up and pulled her slacks back on, she looked at him.

"We belong to each other, don't we, Hop?"

"Did you ever doubt it?"

"No . . . not really. Not now. No matter what happens, I want you to know you are everything to me."

"And you me, Magnolia. Everything."

In the distance they could hear the first air-raid sirens start. They both reached for each other's hand. Suddenly the door flew open and two enormous men dressed in brown uniforms began shouting and waving guns at them. They were the blackout wardens.

"You come," said one. "Now."

Hopper waved them away. The sirens screamed louder, and in the distance they could hear the drone of planes coming in. Then the beams of the spotlights shot upward, crossing and recrossing until the whole sky was covered with a luminous plaid design.

"NOW!" roared the men. Kate and Hopper found burly arms pinning their own arms down, and though they struggled mightily, they were no match for the wardens. As the bombs dropped overhead, both Hopper and Kate were hurried to the basement where all the hotel guests and staff were made to go—to safety.

When the all clear sounded, she rushed up the stairs and into their room. One of the cameras had fallen over and the lens was shattered. The other two stood secure where she had taped them. Inside the film was as blank as when she had put it there. She fell down on the floor and sobbed. She had missed the big moment.

They spent all of the next day trying to secure permission to stay in the room while the bombing was going on, but the Russians were nothing if not thorough in their ability to adhere to government policy. As dusk approached and with it the sureness of another attack, Hopper suddenly clapped his hand to his forehead.

"It's so simple, why didn't I think of it before!" he exclaimed. "We'll just hide."

"Hide! Where?" She eyed him in frustration.

"Hide anywhere. Pretend you're playing hide-and-seek. Pretend your big brother is coming to look for you, but he isn't so smart, nor does he really care where you are, but your mother had told him to go look." He winked at her.

The sirens started up again.

Kate, her heart racing, plunged under the bed. Hopper, who was too big to crawl under the bed, grabbed the bear rug. Kate couldn't see what had happened to him, but she could hear the wardens coming down the corridor and doors opening. She held her breath. The door to their room swung open and a flashlight roamed the room. Two voices spoke urgently to one another—finally one said, *"Nyet."* The door shut firmly behind them.

Kate didn't move for a minute, then she cautiously peeped out from under the bed. It was dark and she couldn't see Hopper.

"Hopper?" she whispered. "Are you there?"

"Gr-r-r-r-r-r" came the low reply. Kate peered into the shadowy corner of the room. Sitting in all his dignity behind the sofa was an enormous stuffed white bear, only it was stuffed with Hopper. Outside the first bombs started to fall. Inside, two people were crawling toward the window, both of them in peals of laughter.

And so they fell into a pattern. At dusk they would hide until the wardens had gone. Then Kate would creep onto the balcony, lying low so the guards in Red Square could not see her and she could position her cameras. Meanwhile, Hopper would move furniture against the far wall and stow all bric-a-brac and art under the piano; otherwise they ran the risk of being knocked out by a brass lamp or agate inkstand. Once the bombing started, Kate worked nonstop viewing streaks of light in the night sky through the ground glass of her camera lens. Hopper made notes. When the bombing stopped, both she and Hopper would make their way to the radio station a few blocks away. Hopper was allowed only ten minutes of air time. As he improvised from his notes, Kate would time him, signaling for him to speed up or slow down so that his broadcast fit the time allotted to him. They worked in perfect harmony—and they were making history.

Afterward they would creep back to their hotel room and crawl into the luxurious bed. There they would hold each other and talk in whispers. They played word games and told each other secrets about themselves that each swore they had never told another. They talked of home—the farm with the big warm kitchen and the pretty garden and the cats curled up in their baskets by the fire. They talked of the child they both wanted. Their child who would have the best of everything. A girl, Hopper decided, with Kate's red hair and a mother to teach her how to see, really see, the world and a father to show her how to care deeply for her fellow human beings. When they talked of the child, Kate thought of herself as a child, all snug in the big bed in the black night, because with Hopper, she had her family back again. Life was so good and sweet in that make-believe world just before dawn, when at last they would both fall into a deep sleep. By early afternoon Kate would be in the enormous bathroom filled with dripping films hung from cords which she had stretched back and forth between the high water pipes and pinned to the edges of towels and window curtains. Hopper worked on his broadcasts, and nothing was ever said about the nocturnal child who got born over and over again in the wee small hours.

After a few days the wardens got wise to the subterfuge, and once again Kate and Hopper were dragged bodily from their room to a shelter in the subway. Frustrated and angry, Kate appealed to the American embassy, but the ambassador could do nothing except give her permission to photograph from the embassy roof where no Russian wardens were allowed.

Hopper tried to talk her out of it. "After all," he insisted, "you've got hundreds of pictures of the bombing. Why risk trying to get more?"

"Because I haven't got the one I want" was all Kate said.

But Hopper didn't see. He didn't want to break their routine. Nothing about the bombings, indeed nothing about the war excited him the way it did Kate. War disgusted him. There was no justice in war, only ugly truth. Excitement, heroics, adrenaline—none of it appealed to him. It was all too immediate and gave him no time for reflection. Hopper wanted to go home and he wanted Kate to come with him, but instead of stating this simple and quite reasonable fact, he accused her of aggrandizing death and destruction. War sickened him, he said. She was risking death and for what? Kate insisted she wasn't aggrandizing anything. She was merely recording history. She dismissed his notions and proceeded to set up her equipment on the roof of the embassy.

That night she stood alone. Hopper refused to venture out. For a brief moment she forgot her camera, forgot Hopper, forgot everything. The spectacle from the roof was ravishing. Brilliant color flashed about her and in the distance she could hear guns and the drone of airplanes coming in low and fast-dropping flares which appeared to her like blazing parasols floating to earth and lighting up the whole central section of the city. She had never before witnessed such magnificence. This, she knew, would be like no other night.

As soon as she got behind her camera, her body chemistry changed. She was relaxed, concentrated, tireless, and fearless. She was immune to death and danger, but then like a deer in the meadow, she lifted her head. Nothing had changed, but instinctively she knew that something larger and deadlier than

anything she had ever known was heading toward her. She
climbed back into the window of the embassy, and shielding
her camera under her, she ran to the far side of the room and
crawled under the heavy carpet. Then it came. A bomb exploded not fifty feet from the building, blowing every window
in so that broken glass rained down on her. A heavy ventilator
blown in from the windowsill landed not two feet from where
she lay. She was still for only a moment, and then she was up,
picking her way through the glass and debris once more to the
window. What she saw was truly astounding. An enormous
plume began to rise into the air. It seemed to hang there frozen
in the moonlight and then out of the thick, billowing smoke,
stones and boards began to drop out of it. Kate raised her
camera once more and took one last picture. Shaken but sure,
this time she had the picture she wanted.

Hopper was furious. When he saw the broken glass knee
deep and the destruction of the upstairs room, he wept. She paid
him little attention and ignored his concerns. All she cared
about was developing her film. Hopper leaned against the wall
watching her as she bent over the tub. She was silent and intent on what she was doing. The smell of the chemicals made
him feel faintly ill. There was no light in the room except for
the dim red glow of the safelight, and she looked to him like a
witch. The deep shadows made the angles in her cheekbones
and the hollow of her cheeks ugly and almost inhuman. Her
mouth, the wide full mouth that laughed so easily and was to
him the sweetest mouth to kiss, was taut now as she waited for
the first images to appear, and it seemed to him thin and hard.
He saw that a band of perspiration had broken out on her upper lip, and she looked almost carnivorous, a hungry cat about
to pounce on a small and defensless prey. In that moment he
hated her, hated what she had done to him, hated himself for
following her halfway around the world so that she could
"get" her picture. He had given her everything—his dreams,
his heart, his whole attention—and she had repaid him by
risking her life, the life of their unborn child, their whole future together so that she could lean over a bathtub filled with
smelly chemicals with that sickening expression.

At that very moment she let out a whoop of delight. "My
God, Hopper. It's wonderful. It's incredible. I can't believe it.

Come and look." And she grabbed his arm and pulled him over to the tub.

The finished photograph floated in the bath. In the inky blackness were the spires of the Kremlin illuminated by incandescent zips and melting blobs of light. It was as though the Russian antiaircraft gunners and the German pilots had been handed giant paintbrushes dipped in paint and were executing abstract designs with the sky as their canvas. It was magnificent.

She hugged him with all her might, and she felt so alive in his arms. Her eyes were radiant—and he felt lost.

PART FOUR

1942

"We'll meet again,
don't know where, don't know when. . . ."

CHAPTER TWENTY-SEVEN

"MR. DELANEY. WE'RE about twenty minutes out of Pittsburgh. I hate to wake you, but we got to prepare the room." Hopper opened his eyes. Had he been asleep? Dozing maybe. He glanced at his watch. It was five in the morning, and outside the train window he could see the dawn just beginning to break over farmland. He rubbed the stubble on his cheek and came fully awake, piecing together the last twenty-four hours. Chicago . . . all those reporters . . . that college girl . . . sweet girl but so young, too young . . . Pittsburgh? Yes. He had to give up his room, and then what was he supposed to do? Stand the rest of the way into New York? But the porter assured him of a seat in the bar car. "They closed it down at midnight. Yessir. Too many kids on board gettin' drunk. You go on down there, Mr. Delaney, two cars down. My friend Al is expecting you . . . he's got coffee."

For some inexplicable reason Hopper's eyes filled with tears. He coughed and cleared his throat and then stood and reached for George's hand. "Thank you."

The bar car was empty except for some of the porters and trainmen taking their breaks. Al was expecting him, and the hot coffee and toast set before him was restorative. He used

the bar car lavatory to shave and wash up and then came back
to an even bigger breakfast. In Pittsburgh he watched the dra-
mas played out in the station. Boys in uniform leaving, girl-
friends crying, mothers and fathers trying to look brave.
These were the long goodbyes of war played out, he supposed,
all the way back to antiquity.

He thought of his own goodbye. "You can't leave, Kate.
You can't leave *us*." Why did he have to keep remembering
that damn phrase?

It had started out such a good evening. He had come in
from his studio, a tiny writing cubicle he had built himself in
the back of the garden along the order of George Bernard
Shaw's writing shack. Nothing architectural to speak of but
an engineering dream. The shack was built attached to a center pole, which meant you could turn the entire structure so
that its large front window could always face the light. It
virtually eliminated the need for electric light or heat, although both were installed just in case. The novel he had
started some months before had not been going well. He had
returned from Russia in a state of exhaustion and had ever
since been fighting his work. This battle he kept to himself
because Kate did not like to hear when his work was not going well. Her work was always going well, and she was so
busy now that America was in the war. On December 5 they
had celebrated the astounding news that the Russians had
managed to hold back the Germans on the very threshold of
Moscow. The tide had turned, and snow, brutal cold, and Soviet determination had stopped the Nazi blitzkrieg dead. Two
days later the Japanese attacked Pearl Harbor. America declared war on Japan, along with Japan's allies, Italy and Germany. And now here it was, almost a year later, an autumn
evening in September of 1942.

America's declared war galvanized Kate to even greater
heights of achievements. Now she crisscrossed the nation on
lecturing junkets raising money for the war effort. Of course,
Hopper was invited, too, and occasionally he joined her,
which always caused a stir, but she was really the draw. People
came by the hundreds to any hall in which she was booked.
While Kate thrived, Hopper found that traveling only made
coming home to his work all the harder. "You stay, darling,

and get back to work," she said, and so he did, wondering why the work was not going well but now, this very day, he had begun to see that what he had conceived of as a novel was in reality a play, and all of a sudden the dark veil blocking him from inspiration had been lifted. A play! He had adapted *Belle* to the stage and had drafted the first of many scripts for the film version of *The Road to Nowhere,* but he had never written a play in and of itself. Like a scientist who finally breaks a code, the ideas and words fairly tumbled out of him. He worked all afternoon without pause and was exhilarated the way one always is when things are going your way. He could hardly wait to tell Kate. His working title—*Scorched Earth*—was a phenomenon they had witnessed firsthand in Russia. As the Germans advanced, the Russian people rose to defend their homeland with a ferocity that astounded those foreigners still in the country and soon the whole world. Old men, women, and children burned their own houses and factories. They blew up bridges, dynamited huge dams, destroyed livestock and food supplies—everything that lay in the path of the Germans became scorched earth so that not so much as a single grain of corn would be left to aid the enemy. His play would center on a family torn by wars that raged not without but within the human heart.

When he came into the house, she was standing in the living room mixing cocktails. She didn't hear him at first, and so he paused just to look at her. Everything about her was familiar, and at the same time he marveled at how she continued to fascinate him—her hands absorbed with the mixing and stirring of the liquor, her face glowing as the last rays of the sun filtered into the large comfortable room. Then he noticed that she was wearing evening clothes, a lovely long green dress with her hair rolled high off the brow.

"Hello, there," he said. "You're all dressed up. Very pretty, too."

"What do you mean, 'very pretty'?" She came over to him with the drink, laughing. "I'm perfectly gorgeous, and you know it. This is a new dress; I have a new hairdo and the very latest color in lipstick, Jungle Red. Do you like it?"

"Hmmm. I like the mouth it's on even better." He put his arm around her and started to pull her to him, but she laughed again and pushed him away. "Not until you're bathed and dressed up as pretty as I am. I have a surprise for us tonight. I'm taking you on the town."

They were extravagant. A hired car and driver took them to New York to El Morocco. He hadn't been to his once-favorite haunt in ages. The maître d' gave them a ringside table as of old, and as they were seated, Hopper watched the men at surrounding tables admire Kate, which pleased him because she was his.

They ordered champagne, which was very extravagant because you couldn't get champagne much anymore due to the war, and when it was cooled and poured, Kate touched her glass to his and said, "To us," and he answered, "Yes. Always. To us." It went on like that through dinner. They danced and told themselves what good dancers they were until both of them felt inspired to try new steps they hadn't tried before and marveled aloud how perfectly they executed them. It was the kind of evening where everything meshed to perfection. The talk was light and they laughed a lot, they saw people they hadn't seen in a long time and waved. The orchestra seemed to know all their favorite songs so that they kept springing up to dance again. Some of the tunes made them remember something, and they said to each other, "What does that remind you of . . . ?" And the other one always knew.

And then, just when the evening was at a high point, Hopper realized that Kate had some special purpose in it, that she had staged this evening deliberately . . . and his breath caught. A child. She was going to tell him she was pregnant with their baby.

"There's something I want to tell you," she said to him at last, "and it's going to be hard."

She lifted her eyes and met his steady gaze.

"I've got a new assignment . . ." but he didn't listen. He felt his heart lurch in disappointment, and now his steps on the dance floor were clumsy. She was talking, telling him something, but he would not listen to her, not here, not now in this crowded room filled with uniformed men and their women looking ever so chic. He took her by the arm. "Let's get out of here."

They spoke little in the car going home, but once back in

their house, she turned to him. "Hop, don't make this any worse than it is. I'll only be gone a few months."

"You toss out 'a few months' as if you were referring to a few days. What do you think 'a few months' means to me?"

"I don't know."

"I'll tell you, then. When you're gone, I can't work. I can't stay in this house."

"You could move back to the city until I get back."

"Go back! You think I could find my old life again? This is my life now. You are my life."

"Hopper, don't say these things to me again. We've been through this hundreds of times. I can't live without my work and my job is to go where the stories are. I have to be there. Once I get to England I'll be looking for some way to get to a battlefront. . . ."

"But you were there, for God's sake. You almost got killed in Moscow. You saw the bombs. You took hundreds of pictures of death and desolation and starvation. By God, you've cornered the market on weeping women and orphaned children. How much more do you have to do? And why?"

"Because I need to be where the action is. I need to be where it matters most, and right now, what matters most is not you or me but the courage and nobility of ordinary people coping with the most extreme situation imaginable. If I can put down in black and white the tragedy of war, if I can make people see how horrible war is, then perhaps I will have done my little bit toward ending wars for all time."

"Come off it, Kate. Don't let's get noble. It doesn't suit you. You want to get in this war because you are so competitive and aggressive you can't bear someone else getting all the cover stories at *World*. Isn't that it? Why not be honest for once? You haven't had a cover in months—they've all gone to the war boys. And while we're at it, it isn't the issue of war that makes you want to go, it's the thrill and danger and adventure of war itself. It's plucky Kate Goodfellow, girl reporter on the front lines, darling of *World* magazine. How many more times do you have to see your name in lights? What about us?"

"Us? The world's going to hell and what are we doing about it? Lecturing? Giving blood? Lending our names to a few committees and causes? Buying an ambulance for Britain? I can't do that anymore, Hop." She saw the look on his face and quickly added, "You act as if I'm leaving for good. This assignment is over in two months."

"You've said that. And do you expect me to believe that in a few months you'll come home? A few months, is it? I'd say you're ready to fight the whole damned war down to the bitter end! How long have you been planning this?"

"I didn't tell you because I knew you would react this way. Otis has been working for months on getting special privileges for *World* reporters as war correspondents. Now he's got them. We've all been made lieutenants in the Army." Her eyes were dancing with excitement. "Don't you see? Now I can go anywhere the army wants me to go. So much easier than as a civilian."

"So you *have* known about this? And now you waltz in here pleased as anything with your military rank and announce you're leaving me? Do you know that for one brief moment I thought the whole setup of this evening was a preamble for you to tell me you were pregnant?"

"Oh." She was momentarily caught off guard. "Oh, Hop, I'm sorry. It never occurred to me—"

"Of course it didn't. And speaking of which, what about having a baby? In Russia you were all for it. Phoebe. We even have her named. She's as real to me as if she were already born. You said when we got home. Then you said after this trip or that trip or any trip. And now a year has passed and you're leaving for two months."

"But don't you see, you act as if the whole world revolves around you, what you want, what you need, how you work. You married me, Hop. Not some dutiful wife. You thought marriage would give you some sort of possession over me, but I can't live like that. And I can't live with this constant Byzantine struggle for control."

"It has nothing to do with control, but it does have to do with need."

She opened her mouth and then closed it, walking over to the bar as if to pour a drink. "Need. What about what I need. I can't explain it to you. I can't even explain it to myself. I just know I have to go. I can't stay here, I can't do what you want me to do. I can't teach photography or write books or lecture. I've tried. I've tried everything I know to be the person you want me to be, everything except having a baby, and I can't do that now. It would be wrong, terribly wrong. Babies should come when they are wanted, and right now I don't want to stop what I'm doing. I have to go, Hop. I have to."

"There's no use in all this talking. Marriage is a life for two, not one. We deserve more from each other."

Kate turned away impatiently. "Can't you see that this is all so much bigger and more important than us? You're asking me to turn my back on the biggest story of the century, but I can't. I'm a reporter. It's in my blood. Yes, I like excitement. I need it. The problem with you is you don't love your work anymore. You say you need me here with you so you can work, but you don't write, you putter. You seem content to bask in the old glories. I hate that. I loathe it. It's phony and unreal and has nothing to do with the man I fell in love with and respected for his passion and strength of will. You've lost all your passion, and now you want to drain me of mine."

"Drain you! I want to have children with you. I want to fill you up and create a future with you that has some meaning to it. Instead you seem to find it more worthy to dress up in a uniform and go rushing off to find a battle, any battle, just to say you've been there. It's never about the future, it's only about now. You have turned this marriage into a dismal apparition. Passions don't die, Kate, they just change."

"Hopper, *listen!*" she cried out. "If you wanted a family, you should have married someone—anyone—but me. You knew what mattered to you from the beginning."

"I thought I knew. I still do. I've waited a long time, Kate, for something better than this. After Moscow, you said. Now you're telling me you have to go back to Europe to show the world the horrors of war? Christ! The world knows that! And believe me, thanks to you photographers, they will know it in sickening excessive detail before this is over."

She shook her head and then turned and went upstairs. The first light of dawn was shining through the trees of the garden. Hopper stepped out onto the terrace, and the cool morning mist enveloped him as if he were in a dream. He stood there for a long time, and when he heard her coming down the stairs, he turned. She was wearing a uniform. At first he wanted to laugh. Instead a weary patience overtook him. She started to say something, but he held up his hand.

A lock of his hair had fallen over his forehead, as it always did when he got excited or agitated, and she saw that it was no longer the black hair she always pictured it to be, but now it had a peppering of gray. She wanted to reach out and smooth it back. His eyes found hers at that very moment of softening. "For God's sake, Kate, don't leave. Don't leave *us*."

Kate broke his gaze. She could feel the tears of frustration, and she fought them down, staring out the large bay window to the garden. It wasn't a formal garden but one which meandered through a pretty wood and now it was beautiful in the early dawn light. Her idea of gardening was to discover something wild in the woods and weed around it with utmost care until it had a chance to grow and spread. Now she saw the fruits of her handiwork. The rising sun cast a stream of light over the dark floor of the woods showing a carpet of wildflowers and ferns, their lives so short-lived that the sight of them now was almost painful. She wanted to rush out and hold the flowering back with her hands, pin the tiny blossoms so they might stay just as they were.

She turned back to Hopper and she did weep now. "Sometimes the things you fall in love with people for are the things you like least about them in the end. I belong to my work and nothing ever seems to change that—no matter how hard I try." She picked up her canvas bag and stepped toward him tentatively, hoping he might relent, but his face was immobile. She put her hand to his cheek and kissed him, knowing he would not respond; knowing he might never respond to her again.

"I did try, Hopper," she said miserably, "and I love you. But I have to go. And there it is."

CHAPTER TWENTY-EIGHT

AND THERE IT is. It was one of Kate's little expressions—one that had irked him over the years because it was always delivered with such finality. *There it is*—there is no more. Hopper stood at the window of Otis Bennett's large corner office staring out over the city. He couldn't bear to look at these people gathered in the room. He couldn't bear the look of misery and all the bloody heartfelt sympathy they directed his way. And so he stood at the window and stared out. Instead of skyscrapers and churches and brownstones, he teased his mind into thinking of them as chessmen, advancing, retreating, until the whole city seemed as if a grossly outsized game board. Housed out there were all the players, each one hoping his or her next move would bring them closer to the mark, the dream, the goal. Out there, some would be winners, but most were doomed to lose, lost in misery, envy, heartache, fear, and confusion. He looked at the city and saw it all. Six days and on the seventh day they will put her to rest. *And there it is*.

Six days, a roller-coaster ride of hope and hopelessness. The casualty list was not complete. Perhaps it never would be. At least half of the people on board the torpedoed ship had survived, all of them picked up by helicopters and hospital ships by the second day. The rest? Unconfirmed dead or missing. Overcast weather, rain, and fog had hampered search efforts, and now the word from Washington was that all official search had been called off.

"Hopper?" Otis was standing next to him. "We'd like you to see the mock-up."

He turned back into the room. There they all were, each with his own thoughts, and he wondered what they might be. Virginia York—kind, thoughtful, efficient Miss York. He had never called her by her first name, almost no one did, even after she had been promoted to a staff position. What was it? The negatives editor. He remembered coming in the office one day and finding Miss York sitting over a table with a light underneath it. Beside her was an enormous magnifying glass so that she looked like some comic-strip version of a private eye. She had laughed at his observation and said that was exactly what she was. Her job, it seemed, was to go through the hundreds of exposures any given photographer might send in on a story and weed out forty of the best for the pictures editor, Rolly Stebbins. Kate said this made photographers look better than they were. Their failures—the stupid shots, bad exposures, vulgarities, and all that was unimaginative and dull were discreetly discarded by the ever-tactful Miss York. She looked as she always did, very neat and prim. He wondered if there was a romance in her life, a lover who penetrated that exacting exterior, who mussed that perfectly marceled hair, who caused her to weep uncontrollably or cry out in pleasure and passion. He supposed he would never know.

They were all standing, staring at a cork-covered wall. Virginia was tacking up pictures. He had seen them do this before. Each spread in the magazine was pinned up on the wall so that it could be viewed as a whole. Rolly, Otis, and Diz all stood peering at the wall. The cover photo went up first with its big, bold red and black letters at the top. Virginia stepped back, and there for all to see was a portrait of Kate in her war correspondent's uniform, the insignia sparkling on each lapel of the tailored jacket. On her head she wore a cap set with jaunty aplomb to one side of her head. Her hair swept up away from her face seemed to glow with highlights of color, although the picture was black-and-white. Her eyes gazed to a far horizon, and her mouth was slightly parted, as if she were about to speak or laugh. He focused on the mouth. It was a mouth made for passionate talk and love. Everything in her face—the angular cheekbones, the intensity of her expression, the long, narrow nose, the vivid hair and white skin—were all softened by her mouth. It was full and expressive. He recalled how it quivered like a child's when she cried, and when she smiled it was so indescribably sweet that he was reminded of a girl in a Renoir painting. To the side of those lips in the margins of the page were bold black letters: MISSING.

Virginia stood quietly waiting for some signal to continue, but none came. The silence seemed painful. Then she started tacking up a series of pictures. The years of Kate's life were gathered in a neat stack in a wooden tray culled from archives and collections and scrapbooks and newspapers. Kate, waving from an airplane just before boarding for her last trip to London (*Herald Tribune*)—Kate catching a few hours' sleep on a desk in a news office in Louisville, Kentucky, in the 1936 flood (*Courier-Journal*)—Kate, in a miner's hard hat about to go down a mine shaft (Mrs. Oley Johnson, Finger Gap, West Virginia). From the Cleveland *Plain Dealer* there was the famous shot of her perched on the girder of the Weston Building, her hair blowing in the wind. There were dozens of pictures of Kate and Hopper extracted from the albums they kept— one taken on their honeymoon wearing matching mountain climbing outfits complete with mountaineer pickaxes and jack-boots—another earlier shot in front of a sign that said THE SAVE YOUR SOUL GOSPEL CHURCH, SAVIOR, ALABAMA—the working Kate in an Eskimo caribou parka on board S.S. *Diligence* in the Arctic Ocean; the famous Kate receiving the Woman of the Year Award from Mrs. Roosevelt; the private Kate making a terrible face at the camera, disturbed from her sunbath in the garden in Connecticut. There were more. Dozens and dozens more. Kate's high school yearbook picture, Kate standing with her father next to a gigantic printing press, a teenage Kate holding up a long black snake, a baby Kate enfolded in her mother's loving arms. Virginia tacked them up. When she had finished, the pictures ran more than twenty feet along the wall.

"What's that one, Miss York?" Hopper stepped closer to

the board and peered at an image he had never seen. In it Kate with bobbed hair and a cloche hat was holding a large black box of a camera.

"We're curious about this one, too. It was sent in early this week from a school." Virginia consulted her notes. "The Browning School for Boys in Jamestown, New York. But the date confuses us. Did Kate teach when she was in college?"

Hopper shook his head. "Kate never talked much about college days except to say she had worked her way through taking pictures of the campus."

"Yes. They sent some of her work also. Very romantic views. Not her best work, but then far better than anyone else her age. Do you want to see them?"

Hopper stared at the photographs a moment longer, then turned away. Then he looked back. There was something about the picture that bothered him and he didn't know why. He stared into the familiar eyes and the wide, open mouth. A young face, innocent and naive. She was certainly pretty enough. But a teacher? Then he saw what it was that had bothered him. She held the camera up in both of her hands. On the fourth finger of her left hand there was a single band. A wedding ring. He stared at it for a long time, and then he looked up to see that Rolly was watching him.

"Was it you?" Hopper asked.

Rolly smiled sadly. "No. It wasn't me. I didn't know her until she moved to Cleveland. But I knew about him." Rolly glanced around. "She never wanted anyone to know. She was married in college and for a year or so afterward. It didn't work out. She was divorced just before she came to New York. It was something she wanted stricken from the record, so to speak. It was very painful for her. She couldn't live with failure and she loved him very much." He glanced back at Hopper.

"What was his name?" Diz asked.

Virginia was looking at Rolly closely and suddenly she knew. She knew who this first love had been. "The colonel. Chester Edding. That's who. That's why you looked so surprised when I read his name."

Rolly nodded. "I was surprised. I only met him once. He

came through Cleveland on his way to Chicago to take a job, I forget doing what, and he came to the studio. Kate wasn't there. She had gone out to dinner with the client. He stayed for a while and we talked. I tried to get him to stay until she got in, but in the end he left. He made me promise not to tell he'd been there. Said it wouldn't do either one of them any good. I thought him a good man despite their problems."

"I guess everyone has a past," Diz finally commented.

"Not really a past. They were very young. Too young for marriage, too young for each other. It simply didn't work out, but Kate carried the torch for a long time. She tried awfully hard not to let anyone into her life after Eddie. She once told me she would never again let a man change her plans, and I got so I believed her. Eddie and I kept in touch for a time. He married again and had a child, but there was some awful accident and they died. He stopped writing after that."

This being the longest speech Rolly had ever made seemed to accentuate the silence in the room. Hopper felt everyone was waiting for him to say something. He shifted his weight. There was nothing to say.

So they met again in England, and he got her the orders she wanted. It was thanks to him she had been on that ship on her way to cover the invasion. Kate always said that whenever she needed something, along came just the person who could give it to her. And so it was. Only in this case not just any person, but someone deeply embedded in her past. A secret someone. If Kate was dead, then this someone will have meant more to her at the end than Hopper did. He felt his blood rush. It wasn't that she had been married before, a fact that made not the slightest difference to him; it was the secrecy. What other secrets did she harbor? Who was she, really? He would never know. He looked around the room. Silence. The world was a noisy place full of silence. He wondered if everyone in the room would carry their own secrets in silence to the grave.

Rolly then began working over the spread slowly and carefully. His job was to select the significant photographs of Kate's life and create a picture essay. He pulled from the collection, shaping, melding, condensing, editing. When at last he stepped back, Hopper could see why they called him a genius. Rolly had sorted out the material so that Kate's life unfolded before him not just in chronological order but with a logic all its own that propelled the eye as well as the senses. The overall effect had a rhythm and drama to it. It started with a chubby sixteen-year-old Kate with a snake wrapped around her neck, grinning delightedly into the camera as if to say, "Look at me, World, and look out!" There followed a fast series of shots of the girl and her early work building to a showstopping, double-page spread of a path of sparks flying as molten metal streamed from the great ladle in the steel mill. Then came an action lay-out in which Kate seemed to race from one turbulent assignment after another, but this sequence skidded to a halt in the face of two little Negro girls, twins sitting on a bare mattress in a paper shack somewhere in Georgia. From this picture on to the last, one felt the photographer mature. The final picture in the story was one from the last photo essay Kate had filed— a story about the Flying Fortresses, the pride of the Air Corps. Kate's last work was filed with these notes.

The Bombing Mission. What's it like up there? I ask. One of the boys was an editor for his college newspaper, and he is more articulate than the others. "It's just you and the sky and the engines. It's like a dream." "And the actual bombing?" I say. He's quiet for a minute. "Then everything changes. Once you're in enemy territory, a prickly sensation creeps up your spine until it wraps itself around your neck. The action starts with little black angels from below. Deadly puffs. Planes are coming in at you. You can smell the sweat on the other men. You see the enemy. Dodge. Weave. Nothing matters but the target. The bomb doors open. The target comes into sight. The countdown starts. Release. It's done. You pull back on the stick, and the plane soars like a balloon cut loose from the tether. You're up in the sky like a bird. Then head for home."

In the offices of *World* magazine they stood looking at the mock-up, each person in the room alone with his own memories. No one said anything.

CHAPTER TWENTY-NINE

THE BABIES WERE mostly dark with wet black hair and dusky faces. Viewing them was like looking through a window into the future. Row upon row in their little baskets, each baby so perfectly formed, each one coming into the world despite wars and bombs and death, each one with all the hope of tomorrow and no mistakes yet made. Now, for a few days, at least, they were safe, encased in the white wicker cocoons of the maternity ward like a row of bottles she had once lined up on a windowsill.

She liked the word *cocoon*. Such a pleasant place to be, warm and protected from danger. Her thoughts drifted and she was a child again, raising insect pets and caring for them so tenderly, the way other little girls cared for their dolls. In each bottle a twig bearing a white praying mantis egg case the size of a golf ball. She had stayed home from school for days just so she could be there for the hatching of her eggs. Emerging insects, she knew, waited for no one, but followed a mysterious timetable known only to themselves. She had hardly dared move from her vigil for fear she would miss the moment of birth. Then, almost without warning, a signal ordained by the cosmos unlocked the tough outer shell of the cocoons, and as she watched, the first baby mantis wrestled its way free. Then came a pouring river of the creatures slithering out of their protective sheaths; as if propelled by the devil himself, they climbed up with great effort on their new and tender legs, dragging themselves upward to air and light, and once perched free of the cocoon, there they rested, hundreds of them, each smaller than her fingernail. Each one perfect.

Kate rested, putting her head against the sill of the maternity ward so that it was now on a level with the baskets, and her eyes concentrated on the baby nearest her. Peeping out from the tightly wrapped swaddling was a fat little moon face with two or three chins and jet curls laid across the forehead like a midget Roman emperor. The baby's eyes were two fine slits edged in black lashes, and the mouth, pink and round as Cupid's heart, puckered involuntarily at the air, seeking nourishment. Kate suddenly felt herself go all quivery inside, as if some steel rod had snapped and left only trembling intangible vibrations in its place. A soft cooing escaped her lips.

They had brought her in with the other women to the only place available in crowded Algiers—the maternity hospital. There she had fallen into the first real sleep of seven days. Later she had been told about sleeping through a night raid and being awakened for meals, but she had no recollection of any of it. All she knew was that she was alive. That an Albatross seaplane en route to Algiers from Portugal had spotted the small boat bobbing in the water not ten miles from the Strait of Gibraltar. The boat had appeared empty, but the pilot had circled just to make sure and in that moment had seen signs of life, hands waving, faces lifted. All the rest was a blur to Kate. She was badly dehydrated and suffering from exposure. She slept the sleep of the dead for three days.

"Hi, kid. How are you doing?"

Kate looked up from the baby reluctantly. Then she smiled. "Pat. I was wondering if you were here." Kate reached out a hand to the friendly nurse who had shared the lifeboat, and for a moment they just gripped each other. "How are you?"

"From the looks of it, about as good as you." Pat tried to laugh but couldn't quite get up the energy. "I guess none of us are ready to be cover girls—not just yet anyway."

"How many of us are there?" Kate asked.

"Well, I don't know about the men, but I suspect they all made it. You and me and the two English nurses are here. They're okay. I guess we all made it, though I wouldn't have bet on it a day ago."

Kate's eyes teared. "We all didn't make it."

Pat sat down beside her. "Yeah. I've been thinking about Maggie, too. Poor kid. I guess her family knows by now and that fella of hers. What was his name?"

"Jamie. Jamie Lloyd. Jamie with the big ears. That's the way I thought of him. I wondered how anyone could love a man so much who had such big ears."

Pat sighed and put her head against Kate's. "You were wonderful to her, Kate. You were her friend. I'm glad she had you with her. Not many people have a true friend with them when they die."

"I wish she hadn't died," Kate said. "She wanted to live so much. She wanted . . . wanted this." And her eyes went back to the babies. "She wanted life and to make life."

Pat nodded. "I guess we all want that."

Kate was silent. Her baby, the little fat Roman emperor, was stirring now. A big yawn and then a few tentative smacks of the lips, then a wrinkled nose and a frown, then more wiggling inside the swaddling of white muslin and more smacking.

"If I had any money," said Pat, "I'd lay you ten to one that one there is going to let loose with the biggest bawl in just about two seconds." They both peered intently at the baby, and sure enough, the mouth opened and out came a high-pitched wail at full volume. A nun appeared in the nursery with a severe look of disapproval on her face.

"Pick her up," Kate muttered under her breath. "Why don't you pick her up?"

"They don't, you know. These are orphans. The hospital takes them in for a few weeks, and then they get sent along to other care centers. A lot of these babies are going to America and Canada, but until then the nuns don't pick them up. They feed them and diaper them, but I watched them all morning. They don't hug them or kiss them or anything. I guess it's against their religion or something, but babies need hugging."

"Miss Goodfellow?"

Kate did not turn around. The baby was now bellowing, its face red and blotched. "Yes. What is it?"

"The car is here. Are you ready to go?" It was one of the French nuns, the one with the unbelievably sweet, high voice just like a child's, who had been one of Kate's nurses. She held out her hand to help Kate to stand. Kate ignored the hand.

"Is it a boy or a girl?" she asked.

The sister peered over her shoulder. "Ah, yes. A little girl."

Kate smiled. "I was a fat baby, too. They say I weighed ten pounds when I was born."

The nun nodded her head agreeably, but Kate knew she had not really understood. "The car . . . ?" The Sister gestured down the long, wide corridor with its polished marble floors. Kate sighed and leaned her head once more down to the sill.

"Goodbye, baby," she whispered. "Goodbye, little fat girl." The baby stopped crying, her face still furious like the imperious Queen of Hearts in *Alice's Adventures in Wonderland*. Yet she opened her eyes—deep pools of purple liquid swimming with wisdom—and looked straight into Kate's. Kate stood up, and with inexplicable tears she hugged Pat Sommers. "Good luck," they both said at the same time, clinging to each other. Then Kate followed the white hem of the nun down the hall and stepped out into the blinding sun.

Once out of the hospital, the army had arranged for her recovery in an exotic villa overlooking the Mediterranean. It was, by anyone's standards, more a palace than a villa, standing on the edge of the sea in a series of tiled terraces and rich trims of gold and purple. There was even a brook, which ran right through the center of the house. The villa had been requisitioned by the Allied Air Command for their topflight people and served now as a headquarters for the activity in North Africa.

No sooner had she stepped inside the front door to a cool reception hall than she collided head-on with Colonel Chester Edding. He broke into a wide grin. "Kate. Lord, you don't look like you've been bobbling about in the ocean for seven days." He took her hands in his and held her arms up as if she were a child in a new party dress. "You look wonderful. It must have all been a publicity stunt."

Kate laughed and then almost immediately felt the tears

well up in her eyes. "Yes . . . no . . . I don't know. Look at me. I've been crying like this for days. I'm sorry. It's just so good to see a familiar face."

He put his arm around her and led her to a small divan and waited until she had calmed down. "What you need, Kate, is some rest and some good food and a good belt of my special blend of Scotch. The United States military has instructed me to provide anything you desire, and I don't intend to go against orders. I think rest comes first, then we'll toast your safe return with the Scotch. Come with me."

He got up with a very determined air, but she laid a hand on his arm. "Eddie. Have they been told in New York? I mean does anyone know I'm alive?"

He shook his head. "No one except possibly the entire United States. It's going to take you the rest of the war to read all your cables. They finally had to stop them. It was clogging military channels. They tell me, though, that they'll send them all on through a military packet from Washington. I can't tell you how many people are glad you are alive." He stopped, his voice betraying the emotion he felt. "Me included."

She nodded. "Thank you. Well . . . maybe I will have a little rest now."

In her room a nurse helped her to get undressed. Kate had no inclination to notice the furnishings, which were lavish and splendid Moroccan carved pieces like something out of *The Arabian Nights,* or the view of a terra-cotta terrace and azure sea beyond the French doors with white curtains so thin they floated in the warm air. Nothing, it seemed, was coming into full focus. Except for that baby. She sank down on the edge of the bed. The nurse was taking off her boots. They had found a small soldier's uniform and boots for her to wear out of the hospital with a promise of sending a military tailor around in a few days. It was this or Algerian costume, and everyone thought she would prefer the military. As it was, she preferred not to think about it.

By the side of the bed on a funny octagonal little table inlaid with mother-of-pearl lay a small stack of cables. Kate picked them up, and they were heavy, like lead bricks. She held them for the longest time. Then, very slowly, she opened the one on top. It was the only one that mattered.

The tears fell steadily as she tried to read and she had to keep wiping her eyes and her nose and her chin. It was as if her whole face had become a sea of tears. Hopper's cable read:

WE'VE BEEN GIVEN THE GREATEST GIFT OF ALL STOP
A SECOND CHANCE STOP I'M COMING FOR TO CARRY
YOU HOME MAGNOLIA.

The nurse put her in the bed, and she fell asleep clutching the paper in her hand. Her body rocked as if still in the lifeboat.

When she awoke some five hours later, she wondered where she was. Surely this was some fantastic dream and she was hallucinating. Then she turned her head, and there Eddie sat reading a book in a chair pulled close to the bed. She looked at him for the longest time trying to see the Eddie he had been when she had married him. He had aged in a nice way. The uniform and the regulation haircut, of course, gave him a man's look, but it was something else she saw in him. A sort of wisdom.

She licked her lips. "What are you reading?"

He looked up quickly and grinned. "Awake at last, lazy bones. The very latest book." He held it up. "It's called *The Human Comedy* by William Saroyan."

"I like the title. Is it funny?"

Eddie shook his head. "No. It's too real to be funny. Hey, how about some food? Doctor's orders, Lieutenant." He got up and brought a tray over to her bed, laying it carefully on the end while he plumped up her pillows and eased her to a sitting position. "The nurse said for me to ring for her as soon as you woke up, but I like doing this myself."

"I remember. You used to always make me breakfast in bed back when . . ." Her voice trailed off. It seemed so very long ago, but she remembered the bedroom in their tiny apartment flooded with sunlight on a Sunday morning and Eddie in his striped pajamas and a tray heaped with pancakes and hot steaming coffee. She looked down and saw a cold jellied broth, a perfect pear, and a silver flagon.

"Is that the Scotch?"

"No. Not yet. They tell me you're going to have to eat and

drink lots of fruit juice before you're ready for the hard stuff. Are you hungry, Kate?"

"No. Funny, isn't it? I was so hungry at times out there I thought I could eat shoe leather. We scraped seaweed off the bottom of the boat and ate that. We even ate the jar of Vaseline that was in the first-aid kit. I should want this, shouldn't I, but I don't."

Eddie was having none of it, though. He spoon-fed the jellied broth into her mouth and patiently made her take sips of juice and tiny bites of the pear. And all the while he filled her in on what was happening.

The three Anglo-American landings made at Casablanca, Oran, and Algiers had been a success. Troops, tanks, and tons of supplies had been put ashore from the vast fleet that had survived the storm and German torpedoes. It was a magnificent feat and the mood among the Allied commanders was electrified. Everyone felt the war switching gears. The invasion of North Africa had been a complete surprise to the Germans. Rommel's army was now trapped between Montgomery in the east and Eisenhower's army in the west. Hitler was preparing to pour thousands of airborne troops into Africa to defend his position and the Flying Fortresses were being readied to attack any day now.

"The Fortresses are going to make the difference, Kate. And by the way, your boys are safe. *The Flying Flashgun* went down at sea, but all of the boys, all of them, were rescued. We fished some out of the drink and the others parachuted into the Netherlands and were airlifted out. Without us, the land troops can't . . ." Kate watched Eddie talk. She heard the words . . . secret base in the Sahara . . . troops massing . . . It was hard to believe it had been only two weeks ago that she had christened that airplane with a bottle of Coca-Cola. Two weeks, a lifetime, an eternity. She had lived and died and lived again in that time. She wasn't the same woman anymore. Troops and battles and bombings . . . it was a human comedy all right. Only she didn't even feel like smiling.

Still, she was glad Eddie was there, glad to have him talking and feeding her food. There was a strength in Eddie now—the kind of strength that often happens to people when they live through a tragedy. The night they thought the crew of the *Flashgun* had been lost he had filled her in on his life. The job teaching boys in a settlement house, the marriage to a girl in Chicago named Alice he'd met when he had taken his boys to the Museum of Science and Industry. "I loved that job," he told her. "And Alice, she didn't mind the low pay. She was even willing to live on the South Side, but after the baby came . . . well, I wanted them to be . . ." He had struggled with the word. ". . . safe." He told her he had joined the Army Air Corps after his wife died. His wife and his little girl. They had been killed by a hit-and-run driver not half a block from their new home in the suburbs. Poor Eddie. She wondered how anyone could bear such a loss.

But she couldn't think of Eddie now. Kate knew she had to sort out her own life right now, and for the very first time she didn't feel equipped to tackle the problem. There had been no more cables from Hopper because they would not let them through. She learned he had tried to get clearance to actually come for her in Algiers, but there was no civilian passage, no matter how many strings he had tried to pull to Lisbon, London, anywhere within range. She felt, even thousands of miles and an entire ocean away from him, the sheer force of his will. For now, however, she was much too content to drift in and out of sleep in her luxurious bed and let someone else do all the thinking. Eddie would think for her, at least for now.

Eddie had been right when he said the cables addressed to her had clogged military channels. Her rescue was the biggest news in America short of the whole war. They had even stopped the presses on *World* magazine for the first time ever in its seven-year history. General Jimmy Doolittle came to see her, to see how she was and to tell her that the army would do everything in their considerable power to see that she had the finest care. When she was ready—the doctor advised a week— safe passage was hers, "by air this time" home. And when she got there she could expect a hero's welcome.

Home. The word was at once as dear as the dearest word and yet so distant. It was so far away, not just in the miles that lay between her and home, but in the notion of it. Home. Her home. She immediately felt a kind of strength flowing back into her veins. A week seemed a long time.

By the third day she was too restless to stay in bed, and she had ventured out onto the terrace off her bedroom. She tried to sort out her feelings, but she could not. About the best she could do was complain to Eddie that boredom had started to creep into her life at the villa. Eddie said that was a good sign. She was too pampered, she said. It made her feel uncomfortable. She couldn't move without some attendant rushing to her side and thrusting cool drinks or hot teas or soothing hands at her. In the evenings at dinner there were transient brass from America and Britain who were delighted to meet the famous Kate Goodfellow and hear her story. Then the talk would turn to other matters, important war matters, and Kate's moment would have passed. She was beginning to feel like the warm-up act.

Eddie came less and less, which made their meetings more immediate and intense. She seemed the only person uninvolved with the great Operation Torch, as it had been dubbed. So boredom, like an enemy infiltrator, worked its way into her life. She had a new camera, thanks to Eddie, who had requisitioned it especially for her. A Rolleiflex, a much smaller camera with a square negative, but for the first time in her entire life she could not focus her concentration. She wandered restlessly about the villa, unable to create an objective, a stalled car whose ignition would not spark.

She insisted on sleeping outside on the terrace near a reflecting pool so that she could see the stars. They had accommodated her with an elaborate wicker *chaise longue* with a little fringed half-canopy on top. It was wide and luxurious, and was made up with bright striped cotton bedding and a place for a candle on each armrest. It was also on wheels so that she could roll it to whatever spot she wished to view the night sky, and there she would drowse off as the endless drama of the heavens passed over her. Then she would wake for a few moments and see that the stars had moved; again to sleep, and awake to find the moon had risen. It was only then, looking at the stars at night, that she was at peace. At the first hush of daylight Kate's agitation returned.

The end of the week came, and with it a delay in passage

home. She felt well; she *was* well. It was time to move on and now this hitch. A dispatch bag from Washington gave her another stack of cables, and they went straight to her heart. Otis, Rolly, Virginia, Diz—they were all so touching. And Hopper. She read his longingly. They were funny, some of them . . . COME HOME IN TIME FOR SUNDAY DINNER STOP I LOVE YOU. *Come home. I love you.* Such simple words. But every time she thought of them, she didn't know . . . if she left now, it would change her life forever. If she stayed and went on with her work, she would lose her life forever.

On Thursday two things happened that forced Kate to realize she must decide what she was going to do. Word came that she had a ticket on the ten A.M. Pan Am Clipper on Friday for New York. Tomorrow morning. Eddie sent her a note asking her for dinner tonight. He had "something important to tell her."

Without warning her heart gave one of those surprising lurches. Something important. . . . Eddie arrived in his jeep to pick her up early. He wanted to show her Algiers, a sightseeing tour, he said, and then they would go for dinner. As they drove away from the villa, she looked at his face out of the corner of her eye. It shocked her slightly each time she saw him. He had lost that boyish jauntiness and good-natured appeal that had been the Eddie she married. Eddie's face reflected the fifteen years between then and now. It had become a strong face, full of purpose and determination, but no longer merry. Still, the eyes were the same. The very same. Inquisitive, curious eyes. And the mouth. It still slanted up at one corner lopsidedly when he smiled. In fact, when he smiled, which was not often enough, he did look like the old Eddie, and she was warmed by the look as she was warmed by the man.

She wished he would smile now, but as they drove his look was intent and he seemed deep in thought. No one wanted to call it a farewell dinner, but, if all went as scheduled, she wondered if she would see Eddie, or indeed, the war, ever again.

She would not think about it just now and willed herself to relax and enjoy their expedition. All around her the streets of Algiers moved with teeming life. The sounds and smells were intense and colors everywhere so vivid they seemed to take on a life of their own. The air was filled with the sharp dung smoke from open fires and the aroma of exotic spices; mules and camels moved in the dusty streets.

"This looks just like the pictures my mother and I used to look at when I was little. Oh, how we loved the idea of camels and the desert and women in black veils. I'd love to drive out into the desert, Eddie. Just to see if it's at all like I imagined it to be."

"Sure," he said easily. "One desert, coming up."

They drove in silence for about a half-hour until they came to a crest in the road, where he pulled the jeep over to a stop. There she saw laid out before her all the magnificence of a vast landscape of sand and dunes. The horizon was a sharp edge against the sky and the windblown sand cut intricate patterns as if sculpted by a master craftsman. There was nothing in sight for miles. Behind them the sun was setting so that purple shadows cast long columns in the sand. In the rich silence neither one of them said anything, content to let the falling night envelop their thoughts. The play of nature and the light of the setting sun was as grand as the most opulent orchestral symphony.

The dark came quickly and Eddie started to turn back to town, but Kate stopped him. "Let's stay here a while. I don't think I'm quite ready for dinner."

"Okay." He twisted around and lifted a bottle of wine from under a blanket along with two tin canteen cups. "Best I could do without stealing. The wine's just about as bad as the cups." Then he swung his legs over the side and walked around to the front, spreading a handkerchief on the hood. And all of a sudden she remembered the day Eddie had taken her flying. The very first time she had ever been up in an airplane. She remembered how she had felt, how giddy and fantastic and daring. She got out and went to stand beside him. He uncorked the wine and poured the deep red liquid into the cups. Then, quite ceremoniously, he handed one to her and held his up to it.

"To you, Kate."

"Why me?" she said. "Have I done anything?"

"Oh, not much. You've only survived against all odds."

"Luck more than anything. I don't think I contributed much to my surviving a torpedoed ship."

"Luck is a mystery, isn't it? But I didn't mean *that* survival.

I mean you've survived your life. You've flourished. You stuck to your guns and carved out a place for yourself, an important place."

"Have I, Eddie? I wonder. I've been wondering about that for a week now. I wonder whether anything I've ever done or believed in was right. I'm not so sure. . . ."

Eddie looked at her hard, and then he smiled, a sort of sad and gentle smile. "You who were always so sure. After our marriage broke up, it was the one thing that kept me going. You were so sure of what had to be . . . and I was helpless then. All I wanted to do was find you again and cling to you because you were the only sure thing I had ever known."

"But, Eddie, you never even wrote to me. Only that one letter when the divorce papers had to be signed. And after you moved to Chicago, I wrote to you often. It hurt me terribly that you didn't care." And it had! She could feel it now, an old ache welling up from inside.

The shadows in Eddie's face made him look almost like a statue. "And there I was caring so much I thought I could die from it." He drained his cup and then looked at her again with that crooked smile. As if she were a child with mussed hair, he reached over and picked up a few strands that had fallen over her forehead and smoothed them back. "I never answered the letters because they were so full of your new life, your new life without me. It nearly drove me mad. I couldn't bear the thought of us being friends. I had all sorts of fantasies about arriving on your doorstep and sweeping you up like something out of King Arthur. In fact, I did arrive on your doorstep. Did your friend Rolly ever tell you I came to see you?"

"You did? When? In Cleveland? Rolly never said a thing."

"Well, I asked him not to. Some sort of masculine pride, I guess. I went to your studio over the camera shop. I was so proud of you, Kate, it was just as you said it would be. Rolly was working in the darkroom and he was very kind."

"Did you tell him about us?"

"Yes, I did. After we got to talking. Not at first. But I got the feeling he knew all along. You were out with some steel magnate, a big deal, Rolly said, and he showed me the photographs you had taken in the steel mills. We talked for hours. You never came back that night. But it didn't matter. All I needed was one last touchstone. Our marriage really ended for me that night. At least it was the turning point for me to go on. He was a good man. Whatever happened to him?"

"Rolly? Why nothing happened to him. He's very much a part of my life. He helped me set up my studio in New York after the crash. He was my partner and then, when I went to work for *World,* he came with me. I don't know what I would have done without him over the years."

"I think he was a little bit in love with you, too."

"M-m-m-m-m. Maybe. Were you still in love with me then?"

"Yep. I'm not so sure I'm not in love with you now. You're a hard woman to get over." He was teasing her.

"Well, you weren't so easy, either, bub. I was determined never to love another man again. At least not until I was thirty. I figured I would know everything I needed to know by the time I was thirty."

"And?"

"And . . . as a matter of fact, I was just thirty when I met Hopper." Hopper's name hung in the air between them. Now they were both silent in the dark of the desert. Then they turned toward each other. "Eddie . . ." and she started to say "kiss me," but she didn't have to. He had taken her in his arms, and she felt herself melt into his embrace as if they had been kissing each other for a long, long time.

CHAPTER THIRTY

"EDDIE, AM I a little drunk? I feel like I'm floating."

"Good for you. You probably are a little drunk. This is our second bottle of wine." They were sitting on a banquette of cushions in the corner of a tiny restaurant splendidly draped in colorful strips of cloth. It was like being inside an exotic desert tent and it suited their mood. The restaurant was in the Medina, the old part of town, where the streets ran narrow and winding and one could imagine all sorts of mysterious comings and goings behind the wood carved doors that led into interior gardens. They laughed and reminisced a great deal and the sense of having rediscovered each other had them both euphoric.

"Do you remember the day you took me up flying?" she said. "That's the way I feel. It was one of the best days of my life. Actually, it changed my life because for the first time I was living the way I had always imagined, high, wide, and free, even if it was only for twenty minutes."

"I remember. I was a damn fool. I don't think that so-called airplane ever flew again." He reached over and took the lid off the large clay pot that sat in the middle of their table. The aroma of chicken baked in spices and olives and lemons filled up their senses, but Kate shook her head. "I can't eat any more, Eddie. I am wonderfully, happily full to bursting."

Eddie signaled for the waiter to clear the table, then he sat back, suddenly serious. "Kate, I don't know whether you want to hear this or not. I've been wondering whether to tell you at all because I know you're scheduled to go back to the States tomorrow, but . . . they've given you clearance to go on a bombing mission."

Kate said nothing. She drew a deep breath. "Talk about timing . . . I waited so long to get permission, I'd sort of forgotten all about it."

"Well, they figure since you've been torpedoed you might as well experience everything. The missions will start in about a week. You'd have to go through some training. It's going to be dangerous work because Hitler's going to give us everything he's got. You know if this thing is a success, we'll control the Mediterranean, and that means an invasion of Europe. Africa is the turning point. If we win this one, we win the war. Maybe not this year or next but eventually."

Kate didn't say anything. Eddie waited. He knew she was fighting a battle inside herself. She wasn't looking at him but away to some nonexistent spot in the room. Finally her eyes still on that spot—

"I can't, Eddie." Her voice was low but definite.

He nodded and said nothing for a while. "I don't blame you for wanting to get back home." Long silence. "What's he like, your husband? You've hardly mentioned him."

Kate held her breath for a second, then sighed. "I love him, Eddie. He's in my blood. I fought it from the minute I met him, but I can't fight it anymore. He's a wonderful man. Difficult, complicated, but wonderful. The trouble is he and I have never quite figured each other out. I guess that's about as easy as I can say it. Our whole relationship has been sort of one step forward, three steps back, but when we're in the forward mode . . . well, it's like there's no one else in the world. The trouble is all the reverse modes. We've gone down our share of bumpy roads." She shrugged and then forced a smile. "The roving life is great but only for the one who's out there roving. It's hell on a marriage. I'm not so sure I want to keep making that hell go on."

She leaned back on the cushions, her thoughts far away. "You know, when I was out there in that boat thinking I would never see anyone again, when Maggie died . . . my life, well, it didn't flash before me or anything like that, but something came into focus. It was like looking through the lens and seeing myself at the other end. I realized that I had never asked myself what it was all adding up to. Photographers live through things so swiftly. All our energy is focused on finding that all-significant perfect moment. It occurred to me out there bobbing about that all the excitement and adventure I have always craved so much has to be balanced with something deeper, something more than just the next assignment. Otherwise, what is it all about? It's like a tree. In order to reach to the sky, the roots have got to go down deep. With Hopper, it seems no matter how finished it is, it's only the beginning."

"Everything has to be balanced against a personal commitment to something," Eddie agreed. "A person, a moral, a country, an ideal. But you still have to make your own life worthwhile. Otherwise you betray your soul. What will you do when you get home, Kate?"

"Hopper said to me before I left that last time, 'the passions don't die, they just change.' He wants a family."

"And you? Do you want a family? Is that what you want?"

A vision of the little fat baby in the maternity ward swam before her eyes, and she remembered the almost unbearable urge to pick her up and hold her close. She looked up at him. "I want it all, Eddie. I always thought that the trouble with most people was that they never knew what they wanted, whereas I have always known exactly what I wanted. And that's been my trouble. I've always been so sure of myself that I couldn't make room for someone else. I want everything life has to offer, but up to now, I've wanted everything my way. Well, it isn't about having it my way. I probably had no business marrying Hopper, but then maybe I don't know what my real business is. Hopper and I have gone through the fire together. I feel I owe him and myself the next round."

"Owe? I'm surprised to hear you say that. No one owes anyone."

She shook her head. "You're wrong. We all owe each other

everything. We owe each other respect and caring. Most of all we owe each other love."

"We do. We do, indeed," he said. "I love you, Kate, and because I love you, I'm now going to make a speech. Do you mind? Well, it doesn't matter whether you do or don't, because I'm going to make it anyway. There was a time when I would have given my soul to the devil to hear you say to me what you've just said about Hopper. But not now, Kate. There's something more important to you than Hopper or me or any other man. It's your work. It has always been your work. It's what makes you tick. You can't deny yourself that. The work comes first and it has to. You're not a tree, with roots dug into the ground. You're a traveler. You set off on the journey a long time ago—a journey toward an ideal self and an ideal accomplishment. If you stop now, the rest of your life will be a series of *what-ifs* and *if-onlys*. You're a child of the sea, Kate, and your life is an adventure on that sea. Sure, it takes courage, real courage, but you've got that. Any man who would want to harness that courage is wrong. I was wrong, and Hopper is wrong. You, Kate Goodfellow, are not built for the curtained windows of domestic life and the firesides of tradition, because you're not like the rest of us. There's no ending your adventure. Let the rest of the world search for romantic happy endings. But not you. Don't give up, Kate, don't ever give up."

Kate stared at him, then she started to giggle. "You are drunk, Colonel Edding."

He laughed. "How true . . . how true."

They left the restaurant and walked into the crowded narrow streets of Algiers arm in arm. "Let me buy you something, Kate. It's been a fantasy of mine ever since I've known you to be able to buy you something beautiful. You will let me, won't you? Come on, let's go see what we can find."

They wandered into the souk, a labyrinth of alleys and tiny streets covered over with tin roofs or brightly colored cloth, where hundreds of shops and booths and peddlers with their goods spread on the ground composed a lively midnight market. With the advent of English and American troops, it was teaming with activity. Each part of the souk had its own specialty—the tinsmiths, leather goods, carpets, shoes, cloth, pottery. Kate gasped in delight when they turned into a narrow lane devoted entirely to spices and herbs displayed in hundreds of beautiful wooden bowls, each piled to near overflowing and every color of the rainbow. Coming into yet another canopied lane, they reached a row of tiny shops selling gold and silver jewelry. A sharp-eyed merchant spotted them and hurried out with assurances that his goods were far superior to any others. The shop itself was gaily decorated and crammed to the ceiling with trinkets and baubles of gold and silver, but no business could be transacted until the jeweler was assured that they were comfortable and relaxed. He soon had them settled on folding chairs sipping thimble-sized cups of thick coffee. Kate asked to see a tray of silver rings, but he waved it aside, indicating that it was of a lesser quality. No, no, and no, he insisted, the beautiful lady must see his treasures. With that said, he ceremoniously brought out three small cases carefully wrapped in linen. These were his finest pieces, he assured them, and once unwrapped and laid out for them to see, they had to agree. They were lovely, both Kate and Eddie exclaimed, but, as it turned out, very expensive. Kate protested. "I've never liked expensive jewelry. Just buy me a souvenir, Eddie."

"Nonsense," said Eddie. He picked up a bracelet. It was old, two hundred years or more, said the dealer, set with two large, deep purple amethysts clasped in delicate tracery woven in three colors of gold.

"Whoever made this bracelet two centuries ago," said Eddie, "made it for you." He fastened it around her wrist and then, with a flourish, laid down a stack of bills on the counter to the bewilderment of the shopkeeper, for he was prepared for a lengthy bargaining session at which he was a master. Kate and Eddie didn't notice. She held her arm up to the light. It was a beautiful glowing thing, mysterious and old and eternal.

They drove back to the villa and sat for a time in the jeep, neither one wanting to say good night, each knowing it had to be.

"Kate . . . tomorrow . . . you could still change your mind . . . ." he started to say, turning to her.

"Don't, Eddie. Don't say it." Her face was soft in the moonlight. She reached for his arm, found it, and laid her hand on his. "Let's not say anything. Tomorrow I'm going home. Tomorrow you're going to some secret spot in the Sahara."

"Do you know what it's called? It's an oasis out there in the middle of nowhere, and they call it the Garden of Allah. How about that! I'm told the finest dates in the world grow there. Did you know I've been promoted to brigadier general?"

"Eddie! No. How wonderful!"

"Yep. I'll be flying out with my men in about a week."

"You're flying the mission?" Kate picked at nonexistent lint on her trousers.

"Sure am. I knew I could only stand that desk work for so long. I know I shouldn't say this, but . . ." He shrugged. "I had hoped you would be with me. It was something I cooked up back in England. I figured if I got you as far as Africa, they would let you go on a mission. So I put in to fly again."

Kate's heart was pounding. "Eddie, I don't know what to say."

"This was just my way of saying I'm behind you, I'm with you. And I'm for you, Kate. I've wanted to say that for a long, long time. You're one of the rare ones."

Kate reached for the door handle. Eddie jumped out of the jeep and came around to take hold of her arm. "Kate, I'm not trying to come back into your life other than as a friend. Our time together was a long time ago, and who we were then is sometimes hard to even remember. We've both been through a lot over the years. I just want you to know how much I believe in you. I understand why you're going home. Really I do. When my wife and child died, the only thing that kept me breathing was the fact that we had loved each other so much. I hope to God I can find that kind of love again, but even if I can't, it will have all been worth it just to have known it at all. I wish you safe journey home. I wish you every happiness. I wish . . ." but Kate broke from him and ran to the top of the stairs of the villa. Then she turned and raised her arm. He was in the jeep. His foot raced the motor briefly, and then he was gone. She stood on the stairs for a long time listening to the noise of the motor fade into the night.

The Pan Am Clipper was leaving at ten A.M. They awakened her at seven for breakfast and a bath and a leisurely ride to the airport, where bedlam seemed a mild word for the chaos

of the confused, frightened, desperate masses of people trying
to get out of Algiers. Kate waited in her line unencumbered of
baggage, only a canvas bag with her camera in it and a change
of clothes still in the bag from the tailor's slung over her
shoulder. They had delivered to her that morning an officer's
uniform tailored to her size, but she had decided to wear the
much more comfortable blue cotton Air Corps jumpsuit for
the long flight home. Before landing, she would change into
her uniform, as she knew there would be a big reception waiting for her at Idlewild. As she waited, confident of her seat on
the plane, she noticed a small cordoned-off area where a few
nuns were standing watch over the now familiar small white
baskets. She strolled over. The baskets held babies, as she
knew they would, as many as a dozen in all. She motioned to
one of the Sisters.

"Do you speak English?" she asked.

The Sister looked at her for a long moment but finally nodded. "*Un peu* . . . a little."

Kate gestured to the babies. "Where are these babies
going?"

The nun looked doubtful as if there might be some problem, but then she brightened. "Ah, *destination*," she said with
pleasure. "These go America. Many, many babies . . . they
have home in America." She beamed. Kate peered into the
baskets nearest her wondering if her little fat girl was in one
of them, but she wasn't and just then, over the din of the airport, she heard the boarding announcement for passengers
holding tickets on the Pan Am flight to New York. She backed
away from the smiling nun and stood absorbing the scene all
around her, as if wanting to memorize it. There was a band of
native children scurrying about in the hubbub with their arms
outstretched, begging for coins. She could hear their high-
pitched cries over the din: " . . . *baksheesh . . . baksheesh . . .*"
and for the briefest moment she remembered a scene she had
long forgotten from her own childhood. She was with her father in Montreal. A girl with a camera. A big box of a thing, so
clumsy and heavy; yet capable of transforming the world
through the magic of light and dark. *Hold the coin up, Dad, so
they can see it.* And then, uncapping the lens, came the shot
she had wanted. The perfect moment.

Kate smiled, remembering, and then she turned and walked briskly toward the door that was calling to her.

Brigadier General Edding looked up from the transport plane where he was checking supplies on the loading ramp. Overhead the big Pan Am Clipper roared into the sky bound for America. He followed its path for a few minutes and then turned back to the job at hand. That day he would fly into the desert to the Garden of Allah, a windswept oasis of a few buildings in ruin. Here the final preparations for the mission would be made. He knew the time ahead would be dangerous, many would die, but he thrust that thought as far to the back of his mind as possible. In the field of preparation, one did not think of death. It was hot, even at ten in the morning, and his eyes were filled with sweat. He reached for a handkerchief and mopped his brow. Then he blinked his eyes, squinting against the white sun and shimmering heat rising up from the tarmac. In the distance, walking toward him in a blue jumpsuit, he could just make out the color of her hair.

POSTSCRIPTS FROM THE PRESS

❧❧

December 1943. Miami Tribune. Novelist and play-
wright Hopper Delaney honeymooned today in Key
West with his twenty-two-year-old bride, the former
June Michaels. Their marriage publicly revealed for
the first time that he was divorced from the noted
photojournalist Kate Goodfellow. The bride is a recent graduate of Northwestern University, where she
majored in school dramatics.

May 1944. Stars & Stripes. Brigadier General Chester
Edding, Commanding Officer of the 97th Bomb
Group, was killed in action in a bombing mission over
Southern Italy. The Brigadier distinguished himself in
the North African campaign.

April 1945. The New York Times. General George Patton's troops marched into the German concentration
camp at Buchenwald a mere two hours after the
Nazis departed. Noted *World* photographer Kate
Goodfellow documented the liberation efforts. For
the first time, Americans, and the world, have proof
of the shocking extent of Nazi atrocity. These images
are now etched in memory forever.

AFTERWORD

INSPIRATION FOR THIS book began with reading Vicki Goldberg's excellent biography of Margaret Bourke-White, whose true-life adventures, love affairs, and feats of daring were truly astonishing.

Bourke-White's photography has been published in many collections and is fascinating to see. Her early industrial work dramatizing the nation's steel mills and production lines in *Fortune,* photographic essays in *Life* (the Dust Bowl, the Arctic, and the bombing of Moscow among them), and the social documents published in collaboration with her then-husband, Southern writer Erskine Caldwell, offer magnificent insights to her talent and the era in which she lived and worked.

She was a woman of "firsts," pioneering photography over text as a way to tell the story. In World War II, Bourke-White was the first woman to fly a bombing mission. She worked on the front lines of the Italian campaign, and followed Patton's troops into Buchenwald. Her photographs of the concentration camps were among the first seen by Allied civilians.

After the war, she was assigned to cover the birth of the new nation of India. Her photograph of Mahatma Gandhi, seated at his spinning wheel, has become one of the most widely reproduced images of him ever made. In the movie *Gandhi,* Candice Bergen played Margaret Bourke-White.

Later assignments included the Korean conflict and an exposé of the South African diamond industry, where she was the first woman ever allowed down in the mines. In 1955 she asked *Life* publisher Henry Luce to promise her the assignment for the first trip to the moon. Soon after, she was diagnosed with Parkinson's disease—a condition she battled with little success. Toward the end of her life she wrote in her autobiography, *Portrait of Myself,* that she had built her life on a plan, but had missed out on two major items—a family, and a stable home life. Final entries in her diary record the statement: "In the end, it is only the work that counts." She died in 1971 at the age of sixty-seven, and is remembered as a groundbreaking artist, a glamorous personality, and a woman of unbridled courage.

Writing this book was a great journey into the life of an American original. On a more personal note, I thank Paul Bresnick, an encouraging friend and superb agent; Susan Duff, my greatest cheerleader; Maria Robbins, who was part of the beginning; and Bill Henderson, who is always there for me, recovering treasure from trash.

Genie Chipps Henderson

ABOUT THE AUTHOR

Genie Chipps Henderson writes and produces documentaries for regional television on the East End of Long Island. She is also the coauthor of two nonfiction books, *The Woman's Guide to Starting a Business* and *Supergirls: The Autobiography of an Outrageous Business*. She lives in East Hampton, Long Island, with her husband, Pushcart Press publisher Bill Henderson. This is her first novel.